NIKOLA SCOTT

My Mother's Shadow

REVIEW

First published in Great Britain in 2017
by HEADLINE REVIEW
An imprint of HEADLINE PUBLISHING GROUP

First published in paperback in Great Britain in 2017
by HEADLINE REVIEW
An imprint of HEADLINE PUBLISHING GROUP

1

Cataloguing in Publication Data is available from the British Library

ISBN 978 1 4722 4116 0

Typeset in Garamond MT Std by Jouve (UK), Milton Keynes

Printed and bound in Great Britain by CPI Group (UK) Ltd, Croydon, CR0 4YY

MIX
Paper from
responsible sources
FSC® C104740

Headline's policy is to use papers that are natural, renewable and recyclable
products and made from wood grown in well-managed forests and other
controlled sources. The logging and manufacturing processes are expected
to conform to the environmental regulations of the country of origin.

HEADLINE PUBLISHING GROUP
An Hachette UK Company
Carmelite House
50 Victoria Embankment
London EC4 0DZ

www.headline.co.uk
www.hachette.co.uk

Praise for *My Mother's Shadow*:

'An intriguing twisting story with a lush opening and beautifully descriptive writing throughout. I loved it' Dinah Jefferies, author of *The Tea Planter's Wife*

'A compelling family story . . . beautifully written and evokes vivid pictures of an English summer in the 1950s' Sheila O'Flanagan

'A gripping family mystery told in lush, evocative prose . . . will transport you to another time and place but the heartbreak makes itself felt across the decades' Erin Kelly, author of *He Said, She Said*

'Compelling, atmospheric and beautifully written . . . a profoundly moving debut that trembles with family secrets. By turns heartbreaking and hopeful, it shines a light on the bonds between women and the incredible hidden pasts of the people we love. I adored it' Victoria Fox, author of *The Silent Fountain*

Born in Germany, Nikola Scott studied English and American literature before moving abroad to work as a fiction editor in New York and London. After over a decade in book publishing, she now lives in Frankfurt with her husband and two sons. *My Mother's Shadow* is her first novel.

For Paul

1958

There are many things this house has seen and many secrets it has heard, whispered things in the night that drift on the breeze and curl around chimneys and slate-covered gables, mullioned windows and white pebbled paths, wind their way through roses and rhododendrons and the trees of the old Hartland orchard. Loves found and lost, the pain of unexpected death and the deliciousness of forbidden trysts. Midnight tears and laughter in summer nights, all the dreams to be dreamed and all the worlds to be found. The house has kept them, without question, without judgement, preserving them in the shadows of its walls.

And these days, life at Hartland is rife with memories. The war, and the death it brought, is still fresh in everyone's minds. It's not been so very long, after all, since England came out of the bleak years of rationing, bombed-out houses and Nissen huts, blinking against the unexpected onslaught of new luxuries and sweets in the sweet shop and jangly new music everywhere. But the future is bright now, and so it's little wonder that they grasp at life with both hands, these young people of 1958, that this country house summer has made them all a little giddy with the promise of having it all.

Or maybe it's the moon that has made people giddy tonight, the way it hangs in the sky as if pinned there, low above the stables and bursting full with a strange orange light. You only need to look at it, you only need to taste the champagne prickling against the roof of your mouth and smell the heady scent from the rose garden, and you'll feel a pull at the bottom of your stomach, a reckless moon-madness that speaks of endless possibilities, of making the world your own. Lanterns are strung up all around, waving and twinkling in the evening breeze like so many coloured fireflies, and 'Magic Moments' is crooning around the couples swaying and laughing and smoking, perched on the low walls of the terrace with gimlets and lemonade to cool flushed cheeks. One of the girls hired to help for the evening stops to watch as she tops up the lemonade pitchers and punchbowls, sets out a new platter with puff pastry squares, marvelling at these golden young men and women who seem to have no care in the world other than to celebrate a seventeenth birthday, to cheer on a young girl's entrance into adulthood.

Two people are missing, though, two have slipped away from the terrace, made their way past a croquet mallet lying forgotten among the rhododendrons, down garden paths and through the trees, hands across mouths to hold back laughter and the occasional gasp as a stray branch hits the backs of bare legs. One is the birthday girl, seventeen today, who has in her short life already known too much heartbreak and for whom much worse is still to come. But tonight the girl has shed all her worries and fears, and she knows, deep down, that life can never ever be as deliciously forbidden, as wonderfully new as this summer night. So yes, she, too, is grasping at life with both hands, and who can blame her, holding on to the hand of a man who's been smiling at her for days, lazy, bemused smiles with drops of sea-water clinging to his lashes, wide innocent grins when others were watching, and secret, promising eyes when they had a brief moment alone in the Hartland rose garden. She can't see the smile in his eyes tonight, only moonlight and firefly lanterns, but she can feel him close to her, so close that his skin is warm against her arm and the smell of him mingles with that of freshly mown grass and the darker, more mysterious night smells of a garden unwilling to be disturbed, even for a first love as urgent as this one. Here, among the trees in the orchard, the air is cooler and involuntarily the girl shivers, and that's when he slips his arms around her and gathers her close, tips her face up with his other hand, and in this one single moment, life is perfect.

But already, and the house knows this, trouble is in the air, and the golden facade of this perfect summer, the glow of the heady, fragrant night, is about to be tainted. The house has always been a faithful keeper of all its secrets, and so it won't now give away what lies ahead. Instead, it takes the fleeting memories of a girl's first love, to keep them safe forever.

Chapter One

Death is a funny thing. Not *funny* funny, obviously, and really not funny at all, but strange. By rights, it should come with a bang, announcing its cataclysmic blow with machine gun harbingers of doom; instead it sneaks up like a thief, waiting for a too-eager foot stepping out into a traffic light or that single rebellious cell in our bodies that suddenly decides to start its devastating multiplication. Death always watches, biding its time until it strikes, and when it does, nothing will ever be the same.

Given the disproportionate awfulness of death, I don't remember much at all about the day my mother was hit by a lorry. Disjointed little bits, maybe, like the absurd amount of glass the lorry had showered across Gower Street and my father's pinched face as we waited for the taxi that would take us to her body; my sister Venetia arguing with the policewoman who, surely, had made a mistake, and was no one doing their jobs properly anymore?

The one thing I do remember, very clearly, was the moment I was told about it, because it was in this moment — I was standing in front of the dairy fridge holding sixty-five eggs for the day's meringues — that all the tears I might have cried vanished, and my eyes suddenly and inexplicably dried up. And dry they remained, through weeks filled with coroner's statements and my mother's favourite Countess roses on her coffin and making sure my father got up each morning over at the big, now-empty house on Rose Hill Road; all throughout, I never once shed a tear.

Some people simply don't cry very much, so this in itself was perhaps not a true measure of one's grieving abilities, but I had never been one of those people. On the contrary, I used to be particularly good at crying, in fact, it was one of the things I excelled at. When I was little, I cried so often and so readily that my mother claimed my body had to be made up of two-thirds salt water. My very own vale of tears, she said. I cried over molars accidentally flushed down the sink and white spots at the back of my throat, I worried about what lurked in my wardrobe and under my bed and at the bottom of the swimming pool. I followed stray cats and collected baby birds that had fallen out of their nests and wrestled with their fates for days.

For heaven's sake, Addie, my mother would say and push a handkerchief my way, twitching impatiently when my eyes got big and shiny and my throat was working to swallow back those sobs that were so weak and futile when one should be strong, square one's shoulders, get on with things. *Buck up, darling. Look at Venetia, four years younger and you don't see* her *cry.* I must have been an immensely exasperating child, because so many things about me brought forth that twitch on my mother's face, a sort of lifting of one cheek and compressing of her lips into small, white folds, that I'd started hiding when I saw it coming, mostly in the downstairs loo, which was always warm and smelled of Mrs Baxter's lavender cleaner and was rarely visited by anyone. Years later, after I'd moved out and bought my own apartment, one of the things I loved most about it was the absence of a downstairs loo.

And now, when my old nemesis, my private vale of tears, actually had a chance to shine, in a perverse twist of fate, it had gone and the most I was able to procure was a choked sobbing, swallowing convulsively to dislodge a strange lump that seemed to have got itself permanently stuck, like a fat little troll, at the bottom of my throat. It wasn't that I didn't miss her. Of course, I did. Who in this sad world doesn't miss their mother when she's gone? But the more Venetia mourned, as a golden child does, by losing weight and turning wan and shadowy, the more mutinously dry my own insides became. This worried me a great deal, until it occurred to me that maybe I was actually doing exactly what my mother had always wanted me to, being strong and squaring my shoulders. Were my eyes staying heroically dry from some deeply ingrained impulse to ward off the white-lip mouth-twitch, nurtured through forty fractious years with my mother? Was somewhere deep inside me a little girl smiling, because all the way into the grave, her mother would finally be pleased?

* * *

Venetia, who expected me to pay appropriate homage to our mother, was inevitably disappointed by what I produced instead. Newly pregnant and dangerously volatile, she swanned in and out of Rose Hill Road with homeopathic remedies, shop-bought chicken soup and lots of unnecessary advice. I tried to stay out of her way as much as I could, because while she held centre stage with her pregnancy and her bereavement counsellor, my father had gone very quiet in the side wing.

The one time he broke down, about two weeks after the funeral, was completely unspectacular in that he simply didn't get out of bed. Finally, on day four, when his bedroom door was still closed at five in the afternoon, my brother Jas and I took him to the doctor and then the hospital, from where he emerged a week later almost eerily calm. With some relief, my siblings went back to their own grief and respective careers and impending families, but I lingered, unnerved by the look in my dad's eyes. It was hard to believe that this was the same person who'd taught me chess when I was ten, who'd re-enacted the Allied landing with a stapler, two pencils and a hole punch when I needed help with my history homework and who was always game to get a flashlight and study those white spots at the back of my throat. *It's not a tumour, Adele, I'm sure of it. It's germs fighting a battle with your body and, open wider, just a bit wider, yes, I think your antibodies are currently in the lead. Here, maybe a Polo mint will help.*

Now, more often than not, we exchanged polite news of our week over tea or stared out silently at my mother's garden wilting in the back, and the chessboard hadn't seen the light of day for ages. Sometimes, I had to resist the urge to pinch him, very hard, just to make sure that he hadn't also died and left his body behind to get up and go to work and return for cups of tea, the cold dregs of which he left all around the house to be collected by Mrs Baxter, who came in four mornings a week to keep an eye on things. Still, I was hoping that maybe one day soon he'd be waiting for me, holding two cups of tea, throat-scaldingly hot, the way we both liked it, his face creased in a smile. *Addie! There you are. How about a game of chess with your old father?* So I continued coming to see him, making my way across North London after work, at first through too-bright summer dusks and then autumn evenings and eventually sharp and wintry nights that turned once more into a beautiful London spring, ticking off the twelve months after my mother's death by the way the bark changed on the trees on Hampstead Heath and the shadows of the little supermarket outside the Tube station had lengthened when I rounded the corner towards my parents' house.

Long before Venetia had started throwing about ideas for how to mark The Day of her Death, I'd started to dread it. But the calendar that hung in the patisserie kitchen had a big red splat on the corner of 15 May, raspberry sauce I think, which seemed to grow in size whenever I looked up from decorating Mrs Saunders' birthday cake with seventy-five pale pink fondant roses, forcing down the swallows that rose up my oesophagus like sluggish bubbles on a pond.

Venetia had wanted to get some of the family together – Jas and Mrs Baxter, my father's brother Fred, and a variety of other family flotsam who lived in the vicinity, to 'draw solace from each other's company', and 'let this day go by amongst close family', which, according to her bereavement counsellor, would be an important step towards Stage Five in the grieving process. Rather over-optimistic, in my opinion, because my father had barely progressed past 'Denial' yet and even though I generally tended to go along with things, especially where Venetia was concerned, this time I did try to argue. Being in our big, bright kitchen where my mother was so conspicuously absent was not remotely the way I wanted to spend the day, and I was fairly certain my father didn't either. Venetia overrode all objections, however, made me swap shifts, ordered an indecently large box of pastries from the patisserie and made sure I left on time to deliver it to Rose Hill Road.

And now I was here. The door gave its usual soft groan as I stepped into the front hall and involuntarily I held my breath. But it was very quiet, the grandfather clock ticking in the corner as it always did, and it smelled the way it always had, like books and dust and Mrs Baxter's lavender cleaner, even though this time last year my mother had died. To my right, jackets hung on the ancient coat stand in the corner and several umbrellas dripped onto the stone floor tiles, indicating that the family had come together only a short while ago.

Silently, I crept across the front hall, eyeing the light that spilled through the door to the downstairs kitchen. A subdued mumble floated up, then a laugh, quickly stifled into a discreet cough. Uncle Fred, I thought, my father's brother, who lived in Cambridge with his three dogs and a collection of rusty cars he was forever fixing up. I strained my ears hopefully for answering sounds from my dad, but his deep, slightly hoarse voice couldn't be made out amidst the low thrum of conversation. He'd been working more than ever lately, and from what I could tell, his heartburn had got a lot worse. I hoped he'd gone to the doctor yesterday like he was supposed to. There was another mumbled question. Jas, probably, who must have come straight from the hospital in his rush to do Venetia's bidding.

I dug my toes into the sisal matting at the thought of them all draped around the big kitchen table. Venetia's bereavement counsellor had said to leave our mother's chair empty, as a sign of respect. I hated the bereavement counsellor, who was a cadaverous-looking man called Hamish McGree, and I hated the thought of that resolutely empty chair, with its curved armrests and straight back and the jauntily chequered wedge that my mother had stuck under the lining to help her bad back. I tried to remember when I last saw her sitting there, looking at her garden, her expression faraway in contemplation of the day's to-dos or frowning as she scanned the newspaper headlines. But I couldn't. Her face remained blurry and unfocussed, and all I could see were little bits of her: her hands, long-fingered and slightly tapered like mine, or the strands of her hair falling forward as she bent to blow on her coffee, which she had liked tepid, almost white with milk. It'd been like this all through the year. As people around me recalled funny moments and entire conversations and whole afternoons spent in her company, I was still working on simply remembering her face, the way she'd put on her lipstick in the morning, the twitch of her mouth when she was impatient and the tight set of her shoulders at night when she was cold and looking around for her scarf. It was a shrapnel rain of memory fragments that my mind seemed to be expecting me to put together when my ability to remember her was stuck in the same barren place that my tears had disappeared to, a dried-up riverbed of disabled grief, where memories were barrelling along like tumbleweed, never connecting, never whole and, somehow, rarely good.

More subdued laughter, turned discreetly into a cough, and, just like that, I realised that there was no way I was going to walk down those stairs, to that empty chair and the blurry echo of my mother's face. Backing away from the kitchen stairs, I dumped the cake box onto the hall table with a squishy thud and shot, sodden jacket, bag and all, through a door on the right where I sagged against the wall and, for a long moment, simply stood, savouring the cool darkness against my pupils after a long day staring at the raspberry splotch on 15 May. The ticking of the grandfather clock was louder here, because its back was against the wall, but it thudded in a comforting sort of way, like a heartbeat, and finally I exhaled and opened my eyes, pushing down a twinge of fear at my own daring. Venetia would be livid.

My mother's study. I hadn't been in here for a long time, not since Venetia and I had come and gingerly poked through the desk for her address book to do the death announcement cards, practically exiting at a run. Every now and then, Mrs Baxter would suggest having a clear-out, but every time Venetia dismissed the idea out of hand, so the room had remained exactly the same as the morning my mother had left to teach her popular seminar on 'Emerging Creative Outlets for Women Writers' for the last time. Books and folders and papers were lined up neatly along the shelves, post-its daring only occasionally to stick up here and there, pens stood ramrod straight in an old mug that was too good to throw away, as if they were waiting for my mother, who liked her pencils straight and sharp and ready to go. There was her telephone, the old mustard-coloured kind that still used a rotary dial, and her roll-top desk hulking against the wall, with drawers and cubby-holes and gadgets we'd made her for Christmases and birthdays because we knew that she liked things orderly and put away.

She'd been in here every evening, a sliver of her visible through the half-open door as she worked on lecture notes, student essays or manuscripts or, more mundanely, read the newspaper. She read that paper with an almost religious fervour, every single night, whether we were asleep or awake, in bed with chickenpox or out on the town. Sometimes, watching her unfold it to cover the entire desk, I wished that she'd look at me, or at the very least at the burglar in my wardrobe, with half the focussed attention she gave the small advertisements in the back and the obituaries and the robber held at a police station in Leeds. But things between my mother and me had been difficult. It was mainly my fault, really, because I was too soft, always had been. I didn't put myself into life's driver's seat, I didn't square my shoulders enough. My mother wasn't soft and she wasn't weak, she was like a hard, shiny gem, and however much we both tried, my soft, desperate-to-please self and her brilliant one could not but rub each other the wrong way, all the time, relentlessly, like stroking a cat against the grain, like golden vanilla custard splitting into a curdled mess. That's how things had been, between my mother and me.

I'm not sure how long I stood there, on the threshold of her space, breathing in the faint echo of books and determination that had been the very essence of my mother, waiting for tears and wishing for at least one small good memory of her, because today, of all days, I should remember her face, I should remember *her*, properly and whole.

Obviously, something had to happen, and something did.

The phone rang.

Chapter Two

The sound was so odd inside the gloom of the study that it was like hearing a siren underwater. For a second I froze. Too soon, it rang again, and when I heard the echo of the main unit in the hallway, I dived towards the desk and snatched up the receiver.

'Yes?' I whispered, looking nervously at the door. I'd very much prefer not to be found skulking in the darkness of my mother's study while I was supposed to be helping with the mourning downstairs.

'Mrs Harington?'

I'd been pressing the handset hard against my ear and the voice on the other end arrowed straight into the left side of my brain. Suppressing a small scream, I wrenched it away and the mustard-coloured receiver clattered onto the surface of the desk.

'Mrs Harington? Are you there?' the phone squawked. It was a man, speaking in a slow and gravelly way. Reflexively, I opened my mouth even though Mrs Harington, well, she wasn't exactly – here.

'I'm sorry, yes, what was that?' I said hesitantly into the phone, looking at the door again and clearing my throat.

'I know you prefer not to be contacted here,' the voice on the other end said, 'but you haven't been answering your mobile these last few weeks. I wonder, is it turned off? Nothing's come in for a long time, so as per your request I've not been in touch. But then, out of the blue, I got a rather interesting letter, which I'd like to get to you soon, and since you asked me not to send anything without prior warning . . .'

Mrs Harington is not here. Tell him, Addie.

'A letter?' I said to the stranger who was calling my dead mother on the telephone.

'I'm not sure about this one, because it could well turn out to be yet another dead end, but . . .' He stopped for a second and, instinctively, I leaned towards his voice. 'The connection isn't terribly good, I'm afraid, so do excuse the brevity, but you'll get the letter soon. In any case, on the fourteenth of February,' the line crackled, 'there seems to have been—'

The fourteenth of February? I frowned and opened my mouth to ask the most obvious question, but just then, there was another noise. The telltale squeak of the kitchen door, then footsteps on the stairs.

'Excuse me,' I whispered into the phone, 'I have to go. I'm so sorry. I'll call you,' I added for good measure.

I hung up just as I realised that I didn't, actually, have this person's number or his name. Nor did I know anything about what he wanted. And had he really said 'the fourteenth of February'? That was strange because . . . but what would he know about 14 February? And, come to think of it, who was he? I frowned at the phone, forgetting the dry sting behind my eyes and the troll-like lump in my throat. Mrs Baxter might know. I'd have to ask her.

Voices in the hallway. Shoes scuffling across the tiles, heels clacking into the loo and back out, the front door groaning.

'I'll see you soon, then.' Jas's voice came through the wall. 'Uncle Fred, I'll give you a lift to the station, shall I? I have to pop back to the hospital.'

'I have no idea *where* Addie is. She *said* she was going to be here.' Hoarseness blunted Venetia's sharp voice but there was a distinct edge to it, and in my hiding place, my hand still touching the mustard-coloured phone, I cringed, thinking of the inevitable moment when she would come to find me.

After some shuffling back and forth, silence fell at last and I strained to listen. Maybe Venetia had gone too, leaving the kitchen for someone else to clean up, and I could slip out, find the cake box and Mrs Baxter and my father. We'd had *Biscuit Roulé* as a special today and I'd made five of the fluffiest sponge cake rolls, scented with vanilla and studded with tangy, ruby-red raspberries. I'd added some to the cake box because at the end of a long and trying day, there was nothing better than a cup of Mrs Baxter's golden Oolong and a rolled-up cream-filled slice of *Biscuit Roulé* heaven.

My black Whistles tote was on the floor, and my jacket, which I'd dropped onto the small armchair when the phone rang, had slipped onto the floor, scattering a couple of coins across the carpet, small pockets of mess in the otherwise tidy room. Quickly, I knelt to scoop them up and was just about to straighten when my eye caught something below the desk. All the way at the back, tucked neatly between the legs of the desk, the clasp occasionally catching a random ray of light, was my mother's handbag.

I looked at it for a moment, then, before I could change my mind, I stuck out my hand and eased it forward. Graphite grey and elegantly sturdy, it was a vintage Hermès bag; well, it was vintage now anyway even if it hadn't been when she'd got it back in the early seventies. She'd bought it with the money from her first ever award, something about contemporaries of Jane Austen who, apparently, had been much more successful at the time but were now largely forgotten. I stroked the side of the handbag, feeling the leather ripple underneath my fingertips. I had no idea what it was doing here, but then again, where else would it be? My father still slept on the right side of the bed with her pillow and blanket made up next to him, her book splayed open by the foot of her lamp. Venetia, despite being brisk about life in general and my many shortcomings in particular, was so erratic about our mother that she would have liked to wrap the entire study in cling film to preserve it for eternity. So we'd left my mother's gardening gloves hanging over the side of the bucket, permanently moulded to the shapes of her hands, and *The Prime of Miss Jean Brodie*, swollen with dried moisture, behind the U-bend of the sink in the upstairs bathroom; we'd left her coat on the coat stand in the front hall and her shampoo in the shower. Someone should write a letter of complaint to Hamish McGree.

I set the bag onto the desk. If we ever did get around to clearing out her things, then Venetia would probably take the Hermès bag. She and my mother had shared the same simple, understated chic; they'd both loved being beautiful and all the small luxuries that brightened one's day. Venetia always unerringly knew what to give my mother for birthdays, and my mother always unerringly loved what Venetia had given her. Watching her unwrap my dad's thoughtful gift and Venetia's stylish one, I would sit on my hands to resist the impulse to hide my own laboriously selected and agonised-over present because I knew it wouldn't be nearly as perfect or as beautiful as the cashmere shawl that Venetia had got her for chilly evenings.

Oddly enough, my mother and I actually looked a lot more alike than Venetia and she did. We were both small and compact with a high-maintenance cloud of dark curls and slightly slanted grey eyes, set wide apart over a small nose. But being a pastry chef meant bulky aprons and hairnets, scarred hands and clothes that were always sticky with fondant and blueberry pie filling. My mother had taken meticulous care of her clothes, because she hadn't had much money when she was young, and even though I'd tried to clean myself up before I came home from school and then later, when I came over for lunch on a Sunday, inevitably she'd discover a stray dusting of flour on my back or a rip in my sleeve and would frown at my carelessness.

But the Hermès bag was a rare exception. When we went to buy it, Venetia had fallen asleep in her buggy on the way, so it was me who helped line up all the contenders on the worktop, who pointed out the compartments inside that allowed her to keep things organised, who was smart enough to think that the grey would be more practical than the light beige. Soon after, Venetia had started walking and talking and doing all sorts of amazing things, and by the time I was ten and she six, she had firmly and effortlessly claimed my mother for herself. And my mum, who was always so impatient with me and seemed to have to spend an inordinate amount of energy getting me to square my shoulders and stop shilly-shallying, very readily gravitated to Venetia, who was quick and sure and confident. It took me a while to realise and then to accept this fact, and only a little bit longer to stop trying to measure up to my clever sister, as she went on to become an architect with her own small firm north of Regent's Park. And when Jas, who was born with a stethoscope in his hands and bucket-loads of determination, turned out to be the youngest ever hand surgeon in the London metropolitan area, I stopped vying with my siblings altogether and settled down to my own modest life as a pastry cook at a small patisserie start-up in Kensington. *All the world open to her and what does she choose to be? A baker*, I overheard my mother say to my father more than once and I eventually stopped bringing cake and sweets and breads home for Sunday lunches, figuring they could only ever be reminders of a mediocre career that had fallen far short of her expectations.

I hesitated for a second before lifting up the Hermès bag, feeling the solid heft of the leather against my shoulder, the straps hugging my arm. My mother had bought other bags after this one, but she always kept coming back to the Hermès. *It reminds me of how far I've come*, she'd said once, and whenever I saw it hanging off her arm I felt a small ridiculous twinge of happiness, irrationally convinced that the one afternoon of choosing it with her made me complicit in its wearing and in how far she'd come. For some reason, I was loath for the bag to go to Venetia. I should just ask her—

Sudden footsteps and a loud hrmph of annoyance heralded Venetia's imminent arrival. It was in this moment, the split second before the door to the study opened, that for some unfathomable reason I decided to hide my mother's handbag from my sister. Swinging it around my back, I snatched up my jacket to cover it.

'Adele.'

Venetia was eyeing me through black horn-rimmed glasses. Her hair was pulled back into a ponytail and, with the exception of a perfectly round bump that looked like she'd stuck a large basketball underneath her expensive maternity dress, she looked so thin and hollow-eyed that I felt a squirm of guilt at having left her in the lurch. I shifted the Hermès bag further behind my back, fumbled awkwardly for my own large Whistles tote and hung it off my other arm.

'I'm so sorry, Vee, I don't know, I was so . . .' I saw her mouth twitch impatiently and automatically forced myself to stop waffling. 'How is Dad doing?'

'He could have used your company today, and I could have used the help. Not to mention the cakes, which I paid a fortune for,' she snapped.

'Vee, I'm sorry . . .' I reached out to touch her shoulder, but she twisted away and frowned, looked around.

'I keep waiting for it all to get easier. What are you even doing in here? I thought we agreed we'd leave things alone for the time being?'

I'd been about to nod but then I suddenly said, 'Perhaps it wouldn't be such a bad idea to start clearing out some of her stuff? Maybe Dad needs not to be reminded of her all the time.'

Venetia frowned. 'Addie, I'm telling you, we aren't ready. And you know full well that Dad isn't remotely ready.'

How would she know who was ready or not, when she was only ever briefly around to dispense Hamish McGree's dubious wisdom and even more dubious chicken soup?

'Come on, then, let's have some of your cake,' she said when I looked away, striding ahead of me, the only woman in her third trimester who could still walk in three-inch heels.

I hesitated, already regretting my inexplicable impulse to take – well, let's face it, steal – the Hermès bag, but there was no way to put it back now without attracting attention to the fact that I'd taken it in the first place. Not that I didn't have some claim to it, but Venetia was funny about things. She turned and I twitched but all she said was, 'Did I hear the phone earlier?'

'Yes, well, you know, it was——' I started, then stopped, because, really, what had it been? A stranger calling my mother? Me pretending to be her?

'Er, it was nothing. Just a spam call.'

Unnerved by the lie slipping so easily from my mouth, I shuffled her out into the living room ahead of me, using the opportunity to stuff the Hermès bag deep inside my large tote. 'Do you know if Dad went to his doctor's appointment yesterday?'

'Doctor? Why? Close the door, will you?' Venetia was waiting for me in the hall, awkwardly holding her bump to ease the strain on her skin, her shoulder blades sticking up inside her dress.

'He's been having that heartburn stomach thing again.'

'No. I don't know. He didn't say.'

'Did you ask him? You have to ask. He doesn't say anything on his own.'

'Adele, I had no idea he was going, so how could I have known to ask?'

Before we could continue this highly productive conversation, the door to the kitchen stairs opened and Mrs Baxter emerged, closely followed by my father, who was carrying a cup of tea.

'Addie!' Mrs Baxter's face lit up and she surged forward to give me a quick one-armed hug, holding her handbag and a pack of cigarettes in the other. 'We thought we'd lost you. How're you doing, love? Look who's turned up like a bad penny, Mr H.'

Keeping her arm around my shoulders, she turned me towards my father, who obligingly said, 'Addie,' then added, 'we were wondering where you'd got to.'

Mrs Baxter gave my shoulders another affectionate squeeze. 'It's so good to see you, Addie, love. I was just about to leave, give Mr B his dinner. But I could stay, make us all another pot of tea?'

My father looked longingly down at his cup, which he'd clearly intended taking away somewhere private, and I quickly said, 'I'm fine, Mrs Baxter, I just came from Grace's. And I'm so sorry I was late and . . . but how are you, Dad?'

I didn't hug him, we weren't a family who hugged or kissed or touched much at all, but I surreptitiously ran my eyes over his face, checking for the repeated swallowing that would indicate his heartburn or a deepening of the grooves around his eyes that meant he hadn't been sleeping again. He used to play cricket when he was young, 'his village's hope for national glory' his mum always said, so no amount of grieving and non-eating and working too much could possibly diminish the solid set of his shoulders or the length of his stride. But when you looked closer, he seemed to have shrunk somehow over the last twelve months and his face had a worn look, sort of threadbare, the soft tissues of his face folding in on themselves to create craterous lines in his forehead and around his mouth.

'Just on my way up,' he said, cradling his cup of tea. 'Some papers to look through.'

'But surely you don't need to work today of all days,' I said worriedly.

'Leave him be, Addie,' Venetia said, hrmphing at a wet umbrella someone had left on the hall table. 'People do need to do their own thing, you know.'

Ignoring this blatant display of hypocrisy when she was forever at me about one thing or another, I kept my eyes on my dad, trying to find something to say that didn't involve my mother. 'So, er, how was the doctor's appointment yesterday?'

He looked blank for a moment. 'Oh, I ended up having to cancel, I had so much on at the office. Walker was off sick and I had to take a meeting for him. But it's just the occasional twinge, nothing to worry about.'

'Dad,' I said exasperatedly. 'It takes weeks to see that specialist. Jas pulled all sorts of strings.'

'Addie, I'm fine.' He sounded irritated now and I heard Mrs Baxter give a small sigh next to me because my dad was always 'fine', whatever the occasion. Sometimes he elaborated and was 'really fine', other times 'fine, really'; occasionally 'things were fine', or, if he wanted to sound particularly jubilant, 'all was fine'.

'I'll be off, then,' she said resignedly. 'As long as you're sure you're *fine*, Mr H.' She raised her cigarette in a sarcastic salute. 'I'll see you tomorrow, then, shall I?'

'Yes, of course. Thanks for everything, Mrs Baxter. Give my regards to your husband.' My dad's itching to be gone was palpable, a straining emanating from his very pores, and he already had a foot on the bottom step when he stopped, turned to me and said, very quietly, so that no one else could hear, 'Are you all right, though, Addie? Today, I mean?'

He looked straight at me when he said it, and his eyes were so full of sudden anguish and love and loneliness that almost instinctively, I moved forward to throw myself into his arms the way I used to do when I was a little girl. But just then, there was a small kerfuffle and a shriek from Venetia as Mrs Baxter tried to shake out the forgotten umbrella and it popped open, nearly spearing Venetia's bump. My dad, obviously realising that human contact of any kind might force him to be part of the world again, instantly retreated and cleared his throat awkwardly.

I stopped in my tracks. 'I'm fine, Dad, just fine.'

Oh for the love of god. When would we all just stop being *fine*?

'Well, I'm glad you came anyway,' he said, sounding vague now. 'I'll see you tomorrow maybe?'

'Yes, Dad. Hope you have a good evening.'

Still clutching his cup of tea, he walked up the stairs. I heard a door open, then close and he was gone.

Mrs Baxter had come up next to me and I saw that she, too, was watching him go, her hands clamped around the wet folds of the umbrella. When she caught me looking, she pursed her lips and shook her head.

Venetia, who was inspecting her bump with a worried expression, hadn't noticed anything amiss. 'Mrs Baxter, how could you? We'll have bad luck raining down on us in heaps, and right next to the baby, too. What if—'

But we would never learn what, exactly, the bad-luck umbrella would do to her unborn child because there was a sudden noise by the front door. Someone was coming up the steps. We turned as one, waiting for the bell, but the footsteps went back down the stairs. Then came back up again.

I looked at Venetia.

'I bet that's Uncle Fred and this infernal thing is his,' she said darkly. 'Quick, let's give it to him, maybe the bad luck will transfer.' She wrenched open the door. 'Here—'

She'd been about to thrust the umbrella through the door but stopped midway because the visitor was not, in fact, fat, bearded and jolly Uncle Fred.

It was a woman.

She stood silhouetted against the last light of the afternoon, leaning forward slightly to escape the raindrops dripping from the wisteria above. She was tall and thin, and her face seemed to consist mainly of angles and sharp jutting cheekbones rising and falling around grey eyes. Her skin was pale and her hair, drawn back tightly, pulled at the sides of her face. I'd never seen her before.

There was a moment's silence as I waited for Venetia to greet this person, whom she must have invited for the afternoon's gathering, and I'd actually turned and picked up the cake box, intending to start moving things downstairs, when I heard Venetia say, rather impatiently, 'Yes? Can we help you?' She was shifting from foot to foot, clearly dying to sit down.

The woman looked between Venetia, holding her belly and the

umbrella, and me, laden with my bulging bag and the large cake box with its jaunty red and white stripes and Grace's Patisserie emblazoned on the side.

'Yes,' the woman said and her voice was unexpectedly melodic against the sharp, symmetrical lines of her face. 'That is, I'm not sure. I hope so.' She paused again, looking at Venetia and me, then gave herself a visible push.

'I'm so sorry to barge in, but I'm looking for Mrs Harington. Elizabeth Sophie Harington. She used to be Elizabeth Sophie Holloway. I wondered if I might speak with her?'

My head whipped up and I turned back to the door. This was the second time that someone had asked for my mother, whose death we were remembering today.

Seeing our frozen faces, the woman faltered for a second, then rushed on, squeezing out the next sentences quickly, so that the words jumbled over each other. 'I think that she . . . well, I just found out that . . . Elizabeth. You see, she's my mother.'

Limpsfield, 17 July 1958

I bought a new journal today, from nice Mr Clark on the high street. He had a new colour in, frosted pink, and he showed me the little clasp at the front and the flowers on some of the pages. Perfect for a pretty young woman like you, he said with a wink. He meant well, I'm sure, but I didn't want that one. Instead, I got the darkest grey, black almost, because I know full well that it isn't going to be a frosted pink kind of year. I chose the slightly thicker paper too, even though it was more expensive, because I have a feeling I'm going to need thicker paper this year. Thick, thirsty paper to soak up all the thoughts and the tears and all the awful things that are happening at my house.

On the bus home from school, I wrote my name in the front, like I always do, Elizabeth Holloway, and the year: 1958. And then I realised that by the time I've finished this journal, when I've covered all the thirsty pages with all the things I'm thinking and supposed to be doing and not allowed to be doing, when all the awful things that I know are happening will have happened, my mother will be dead. She will have perished, she'll be deceased. She'll be buried. She'll be gone.

Stupid Mrs Farnham, when I met her at the butcher's the other day, called it consumption and told me not to get too close to her or we'll all be razed to the ground in a matter of days. I left her standing in the queue, even though I'd offered to run out for the bones and chicken feet for Mum's broth. I can't stand stupid people like that. I don't see how she has any business to talk about my mother in the first place and, in any case, it isn't consumption. I listened at the door when the nurse was in, I looked it all up in the school library and I know exactly what it is. It's a growth in her lungs. I think it comes from the winters when the fog starts being bad and people every-where cough until spring. Except that Mum continued coughing all the way through summer and another foggy autumn and yet another winter, until it became what it is now. An incurable growth. Cancer, they called it when she finally went to hospital. Incurable, plain and simple; as plain and simple as being dead and buried and gone.

My father's not talking about it, he doesn't ever talk of what is now and what's to come. Maybe he believes that a sixteen-year-old girl mustn't know about things like incurable growths and bedpans and morphine injections, but how on earth he can possibly think that I can't hear my own mother coughing herself to death is unfath-omable to me. She coughs in dry, racking gasps, which I know must be painful; they take so much obvious effort, and grow weaker and more laboured every day. At first, I was dreading hearing the cough, was waiting for it and relieved when it was a good night, when all stayed quiet. Now what I dread most is not hearing the cough at all anymore. It's become a measure of my life, a fragile barometer of hope and despair, and I can feel it all around me, creeping into every room, dogging my footsteps when I run up the stairs to my mother's room. It has seeped into the curtains of the front parlour and the carved backs of the dining-room chairs we rarely use anymore, it's settled on the flagstones of the kitchen floor where only Dora bus-tles about these days. It hangs in the wet air on wash days and crackles in the fire when my mother brushes my hair for me on Friday evenings, which I still let her do even though I am not a little girl any longer, because I know that soon she won't be here to do it at all anymore. The cough is the last thing I hear when I leave for school in the morning and the first thing when I open the front door in the afternoon, having jumped off the bus and hurried down the road to make the most of the precious time I have alone with her, before Father returns from the bank and sends me to my room, before the district nurse comes for the evening injection and my mother falls into an uneasy haze of pain and morphine.

I'm sitting here now, waiting for Sister Hammond to leave. I got out a new book from the library, which is called *I like it Here* and looked funny enough to take my mind off things. I should probably be working on my Latin verbs if I want to do well after the summer holidays and eventually go on to university like Mum and I have talked about. But I can't settle down to my book or my verbs at all as I listen to Sister Hammond's voice down the end of the hall, and I can't settle down to even think about the future, with all these other worries and fears crowding my mind. Writing them down and shutting them away between these thirsty pages is the only thing that keeps them from spilling out and taking over everything, and so I've decided that my verbs will have to wait. I'd rather write about the street below, lying hot and dusty dry in the late afternoon sun. The travelling salesman four houses down, who is sweating in his suit as he goes from door to door. The children from number four racing down the street and calling out to friends as they go.

Everyone at school is excited about the summer holidays, going to places like Brighton and Blackpool and Torquay. That's where Judy is going, to Torquay, and a while back her mum had kindly asked me to come along. But I said no right away and I didn't even mention it to Mum because there is no way I'll leave now. Judy's mother didn't press me. She lost two brothers in the war and I think she understands that time slips away fast when someone's dying, like quicksilver, like water through a fork, and that I need more of it, more time with Mum, if I want to survive the rest of my life without her.

I've made a list of books I know she still wants to read, like The Long View, which is a bit sad, and The Grass is Singing, which Father won't like us reading because he says it is communist nonsense. I've marked up the Radio Times with programmes we'll listen to, and that's how I'll spend the summer of 1958, cramming in all the reading and listening and talking that was meant to last us a lifetime.

That's the front door closed and there goes Sister Hammond on her bicycle. She looks up once and I wave but I'm not sure she can even see me, sitting up on my windowsill, half-hidden by the curtains. She passes Mrs Peckitt and Mrs Smith from across the road, who've settled in for a chat across their doorsteps, and stops to ask a question, then peers into the throat of the toddler clinging to Mrs Peckitt's skirt. I like Sister Hammond, she's always honest and direct, and she stands up to my father when he tells everyone what to do. And I'm sure, after all the quiet and death in here, she must be relieved to be looking at life, even if it comes in the form of a dirty, red-faced child fidgeting out on the hot street. Still, I'm amazed that after seeing my mum only minutes ago, she can now laugh so easily with Mrs Peckitt, whose curly hair bobs in the evening breeze, and Mrs Smith, who is holding a broom. They look so comfortable, the three of them, oozing life and bursting with health, so competent and cheerful and rosy-cheeked, with their unending supply of tea for sore throats and iodine for grazed knees, simple remedies for simple illnesses. So different to my own mum lying just a few doors down, pale and racked by coughing, drifting away from me on a wave of morphine.

I envy them, all those families with all their jolly children. We've always been greeted politely enough and Mum has made a few acquaintances along the road, but the neighbourhood is a strange mix of old houses that have been here forever like ours, and terraces and new builds, and somehow there's always been a slight wariness between us and our neighbours. It's my mum, who is smarter and brighter and funnier than any of the housewives here, who has help to clean the windows and do the washing on a Monday and take delivery of groceries when most other mums are on their knees to scrub the flagstones themselves or trudge down the road with a shopping bag several times a day. It's me, who is an only child, a grammar school girl, who goes off on the bus each morning, so conspicuous among these large broods who spill in and out of each other's houses in cheerful chaos, whose children troop off to the local primary and the secondary modern. And it's my father, who rejects any social advances, who hates these bright new years of having it so good, who seems to despise cheerfulness and lightness and frivolities, feeding his complicated memories of war and death with the piety of his moral high ground.

But most of all, I know it is Death himself, who has started his

23

slow, inevitable descent on this house, who is hovering above our roof and telling everyone that we are not good company.

Sister Hammond is cycling away down the street now, and I can see Mrs Peckitt and Mrs Smith say their farewells, herd their children inside for tea. Soon, the road will quieten down, and in those houses lucky enough to have it, families will perch around what I can't see from up here but know are television sets. I imagine them watching *Hancock's Half Hour* and Marguerite Patten's cookery programme or maybe the sport. Girls at school talk about music programmes, *Six-Five Special* and something called *Cool for Cats*, which sounds like fun. But I don't keep up with it at all. My father doesn't approve of television, he doesn't approve of much on the radio either, and he certainly does not approve of rock 'n' roll. I don't care so much for all that myself, but I would quite like to watch *The Sky at Night*. Miss Steele at school has told me about it and I love the sound of it, given how often I'm sitting on my windowsill looking up at the sky.

I'm waiting for night to fall properly now and for Father to retire to bed so I can slip down the corridor, sit in the chair next to Mum's bed and talk to her or read if she wants to. But he's still in her room, even though it is coming up to nine o'clock now. I can hear them talking, my mother's raspy voice punctuated by coughing, and my father's impatient staccato bark. I wonder what it is they're talking about. I often wonder what it was that brought them together in the first place, because no two people in this vast, wide world could be more different than George and Constance Holloway, respectable residents at Bough Road, Limpsfield. My father was born in this house, his parents lived in this house before him and he himself will eventually die in this house, the same respectable resident he's always been, off to the bank in his dark suit and bowler hat in the mornings, back home for supper with his wife and daughter in the evenings. He doesn't need change, he doesn't ever, ever long for more. He doesn't want the moon, not like my mother, who always tells me that as humans who've survived two versions of hell, we are now obligated to make something good of this new world. 'Go and get the moon, Lizzie.' That's what she said when I sat my exams at eleven, or when she saw me off on the bus on my first day at grammar school.

I don't think my father even knows what that is, the moon, because at Number Seven Bough Road, the velvet curtains – hung there since my Great-Grandmother Alice put them up before the Great War – are drawn at eight o'clock and he retires at half eleven, not to rise again until a quarter past six in the morning, every day, without fail. What has made my mother flutter into his life, then, like a neat, happy bird, curious and eager, what has made her come to roost in this house that is so full of him, that oozes my father from its silent walls and polished floors and dark corners? My mother and I like to visit flower shows and the circus, we go to the panto at Christmas and to the sweet shop to pick from the jars. We pretend to be fancy ladies having cream tea at stately homes' open days, and at the bookshop my mother always goes quite mad and spends too much of her pin money on books, which she then has to hide from Father to avoid a lecture on gratuitous luxury. Sometimes, I feel that both my mother and I are merely guests here, small fluttery birds in a cold, dark, red-brick house, looking at the moon through a crack in my Great-Grandmother Alice's velvet curtains.

It's getting dark now and in a moment I'll switch on my light, hide my diary safely away beneath the edge of the little rug by my bed where Father could never find it. But I want to sit by the window until the very last moment because it's so warm out there. The roses in our front garden send up little bursts of scent, the night air lifts my hair and makes me smile and the last light hovers on front steps and bay windows and mossy roofs as the street tucks itself up for the night. It's the kind of evening you want to reach out and hold on to, because when darkness finally falls and it gets quiet, the coughing will start up again.

Limpsfield, 18 July 1958

I now know what it was they were talking about last night. And to think that only this morning, I ran off to school so much more cheerful than usual because it was the last day before the summer holiday, and that I came home so much happier than usual because I was done for the summer. But then I saw that Father had come home early and he was looking over the car, and I had a feeling, a very bad one, that something was going to happen. He never, ever comes home early, not when he needs to set a perfect example for everyone else at the bank.

He called me into the front room as I was passing later and told me that I needed to pack a suitcase because I'm being sent away tomorrow to spend the summer in the country. Away for a whole month at least, he said, maybe six weeks, then went on for a bit about the benefits of the country air and hopefully doing something useful with my time, and somehow he seemed to think that he was doing something nice for me, expected me to say all the right things, to be thankful and polite. Instead, I was simply stunned and just stood in the door and didn't say a thing, hiding the new *Radio Times* behind my back because I didn't want him to see all the things I was going to listen to with Mum. He's not used to arguments in any case, not from me nor from Mum, so after he'd delivered his message he turned back to his newspaper and left me standing there looking at him and trying to finds the words to say no.

Now that I'm back up in my room, all the words that I should have said come to me. I'm not going to do what he says, I simply won't. I vow that here and now in these pages, and I'm going straight into Mum's room to tell her so, to tell her to stand up for us and convince him he's wrong.

Later

Mum was sitting up when I came in. I thought she looked better today, she seemed to have more colour than usual and her face wasn't quite so ravaged looking. My heart lifted, it always does, because Hope is stupidly indestructible like that, and I went to sit with her, showing her the *Radio Times*, and asked whether she was ready for *Mrs Dale's Diary* or wanted me to go down to the garden.

A few months ago when spring was finally here, she started talking about her garden, about needing to check on her plants and vegetables and whether the espaliered apple had taken or not. But she couldn't really, because the exertion made her breathing so much worse that she had to stay inside. So when she gets too restless I move her armchair right next to the window, where she can look down and write into her notebook what is blooming and what needs doing and then send me down with a list. Sometimes she'll call instructions from the window and I stand below, at the ready with the clippers. We do have a gardener who comes in for the big things and Father doesn't like it when she shouts out of the window; he thinks it entirely unsuitable for a woman to shout like that, not to mention a woman who is dying to boot. But she's happy doing it and she loves her flowers, so no matter what Father says I collect big bunches of them to bring up to her, sometimes two or three vases full that I put around the room.

But today wasn't a garden happiness sort of day, because I really am being sent away for the whole of the summer holidays to stay with a family they know, the Shaws, who live in a place in Sussex called Hartland. Mum put her book to the side when I came in and already when she looked at me I knew that it was a done thing. I hadn't even opened my mouth when she said, in that terrible raspy, hoarse voice she now has, 'I want you to go.' She was struggling for breath and I automatically got up to check the kettle, which we keep boiling over the fire to make the air easier for her to take in. But she held me back. 'I want you to go, Lizzie darling, I want you to have a wonderful summer away from here. You've been such a good girl, such a joy. You deserve it.'

'But I want to be with you,' I told her, trying very hard not to cry. She doesn't like it when I cry, she wants our time together not to be wasted on tears or bemoaning the inevitable. I know she's trying to teach me how to be strong for when she's gone. But I am not strong, not always, and certainly not now. I tried to say I didn't want to leave her, but she held my hand very tight and said that she knew, she knew this would be hard, but that I would like the Shaws and that she'd been to Hartland herself when she was younger and it was beautiful, close to the Channel, and on windy days, you could sometimes smell the sea. 'It's a lovely place, Lizzie, a real country house, big but cosy, too, surrounded by trees and lawns and beautiful, beautiful gardens. You can go for walks, there's a rose garden just like the Rossetti poem. This is not just Father telling you what to do; I want you to go. I want you to be happy. It'll be good for you to be among people your own age, not always cooped up with your old mother and hardly ever leaving the house.'

But what is she going to do with him gone all day? She's always tired and yet restless also, tossing and turning in her bed, and I know how to talk to her, to soothe her. He doesn't care for her the way I do, bringing her tea and holding her hand when she rests. I read to her, too, but you need to go slow and quiet so as not to hurt her head, with lots of pauses to let her cough. He won't read her the novels she likes, Graham Greene and Doris Lessing and Agatha Christie. And he might not know how much she loves poetry. He'd be embarrassed by all the yearning and love, refuse to indulge her, even if Rossetti is so very respectable and solemn. I read from the newspapers, too, not the bad news about nuclear armament and the Cold War and Asian flu, but the good bits, about Teds dancing in the aisles of cinemas and being chucked out by the police, about Hillary reaching the South Pole and women finally allowed in the House of Lords. He might put on the BBC Symphony Orchestra and *Gardeners' Question Time* for her, but not *Saturday Night Theatre* or the poetry readings on the Third because he thinks they're indulgent and silly.

Thinking about my mum all alone with only him, Sister Hammond and morphine injections for company is almost more than I can bear.

'I will miss you, so much,' she said then, as if she knew what I was thinking, 'but I want you to be a good girl and have a lovely time, you hear me? You hear me, Lizzie? I want you to be happy.'

She said the last bit urgently but it doesn't make things any easier at all. I know that he doesn't want me to be here at Bough Road. I'd like to think that he wants to spare me from watching my own mother die, but really he simply doesn't know what to do with me rattling around the house now that school is finished. Or maybe he doesn't want to see it himself, the way my mother deteriorates, maybe it brings back terrible memories from the front and watching men die in the trenches and I should pity him. But I don't have it in my heart to pity him because we both have to cope with it in some way or another, we'll both have to be strong and live with it soon. I hate that he decides how I should cope, that I have no choice but to do what he says. And I hate that I cannot turn away from what Mum wants, not when she says it so urgently, holding on to both my hands and putting her forehead right up against mine, so I can feel her once-smooth skin that's now so fragile and papery. Up close, seeing only her eyes and not her thin, sick body, I can sometimes forget, just for a moment, what is happening to her, and it's just me and her, the way it has always been.

But when she pulled away and looked out of the window, I suddenly understood. I saw, or at least I think I did, that she wants me to escape from all this, from this dusty-draped dark house that'll be so much darker before long, from the garden that she's not able to tend, from the other people in the road who won't come near us because they are afraid of the way Death is eyeing up our house. That she wants me to be free, at least for a while.

I didn't say anything else then, and we read together for the last time and I was trying very hard to make it sound good for her, and not to cry because she hates me crying. But I challenge anyone to read Christina Rossetti without crying when your mother is dying.

Chapter Three

Elizabeth Holloway is my mother. The woman's words fell across the threshold, into the hall, and reverberated off the walls until they had reached even the darkest corners.

'I'm sorry,' she said and edged closer. When she held out her hands in a sort of conciliatory gesture I could see that her fingers were trembling slightly. 'I know it's sudden. I'm sorry for . . . just showing up here. I came all the way from Solihull, and then I was suddenly afraid to ring the bell. It's not quite how I'd –' Her voice lost some of its melody, got thin and reedy and then trailed away altogether.

There are a million and one things to say to something like that, but shock has a strange effect on people, a recoil of denial, paired with a bewildered floating-above sensation. I watched her mouth open and speak again, haltingly at first, then more decisively, pulling out a thin folder, pointing at something inside it and holding it out to us, but the neural impulse of the sounds refused to take on concrete meaning until I heard Mrs Baxter speak.

'This is your birth certificate?' Mrs Baxter frowned and brought it closer to her eyes, patting her front for her spectacles.

'I know it doesn't mention her, but I don't have the adoption records. Yet.' The woman cleared her throat. 'I've contacted the local authorities but it's a bit of a complicated process because I'll have to work with an advisor. But I also have this.'

She reached into her bag and pulled out a bundle of rags. No, not rags. A linen bag, held together with rough, uneven stitches, as if its maker hadn't been entirely sure what she was doing. Yellow with age, it smelled slightly musty and the embroidery at the top, a crude pattern of stitches crisscrossing along the edge, had faded into an indeterminate colour. The woman reached inside and brought out a little green jumper, a small woolly hat with a bobble on top, a pair of balloony shorts made from the same scratchy green wool. And finally, a slim notebook, more of a booklet, really, which looked worn with handling and soft, as if it had been held and read many times. Reflexively, I reached for it, but Mrs Baxter was faster, jamming her spectacles onto her nose as she took it and quickly skimmed the pages. Through a strange whooshing sound in my ears I saw that her face had gone very white.

'Where did you get this?' she asked, pronouncing every word carefully. Her voice now had a distinct edge to it and I noticed her hand gripping the booklet so hard that it bunched up at the corners.

'My mother. My adoptive mother, that is.' The woman was still holding the baby clothes and she watched Mrs Baxter's grip on the booklet with obvious concern, hesitated slightly, then held out her hand for it. When Mrs Baxter didn't immediately give it back, the woman stroked the little jumper. 'I'm sorry,' she said. 'I really *would* like to speak to her, if, I mean, if it's at all possible? I know this is a little unorthodox and I hadn't meant to come by here just like that. I'm not usually like this. But I simply couldn't sit at home, waiting and waiting for something to happen. It's hell, not doing anything. All I've been thinking about is being able to talk to her. God, I'm making such a ridiculous mess of this,' she added with a self-deprecating laugh. 'I'm so sorry. I'm Phoebe. Phoebe Roberts. Are you, I mean – are you her daughters? Her family?'

She held out her hand, but just then, there was the sound of a door opening upstairs. At this, Mrs Baxter seemed to finally come to her senses. Ignoring the woman's outstretched hand, she motioned her backwards, then pulled Venetia and me through the front door and out onto the footpath below. After raining most of the morning, it had finally stopped and Mr Field across the road was clipping his hedge, as he always did, the familiar clip-squeak-clip-squeak of his rusty garden shears drifting across the street.

'I'm sorry, Miss, er, Roberts?' she said, checking the birth certificate again. 'Today really is not a good day at all. We need just a minute. Venetia, love. Addie. You'll have to look at this.'

She handed us the booklet, keeping the paper in her hand. Venetia shook her head, but involuntarily my hand came up to take it, open it, turn the page. I drew in a sudden, sharp breath.

Blue ink, iridescently, impossibly blue, swirls and whorls that rose and fell in girlish loops on each page, some of the straight lines pressed down into the soft paper hard enough to create tiny little grooves. *Weight: 8 st 6 lb . . . Moving a lot . . . Feeling faint 36 wks . . .*

It was a lot less confident than I knew my mother to have been and the letters were rounder, more carefully executed than when I'd last seen them, but it couldn't have been more clearly my mother's hand-writing if she'd appeared from the back of the house just now, the day's paper clamped beneath her elbow, pushing her spectacles up into her hair and smiling at the postman as she signed for a delivery, and it made me finally open my mouth, meet the woman's eyes and say the one thing that hadn't yet been said.

'My mother died, a year ago. It was an accident. Very sudden.'

For a moment, the woman stood, her eyes on my face as if she was looking right into my heart and saw my mother there with her news-paper, the lenses of her spectacles glinting through her curls. Then her face closed up, the angles of her cheekbones tightened.

'No,' she whispered. 'Oh no. I didn't know.'

Her voice sounded so bleak that I involuntarily made a move but Mrs Baxter had already stepped forward, put an arm on the woman's shoulder and steered her over to the bottom of the front steps, where she sank down, hunching over her bag. Across the road, Mr Field was still clipping his hedge, clip-squeak-clip-squeak, the same way he'd done for decades. My mother had once gone over and anonymously left a small can of machine oil on his doorstep.

Then, loud and clear: 'I don't believe you.' Venetia had recovered and her face was set. 'Our mother is dead. She's gone. Leave us to mourn her in peace and take your story elsewhere.'

The woman lifted her head and when she saw Venetia tower over her, she got up, cautiously but by no means afraid, and a small part of me took a moment to admire that fact.

'You don't? Then have a look at this.'

Her face was very white and her cheeks seemed to have hollowed, as if someone had carefully extracted all the flesh underneath her skin, leaving her face stretched tightly over her cheekbones. She turned out the seam of the linen bundle, her thumb caressing its length, until she found what she'd been looking for, painstakingly stitched, the letters ESH. *Elizabeth Sophie Harington.* Venetia made an incredulous sound in the back of her throat, and might have said something along the lines of 'bah', but the woman calmly took the little booklet and opened it, held it up right in front of us, turning the pages until she came to the very end. A large-lettered column that listed words, one below the other, in my mother's handwriting.

Flora. Beatrice. Hester. Dona. Baby names. And then, on the very last line, *Venetia.*

Venetia had always been supposed to be 'Flora', after Flora Poste from *Cold Comfort Farm*, but my dad had intervened, and Jas had been allowed to be 'Jasper', instead of 'Fitzwilliam', which had been my mother's favourite and which my father had also vetoed, along with things like 'Winifred' and 'Galadriel' and 'Sylvester', thus supporting the fact that English professors, particularly those with a penchant for Georgette Heyer, should never be allowed to name their children. I frowned at the careful swoosh of the V, like a big check mark that had anticipated Venetia's arrival, and resisted the urge to turn the page. Surely, the list would continue on the next page. There had to be more names, like Adele. Or Adelaide. Adeline?

'"Venetia", that's you, isn't it?' The woman emphasised each syllable carefully. 'And, if you still don't believe it, then it might come as a big shock that it's not just me. I'm fairly sure that there is also someone else—'

'How dare you,' Venetia hissed, her eyes flashing, 'how dare you show up here, today of all days. And where the hell did you get all this? Did you steal it?'

The woman gave Venetia a look of contempt. 'A nurse gave it to my mother the night I was adopted. I read that mothers were encouraged to make clothes for their babies to take with them to their adoptive families.' She exhaled and her shoulders sagged. All the fight seemed to have gone out of her now as she slowly refolded the little shorts and the hat and put everything carefully back into the bag. 'My parents kept it at home all these years. I found it last week by pure accident when I was looking for an old winter jacket.'

I watched her shut the little booklet and in that split second, when my mother's blue handwriting disappeared, I felt a jolt of grief so unexpected and so razor sharp that it almost knocked me backwards. An arm came around to steady me and I leaned into Mrs Baxter's familiar scent of lavender water and stale smoke.

'How did you find us?' she asked, and I could feel her breath on my hair. She still held one of the papers in her hand but I noticed that she'd turned it over so I couldn't see what was on the front.

'I had her name, found her in the marriage register. It took a little while, to be sure, but once I knew her married name, it wasn't hard to find her address. She was so young, it never occurred to me to look in the death indexes. And,' she jabbed her thumb at the house, 'she's still listed in the phone book . . . everywhere.'

I looked up to where my dad would be sitting over his cold cup of tea and, involuntarily, I nodded. That made sense.

'My mother wanted me to wait,' the woman continued. 'Talk to the counsellor first, approach it the right way. But I didn't want to. I couldn't wait, not when I had her name and everything right there. Turns out, it didn't matter—'

She abruptly stopped speaking and there was a brief silence. Even Mr Field's shears were quiet.

'When is your birthday?' It took me a moment to realise that I was the one who'd spoken. Mrs Baxter's arm stiffened around my shoulders.

'No, I'm done with this,' Venetia said dismissively. 'Come on, Addie, let's go back inside. I really need to sit down.'

She tried to pull me back, but I didn't move and the woman looked up, still holding the bundle. Her voice, when she spoke, was hoarse and she was still breathing hard.

'My birthday is February the fourteenth,' she said.

Venetia gasped but the woman ignored her because there must have been something in my expression that made her focus on me. Her eyes roamed across my face, took in my hair, then locked onto my own eyes.

'February the fourteenth, 1960,' she repeated slowly. 'Why? Do you . . . do you maybe know the other one?'

'The other one?'

The roaring in my ears was deafening. The Whistles tote slipped down and onto the ground, where it landed with a thud, and for a brief moment, bereft of its solidity, I swayed. My eyes were wide open as if to help me understand what she'd said and the unbelievable thing she claimed to be, until the pressure inside my forehead and at the bottom of my throat was burning, like I was suffocating and drowning at the same time. An excited clip-squeak-clip-squeak drifted across as Venetia moved towards the woman so quickly that she was forced to step out into the road, but still she looked at me. I saw her mouth move and Mrs Baxter was holding Venetia back and Venetia shouted and the woman stood wedged between two cars parked along the street and looked only at me, because she alone had understood immediately what none of us seemed able to grasp.

That 14 February 1960 was my birthday.

Chapter Four

My mother used to adore amusement parks. When we were young, she could think of no more fun, no more exciting family outing than the Bembom Brothers White Knuckle Theme Park in Margate. It seemed incongruous, whenever I thought about it now, because she was so frugal and neat and cerebral, and she hated chaos and cheap thrills. But she did love bravery and daring and going for it hell for leather, so perhaps she had to find an outlet somewhere and that outlet was roaring down the triple loop of Celestial Cyclone.

Risk-averse to a fault, I was, perhaps not unsurprisingly, not a natural rollercoaster rider. While Venetia counted down the days with her best pink pen on a piece of paper stuck to her wall, all I could see were mangled bodies falling from the sky and there was nothing I dreaded more than the moment we'd step out from behind the till, my mother stuffing the tickets into her pocket and clapping her hands excitedly while I shrank back, hoping for the sudden onset of a fatal illness. *Right, let's start with Celestial Cyclone. Cyclone really is the best. And then Thunder Swell if the queues aren't too long? Come on, Addie, not another loo break. Let's go!*

My father, always the bag-carrier and Jas-minder, drink-procurer and queue-keeper, tried to prop me up when he noticed my distress but my mother's enjoyment always came first and my mother wanted us to ride the rollercoaster together. Absurdly, the more I shilly-shallied the more stubborn she got, until it became a fixed idea of hers that rollercoasters were the very thing to cure her anxious first-born daughter of all that useless agonising. *Chin up, darling, for heaven's sake. We're not even all the way up yet. Open your eyes!* Even if I had been less of a shilly-shallier, even if I'd squared my shoulders more, I'd never have stood a chance against the combined forces of Venetia and my mother at the bottom of Celestial Cyclone. Longing, above all, not to spoil my mother's day, which she had set aside especially to have fun with us, I let myself be dragged through the turnstiles again and again, at Belle Vue and Blackpool Pleasure Beach and Tucktonia. Sitting between my mother and Venetia, I felt their hands gripping me as if they wanted to keep me from making my escape at the very last moment, then the soaring and swooping of the rickety carriage, the inevitable plunging, the terrifying sensation of free fall. And then, just when I thought my thirteen-year-old heart would fracture into a thousand pieces from adrenaline and terror, there came that one short tantalising moment when the world righted itself at the top of each loop, for a fraction of a second, half a breath – relief – only to be off again on its madly careering, deadly course.

I went from being a risk-averse child who rode Celestial Cyclone to make her mother whoop with joy to being a risk-averse adult, an average sort of person, who didn't cry much at all any more, but who stuck around London when she could have been backpacking in Thailand, had a foot on the property ladder at the less angelic end of Angel and a string of equally average boyfriends, and who, to her mother's eternal dismay, baked not only for a living but all other God-given hours in the day.

I never went on a rollercoaster again, but the night after Phoebe Roberts came to Rose Hill Road, I unexpectedly dreamed about it. It was a dream entirely without story, a lateral terrorscape of endless looping and soaring, of free-fall plunges into bottomless, velvety black nothingness, my mother's face a flash of white next to me, her nails digging into my palms, her hair streaming like a halo around her head as we plunged down the tracks, her mouth that brief 'o' of delight that had, for one moment, always made my terror utterly worth it. I woke in the half-darkness of the early morning, tangled in my blankets and sheets, my arms clenched hard around my pillow, and with a squeeze of my insides everything that had happened the day before dropped back into my mind. I fell back against my pillow, closing my eyes against the woman looking back at me across the rainy footpath in front of my parents' house.

Do you know the other one?

It took the better part of a pot of coffee, dark and hot and very strong, and all the lights on, for the Cyclone dream to fade and for me to start thinking, in some preliminary way at least, about the appearance of a woman called Phoebe Roberts. When I'd finally looked at her birth certificate yesterday I hadn't taken in much other than the date of birth: *14 February 1960. Phoebe Charlotte*. My mother's name hadn't been anywhere on that birth certificate; instead it had said *Someone Someone Roberts*. And another *Someone Someone Roberts*. My own birth certificate, on the other hand, which I'd unearthed after some digging, was vastly different-looking, stating very clearly and completely unequivocally that I was the daughter of Elizabeth Sophie Harington, formerly Holloway, and Graham Alexander Harington. There was nothing on here, nothing at all, that linked me to Phoebe Roberts, that made me an 'other one'. Except our birth date, obviously. And the place. We'd both been born in Brighton.

Standing at my kitchen worktop and listening to the rain bucketing down outside, I picked at a white chocolate cake I'd been experimenting with a few days ago and studied the paper in front of me, willing it to release some information, anything really, on how a forty-year-old woman showing up on my parents' doorstep could possibly be who she said she was. And how this woman could have disappeared the day we were born. And how my parents, my mother especially, who was always so strong, who whooped at the top of Celestial Cyclone, could have been a part of this, at the heart of all this, had given away a baby, my other half, and then never told me.

My parents were married in 1959. There was a picture of them in Rose Hill Road, my mother looking slender and fashionably pale in a light-coloured suit, her hair much shorter and curling softly under a small hat, my father young and nervously happy in a black suit with a blurry flower in the buttonhole, his hand tucked through the crook of her elbow. My mother's parents were already dead then, and my dad, whose family was from the Midlands, obscenely large and hard to quell, always said that he hadn't wanted to overwhelm his young bride with a celebration dominated by hundreds of boisterous Haringtons they had no money to cater for. So they married quietly at the Southwark Register Office on a sunny May day in 1959 and barely a year later I'd come along.

Maybe to make up for the modesty of the actual day, my father had always carefully planned their anniversaries, often asking Venetia's opinion because she was so good about presents for my mother. Would she love tickets for a concert or a blues club? Or maybe the ballet? Or this special flying circus troupe that was in town? He'd have a present ready for her, too, a framed print he thought she might like for her study, a bouquet of roses, sometimes jewellery, painstakingly wrapped inside a small box. My dad was a surprisingly good present wrapper, with perfectly sharp corners and the tape lined up in parallel lines, neatly, carefully. He would be tapping around the front hall in his best suit and dark leather shoes, pausing to check his reflection in the hallway mirror and making silly, un-Dad-like grimaces when he caught me spying from above. And when she did finally come down the stairs, his face would light up and he'd offer her his arm, maybe give her a theatrical twirl for my sake, and they would leave together, a small white rose in his buttonhole, laughing and remembering the happiest day of their lives. I'd always secretly loved that day in May, the continuity of that happiness and its unchanging reliability, and it became one of my childhood years' bright little milestones as I grew up, like Pancake Day and the May bank holidays, my birthday and the beginning of school, Bonfire Night and ham sandwiches on Boxing Day.

An involuntary smile lifted the corners of my mouth at the memory of the buttonhole rose but then faded almost instantly when I remembered the same suit and black leather shoes and the very different man at the side of the grave, with the small bunch of flowers he'd brought, and which I eventually took from his hands and gently laid on top of the coffin myself. In a sad twist of fate, my mother died just a week after their fortieth wedding anniversary, which we'd celebrated in a big way. A Ruby Wedding at the Red Velvet Club off Marylebone High Street, planned around a ruby-red theme by Venetia, who insisted that I put together a red buffet: beetroot salad cups with slivered almonds and pomegranate seeds, salmon skewers with sundried tomatoes, red velvet cake and strawberry parfait. Pomegranate Martinis to greet the guests. Gallons of red wine to finish them off. Venetia was mad like that. A lot of the condolences, particularly those from party guests, had later mentioned the fact that my parents had been married for forty years, just in case he might not be aware how acute her loss had to be after *four wonderful decades together*. I'd never shown him any of those cards.

I put down my coffee cup slightly harder than I'd intended and looked down at the birth certificate again. All perfectly straightforward, all very ordinary. There was no way that my father would have given away a twin sister. It simply wasn't true. He'd have been thrilled to have something as special as twins, double the wonderful thing that he was sharing with the woman he loved most in the world, the woman he was going to take out every May for forty years in his good black suit and a buttonhole rose.

But tiny doubts started pinpricking me again; there was also nothing that definitively and unequivocally said it *couldn't* be true. At least not judging by the actual information I had on the particulars of 14 February 1960. There was no family lore about my birth, the kind my friend Andrew's mother, who adored her only son, very readily shared, making him squirm with embarrassment. *The blood, Adele, you could practically hear the skin rip. It was carnage, complete and utter carnage. The doctor took fifteen minutes to stitch me up. And don't get me started on how things* down there *were never the same. Sorry, Andrew, but women everywhere* must *be warned.*

I slid the birth certificate right underneath my jacket, which was lying in a jumble with my bag and the pastry box on the worktop where I'd dropped them when I came in the night before.

My father had never really talked much about my birth or the first few years of my life and my mother hadn't either. Although the latter might not necessarily mean anything out of the ordinary because my mother didn't go in for sentimental talk, at least not with me. She just wasn't that kind of a person, the coffee and cosy chats about first kisses kind of mother. She was fiercely private, for one, and she'd had too much to do, too many places to be, for another. I remembered her leaving for one of her many work trips, off to give a lecture at another university or do research at a far-flung library. She'd grip her case and turn one last time at the door, her smile quick, eager. *Be good for your dad and Mrs B now, you hear me?* And her expression, in that second before she actually closed the door, was one of – relief. Relief to be free. Had my mother, expecting twins, felt overwhelmed and wanted to be free? But she wouldn't have been free; they still had one baby, they still had me.

Suddenly, a loud buzzing came from beneath my jacket. I jumped, spilling coffee on the worktop before somewhat wearily extricating my phone from my pocket. There was only one person who'd ring me at 6.30 in the morning and she would simply continue calling until I'd picked up.

'Addie!' Venetia's voice broke onto the morning like a tidal wave. 'Are you awake? I wanted to make sure you were all right. Are you?'

'Bit tired.' I reached across to the sink for something to wipe up the spilled coffee. 'And, well . . .'

'It's completely ludicrous, you know that.' Venetia's voice briskly cut to the chase. 'Tons of babies are born every day in Brighton. This woman could be anyone's child. What if someone at the hospital, another mother, really did give away her baby while Mum was there and somehow Mum's stuff ended up with that baby, rather than with you? Just think of it, this woman has been in possession of *your* bundle all these years.' She huffed indignantly into the phone. 'It's outrageous, really. We should sue the hospital.'

'But that look in her eyes.' I moved the cloth in small methodical circles across my stainless-steel worktop. 'She seemed so sure.'

'You know Mum. You *know* her.' Her voice was sharp and I held the phone away from my ear. Conversations with Venetia were generally better had in person because over the phone she came across just a little bit sharper, just a little bit shriller than any sane person could stomach at 6.30 in the morning. 'She would never do that. Think how she grew up, an only child. Mum wanted a big family.'

That was true. She had no siblings and after her parents died she'd barely had enough to live on, was working as a secretary for a while, any jobs that came her way, taking in extra typing at night before eventually going on to university. Later, she would make us work for our luxuries, too, forever lecturing us on the softness of our generation, which had enough boots and sausages and possibilities to never want for anything.

'We were *everything* to her. She would have done *anything* for us.'

Venetia's voice warbled on the last word and a small sob choked down the phone as she waited for me to chime in. I blinked my own resolutely dry eyes and wished for at least half my sister's easy, uncomplicated faith in our mother's maternal devotion.

She blew her nose into the phone with an annoyed honk when I stayed silent. 'Well, I'm not entirely sure why you're so ready to believe a stranger over Mum, who, might I remind you, is dead and gone and unable to defend herself from these unfounded accusations, but . . .'

'Look, Venetia, I have to go to work.' I tossed the rag into the sink and fished for my bag to find my diary. I was due at the patisserie this morning, although not for another hour or so, but I wasn't going to tell Venetia that. My boss, Grace, had even kindly offered me a few days off altogether but I'd declined, wisely as it now turned out, because anything was better than staying here, polishing the worktop, listening to Venetia and trying to make sense of something that didn't make sense at all.

'. . . I, for one, won't have her sullying Mum's name and creating all this emotional chaos for everyone when we have enough to be going on with. We just have to make sure she doesn't run into Dad.'

'What? Why would she?' I stopped, my hand on my bag. 'He didn't see her, did he, after I left last night, I mean?'

I imagined my father walking down the stairs and seeing us out there, standing on the street with a woman claiming to be his long-lost daughter. Involuntarily, I shivered. Things were just about hanging in the balance, between his work, Mrs Baxter and myself, but only just.

'No, I managed to head her off. And I did *tell* her not to come back, very clearly, but, you know, I'm not actually sure that she won't.' Venetia sounded amazed that there were still people out there not doing as they were told. 'She just had that *look*. What do you think, should we call the police?'

'Don't be dramatic,' I said exasperatedly.

'But remember when he went to hospital last year and then we had to practically move in with him afterwards? I'm having a baby in less than a month, I need to prepare myself, mentally, emotionally. I can't be going over to Rose Hill Road at any given point, staying the night and all that.'

'Venetia, may I remind you, *you* never "moved in with him".' I finally found the zipper on my bag and opened it with an angry slashing movement. 'I agree that we don't want him involved unless it's necessary, but please don't make this about *you* or the *baby*. You can't just come in and throw your weight around because it threatens to inconvenience you.'

I realised that I sounded very loud and closed my mouth quickly, but Venetia, rather than giving me one of her icy retorts, was quiet.

'He's so subdued,' she said then. 'I hardly know him at all. Only last year they were opening the dance floor at their party, in that matching hat and tiara that said *Fabulous Forties*, remember? Dad was actually wearing his hat for the entire first dance and I'd never thought he'd even put it on. And now, I don't know, it's like he's waiting for his own death.'

'He needs time,' I said, trying not to think of my dad's happy smile beneath the *Fabulous Forties* hat and the pride in his face as he was twirling his beautiful wife about the dance floor. 'He's still in there somewhere—'

But then I stopped talking and frowned, because looking down into my now-open Whistles bag I suddenly remembered something that in my Celestial Cyclone nightmare and all-round haze of incomprehension I'd completely forgotten about, something very odd and not very straightforward at all. The strange phone call from the man with the gravelly voice. And then, a woman at the door. And both of them looking for my dead mother on one and the same day, both of them saying the words that connected all of that to me. February the fourteenth 1960.

Chapter Five

Pieces of yesterday afternoon slithered across my foggy brain, trying to click into place somewhere. Of course. The man *had* been talking about getting in touch with her, about information. Regarding February the fourteenth. And what else had he said? *I couldn't reach your mobile.* But my technophobe mother didn't have a mobile. She had a long-suffering secretary called Jessica and a mustard-coloured rotary phone that was still working perfectly fine, thank you very much.

Or did she? And if she did, where else would it be but right here, in her Hermès handbag, which was still stuffed inside my bag. I deliberated only for a second, then quickly, because speed worked well in these kinds of situations, I lifted it out and opened it. Inside, the contents had lain peaceful and undisturbed for twelve months, neatly arranged in exactly the same order they'd always been: a make-up bag, a small black diary, the same brand she'd used for decades, a scarf, carefully folded, a new pack of tissues. There was a lipstick in a pocket on the side, the mother-of-pearl shell tarnished, and inside the make-up bag I knew there would be a tiny hand mirror and a small vial of perfume, both in matching tarnished mother-of-pearl, which had been part of a set that Granny Harington had given Mum as a birthday present. A fountain pen stuck out from the edge, neatly clipped to the inside pocket, and even though you couldn't see it from here, the letters of her name were engraved in gold on the side of the cap. Venetia had spent ages choosing the pen for her fiftieth birthday and my mother had never let anyone else use it.

For one long moment, I stared at the silky lining of the bag, the little compartments, the once-so-familiar items. Here she was, Elizabeth Sophie Harington, formerly Holloway, her life reduced to its very essentials, clean and clear and out in the open for everyone to see, the way she'd always been, the way I'd known her for forty years. I swallowed, squared my shoulders and started laying out the items on the worktop until finally the bag was empty.

Nothing.

I combed through the slippery inside one last time, turned the bag upside down. There was a small thud deep inside the lining. I pulled at the zipper hidden below the lipstick compartment, cursing when it got stuck halfway, then slipped two fingers inside and fished until a sturdy rectangular object fell into my hands. It was a Nokia, bottle green and solid. It looked exactly like my own phone, minus the many scratches, the buttery prints across the screen and the dent in the side where it had fallen down the escalator as I was running for the Tube. This unit was shiny and new, barely used.

I stood, frowning at it until it blurred in front of my eyes. What had my mother needed a mobile for and, even more pressing, was it still working? Jessica and I had gone through all her contracts: her memberships and newspaper subscriptions, her yearly passes and season tickets, right down to her ancient local library card, and between the two of us we'd cancelled every single one of them. So if this phone was still working it could only mean one thing: that no one except my mother — and a strange man with a gravelly voice — knew of its existence.

There was only one way to find out.

Thirty minutes later, I was standing by the worktop where the little phone was now connected to a socket by my charging cable, both willing and not willing it to come to life because it if did, nothing would ever be the same.

There was a small burr from the phone and the backlight of the screen came on. A symbol briefly turned in the middle, indicating its willingness to cooperate; words appeared. *Menu. Names.* Bars were running up the left side of the display to indicate a signal. This phone was most definitely connected.

There was a buzzing sound, then another one, and a few seconds later, the display filled. *Eight missed calls. Six messages.* When I scrolled through the list, the same number flashed by again and again, an 0208 number I wasn't familiar with. The missed calls began about eight weeks ago and I wondered briefly if the phone company automatically deleted any messages older than that whether they'd been retrieved or not. I flicked through the menu to the address book. It only had two numbers stored in it and the words were awkwardly spelled as if the user was only clumsily getting used to the tiny keypad. *Jessicaoffice. VOicemail.* I clicked the latter, waiting with bated breath as it dialled, then replayed the messages, starting with the earliest one.

Mrs Harington, James Merck speaking. It's been quite a while since we were last in touch and I'm ringing to catch up with you on a few matters.

The man from yesterday. Older, I thought. Polite, businesslike.

A week later: *Mrs Harington, James Merck here. I'd be grateful if you could give me a ring back.*

Then, about the beginning of May, a hint of impatience crept into his messages.

James Merck again. Do ring me back at your earliest convenience, Mrs Harington. I've had a letter, which I think you should look at. I know you don't want to receive anything at your house without me letting you know ahead of time, so would you like me to put it into the post? Do let me know. Also, there seems to be an issue with the payment, which I'd quite like to discuss.

A little later, he started to sound distinctly put out.

Mrs Harington, I'm not sure if you've received my previous messages. I am trying to reach you. Please call me as soon as you get this.

The last one had been left two days ago, on 14 May, before he had obviously run out of patience altogether and decided to ring the home phone number, which my mother must have given him as an emergency number, and which, due to some freakish cosmic coincidence, I'd been there to answer.

James Merck. He sounded very serious in his considered, gravelly way. Not particularly warm and fuzzy, not at all chummy. A bit fussy perhaps, a stickler for convention, with his plummy *Good morning*s and *ever so*'s and *Mrs Harington*s. A researcher? A doctor? A colleague? He did sound like some of the fusty academics I'd come across in the span of my mother's university career. But what connection could he possibly have with 14 February, with me?

I squinted at the little screen. I *had* promised yesterday that I'd call him, hadn't I? It was only 7.45, but, really, I should tell him that my mother had passed away, that I'd been confused yesterday and . . . I pressed the redial button.

'James Merck Investigations.' A young woman's chirpy receptionist voice rang down the line and I felt the steel-edged corner of the work-top collide sharply with my lower back. *Investigations*?

'Er,' I said cautiously, pushing my fist into my throbbing side. 'May I speak with Mr Merck?'

'He's away for a few da-hays,' sang the voice on the other end. 'Back on Thurs-day. May I take a message?'

'Oh, I'll ring again, then,' I said quickly. 'I just wanted to—'

'Make an appointment?' the chirpy voice proffered solicitously.

'Well, maybe?' I said cautiously. 'That is, I'm not sure—'

'We offer everything, from adultery to family history, but Mr Merck's speciality is missing persons,' the woman reeled off cheerfully. 'And his diary is filling up fast so—'

'I'll call back later,' I said and hung up.

Chapter Six

So my mother *had* had a secret, several, in fact. A mobile phone, a private investigator. And – a missing person? Which seemed to suggest that – although it couldn't be true, could it? – she had been looking for Phoebe Roberts, while Phoebe Roberts, by a strange twist of fate, had found the baby clothes and the booklet and tried to connect with her at the same time.

I stepped into the back room that served as my manager's office at Grace's Patisserie, took down a clean apron from a shelf behind the door and walked back out towards the kitchen to start my day, the way I'd always done for the last fifteen years. But all I could see was my parents, forty years ago, my mother in a hospital bed, my father sitting by her side, two white bundles lying in a crib, cheek to cheek, noses touching, tiny puffs of breath curling around each other's faces. My mother looking both of us over and pointing her finger at one to keep and one to give away.

I shook my head, pushed open the kitchen door. I couldn't believe it, didn't *want* to believe it, because if my mother had given her away, then so had my father. And yet, one thing was very clear. If she'd gone to such trouble to hide the mobile, if she'd asked James Merck not to send anything to the house without prior warning, then he couldn't have been anywhere in any of this secret searching. Why wouldn't he be looking for Phoebe Roberts, too? And why, by all that is holy on this good, green earth, why would he have let my mother give her away in the first place? How had they let her go?

'Are you all right, Addie?' Claire, the assistant pastry cook at Grace's, regarded me over a shallow basket crammed with rosemary rolls and seeded mini-flutes.

'Yes, fine,' I said, blinking against the bright neon light of the kitchen, the blinding white of Claire's uniform and her neat little cap, then looked

48

up and down the worktop where baguettes, rolls and *pains artisanals* stood waiting in baskets to go out to the shop floor and five large trays of dough balls delivered from the head kitchen sat off to the side ready to be baked. I took a deep breath of flaky croissants and butter brioche and felt a stab of relief, because in here everything was still the same, nothing was different. Flour, sugar and butter still came together to make a perfect *pâte brisée* and I knew where every spoon and every whisk had its place.

'Looks like you got everything under control.' I scanned her baskets. 'Where are we on the breads?'

'I'm just going to take these out to the front.' She tucked a sprig of rosemary artistically into a heap of nubbly brown rolls. 'I've sorted the delivery from the head kitchen already. They didn't send us nearly enough custard tarts, even though they've made us have them as specials today. Is it just me or are they getting more stupid by the day? They did send the four carrot cakes to decorate for Mrs Jenkins-Smythe, and we have some orders for platters. But other than that I think it'll be quiet back here. Oh, and Grace is coming by later . . .'

She looked somewhat doubtfully at the smudgy black circles underneath my eyes and my white jacket that I'd buttoned the wrong way, but I waved her on, quickly fixing my apron and twisting my hair into a hairnet.

'I'm fine. You help with the morning rush. I'll do the custard tarts. I'd be glad to, actually. Saves me from starting on the tax forms.'

Claire disappeared through the sliding doors. There was laughter and chatter from the girls manning the counter up front, and as I went to start on the custard, the quick, automatic movements of fetching cream and sugar and bowls soothed away some of the nameless, restless anxiety that had started building ever since I found the bottle-green Nokia in my mother's bag. I separated eggs and scraped vanilla seeds into the slowly warming cream until they careened across the surface like tiny black speedboats, then started cutting up lumps of cold butter into small squares, tossed them into flour, reached for my pastry blender.

She can't let you go. That's what my father had said the day I moved out of Rose Hill Road, after the worst few months my mother and I ever had in all our years together. We'd weathered my highly disappointing academic underperformance at school and my shockingly unambiguous plans to enrol at the bakery school, before things took a turn for the worse during my last summer at home, just before I was to move out on 1 September. My mother had been deeply disturbed by my choice of career and had, in fact, thought I was joking at first. She flat out refused to even contemplate it, then tried to push me to think bigger and leave London. *For heaven's sake, Addie, baking is not a career, not for someone like you. Look at Andrew, he's got a plan, he's leaving his comfort zone, even if his mum would prefer for him to live at home till he's fifty. The whole world is open to you, go get it. Go get the moon.*

My mother had loved Andrew, his spark and gumption, the way he got the bit between his teeth and went for it, so if I wasn't prepared to lead the charge, then the next best thing would be for me to paddle along in his wake.

When I didn't go for the moon in the end, but for the National Bakery School at the South Bank University and a flat share with a friend of Andrew's, I braced myself for yet another onslaught of get-the-moon talk and undulating waves of my mother's disappointment. But instead, after months of arguing, she retreated and, claiming a deadline for her new book, stayed in her study night after night.

Left to my own bewildered and wrong-footed devices, I started somewhat disconsolately gathering my things. I packed bags with clothes, weeded out my cookbooks, equipped my knife bag and organised other utensils, all the while trying hard to understand why my mother, who'd usually be pottering around the garden during the summer or roaming the city with one of us, had all but disappeared. I was never great with change and I always struggled with assorted end-of-an-era anxieties but the silent, awkward weeks during that summer were enough to send anyone running towards change and ending eras at full tilt.

And then, finally, my very last day at Rose Hill Road arrived. The house was quiet when I came down from my room, carrying my last bits and pieces into the hall to be carted across to the flat in the morning. Suddenly, I heard a noise. It was a strange one, more of a low keening really, but filled with so much desolation and longing and sadness that I stopped and stood in the middle of the hallway, clutching a cardboard box filled with aprons. My heart beat wildly because for some reason, even though it couldn't possibly be, it seemed that the strange, unearthly noise came from the closed door to my mother's study. I'm not sure why I didn't go to her then, didn't fling open the door and find out what was wrong, pull her down into the kitchen so we could spend my last afternoon having a melancholy cup of tea together like any mother and daughter would at the end of an era. But I didn't. Instead, I set down my box noiselessly and tip-toed back up the stairs and stayed in my room until my father came back from the office and called for me to come and eat.

Dinner was a silent affair. Venetia was away at a youth camp and Jas was visiting Granny Harington, so it was just me and my dad, sitting down to shepherd's pie and blueberry scones, which were not at all dinner-like but which I'd made because they were my dad's favourites.

'I'm going to miss your scones,' he said, taking a second one and slathering it with whipping cream. 'I really will, Addie. What am I going to do without them? And your blueberry jam? And your raspberry jam? And the cream.' He gave me a smile and wink before taking another bite.

'Oh Dad, I'm not out of this world. I'll be back to visit. Before too long you'll wish I hadn't kept my key.' But I looked away, the cream and scone bite swelling against the roof of my mouth because there was a lump in my throat that'd been there since the afternoon and refused to go away.

'It won't be the same,' he said and sighed. 'It's never the same. Time moves too fast. You have to hold on to it with both hands. Just like you have to hold on to beautiful first-born daughters who're off to exciting scone-baking adventures and will hopefully return on a regular basis for a game of chess and bring lots of samples of their work.' His laughter sounded forced, though, and he cleared his throat laboriously.

'I'm proud of you,' he added unexpectedly.

'You are?' I was surprised, and very touched. 'Oh, gosh, thanks, Dad.'

My father wasn't the effusive type but now he nodded, as if to make sure I got it.

'Yes. Truly proud. You'll do wonderfully well, I know you will. Just go and—'

'Get the moon?' I said bitterly, resisting the urge to look at the ceiling where presumably my mother was sitting over her manuscript.

'Go and have fun,' he said instead, very firmly. 'Follow your dreams. All those silly greeting card sayings. Live your life properly, *carpe diem* and all that.'

'Yes, well . . .' I said haltingly, 'Mum – I mean, she's not even here.'

I broke off, because in all the curdled years with my mother, I'd never been able to complain to my father about the way things had been between us, because he always and inevitably stood by her, refused to ever listen to a bad word about her, would be moved, at the most, to occasionally ask me to 'be kind'. I was sure, now, that he'd steer the conversation to safer waters but was surprised when he said, 'This has been so hard for her. I know it looks differently; it looks like she's cross or doesn't care. But believe me, Addie, just please take it from me, that that's not the case. It's simply hard for her.'

'The fact that I don't measure up to her exacting standards, you mean?' I said bitterly. 'She really must be disappointed about the bakery school not even to come and be here for my last dinner. She's barely been around at all this summer.'

'You moving out is hard,' he said. 'You were her first baby, special in so many ways, and now you're leaving for good. Things will never be the same.'

'But she *wants* me out there, she wants me to go off and do big things. She's disappointed that I'm not going to New York, like Andrew, to work at some glitzy big restaurant, that I'm playing it safe in London instead. How, then, can she be sad about not having me at home?'

'She does want all that for you, but that doesn't mean that she can't still be heartbroken about you leaving home. She can't let you go, Addie. I suppose this is her way to try and figure out how to. How to let you go. To say goodbye.'

'But it's not goodbye' I said, bewildered. 'I'm still here.'

'I know. Just be kind. She needs it, more than ever, even if she pushes it away.'

He sat up and shook his head, mustered another innocuous laugh to show that that part of the conversation really was over. 'But the most important thing is that you won't forget to come back for a rematch soon. Chess and blueberry scones, Addie, preferably together, and I'll be a happy father.'

The next morning he helped me load the car, blithely ignoring the closed door to the study and talking as though it was nothing out of the ordinary that a mother wouldn't be there to send off her daughter into the world. But we were just about to leave when she did appear. She looked a bit hollow-eyed but otherwise composed and she hugged me and wished me well and said she hoped to see me soon, and when I sat in the car, looking back at the house for the last time, I saw her standing there, not waving, just looking after us on the steps of Number 42 Rose Hill Road, and I wondered whether I'd imagined both, the conversation with my father and the keening sound behind my mother's closed door.

She can't let you go. But was there another one she *had* let go? I drove my pastry blender into the pastry dough. Could she not let *me* go then *because* she'd let the other one go when we were born?

Gathering the dough into a rough ball, I wrapped it up to chill, then turned on the mixer. As the egg yolks churned through the sugar, became pale and airy, I thought of my father and his love for blueberry scones, his love for my mother, his love for me. More than anything, I wanted to talk to him, wanted to hear him say that it was all a strange mistake and that everything was still the way it had always been. But he wasn't any more that chess-playing, scone-eating person, who'd always made sense of things, and I knew I couldn't burden him with this, not a day after the anniversary of his wife's death, not until I was certain what it was all about.

Slowly, methodically, I ran a thin, steady stream of cream over the egg yolk and sugar mixture, whisking in the precise figure-eight movements I'd been taught at school until they slipped through my whisk like golden silk, flowing and swirling against the side of the bowl. Bracing myself on the cool worktop, I let myself be lulled by the soothing, homely normality of it all until I'd almost convinced myself that somewhere, someone had got something wrong.

Hartland, 20 July 1958

Saying goodbye to someone you love is like a small death in itself, a horrible, hard kernel of blackness that lodges itself in your throat along with grief, desolation and abandonment and is impossible to flush away.

Saying goodbye to Mum was probably one of the hardest things I've had to do, because I knew when I returned things would be different. And all through getting into the car and driving down Bough Road and out of the village and down into the country, I felt numb and shell-like, as if I'd left all my insides back home next to my mother's bed, and it was just my body which sat and looked at the flashes of green going by. On any other day, I would have loved being out in the car, which we used so rarely, and only for occasional weekend drives and holidays in the Lake District. But then my mother would have been part of it all, excited and healthy, pointing out all the things on the side of the road, dishing out sandwiches from the picnic basket and making up games for when I got bored.

Instead, it was me and my father, and not really me at all, just my shell-me slumped against the window, my eyes watching him drive, his profile set in concentration as we wound our way out of London and down towards the coast. We could have gone by train, but I think Father hadn't wanted to appear shabby, had wanted to be seen driving his own Morris Minor right up to the house. The drive took a long time, however, because the lanes were bumpy and narrow and ill signed and Father seemed nervous somehow, navigating the maze of little roads with exaggerated care as the map led us in what seemed like never-ending circles.

Finally, a small country lane took us up to a pair of enormous wrought-iron gates. We'd arrived at Hartland. He stopped the car then and got out and walked the length of the gates, clearly unsure of how a bank manager was supposed to approach a place that was obviously a lot more grand than he'd anticipated. Seeing him out of his depth was not something I was used to and it jolted me out of my stupor, so I too got out and we stood there, the two of us looking through the gates at the drive stretching away from us beneath enormous plane trees and the house at the end of its graceful sweep. I pushed my face right through the gate to see it better, squinting in the late afternoon sun, but he pulled me back, told me to behave properly and started giving me a lecture on being a suitable guest. I didn't really listen, because my mind was totally taken up by the house. I'd been expecting a bigger version of Number Seven Bough Road, which is a detached Georgian brick house, compact and blackened with a slightly glowering sooty brick facade. This house was much bigger, although not nearly as sprawling as some of the country manors Mum and I had been to see, and it was not dark and not shuttered at all. There was a wide front area where cars could turn, covered with iridescently white pebbles that gave it a beautiful, almost unearthly glow in the afternoon sun, and the house behind it looked light and welcoming with its honey-coloured walls and windows picked out in lighter stone, topped by different coloured roof shingles and crooked gables and chimneys. Over to the side were a few smaller buildings tucked beneath trees and behind it all I thought I could see the start of grassy terraces falling away towards yet more trees. Those had to be the gardens Mum had spoken about.

I can't recall what exactly I was thinking, standing there by the gates, my father droning on about propriety next to me, only that the house seemed to be a friendly sort of thing, cheerful almost, with its little windows winking mischievously in the afternoon sun, and that it smelled of grass and wind and sun-warmed stone. There were sounds, too, doves in a dovecote and gulls, I think, and the clop-clopping of hooves as someone walked out of the stables leading a horse.

I wanted my shell-me to stay sad because I didn't want to be here, but looking at the house I could feel my body filling with something, becoming me again. You couldn't help it, really, looking at this lovely house and smelling the fresh air and feeling the sun warm on your back. And then the person with the horse, a young man, suddenly spotted us and – it was the most amazing thing – he took a flying leap and was up on that horse and galloping down the driveway towards us. I could feel Father recoil next to me and I did too, just a little, because after Limpsfield and the stiff, silent ride in the car, this rider coming towards us and sliding off the saddle was so graceful and fluid and so very, very alive that you did have to back away to make room for him.

I didn't catch his name but he opened the gates, apologising and talking and waving his hands, and Father eventually got back into his car. He clearly wanted me to do the same but the young man was already ushering me through the gates, asking me to hold the horse away from the driveway as my father bumped through and down towards the house, and then he closed them behind us, saying something about dogs running away, and I watched the huge gates swing shut behind my father's car while the horse stood perfectly still behind me and blew warm hay-breath into my hair. It was the oddest feeling, maybe it was the house or the horrid drive or the sun or everything all together, but when I started walking towards the house, hearing the crunch of hooves on the pebbles behind me, the man talking and laughing next to me, my heart gave an involuntary lift and a squeeze, because for the second time that day, I knew that things would never be the same again.

Father was waiting for us at the house and he was very uncomfortable; you could tell by the way he held his arms and twitched his cuffs that he didn't know quite how to approach a family as grand and easy as the Shaws. Not like Mum, who had been to school with girls from families like theirs and would know just what to say and do, how to smile and be gracious. It's Mum who knows the Shaws through an old school chum, whose children, Harry and Beatrice, are staying for the summer, and it was Mum who arranged for me to come. Father, on the other hand, was stiff, rumpled and ill at ease after the long drive and he looked cross when I handed the horse back to its owner and Janet Shaw came hurrying out to meet us, bringing yet more people with her, all of whom laughed and talked in a babble of voices. A man came and took my suitcase away and another girl came up to greet me. I was buffeted by this little crowd of people, shaking hands and nodding and smiling, and when they realised Father wanted to leave right away rather than come in for tea — which was rather rude of him, I thought — someone was already running back to the gate to open it for him.

I felt it again when I saw Father sidle back to the car, that shell-like daze and the deep, piercing tug of home, and just then, absurdly, I didn't want him to go because he was my last connection with home, with Mum, and the thought of her lying in bed and waiting for my father to return late in the evening, to hear how he'd brought me to this sunny place and all these jolly, loud people, was almost unbearable. I backed away, although I knew it had to be rude, too, and I tried to be quiet about it, but I ran after my father and held on to his arm. He got even crosser then because he doesn't like girls to behave like that in public. It's not very often that I stand up to him but last night I did. I made him promise that he would call as soon as things changed at home. I want to be there if things change; I said that last bit very slowly and probably too loudly because Janet Shaw had come up next to me and I could see her frown. But I looked right into his face to make sure he understood what exactly I meant. He must understand that you would want to be home to say a last goodbye. He must.

He left then and I watched him drive away, and Janet must have shooed all the people away and back into the house because in the end it was just her and me, waving to the car until it had rounded the bend. Then she walked me into the house. She had her arm around me, which made me uncomfortable because she hardly knew me, and I was glad when she had to open a door inside and let go of me. There was a girl hovering to take me to my room, but Janet waved her away and took me all the way there herself and then seemed reluctant to leave, kept asking if I was all right and to tell her if I needed anything, anything at all, day or night. I nodded as if I'd do just that, but of course I won't. Wake her up in the middle of the night because my mother is all alone at home?

It was a relief when she closed the door, although strange as well, because at home I have to keep my door open all the time. I waited till all was quiet and then I peeked out to see if she was waiting there, if maybe there'd been a mistake and I should keep my door open after all. But no one was there.

Hartland, 24 July 1958

I've been somewhat remiss in writing because at first I wasn't quite sure if I was allowed to. After Janet had left me in my room, I hid my diary in the small space between my mattress and the wall. It's not quite as good a hiding place as my ones at home, under the edge of the rug or tied behind my desk with some old string I collected from parcels or inside a vase filled with dried flowers, but it'll do until I find my way around. Father doesn't like people being secretive like that and he doesn't like diaries – fanciful excesses of emotion, he says – so I've worked hard to keep it from him, always writing when I know he's not there or in with Mum, or I scatter a bit of sand on the floor in front of my room to warn me of his approach.

But now that I've been here a couple of days, I'm fairly sure I won't need the sand or the hiding places, and that's a good thing because I have to write almost constantly in order to keep a hold of all the things that are happening and that are so different here, so I can tell Mum about them when I'm back home in a few weeks. Everyone is always off doing something, mostly something exciting, and no one cares what anyone does as long as no one lets the puppies out of the front gate where they can run into the road. No one cares what I do either, and certainly no one seems to assume I'm doing anything wrong. On the contrary, they keep asking me whether I'm all right. Am I hungry? Thirsty? Tired? Did I sleep well? I squirm a bit every time they ask because everyone immediately stops talking to listen to my answer and then they all fall over themselves to make sure I have food and drink and am happy and rested. Maybe I need to try to blend in more; maybe I need to make more of an effort to look happy and spry so that they'll stop checking up on me.

The house is bursting full with people and I'm staying in a room on the second floor. They keep apologising for the size and the location of the room, which apparently is some sort of former servant's room, and when I tell them that I find it utterly lovely and very cosy with its brass bedstead and simple wooden furniture, and that I love the evening sun, the brightness of the honey-coloured stone and the trees outside my window, they nod somewhat dubiously. I don't tell them that being in this bright little room and closing the door to the outside world is a luxury I'm cautiously starting to trust, that lying in my bed in the morning, warm and free and ready for breakfast, writing in my diary and listening to the beautiful airy house wake up around me is strange and wonderful and different. There's a distinct smell in the mornings here, I've noticed: leafy things that have grown during the night and dew collecting on the croquet lawn, smoke from the chimneys, and then the wonderful smell of coffee and bacon and bread toasting. I wish I could bottle it, this early morning, and send it home to Mum, the way the day lies ahead, like a tightly furled bud waiting to uncurl, ready to burst forth with all of its promise and the cheerful bustle of people at leisure. Not like Limpsfield, where Mum is looking out at her beautiful garden she can't tend to anymore and listening to tales from a world of which she isn't a part any longer.

But I mustn't dwell on her because she has expressly forbidden me to do so. A letter arrived from her yesterday, which was so lovely, and she told me all about working her way through the *Radio Times* and that she's thinking of me every time she's listening to *Mrs Dale's Diary*. Dora has brought up lots of new flowers, she said, and a neighbour has been in to read to her. I'm trying to picture Mrs Peckitt or Mrs Smith walking up the staircase and down the corridor into her room, wiping their hands on their housecoats and greeting her with their healthy, competent smiles, and although I can't quite see it, I'm happy to hear it. She wants me not to think of her at all, she says, because everything is fine, and just to make sure I write down all the things I'm doing so I can tell her about them when we see each other again.

There is certainly enough happening here to fill whole diaries or to write a letter every hour, I'm sure, so I do just that, I write and write and write, because I can and because I want to and because no one cares that I do.

There are more people here, staying here, working here, than I've ever seen in one house. At home it's just Dora, who comes in to cook and do the washing and things, and Bridget when we need extra help. We have three bedrooms and a front parlour and a sitting room and a kitchen downstairs. Certainly a lot more rooms than many of the people in our neighbourhood have, but it's nothing, absolutely nothing compared to here, which, apparently, is only a comfortable mid-sized country house. A simple family home, Janet said with one of her big smiles, and she talked about their London apartment, which she says is quite big and very handy. I smiled back at her and went away, but of course I know that there's nothing simple about Hartland or a 'quite big' London apartment whatsoever. They must have no idea at all what other families live like. That living space for the majority of people is precious and rare, that up in London whole neighbourhoods have not yet been rebuilt after the Blitz, that people cram together in terrible hovels or ten to a house, with everyone from Grandma to the lodger slotted into bedrooms like sardines. That those lucky enough might move out to new towns where prefabs and high rises are shooting up like ugly concrete growths. That no one I know lives in a house as grand and open and golden as this one, so very beautiful, just like Mum said, perched amidst green hills rolling down towards the coast, with a great big stone terrace looking down into the gardens and small woods and copses all around. I can see on the map hung in Abel Shaw's study how close Hartland really is to the sea, so close that on some days, you can smell it, a fresh, tangy, salty nip in the air. I can't get enough of that salty breeze when I catch it, and I always wish desperately that Mum could have come here with me, because the fresh air would be so much easier on her poor lungs, the salty breeze so soothing.

Before dinner on my very first day I was met by Beatrice, who is really nice and has taken me under her wing, which is good, because

I would get lost at every turn if it wasn't for her. There seem to be rooms everywhere and for every conceivable activity: a boot room, a billiard room, a still room, a conservatory, bedrooms and parlours and drawing rooms and a library. It took me a little while to realise that the house isn't actually all that enormous, it's just got lots of windy, twisty corridors and stairs that you need a map for if you don't want to be late for breakfast. But what I then found out is they don't seem to care if you're late for breakfast. The eggs and sausages and things are all set out for you, they're kept warm and there's heaps of toast and jams and marmalade, and if anything runs out, someone just shows up with more of whatever you want. I ate so much on the first day I almost made myself sick. Very different from the porridge we always have at home, which I hope Dora makes runny enough and not too sweet, because Mum says it hurts her throat.

The Shaws have a lot of young people staying. There is John and Harry and Felicity and Will – they're all old, twenty and more. Only Beatrice, who is Harry's sister, is my age, and John's cousin, a boy called Bert, who has awful sweaty hands and whom everyone seems to detest. Every day, they come up with outings: riding out and going for picnics, driving over to an old abbey or going for walks, eating endless meals and having tea and drinks on the terrace, playing croquet on the lawn in the afternoons. It's enough to make my head spin, all this jollity, and I worry that I haven't brought nearly enough clothes in my suitcase for all the things we are going to do. They were horrified to find out I couldn't ride, which is Abel's passion (and, I think, his work?), and I'm going to be taught soon so I can join in.

In a couple of days, we'll be going down to the coast to take the boat out and they were even more horrified to discover that I can't swim properly. Everybody gasped when I said it; I suppose it is somewhat unbelievable in their world of boarding schools and hockey matches and cricket and skiing in the winter, but I'm the daughter of a bank manager living in Limpsfield and I 'learned' to swim along with thirty shivering, blue-lipped children at the local baths whenever the teacher got a chance to take us. I am, however, turning out to be very good at croquet, even though it's hard to pay attention when the afternoons are so lovely and warm and the Shaws' gardens smell like a corner of heaven. The rose garden begs for me to wander off and get lost among the trees and flowers with my book. And I do that, whenever I can, I try to slip away to walk among the roses and read. Harry showed me the library and said that Janet has offered to let me take out anything I want. After my room and the gardens, the library is my next favourite place in the house. It's beautiful with a round glass skylight and sofas dotted all around and there's never anyone there because they're always off doing something noisy and lively. There are shelves and shelves of books, must be millions of them, all squeezed in so tight I know no one has ever read them and they look so old and crumbly by now that they would surely fall apart if you tried to pull them out. But there are also others, newer books, possibly belonging to Janet, and there's so much here I'd like to read – Anthony Powell and Graham Greene, Ernest Hemingway and Nancy Mitford – that I'm not quite sure how I'll find time for them all along with everything else.

I discovered quite a good little hiding place today, right up against a wall that's been soaking up sunshine all day and stays warm even in the late afternoon shade from the wisteria. I brought a small rug I found in my wardrobe and hid myself away to settle down with two books, one a wonderful story about a lady exploring Africa called *The Road to Timbuktu* and one of Ivy Compton-Burnett's recent novels. One for fun and one for mind-travel as the late afternoon changes into early evening. But I hadn't sat long when John came to find me. He's the oldest of all of them, just turned twenty-four, he told me, and already working up in London. He'd been sent to cheer me up and not to let me be on my own before dinner. Strict orders of his mother, he told me, can't have you be lonely. His eyes were twinkling when he said it and I think he was laughing. He's always laughing and making everyone else laugh and it's difficult to stay sad in his company. So we went walking, and he was telling me all about the roses and a new variety the gardener had recently grafted, called Janie, after his mother, and I tried to remember everything about it so I could tell Mum, who loves roses. And then he gathered up my blanket and books and towed me off to have tea. I didn't tell him that I liked being by myself, here where it smells so lovely and there is so much space everywhere, space to read and write and think about my mother, in this beautiful place, on such a beautiful evening. But then again, I didn't mind so very much walking back with him and listening to him laugh either.

Chapter Seven

'Someone to see you, Addie.'

After tackling a mountain of paperwork in my slightly airless office earlier I was standing in the kitchen decorating the four carrot cakes for Mrs Jenkins-Smythe's daughter's tea party. My mind had been going round in ever more convoluted circles since this morning and I was now so tired that I was longing simply for oblivion, even if oblivion came in the shape of 85 tiny carrots and 30 bunnies made of brightly coloured marzipan. I'd just arrived at an almost pleasant state of dazed concentration, cutting out shapes of marzipan in foliage-green and carrot-orange, when Claire pushed open the swinging kitchen doors.

'Grace here already?' The orange blurred slightly in front of my eyes as I squinted at the worktop. 'Tell her the tax forms and the new shift schedule are on the desk.'

'Much better.' Claire retrieved an armful of baguettes from the counter and gave me an enthusiastic eye-roll as my friend Andrew stepped into the kitchen, long-legged and tall and disgustingly tanned from a week with his girlfriend's family in Marseille, which had been a gallingly sunny 27 degrees while England was having the wettest May in seventeen years.

'Hey, Ads,' he said, frowning slightly when he saw me attacking the marzipan, my hands luridly orange. 'What're you up to?'

'Oh, you know, the usual,' I muttered, sweeping the knife in an arc that might or might not encompass the cakes, myself and the existence of a secret twin sister.

'Had a nice holiday, Andrew?' Claire was lingering by the door, hugging her baguettes with a simpering smile. 'Just make sure you're not here when Grace gets here. No civilians allowed, really, but I won't tell.'

'Claire, why don't you take those out front?' I said, and with evident reluctance, and prompted only by repeated shouting from the shop floor, Claire finally disappeared.

Andrew studied me.

'You look terrible,' he said. 'I leave for a week and you fall to bits?'

He folded himself against the worktop next to me, a slant of sunlight coming in through the high back windows to highlight his smooth cheekbones and pick out the golden highlights in his hair, which was sandy blond and his mother's delight. He looked improbably fresh and crisp, like a just-ironed white shirt, while I was feeling distinctly squashed and orange, my hair shoving impatiently to free itself from the confinement of the hairnet.

'Thanks a lot.' I turned back to my marzipan, deftly slicing off more small strips for the carrot bodies. 'It's been a long day.'

'It's only one o'clock.' His dark blue eyes crinkled in sympathy. 'How was circle mourning yesterday? I tried to call you a couple of times from the train. You must be glad it's over.'

'You have no idea,' I muttered. For one wild minute I was tempted to unleash the happenings of the last twenty-four hours, before reluctantly deciding that James Merck and my mother and Phoebe Roberts were well beyond the scope of Grace's kitchen and the four cakes in front of me.

'Why're you not in Marseille, charming your in-laws?' I asked instead and when I opened my eyes properly to look at him I realised that he seemed oddly fidgety. 'Things not go well?'

'No, actually. Claudette's brothers didn't particularly approve of me and her mum was a total iceberg. They want her to take over the restaurant as soon as possible and they seem to think I'm standing in their way just because I don't want to move to Marseille.'

'I can't imagine why.' I rolled my eyes, feeling a stab of sympathy for the remote Duponts. Andrew had been in a long-time on-off relationship with a beautiful French caterer called Claudette, who'd been supposed to return to her parents' restaurant for the last three years and was continuing to hang about in London instead, hoping Andrew would tear himself away from his *bisque de homard* and commit. Personally, I felt that some hefty heartbreak would do Andrew a world of good, but all the same I'd never actually warmed much to Claudette, just like I'd never warmed to any of Andrew's girlfriends. They tended to be infatuated until they got fed up sharing him with dead lobsters, skinned rabbits and the finer points of consommé, made masses of hysterical scenes and flounced off in a huff, and Andrew, vaguely bemused by all the fuss, would show up on my doorstep with an armful of wriggling fish in a bag. 'Want to have a go at this new bouillabaisse recipe I read about?'

Andrew and I had known each other for three and a half decades, ever since he'd moved in next door to my parents' house when we were six and had come through the hedge adjoining our gardens to show me how to make proper lemonade. At eight, we harvested our first batch of slightly mangy-looking parsnips and made soup together; at ten, we camped out in the back garden and roasted new potatoes in the fire; at twelve, we offered to cater Jasper's sixth birthday party, a job we took very seriously and charged fifteen pounds for, and at fourteen we started a restaurant scrapbook for a restaurant called Le Grand Bleu, with me as pastry chef, and Andrew – no surprise there – as head chef. Andrew and I couldn't have been more different, but from that very day by the yew tree hedge we clicked, in that easy, uncomplicated way childhood friends sometimes do. We stayed friends through all kinds of hopeless and not so hopeless romances and all kinds of crises, through Andrew's years abroad in Paris and New York on his way to culinary stardom, through my own much more modest quest for the perfect white sourdough roll at the bakery school and my decade and a half at Grace's.

'So things sort of came to a head.' Andrew faux-casually reached for an apron and sidled up next to me.

'Oh no you don't,' I warned him, moving protectively in front of my marzipan. 'Touch my carrots under pain of death. I don't get to do too much work in the kitchen these days as it is.'

'Stop being a manager, then, and go back to being a chef.' He paused. 'Anyway, Claudette's *maman* issued an ultimatum. Claudette has to move back immediately or she loses the restaurant.'

I forgot to shield my carrots and stared at him. 'Seriously?'

Andrew picked up my knife, there was a brief blur, like a Japanese stick fighter, then a tiny perfect carrot, complete with miniature leaves and even a speck of carrot cake crumb dirt, dropped onto the counter. He flashed me a wry grin.

'Oh for pity's sake, Andrew, I haven't slept, I've got a mountain of carrots to make and an even bigger mountain of bloody paperwork, Grace is almost here and I need to get on with things. Riveting as your love life is, do talk, if you please, or else I'll see you later.'

'You do look shattered.' He handed me another knife from the drawer. 'Are you sure you're all right, Addie?' He paused, his eyes scanning my face, taking in the dark rings under my eyes, the tight hunch of my shoulders. I quickly turned back to tend to my carrot bed. He waited for another moment, then added, almost as an afterthought. 'Well, anyway, she proposed.'

'Seriously?' I looked up and realised with a very strange and very sharp pang that I had well and truly underestimated the lovely Claudette. 'Wow. That is . . . well, I suppose congratulations are in order,' I said carefully, carving out a series of tiny green leaves to match the carrot bodies and cover my confusion. 'You're moving to Marseille then, gosh, all quite sudden, huh, I will miss you for sure . . .'

I tried to suppress another very strange and very sharp pang, because wherever Andrew had been in the world over the last three decades, I'd always known that he'd be back eventually, waiting for me at the Seven Bells pub quiz, ready to chastise me for my shocking lack of general knowledge and/or the abomination I was making of my talents, although always happy to be diverted into discussing the best way to float an *île flottante*. But now he'd be in Marseille for evermore, cooking side by side with his beautiful little Gallic wife, followed by a slew of children like so many fluffy, sandy-blond ducklings on a pond, washing dishes and bussing tables at the age of three. I started laying out carrots across the brown surface of the cakes, feeling the morning's anxiety drape itself around me again like a twitchy, itchy cloak.

'I said no.'

Andrew's hands moved around the cake in my wake, adding foliage in a very realistic imitation of a carrot bed. I didn't think I'd heard him quite right, but something inside me must have caught at least the last word because little waves of relief pulsed through an innermost recess of my heart that hadn't quite realised just how bereft I'd be if Andrew left for Claudette's fluffy ducklings in Marseille.

'Oh?' I tried to sound nonchalant. 'But you've been wanting to open your own restaurant for ages.'

'But not in Marseille, not someone else's business, handed to me on a plate. You know, I thought that maybe—'

'So where's poor old Claudette?'

'She decided to stay in Marseille. Things weren't quite so smooth after that.' He picked up a small cluster of extra leaves and tossed them onto the cake where they drifted, perfectly placed, on the carrot bed.

'I can't imagine why not.' For the second time I rolled my eyes at Andrew.

The midday delivery of breads arrived from the head kitchen in Maxwell Corner and I went to pull in the trolleys with the stacked stainless-steel trays and set them out for Claire to take up front, before coming back to Mrs Jenkins-Smythe's carrot cakes and starting to transfer them into their red and white striped boxes.

'You and I could always go into business together,' Andrew suddenly said. 'Finally stop talking about Le Grand Bleu and actually do it.'

When we started plotting Le Grand Bleu at the Rose Hill Road kitchen table years ago, it was to be a place of culinary wonders, with an ever-changing menu that fluctuated with experience and age and whatever we were obsessed with on the telly. Eventually, our professional paths diverged and Le Grand Bleu became the stuff of wine-fuelled late-night dreaming, the kind of exit plan you always talk about when things get rough, but never actually mean to realise. *Le Grand Bleu, baby,* Andrew would say when his head chef had slapped him down for a botched fish stock. *Oh, but for Le Grand Bleu,* I'd sigh when I'd stacked chocolate truffles for half an hour only to discover a cracked one at the very bottom. Le Grand Bleu, that mythical place where all life would be perfect, and which had over the years safely removed itself so far from reality that it was no more than a pie in the sky.

'Good old Le Grand Bleu,' I now murmured absentmindedly, suppressing a yawn as I moved the third cake into its box. God, I was tired.

'Come on, Addie, it would be fantastic. Don't you think?'

'Sure.' I smothered another yawn as Andrew folded a fourth box and held it out to me. 'You should probably go soon. Grace will be here any minute.'

'I still have a couple of days off. I thought maybe we could meet up later? We could sit down and talk about possible areas, look at premises?'

Like the menu and the size of the place, the premises were a well-travelled (if highly contentious) path in the land of Le Grand Bleu dreaming and we'd never got further than debating chic Kensington (Andrew) versus the cosier back end of Islington High Street (me). It was with considerable alarm, then, that I saw Andrew extract something from his backpack. It was a batch of glossy estate agent brochures. I looked from the brochures to Andrew and back, feeling a small twinge of panic. We'd never got as far as this before.

'I know you're busy with your mum and dad and all,' Andrew said, fanning my face with the brochures. 'So I went ahead and got these together this morning. Look, I signed us up at all the usual suspects over on the high street, Flaxton's, Mylor and Steele. There's some good properties around, we just have to do a bit of leg work.'

I put down the last cake. We had *never* got as far as leg work.

'Er, Andrew . . .' Dodging flapping images of open-plan ground floors with oak flooring and white-tiled kitchen spaces faintly reminiscent of mental hospital wards, I tried to inject a note of urgency into my voice. 'I don't really want to sign up with estate agents. I can't just leave Grace, and, besides I like it here. And Le Grand Bleu, you know . . .'

How to explain to someone like Andrew, who was born in the fast lane, that I wasn't the restaurant-opening, Celestial-Cyclone-riding, go-get-the-moon kind of person?

'I'm not really ready for all that,' I finally settled on, admittedly rather feebly.

'You totally are, honestly,' Andrew said urgently. 'It would be wonderful. I've got loads saved, and so do you . . .'

I cursed myself for asking Andrew to help with my taxes.

'. . . and we can get a really good small-business loan. I've been talking to my bank manager about it and—'

Suddenly there was the sound of footsteps from the corridor and with great presence of mind Andrew slid the brochures back into the bag. A moment later, Grace stood in the kitchen.

'Morning, morning,' she trilled, surging forward to envelop me in a hug. 'How are you, my lovely? Are you doing all right? I was thinking of you yesterday, you must be shattered, you poor thing.'

Her eyes fell on Andrew. Gratifyingly, she was one of the few among my acquaintances who wasn't the least little bit in love with Andrew (a feeling, incidentally, she shared with my sister Venetia), so she stopped in mid-surge and her face took on a frosty tinge.

'Have I forgotten to put you on my books?' she said coolly. 'Or why else are you in my kitchen?' She turned to me and said reproachfully, 'Addie, you know the rules, don't you?'

'Yes, Grace, I'm sorry,' I said quickly, feeling myself blush like a kid caught with the biscuit tin. 'He only stopped by to give me something. He was just leaving, weren't you, Andrew?'

Considering that Andrew was wearing an apron bearing her logo and his hands were orange and green from the marzipan carrots nestling on top of four beautiful cakes now sitting in boxes in front of us, this was clearly untrue and my face turned even redder, but Grace decided to take the high road and simply turned her back on him and pretended he wasn't there.

'These the cakes on order? Let's see then.' She surveyed them critically, turning one to inspect the back. 'They look great. Make sure that the platters are perfect too. Mrs Jenkins-Smythe is a long-time customer and I want to stay in her good books.'

'Yes,' I said, 'I know. I'll do my best.'

The phone rang from the office. 'And I saw the forms, thanks so much, Addie. Reliable as always. I'm around here this afternoon. Come in for a chat, will you? And you,' she gave Andrew a stern look, 'will not be here for it. Away with you, and be quick about it. And use the back door, if you please.'

'What's this, *Upstairs Downstairs*?' Andrew hissed incredulously when she'd sailed out into the corridor. Pulling off his apron and hanging it on the hook, he gave me a piercing look. 'How can you stand her coming in to inspect your work, when you've been a pastry chef and a bloody good one for thirty years? She's not even a cook. All you're doing these days is moving ready-made baked goods from the head kitchen into the shop.'

'I do make some pastries still. I decorate cakes. And I did those custard tarts—' I started.

'Fine, throw in the odd custard tart when your head kitchen messes up. But cake decorating for Jenkins-Smythe's tea parties and tax forms? You should be doing the pastries yourself, you should be coming up with brilliant desserts. You're wasting your talents here, I keep telling you. Le Grand Bleu, Ads. It'll be fantastic.'

Before I could say anything else, he gave me a quick and somewhat surprising peck on the check and disappeared out the front door.

Chapter Eight

At just after five, I was finished in the kitchen. We'd set out the empty carts with the steel trays for the delivery van from the head kitchen to take first thing tomorrow, and Claire had restocked the front one last time for the evening rush and left. I was staying until I could finally close up at around eight, a point in time I'd been living for since Andrew had departed with his Grand Bleu talk and estate agent brochures, leaving me with a restless, nameless anxiety I couldn't shake.

'Addie,' Grace called out from the office as I passed. 'A minute?'

'Kitchen's done,' I said and sank into the chair across the small desk, leaning my back against the filing cabinet and tugging on my hairnet with a groan.

I'd started working for Grace over fifteen years ago, when Grace's Patisserie was still one small boutique selling a range of beautiful pastries, desserts and cakes to order, all of which I made fresh on the premises. Over the years, the single room with the kitchen in the back had become a large shopfront, with Grace knocking into the adjoining property, and the one Kensington store had turned into four patisseries with a fifth one, in Marylebone, due to be opened at the end of the summer. Secretly, I'd always loved the first Grace's best of all, the simple shop with the wooden floor and the big glass display case full of cakes and pastries I'd made myself in the back, the smell of croissants and *gâteaux aux pommes* scenting the air when I stepped out in the afternoon to check supplies, say hello to returning customers and mums dropping by for their kids to pick a treat on their way back from school.

As she expanded, Grace had wanted me to manage some of the newer shops, maybe even take over from her at some point in the future, but the most I would agree to was to manage this one where it had all started, and even that I regretted as soon as I realised how many tax forms and staff schedules and order forms it involved.

These days, I spent too much time processing deliveries of breads and pastries that were now mostly centrally produced in our head kitchen, an uninspiring place called Maxwell Corner, rather than doing what I'd always done, what I'd always loved, which was making everything myself, from scratch. I still insisted on making something fresh on site every few days, but already most of the new shops didn't even have a properly equipped kitchen, distributing only what came their way from Maxwell Corner, and lately I'd begun dreading the glint of enthusiasm that seemed to glimmer in Grace's eyes every time the new Marylebone shop was mentioned.

'So Marylebone's bang on schedule for September, you'll be happy to hear,' Grace now said, as perky as she'd been at eleven that morning. 'Perfect for pick-up after the summer hols. That's what I need to talk to you about, though. I'm going to have to spend a lot of time over there and I really want you to take on the other shops now.'

I rubbed my forehead, kneading my temples.

'You're perfect for it, Addie,' she said impatiently. 'All your pastry know-how, you're great with people, you work hard, you're diligent, and you've grown up with my vision, *our* vision. You know what we want. I think this would be the right move for you. It's time, Addie . . .'

She went on for a bit longer but I looked down at my apron, rubbed at a floury spot. Why did everyone always push and prod me to be a better version of myself, to be more than I already was? And, while we were asking these kinds of existential questions, why did everything always, always have to change?

'So what do you say?' Grace said brightly when I didn't answer. 'Come on, Addie, don't let me down. I need you.'

'I'll think about it,' I said finally. 'I'm sorry, Grace, I have a lot on my mind today.'

She was instantly contrite. 'Of course. I'm sorry. You do look shattered, my lovely, if you don't mind me saying. Why don't you go home early today, I'll finish up here. Go, have a decent dinner and,' she eyed my hair, exuberant after its confinement in the hairnet, 'a bath?'

I hesitated, but only for appearance's sake, because after the last twenty-four hours, after Phoebe Roberts and James Merck and Le Grand Bleu and now Grace's offer, I felt distinctly like I'd reached the end of the line. Tomorrow I'd have to figure out how to talk to my dad and eventually James Merck, tomorrow I'd think about Le Grand Bleu and Grace's. Tonight, however, I was done. I'd stop off at the Italian deli on the way home for a roast chicken, have a decent dinner that did not involve any kind of baked good. I would wash my hair and sleep for an age and let the world do its thing.

'If you're sure?' I said, already up from my chair.

'Yes. Be well, my lovely, be well. And talk to me about the shops by the end of the week, will you?'

Trying to figure out a way to say no to a great many people in my life, I absent-mindedly waved goodbye to the girls serving the last customers and exited through the door with a final ping. It was raining again, a soft, cool drizzle that seemed to come from all angles, more like a fine sideways spray than anything else, and I was so busy opening my umbrella and shrugging into my jacket that I didn't, at first, see who was leaning against the wall next to the big French windows of the patisserie. Tall and thin. Eyes huge against the pale skin of her face.

'Hello.'

Phoebe Roberts straightened and came forward with a determined smile. I'd stopped right in front of the door, taken so completely by surprise that I couldn't think of what to say. With so much going on, so much to think about, I hadn't arrived at the part where I would see its key player again, unannounced and so soon. Too soon. Somehow, the sight of her brought to the surface all the things that I had been wrestling with throughout the day, the confusion and anxiety and the not knowing, and I tried to decide whether I could, quite simply, run away.

Phoebe was hugging her elbows close to her body, an umbrella tucked into the crook of her arm. She looked anxious and had obviously been waiting for a while because the tops of her shoes were dark with water and her camel-coloured trench coat glistened with little drops of moisture.

'I'm sorry for just showing up here,' she said tentatively. 'I saw the name of the shop yesterday on the stripy box, and I looked you up as

I was in town this afternoon. This was the third bakery I asked at. The girl said you'd be done soon, so I waited and thought it was better than coming back to the house. I wanted to talk to you. And I wanted to ask you . . . there's so much I need to know . . .'

I shook my head against the onslaught of her needs and wants. Behind me, Grace appeared in the window and gave us a friendly if firm shooing motion because she didn't like her staff loitering in front of the shop.

'Come on, then.' I motioned Phoebe up the street.

'Where are we going?' She fell in step next to me, dodging and weaving around the stream of commuters until I stopped, a few roads away from the patisserie.

'Here?' Phoebe asked breathlessly, looking up at the neon sign. Stanhope Café.

Inside, it was dark, with orangey lights and plastic tables, and smelled predictably of stale grease. I nodded to the young girl behind the counter who waved back cheerfully, and sat down hard on the first chair I saw. Phoebe Roberts eyed the Formica table somewhat doubtfully, then pulled off her coat and draped it over the chair next to her, taking care not to touch the hem to the floor or the table. Only then did she sit down.

'I'm sorry,' she said across the table. 'I can understand that this isn't the best way to go about it. I wouldn't want some stranger following me. I just couldn't sit around at home anymore. I wanted to see you. I need to talk to someone. But I can see that it wasn't the right thing to do.'

'Okay,' I said, taking a few deep breaths. 'What do you . . . I mean, what is it that you would like to do right now?'

Phoebe looked down at the tabletop, tracing a pattern across the scratchy Formica, playing with the plastic salt and pepper shakers that sat next to the vinegar in the middle of the table. Behind the counter, the waitress listened, polishing the same knife over and over again.

'I just want to talk, that's all. I know you don't really believe me, and there's part of me that doesn't believe any of this either, but if there's even a chance that we're related, that we're twins, then don't you want to try and figure this out?'

She nodded at me eagerly and I looked back at her, trying to find a sense of kinship between us, a twin-ness, that would bring us close by the sheer force of our shared genes. But all I could feel were her expectations, her hope, which I somehow felt unable to match.

'I'm not sure,' I said. 'Things with my mother were complicated. And her death . . . it's still a little fresh. I'm sorry if that sounds feeble, but I just don't know exactly what to think right now.'

'Complicated? In what way?' she asked. 'Did you not have a good relationship? What was she like, and how did you . . . I mean, if you don't mind telling me,' she added.

I found I actually did mind, at this moment in time, the idea of dumping forty years' worth of history with my mother on the table between me and a stranger. And she sat so close, too, only a few inches of spotty Formica between us. But when I moved back to find room to breathe, she moved with me.

'Have you asked your father about us?' Her eyes roamed across my features, my upper body, my hair, my hands, as if she was disassembling me for similarities, checking for matches against some invisible blueprint. The back of my neck prickled under her scrutiny and I could feel beads of sweat forming on my forehead.

'No,' I said, trying not to lean back too obviously. 'I haven't asked him. And I'm not sure—'

'He must know something. Maybe I could talk to him? Or we could both go. Meet up and—'

'No.' I pushed my chair back with a loud scraping noise. 'Just hold on a minute. Please. You can't talk to him, I'm sorry. Not like that. I have to find a way to speak to him first.' I brought down my voice with some effort. 'He's not at all well and . . . and I'm just not sure he's ready for all *this*.'

I gestured across the table and she sat back, her hands gripping the salt and pepper shakers like small lumpy weights. The waitress, who looked like she was about eleven and who had been gingerly tiptoeing closer, stopped, reversed. 'I'll give you a minute, shall I?' she said over her shoulder as she went back to the counter.

'All "this"?' Phoebe Roberts repeated flatly, setting the shakers back down with a small thump.

'Yes,' I said, wiping my forehead with the back of my hand. 'I just need time. You've known for weeks. I only found out yesterday.'

'But—'

'Sorry, Phoebe. I need to figure out what to think. And whether it's even . . .' *True* was what I wanted to say and didn't, but she knew anyway.

'Oh come on, Adele. Honestly, I'm forty years old. I have a good life. Why on earth would I be making this up?' Her eyes were flinty now. Over by the counter, the waitress put down her knife and called something into the back.

'I have no idea why,' I said, 'but who just shows up at someone else's house and drops a bomb like that into their laps? On the anniversary of their mother's death. Who does that?'

'Are you calling me a liar?' she said incredulously. 'Like your sister? Are you telling me not to bother you again. *Bother* you?' Her voice rose. 'How am *I* bothering people? I didn't know she was dead, obviously, or else I wouldn't have come—'

'Stop shouting at me,' I said evenly. 'I'm not calling you a liar. All I'm asking for is a little more time to get my head around everything. And I'm asking you not to show up at my father's doorstep without me having talked to him first. Is that so hard to understand?'

'Yes, frankly, it is.' She glared at me. 'Do you know what it feels like to find out that everything you've thought you were was a lie? To hear that your mother gave you away, just like that, and then to show up at her house, only to find her *dead*? And to find that *you* were there all along, that I was given away, and you stayed? Can you imagine that, you and your sister, in your cosy family home, can you imagine how that feels?' Her voice was sharp. 'And now I'm not allowed to talk to your father, just because you don't want to burden him with a cooked-up story about a twin?'

'But we're not twins!'

I had no idea where that came from, but as soon as I said it I clapped my hand across my mouth to get the words back in. The nameless anxiety dogging me all afternoon and the claustrophobia that had filled my stomach only minutes earlier drained all in one go, leaving me vaguely nauseous. Across the table Phoebe had gone very still.

Behind the counter, a dark-haired man in a cook's jacket appeared next to the waitress. They stood, watching us.

'Oh god, I'm sorry. I didn't mean it like that.' I forced myself to look at her, flinching when I saw her face, which was both stony and upset. 'I'm really sorry. I've been going over it in my head all day and I don't know what to think anymore. It's just so . . . hard.' I was stammering now. 'Not hard; what I mean is, I still . . . I find it so hard to believe. Not because you're a liar or anything, just because it's so . . . big. My father, things are difficult for him, if you knew him you'd understand—'

'Adele,' Phoebe cut through my rambling. 'We are twins. We were separated at birth. He's the only one who might know anything about the situation. We *need* to talk to him.'

'He's—'

But she wasn't listening. 'Then again, he might not know anything at all. Maybe she kept it from him. She could have, I suppose, although . . .' She shook her head from side to side as if trying to figure something out.

I gaped at her. 'What are you talking about? Keep what from him? Just go off to hospital one day and return with one child instead of two. *Hi darling, I'm home?*'

Phoebe's head stopped in mid-shake and she frowned in surprise. She kept her eyes on me for a moment and I suddenly got the impression that she was trying to choose her words carefully. 'Adele, our mother spent the months before the birth at a home for unmarried mothers, single women in trouble, that sort of thing. Down in the Brighton area. She must have gone straight from there to All Saints Hospital—'

'What on earth are you talking about?'

'It was in the little booklet,' she said cautiously. 'You know the little booklet with the names I showed you yesterday? I read somewhere that—'

'Show it to me. Right now.' There was an unfamiliar hardness in my voice and the 'please' I tacked on automatically did nothing to make it sound less like an order. Over by the counter the waitress and the cook were still watching us.

'Adele, please calm down, you'll get us thrown out of here.'

'Show me.'

Phoebe rifled through her bag and pulled out the diary. She checked the table, wiped away a non-existent crumb, then put the little black pamphlet down carefully. I snatched at it, fumbling a little, my fingers trembling. There it was again, the blue ink, my mother's carefully rounded handwriting.

Babies active today. Babies. I hadn't seen that page yesterday. *Circumference where it should be.* And then, a few pages in I saw a stamp. *Charitable Sisters of Hope, Brighton. 12 December 1959.*

'I read up on it,' Phoebe said to me from across the table. 'The mothers would sometimes be encouraged to keep a sort of pregnancy journal or write letters to the babies. It was meant to help with the separation later on.'

I leafed through the booklet, ignoring her wince when my fingernail snagged on a page and ripped the corner. 'I don't understand. Why would she be in a place like that? She was married to my dad and—'

'Adele.' She sounded almost apologetic. 'Your parents didn't get married until after we were born. She's using her maiden name, for one, here in the very back, and—'

'No.'

I had finally understood what she'd been trying to say about my parents and, specifically, about my father, and I shook my head vigorously, because the lower part of my face felt oddly sluggish. Images flashed through my mind. My father coming to visit me at my first waitressing gig and eating all my ordering mistakes before I got into trouble with the manager. Winking at a knight in the corner of the chessboard so I didn't lose it. Clapping at the end of *A Midsummer Night's Dream*, where I was the third donkey on the left. Standing below Celestial Cyclone and holding all our bags, wriggling baby Jasper's little chubby fist up at us in cheerful greeting. *You can do it, Addie. Just don't look down!*

'Absolutely not,' I said flatly. 'You, fine, I don't understand where you came from and how you disappeared, and my mother, well, I have no earthly clue what she was ever up to. But my father . . . My parents were married. For forty years. They had three children and a

79

house. A Ruby Wedding at the Red Velvet Club last year. We were a family.'

She opened her mouth and there was something that looked a lot like pity in her eyes, which made me want to pull her up from behind that stupid Formica table and shake her very hard.

'I don't want to hear another thing.' I backed away from those pitying eyes, scrabbled for my bag. Behind the counter, the waitress and the cook fidgeted.

'But—'

'No.' I lowered my voice with some effort. 'Just because your life has been turned upside down doesn't mean you can barge in here and do the same to mine. My mother died a year ago. But my dad is my *father* and nothing you say will change that.'

'Adele, I saw their marriage entry in the register. That's how I found her married name, how I found her. They didn't get married until months *after* we were born—'

'I have to go.'

I pushed back my chair so that it toppled over backwards with a loud clunk, then I thrust my finger into her face. 'You stay away from me. Stay away from us.'

Chapter Nine

Riding the London Underground in turmoil was always a bad idea, but it did cut down on your travelling time. I stomped down the stairs and shouldered my way through the crowd and right onto the train, heedless of the elderly and the pregnant, moved into a corner and hung off the safety strap, scowling at but not really seeing my reflection in the window, seeing instead Phoebe Roberts's face when she told me that my father was not my father at all, but a stranger, who'd been lying to me for forty years, when she had no idea about my family, about my father, when she didn't know how much my father had loved me. I refused to believe that he had lied to me, and *about* me, and about Phoebe Roberts and my parents' Ruby Wedding and a million other things that I might not even know about. After bottling it up all day, after trying to think rationally and square my shoulders and get on with things, I felt the bile in my throat straining to rise acidly up my oesophagus, and I realised that I had to talk to my father.

At my parents' stop, I pushed out of the train and rushed up the stairs, not pausing until I reached the crumbly facade of the house, with my mother's wisteria hanging wet and bedraggled above the door. I banged through the door into the hall, dislodging a shower of raindrops onto the threshold, and tossed my bag on the floor.

'Hello? Someone there?'

A voice came up from the kitchen, followed by footsteps clopping up the basement stairs. A second later, Mrs Baxter emerged, holding an unlit cigarette in one hand and the *Telegraph* in the other.

'Addie! I wasn't expecting you! You must be wet to the bone. This weather, when will it stop? It's enough to send anyone to the loony bin. Have you come for your dad?' She came across the hall towards me, tucking her cigarette behind her ear. 'I called you earlier, love. I was thinking of you and—'

Mrs Baxter's voice petered out when she saw my face.

'What happened, Addie? I've never seen you so . . . Come, let's close the door and have a cup of tea.'

'I came to see Dad.' I looked around her, craning my neck to see up the stairs.

'I think he'll be back in a moment; he just popped out. Here, let's get your jacket off. It's that woman, isn't it? That's why I rang. Talk to me, Addie. I want to help.'

She put her hands on my shoulders. I'd known Mrs Baxter for almost thirty years. With her fierce orange hair and smoker's voice, singing throaty hymns up in the attic or down in the kitchen, she'd held Rose Hill Road together for as long as I could remember. Mrs Baxter had been the one to tell me about women's issues (*pain in the bum, love, ride it out, all you can do*) and boys (*same sort of thing, really*). She'd taught me how to bake endless Victoria sponges and bread puddings and toad-in-the-holes and it was her orange peel obsession that had made my madeleines a signature dish at Grace's before Maxwell Corner took over. She was always there on the other side of a cup of tea and a slice of cake, ready to share outrageous tales from her book club and church poker nights and the caravanning trips down to Italy she took with her husband once a year. But right now I didn't want to look at her, didn't want to be mad at anyone else for knowing more about me than I did.

'No.' I shrugged her hands off my shoulders and she flinched. 'All year I've been tiptoeing around things, never saying anything real. But now, for a change, I need to talk to him, *I* need *him*. We're adults, for heaven's sake, if *I* can handle it, then *he* can.'

'What, the fact that this woman showed up with some strange story?' Mrs Baxter's voice was mercifully matter-of-fact. 'Venetia said—'

'Venetia said, Venetia said,' I mimicked horribly and Mrs Baxter's eyebrows disappeared all the way into her dark roots. 'Venetia has no clue about anything. Sanctifying Mum is her speciality, always was. Do you know what it really *is*? Do you?'

Mrs Baxter shook her head. 'I don't, apparently,' she said evenly.

'It's this woman, Phoebe Roberts, showing up again, at the shop no less, with all this, this information, wanting to know all these things about Mum. And she said,' I groped for air, 'she said that my parents didn't even get married until after we were born, that Dad isn't—'

Mrs Baxter's face had slowly become still but, to my immense relief, there was surprise there, astonishment, even. At least she hadn't known it all along, hadn't been lying to me like everyone else.

'Did you know about it?' I asked her nonetheless, holding my breath. 'Anything?'

'No, I didn't,' she said quickly, but then she hesitated. 'Although, I knew there had to be something because I think she had what I thought were fairly classic symptoms of depression. Not all the time, but definitely after Jas was born. And sometimes in the winter months. After you moved out, after Venetia left. I tried to talk to her about it once or twice, but she, well, you know how private she was.'

I paused for a fraction of a second, then shook my head and said bitterly, 'As it turns out, I don't *know* anything about her, least of all that Phoebe Roberts and I are *twins*, from some man my mother slept with, and that she got rid of her, probably to hurt me, because she never thought I was good enough, did she, and then she just went and passed off her new husband as my father for forty years and no one thought to ever tell me.'

The lump in my throat was growing bigger and I pushed the last few sentences past it so they came out a lot louder than I'd meant them to. Mrs Baxter turned slightly and opened her mouth to speak when her eyes suddenly fell on something behind me and she made frantic chopping motions at me. I whirled around and I saw my father standing in the open door. He must have caught at least some of the exchange because his face was white and the deep furrows on his face stood out like gashes.

'Dad,' I said, heat flushing my cheeks. I looked back at Mrs Baxter helplessly but she didn't seem to know what to say, just stared at him, the cigarette still perched precariously behind her ear.

'Dad, wait.' I stepped closer to him, trapping him against the door. 'Please tell me. It's not true, is it? This woman – she showed up here yesterday, saying that she's my twin. And that you aren't my father?'

83

It sounded so ridiculous that I instantly regretted it and yet, for the few seconds after the words had left my mouth, I held my breath, waited for him to deny it all, for him to take charge again for the first time in twelve months. But when I saw him straighten as if to brace himself, saw the flicker in his eyes, I knew.

'So it is true,' I said slowly. 'And you *knew* all this time?' I moved towards him until he was backed against the old coat stand in the corner.

'Addie,' he said urgently, pushing his fist against his chest. 'I'm your father. He was never in the picture. He wasn't even there. We haven't spoken of him in forty years. But *I* was there all along, and I'm here now; this doesn't change anything about us at all.'

'Oh Dad, you haven't been *here* in twelve months. How could you have kept this from me, how could you not have told me?'

'Addie, it's not like that, it's not—' He paused, his voice very hoarse. 'Mum loved you, she always did. More than you ever knew. I don't know what the woman—'

'She can't have loved me very much because she didn't treat me very nicely!' I was talking very loudly now. 'Always picking on me and hassling me and shutting me out, her and Venetia always off to do things together, but everyone was always too busy pandering to her to notice.' I rounded on him. 'How could you, both of you? I'm forty years old. I've been a twin for *forty* years. She never thought of that, did she? But that's Mum down to the core. She never thought of anyone but herself, she was always at me, it was never enough for her, it was always about her, what she wanted, how she was feeling, right down to riding that bloody rollercoaster—'

The lump in my throat was making my throat close up and I wasn't entirely sure what exactly I was saying anymore, I just continued to talk about all the years spent trying to make my mother happy and seeking refuge in the unshakeable solidity of my father that turned out not to be unshakeable at all. It came pouring out of me in one huge, horrible torrent that I was unable to stop even if I'd wanted to. Mrs Baxter was pulling at me from behind, but I shook her off.

'Adele!' I wasn't sure who had shouted but my dad's face had suddenly turned a terrible colour, sweaty and grey, and his mouth was a thin line. He took a deep breath, and then, just as I opened my mouth again, several things happened all at once. He groaned and gripped his chest, then his face went slack and he fell back. Behind me, Mrs Baxter gave a small scream and, simultaneously, a key turned in the front door. My dad hit the coat stand, which promptly folded under the pressure, sending him sliding to the floor, bits of wood flying in all directions, and Venetia's belly popped through the front door followed by her astonished face.

'What did you do?' she shrieked, unnecessarily so, because she clearly grasped the situation in one glance. '*What* on *earth* did you *do*?'

But I stood in the middle of the hallway and didn't answer her, my eyes fixed on my father's waxen face. Dimly, I heard Venetia's shrieks, saw Mrs Baxter jabbing numbers into the phone, then talking into it, felt her arm around my shoulder, murmuring into my ear, 'It'll be all right, Addie, don't worry,' over and over again, and then the squeal of the ambulance. My brain didn't seem to be functioning properly at all because instead of running to help, I just stood, right in the middle of my parents' hallway, and like a horrible, never-ending slideshow, my life zipped by in front of my eyes. Random moments buzzed against each other, remembered snippets of conversation, bloated and swollen inside my head, memories from when I was eight, ten, fourteen years old, all different now, distorted by the knowledge of this enormous lie that had been at the centre of my life. And – I realised this now with a terrible certainty – ever since the woman had shown up yesterday, I hadn't been able to absolve my mother totally and without doubt from abandoning my twin sister, not the way I had, immediately, unquestioningly, *known* that my father could not have had any part in the whole thing, which in a horrible irony, it now turned out he hadn't. What did that say about my mother and what did that say about us?

And my father, whom I'd always trusted and turned to, whom I'd relied on for the world to make sense, all along he had been someone else entirely. When his eyes rested on me over the paper in the morning, when he chuckled conspiratorially with me rather than *at* me like Venetia, when he handed me a Polo mint for my supposed throat tumour and told me, *better keep the roll,* a part of him always knew that I wasn't actually his daughter. We'd been bemused, sometimes, by the funny Haringtonian genes we shared, being so alike in our love for hot beverages and chess and sneezing in threes, when we were, in fact, nothing alike at all. And he had known it, that we weren't supposed to be alike, that we were strangers, really, and that I was missing half of me, and he hadn't done anything about it, when, all my life, I would have loved to have someone of my own, might have turned out to be a different person altogether if I'd had a twin sister by my side.

I wanted to run up to him and hold his hand and talk to the ambulance men, but I couldn't get my brain to cooperate and all that I could feel as Mrs Baxter patted my shoulder and called Jas to meet us at the hospital, while Venetia pulled on me to get me into the ambulance because, really, she couldn't be expected to go, it wasn't good for the baby, was a sense of disorientation that grew and expanded and filled the entire hallway until it started to swim in front of my eyes.

'Addie, for heaven's sake, get in. How can you just stand there?' Venetia shouted.

'You go,' I said hoarsely. 'You go, Vee, and meet Jas. I'll be there . . . as soon as . . . Take care . . . of him.' I felt a wave of nausea rearing up and clamped my hands to my mouth.

'You're not coming?' she said aghast. 'You're leaving us to deal with all this when it's your fault? I'm having a baby soon and—'

But the paramedic thrust her into the van, flung the doors shut and pulled away and I was shaking my head violently because it felt woolly somehow, the whooshing inside my ears making everything seem faraway. Before they'd even disappeared around the corner, Mrs Baxter had taken my arm and sat me down on the bottom step and pushed my head between my knees. The whooshing bounced around inside my skull, swelling and ebbing, bile straining at the bottom of my tongue, and I thought I was going to be sick, then something cold and smelling of lavender was pressed along the back of my neck.

'I couldn't stop.' I lifted my head and forced the words past my tongue. 'I just couldn't stop talking. Oh god, it all came out, all at once, everything.' I took several short breaths but my lungs seemed to have shrunk because I heard myself wheezing, 'I didn't mean to hurt him. You know I didn't.'

'Don't talk, love, just breathe, keep breathing, in and out, in and out.'

I could hear the note of alarm in Mrs Baxter's voice as she squatted down in front of me and got hold of my arms, breathing in and out so exaggeratedly that her smoker's breath made my hair lift, jabbing her chin up and down to encourage me to follow along. I lifted my chest, sucked at the air around me as she held on to my arms.

'I'm all right, all right,' I finally croaked. 'I'm fine.'

With another creak in her knees, Mrs Baxter lowered herself onto the bottom step next to me and I could feel her stroking my back, up and down, up and down, following the pattern of my breathing. She traced the outline of my spine all the way down my back and smoothed out my hair like she used to do when I was ten, untangling it bit by bit until it hung tidily around my forehead, creating a curtain of sorts that shielded me from the rest of the world and beneath which I could breathe more easily. The roaring faded, the bile retreated, although my tongue still felt furry and slightly too big for my mouth, and at last I lifted my head.

'I swear, I never meant for that to happen, I never meant for him to get hurt.'

Mrs Baxter was quiet, then she said, 'You've had a big shock.'

I gave a dismissive shrug, but she said firmly, 'You can call it what you will, but you've had a lot of different news today . . . and yesterday. Maybe it had to come out the way it did. Sometimes these things just have to.'

'I need to go to hospital, I have to see him, make sure he's all right.' I struggled up from the step, pushed my hair out of my face, but nausea washed over me again and I dropped back down, breathing hard. Dimly, I heard the phone ring, Mrs Baxter's voice.

'Jas? How is he? Yes. Ah. Okay. The Royal Free? Oh good, that's nice and close. And they're taking him in right away? Ah.' There was a pause and I looked up, bracing myself on my knees. *Coronary angioplasty*, she mouthed when she saw me looking. 'Yes, I have it right here. And where?' She scribbled something onto the back of an envelope. 'And is Venetia still there? Ah, good. And you can stay, too? I'll be there in a little bit then, with his things.'

She hung up, turned to give me a shaky smile. 'It was a heart attack and he's going in for an angioplasty, but the doctor thinks he'll be all right. Jas is there and he knows the surgeon personally. He'll be with him all the way. It'll be fine.'

'Oh god,' I said. 'Thank you.'

'Addie, do sit back down, love,' Mrs Baxter said, alarmed. 'You look ghastly, you really do. You sit there for a mo, I'm just going to run up and fetch a few clothes for him. I can take them by on my way home.'

'But Mr B, isn't he waiting for his dinner?' I said faintly. I'd only met the ubiquitous Mr B a few times but he always seemed to be waiting for his wife and his next meal.

'He won't mind.' Mrs Baxter pushed me down onto the step again, then disappeared and was back a few minutes later with a small brown holdall that my father sometimes took on trips with him.

'It'll take a while and they'll be doing all sorts of tests. They suspect he's had angina for a while, which would explain the heartburn and upset stomach he's been having. '

'I knew it,' I rasped. 'I knew something wasn't right. He was working too much, filling in for stupid Walker, and missing the doctor's appointment and all that. Could you hand me my jacket?'

But Mrs Baxter hesitated. 'Addie, I don't think you should go. He's not in immediate danger, but seeing you . . . well, he might become agitated or anxious and want to talk. And he needs to rest right now. Jasper is there and he'll stay with him. I'll take this over to Venetia, and then she can probably go home.'

'But I should be there, too,' I protested, struggling to get up from the step. 'It's all my fault, if I hadn't pushed it, if I hadn't shouted . . . It was unforgivable.'

'Go over tomorrow, then.' She tucked my hair behind my ears, squeezed my shoulders. 'Addie, you've done so much for him this past year and you're not the only one responsible for him. Let others take over.'

I opened my mouth to protest, but right then and there I realised that I wasn't actually able to get up from my step and go. That I needed time, even if it was only a few hours, to collect myself. I reached up for her hand, closed my eyes into her dry palm, which smelled faintly of lavender and cigarettes.

'Can you assess the situation and then call me?' I said hoarsely. 'I'll come later tonight.'

'Of course. I promise I'll call you from the hospital the moment he is done with the procedure to let you know how he's doing. And if there's even the slightest need for you to be there you can jump into a taxi and get there in minutes. Now go upstairs, get a bit of rest and some proper food, there's lasagne in the fridge, and things will start to look different.'

I remained sitting on my bottom step for a long time after Mrs Baxter had left, feeling the silence expanding and the solitude deepening. My outburst from earlier, the shock and the panic, drained away bit by bit, leaving me so empty I couldn't face walking up the stairs and lying down in my old room. Shuffling slowly towards the wall, I rested my cheek against it, just underneath the handrail, and closed my eyes. The slideshow of distorted moments had died down to a background hum and I pushed them away, letting my mind drift back instead to Phoebe Roberts, her face a mixture of wretchedness and pity, as I'd run out on her. My sister. My other half. But also – a stranger. Like my father, a stranger. And my mother.

Around me, the hallway grew quieter and darker as the grand-father clock ticked away the minutes. I jerked upright, then slumped back down, pulling my jacket close around me. No, I had to keep myself awake for when Mrs Baxter called. But he would be all right. Jasper was there. And . . .

I sank back against the wall, my cheek nestling into the little grooves of the wallpaper. It was only 7 but the rain clouds hung low, making it a lot gloomier than it should have been. Outside, the quiet was only interrupted by the occasional hum of a car splashing down the street. The wind threw a gust of rain against the windows. Must stay up, Addie. Waiting . . .

I slept.

Hartland, 28 July 1958

Out on the water today! The most glorious, wonderful thing I've ever done. It was nothing at all like our seaside holidays, which always seemed damp and rainy and uncomfortable, with Dad sitting on a beach chair in his trousers and collared shirt, fiddling with his tie, and Mum taking me for an ice cream. This was glamorous and fun and effortless, much like everything the Shaw family does, I suppose. I tried hard not to be happy about it, ecstatically excited if I am being honest, and where else can I be honest but in here, but I think Mum would have hated me being gloomy out there on the water, where it was so beautiful, so sunny, so unbelievably bright.

Harry insisted on taking me for a few swims in the little lake down past the orchards before we could go out in the boat. The lake is more of a pond, really, and I didn't much like the weeds reaching for my feet and the slimy bottom as you waded in to reach the deeper parts in the middle. It was probably the slimy weeds that refreshed my memories much faster than Harry, who's really nice and very patient, simply because I didn't want to stick my feet into the murky green slush below. They weren't going to go until they were convinced I could keep creditably afloat and I tried hard not to hold up the outing. In the end, we didn't all go, just Harry and John and myself, and Beatrice and John's friend Will with his girl-friend Felicity. They'd made plans to dodge the horrible Bert, so when I woke up to the sound of pebbles hitting my window and scrambled up, I saw them standing below, waving me down. I thought they meant for me to climb out of the window, which I did. I just slid down the wisteria, sending them all into fits of hysteria because the stairs would have been perfectly fine.

We sneaked around to the garage where Will had parked his

new car, and when we drove down the lane that I'd come up with Father only a week ago, the sun was shining and the countryside was starting to warm up. I've rarely seen anything as lovely as the countryside going down towards the coast on that morning, and when we came closer there was a salty smell of the sea in the air, just like Mum had said, and you could hear it too, the wind and the gulls and eventually the waves.

We stopped to pick up the boat at Tideford Cross, which is where Harry and John had left it a few days back. It was the sweetest little fishing village, picture perfect with a pub and ice cream stalls and bucket-and-spade shops and a small bakery where we bought some freshly made buns to add to the picnic basket. Will was carrying the basket and the girls had the blankets and umbrellas, and then we all felt like an ice cream to mark the beginning of a perfect day, so John banged at the door of a shuttered little hut and we ended up getting an ice cream right there by the harbour and walked out towards the boat.

Harry was walking next to me and explaining it all, pointing out the boats in the harbour and the breakwater walls that protected them and how there were smugglers' paths all along the coast, from here to Cornwall. And when you looked back from the breakwater towards the village you could see it spread out, an array of red and grey rooftops that looked so pretty and homely in the morning sun. Will's girlfriend Felicity wanted to take a picture with her new camera so we took a whole bunch, one person holding the dripping ice creams, one person taking the photo and the others jollying round the end of the breakwater. The sun was up now and we were all sticky and sweating and in a great good mood, even though the camera almost fell in the water, and one of the ice creams too, and then Beatrice almost fell in after it, trying to catch it.

Then finally we were out on the water, tuckering along the coast. I don't think I will ever forget this day, the clearest, bluest, most breathtaking sky you could ever see; the wild, open sea below, and us so tiny, bobbing along in our boat in the middle. It was so wide out there, so open, so bright, it felt like my heart would explode with the wideness of it all. How can people live in a place like Limpsfield, in a house like my father's with its dark, narrow corridors, its steep stairs, its dark kitchen and small rooms? How could I bear to go back to queuing behind Mrs Farnham and waiting for bones and chicken feet for my mother's broth, that stupid broth that would never make her strong again, when there was strawberry ice cream to be eaten on a harbour wall and flying along the water's surface fast as anything? How could my mother be dying when there were still things like this out here to see and to do, a whole glorious life to be lived?

I was aching to go home and tell her about it, tell her how we flew along the water. I kept asking John to go faster, and faster still and he laughed at me, but he did go faster until Harry shouted that we'd had enough. And even then he went faster and suddenly my hat blew clear off my head and into the water. I must have screamed, thinking of not having brought nearly enough clothes, but John just turned the boat in a wide arc, spraying us all with seawater, and drove back to where my hat was bobbing on the water and handed the throttle to Harry. Then, I can barely write it without either blushing down to my bones or grinning in a stupid kind of way, then he took off his shirt and dived into the water, vaulting right in, swimming up to my hat and snatching it out, tossing it into the boat. When he climbed back in, everyone shrieked because he was making things even wetter and I didn't know where to look.

It wasn't till later, when we'd moored in a tiny cove and set out the picnic, that I felt able to thank him. He just laughed and told me that no beautiful girl should be without her beautiful hat. It was a silly thing to say and Harry didn't much like it, I could see, coming to sit next to me and handing me a sandwich.

We were all sitting in our swimming clothes on blankets. I'd felt quite nervous last night about what I was going to wear and what I would look like. Janet had found me a swimming costume but it was so revealing, nipped and tucked in every area, that I practically seemed to pop out of it. I was stammering like anything because she was being so kind, but I knew that I really, really couldn't wear it. Father would have been absolutely livid. After some more searching she'd found me what she called a more old-fashioned one, dark blue and less revealing with a modesty apron to cover the top of my legs. But once we'd all got to the beach and Felicity sat there in her daring bright two-piece suit which I had never seen outside a magazine, and Beatrice in her red polka-dot swimming costume, looking glamorous in big sunglasses and hats and perfect make-up, I had a brief pang of wild envy, wishing very hard I was the polka-dot, sunglasses kind of girl rather than a hiding-in-the-rose-garden, poetry-reading, modesty-apron one, until I managed to get a hold of myself again because out there, after all, was the sea.

They didn't want to go in the water after the picnic, preferring to lounge on the beach and be civilised and not get their hair wet or their nail polish scratched. But no force in this whole wide world could have kept me away from the waves that looked so cool and inviting in the midday sun. Before I could feel any fear I was on my feet and ran straight at the water and hurled myself in, hearing only dimly Harry's warning calls. The water was fiercely cold and I could feel the pull of the undertow, but there was no weedy pond slime, no murky green slush, only clear, sparkling water and sand beneath my feet and I splashed and swam by the shallow end of the beach, jumping into waves and diving down to grab whole handfuls of sand, and shouting and waving back at the little group draped on towels and blankets. John had come right up next to me and as I kicked off the bottom and shot up from behind a wave, I saw him smiling at me with a strange expression. I was self-conscious again, because my hair was going every which way, my curls wet and mad, I was chattering a bit from the cold, and water was dripping from my nose and eyelashes. I wanted to smooth down my hair and wash off the sand, but he shook his head and said, very quickly and not very loud, so I had to come closer to hear above the noise of the water, that I looked perfect, just like a beautiful sea creature, a mermaid who'd come up to tease impressionable young men away from the shore. I had to laugh then, and let him pull me further out to right behind where the waves broke. I couldn't feel the ground anymore but it didn't matter because he held out his arm and I linked mine with his and we were bobbing and drifting, looking up at the blue sky for what seemed like forever and it was all quite, quite perfect.

The sun was starting to go down when we took the boat back, having swum and sunned and played ball all afternoon until I felt shrivelled and sandy and burned to a crisp. And when I got home I was so full with all the things that the day had brought, so overfull, that I took the first opportunity I had to sneak away to my room, to be by myself and relive the kind of day my mother would never have again.

Hartland, 29 July 1958

It's strange and quite exhilarating and I cannot help it even though I try, but it's almost as if the day out on the water has changed something inside me, pulled down a dam of some kind, because suddenly I want all this so much, I want to see and do and hear and smell everything as hard as I can and as fast as I can, and I can feel myself reaching and grabbing for Hartland, greedily, like I'm stuffing myself with it full to the brim.

There's still a couple of weeks left here. I cannot wait to get back to Mum, but it's her letters, too, that encourage me and spur me on to be here fully and completely, because, and I hardly dare believe it, but I think she sounds better. She doesn't speak of herself much, she's sending me long letters about all the things we used to do, memories she's been thinking of, and then she's always full of questions about me and all the things that are happening at Hartland. I've asked Felicity, who's been taking photos, if she might give me a few to show Mum when I get back home, and I make it my mission to write down every single thing that's been happening so I can tell her about it, because she seems to be living them with me, through me. And maybe she is living, will be living . . . but there's Hope again, my very lovely and very fickle friend.

I don't seem to need much sleep at all these days. I find myself awake early before hardly anyone is up, and I steal out to catch the

94

sunrise from a bench in my fourth favourite place at Hartland, right where the lawn drops down towards the pond, and then I pop into the kitchens where it's warm and smells heavenly. Cook gives me a bun and a sneaky hot cocoa and I visit the puppies, who are always restless and squirming because they're not allowed out the front gate.

And then another day begins and I read and write and laugh and chat and play croquet and listen to Janet and Beatrice's records and look through all those silly girl magazines that Father would never permit me to read and which Bea has brought to catch up on things. At night we turn on the music or play charades and fall about laugh- ing when even the grown-ups join in. It's Janet as much as the younger people, because she's so glamorous and fun and funny, it's like she's a young aunt rather than their mother. They call her fun nicknames, too, like 'Mother Dearest' and 'Mum Darling' or just 'JJ' for Janet Julia, which seems hardly appropriate for one's mother. I've never called Mum anything other than that, just Mum. But Janet, which is what I call her, likes being one of us and she's so friendly, with all her glamorous clothes and her hair done just so and her nails and lipstick a bright matching red, like a beautiful butterfly, flit- ting around and making everyone feel special and gay.

One thing that is strange is that they don't go to church nearly as much as we do at home, especially with Father being a churchwar- den and all. The one time they did while I've been here, it seemed to be seen as a fun outing and they descended upon the church like so many birds, crowding into the pew, chattering and laughing, with- out any quiet at all. At first, I found myself joining in the dressing up before and the gossiping after, but then I felt uneasy because it wasn't right somehow and I kept half-turning, expecting to see Father's face, his anger at the frivolity and the light-heartedness of it all, or Mum's thoughtful frown because she always says we need reflection, we need the shade with the light and the quiet with the noise, and she often took me to listen to the choir when she was well, just so we could sit in peace, thinking together for a little while.

So I've rather been wanting to go on my own, wanted to send special thoughts up for Mum, too, in case – well, there goes Hope again, she's unsquashable, I suppose – but I didn't know how to ask the Shaws to take me or how to make my own way there.

To my surprise, when I was downstairs early again yesterday morning, I came upon Janet who was getting ready to go to Morning Prayer, driving herself in the motor car. She said of course she'd take me and I changed like a flash, which wasn't difficult because I hadn't worn the dark blue skirt and blouse that I arrived in since I came. I expected Janet to chatter and laugh on the way to church, like she does, but she was quiet and so was the small congregation that had already gathered when we arrived and neither of us said much as she chose a pew in the back. Instead, we sat, keeping ourselves to ourselves in the coolness of the early morning. I was thinking of Mum and asking for all sorts of things on her behalf, just about managing not to strike any precarious deals with God but begging for peace of body and soul. I pictured her in her favourite chair, maybe even right at this minute, looking down at her garden waking in the early morning sun that made the dew sparkle on the leaves.

Suddenly, there was a movement along the pew, a vibration almost, and when I looked across to Janet I was shocked to see that she was crying. She had her head bent and her hair, usually lacquered and sprayed into rigid submission, was softer this morning, falling forward in waves, hiding her cheeks. Nonetheless, you could clearly see the tears running down her face, creating little rivulets through her powder. I forced myself to look away quickly because it was a private thing, as I knew perfectly well, but I was close enough to feel her tense shoulders next to me and I could almost hear her tears falling onto the prayer book. She didn't get up straight away after the service, she just sat, still as a statue, as everyone filed out, and I sat with her, both our heads bowed in our separate grief.

Janet stopped at the top of a hill just outside Porthallow and told me all about it, how her older son, John's brother Christopher, had died at the end of the war, in one of the last battles before it was all over, and that she tried so very hard not to think about it, to go on with things, but that she gave herself the early service every

Sunday to 'fall to pieces', she said, trying to laugh shakily. I didn't see anything funny about that at all. 'You should be able to mourn your lost children every hour of every day,' I told her, but she laughed again. 'It doesn't work like that,' she said, 'because life does go on. It has to. It must. But I miss him, so much, all the time.' She got out her bag and her powder and set to repairing her face, and by the time we turned off the road and on to the Hartland driveway, she was back to being the Janet I knew, ushering me in to breakfast with a big smile and making Beatrice, who was yawning over a cup of coffee, giggle as she read out risqué bits from one of her magazines.

It put a cloud over my day, though, and my heart went out to her and to John and Abel, all of whom had to go on with life while this loss was running right through the middle of it, as every room in the house and every tree and every song had to be a reminder of Christopher, preserved forever at nineteen years old. In the afternoon, John asked me to go out riding with him – he's been giving me lessons and says you must practise daily if you want to get any better at all – and I went with him even though I didn't altogether feel like it. I'm not much good at it anyway, but I was even worse today because as we went cantering across the countryside to the west of Hartland, through a wood and down a country lane, I wasn't paying enough attention to my seat and my reins, instead looking at John who was riding ahead, sitting easily in the saddle, his mouth smiling and his eyes lighting up as he turned to point things out to me and shout cheerfully exasperated instructions across the grassy path. I was wondering to myself how, underneath that smile, he was hiding all those memories of his brother, how he could contain all that grief. He's always so full of life, John is, standing easily and confidently amidst all this lovely splendour, and all of him seems to be here, not like me, where a part of me has to sneak off to the rose garden to be sad, or like his mother, who slips out to church on a Sunday morning to fall to pieces for an hour.

His horse threw a shoe a few miles down the road and we had to walk back, leading the horses along in the early evening sun, and bit by bit, the memory of being at church that morning went away, because he was so easy to talk to, so cheerful and clever. It's easy to be happy in his company when he makes me laugh and capers about, pretending we're taking the horses out for a walk like dogs on a leash, scampering through the meadow with his long legs and sending up clouds of dandelion fluff.

When we came up to the stables, however, we ran into Abel Shaw, who was checking on a mare about to foal, and John immediately stopped being silly. I think he's a bit wary of his father and that is something I very much understand, especially as I don't like Abel much myself with his red and flushed face, and the way he's easily irritated and impatient and always smelling of horses. When he watched us come down the path he frowned and as soon as we'd handed the horses over to the stable lad, he pulled John away towards a horsebox to have a look at something, telling me to run along and play like a good girl. I lingered, though, fussing with some tackle and feeding Aristo, the placid, friendly horse I've been given to ride, who doesn't seem to mind my awkward fumbling with the reins. I was hoping that John might be done soon and we could walk back to the house together and have a few more minutes with just the two of us before we were swallowed up in the group and all the noise again. But the minutes dragged on and the stable lad came to tend to Aristo, and without a horse to fuss over I felt awkward pottering around empty-handed by the boxes. I'd just turned to leave because I needed to change for dinner when I heard them come back through the stables. I didn't want Abel to call me a good girl anymore, because I'm not really a girl, am I? I'm about to turn seventeen, which is hardly girly at all. So I pressed myself back into the doorway to the tackle room and let them pass, and I was glad I had because Abel seemed angry about something. He was talking at John in his gravelly voice, something about 'not alienating her' and 'pull yourself together' and 'trouble', and although I couldn't make out what he was talking about, John seemed to understand perfectly well because he looked both defiant and resigned when he took his leave. I watched him go, all the earlier bounce and capering gone as he trudged back up to the house, and wondered to myself what Abel could have said that had the power to make that happen.

Chapter Ten

I woke up to the sound of the phone ringing. It was dark and for a moment I was disoriented by smells both familiar and strange. The phone shrilled through the gloom and I looked around wildly, wincing at the clicking in my neck, but it took less than a second for it all to come rushing back and I jumped up from my perch on the bottom step to pick up the phone.

'Addie?' Mrs Baxter sounded a bit breathless. 'Just to let you know, he's come through it all just fine, although he'll be staying in hospital for a few days. Some of the tests are inconclusive and they want to monitor him, make sure he's all right. No excitement, no exertion whatsoever, obviously. I'm having a little smoke break downstairs and then I'll be going. Addie?'

'Mrs Baxter,' I said groggily, clutching the phone to my ear and feeling huge waves of relief wash over me. 'That's good.'

'Yes.' She sounded tired but relieved. 'Listen, I came all the way here and realised I didn't bring him any warm socks. So silly of me. It's not the cosiest place. Will you bring a few pairs when you come in tomorrow? And a cardigan, maybe that brown one he always wears with the elbow patches?'

'Elbow patches,' I mumbled. 'Sure.'

'Okay, I'll go then. I've sent Venetia home, Jas is here, and there's no need for anyone else to come. He'll be out for quite a while and I know he'll be happy to see you tomorrow. Come right when he wakes up in the morning, love, I've cleared it with the nurse. And don't worry, all right? All is fine. Right, I'm off. Give Mr B his dinner.'

'S'okay. Thanks, Mrs B.'

I hung up the phone and stood braced on the hallway table. The clock showed just before eight. I'd only slept an hour or so. But when I straightened, stretching my cramped knees and rolling my shoulders, I discovered that the nausea had receded, that my head was clear.

99

The street lamps outside had come on, throwing yellowish pools of light through the windowpanes next to the front door. It was raining again, the dripping on the small roof above the front stairs and the metal bins outside coming together to form a soothing white noise. Occasionally, a car trundled down the street but other than that, all was quiet. I stood, listening. I felt depleted, completely empty, after pouring out all those things I'd always felt, about our family structure and the curdled relationship between my mother and me, while she and Venetia clicked so naturally, about Jas doing his own thing altogether and me seeking refuge with my father, who loved all of us but no one more than my mother, who was always first for him, always. And here was Phoebe Roberts, blowing it all wide open, everything that I'd always accepted as a given, that had been part of me, part of who I was. I felt ridiculous, thinking back to how diligently I'd tried all day yesterday to make myself believe that my mother and my father were exactly who they'd always been, that *I* was who I'd always been. How stupid I'd been not to see it right away. And now . . .

The wisteria branches outside moved and slithered with the wind, throwing black shadow tentacles across the ground and walls inside, a fluid shifting and flowing all around me that made me feel loose and adrift, as if I was floating among the shadows, randomly colliding with memories, without anchor, without direction. It was a frightening feeling, being so completely untethered from everything I knew. In the eerie stillness, the familiar furniture was distorted with bulging shadows, and for a brief, ridiculous moment, I had the feeling that the house was breathing above me, expanding and contracting, like some strange, foreign being. I shivered, shrinking back against the hallway table, wrapping my fingers around its edge. Somewhere in here was my family's true story, was my mother's secret. And somewhere in here *had* to be my own story. And, perhaps, that of another man's – my real father.

But at this last bit I heard myself take a deep breath that sounded very loud in the shifting, shadowy hallway. I didn't want to think about him right now, not with my father in hospital, not with everything I knew up in the air. Right now, I was going to go upstairs and find my father's socks, and I would take it from there.

In the dark, I crossed the hall and headed up the stairs. Pictures followed the curve of the stairs, old school photos, black and white baby photos, formal family shots, all of them so familiar that over time they'd almost become part of the wallpaper. Running my eyes over them on the walk up, they seemed strangely flat now and I was almost surprised when I occasionally caught sight of a little girl with dark curly hair forced into two fat pigtails sitting among various constellations of people that looked vaguely familiar, like people I'd once known and was now frowning to recognise.

On the first floor, bedroom doors lined the corridor. The wind had picked up and the windows facing the street were streaked with rain and above the trees lining Rose Hill Road you could see the moon vainly tugging on the clouds. I pushed open the door to my parents' bedroom and edged my way in until I was standing at the foot of the bed. The alarm clock on my father's side gave the odd soft tick, like a tiny bird tapping across a wooden table, but otherwise it was quiet. I reached to flip on the small lamp on a shelf next to the door, wary of the brightness of the overhead lights, shuffled sideways around the bed, then, after a moment's hesitation, opened the wardrobe. My dad's clothes. Work jackets and old jumpers, mostly greys and browns, soft woollen trousers, faded cords. All was sparse and well worn but clean, pressed and solicitously folded by Mrs Baxter, who always worried that the other accountants might think he was going to the dogs.

On the right, my mother's side of the wardrobe was the same as it had always been. Trousers and blouses hung neatly on hangers, jumpers folded below, the drawers of the dresser still held underwear and camisoles arranged by colour and frequency of wear. Involuntarily, I reached out to straighten the sleeve of a shirt but stopped my hand before it could touch the fabric. Still, as if the air around it had been disturbed, a faint whisper drifted across, a hint of bergamot and vanilla. Chanel No. 5. A classy, timeless scent, contradictory, like her, by turns warm and bright, reserved and enigmatic. The scent pierced the fog of unreality in my mind, a sharp, sweet Chanel No. 5 zing, that arrowed straight into the innermost reaches of my memory where my mother was sending a squirt of perfume into the air and lifting her arms to do a small pirouette underneath, curls moving to gather every molecule of fragrance. I recoiled from the vividness of the image, then cautiously inhaled again, putting my nose as close as I could without actually touching, but already, as quick as it had come, the memory had gone and I was once more cut off, untethered, detached from all that I'd known, a stranger in this house, a stranger in my own life.

Suddenly, a rustling noise. I strained to listen, my heart thudding in my chest. Nothing. Just the house settling down for the night. More rain hitting the windows, the hissing sound of tyres on wet tarmac. Quickly now, I picked through the hangers on my father's side until I found the brown cardigan, a few balled-up socks in the drawer. I selected another shirt I thought he might like and a thin muffler, which had been his only concession to being sick, rolled everything up into a bundle, tied the arms together and slung it over my shoulder. Then I stood back on my heels and looked around the room for anything else he might need. The duvet was neatly folded over the entire bed and bulged slightly over my dad's pillow on the right and my mum's special neck-supporting pillow on the left. There was an old copy of a Daphne du Maurier novel on her bedside table, splayed open at the page she'd last read, and presumably dusted twice a week by Mrs Baxter. *Rebecca*. I picked it up and turned it over in my hands, but it had been forced open in that position for a year and refused to close properly anymore so I quickly set it back down next to a photo of my mum in a silver frame. It had been taken just after my mother had become a senior teaching fellow and she looked almost exactly as I remembered her, in a beautiful if somewhat stilted composition. Her gaze was directed somewhere beyond the camera, her face taut with seriousness, her eyes hidden in the shadows of her lashes, as if she wanted her expression to suit a newly distinguished academic at the near-pinnacle of her career. I was about to turn and leave when I saw another picture, one I'd never seen – or perhaps never paid attention to – before. Half-hidden behind the lamp, an ancient wooden frame showed a girl and a woman. You couldn't see their bodies, just their faces pressed close together, arms around each other's shoulders. I shook my head and blinked my eyes, because if it hadn't been for the old-fashioned wavy hair, the sepia tinge that blurred the edges, this young girl might have been – me.

But when I looked again, I realised almost immediately that, actually, it was a different version of a much younger me, similar features arranged slightly differently, forehead longer, the cheekbones higher. And yet, unmistakably, my mother. My impossibly young mother whose face was next to – straight hair but also dark, a dimple in her chin pulling down her lower lip ever so slightly, like mine, and the very same grey, slightly slanted eyes looking straight at me – her own mother. My grandmother. They weren't smiling, although you didn't get the impression that the mood was sombre, only that they'd been forcing themselves to stand still long enough for the picture to be taken and were dying to be off somewhere together.

Constance had been my grandmother's name, Constance Hollo-way. I knew that much, and that she and my grandfather had died when my mother had just turned seventeen. But my mother had said little else about Constance, and I'd never asked about her. My father's family had always been so very present in our lives that there was little need for another set of grandparents, for another slew of aunts and uncles and cousins, and when information wasn't forthcoming, I'd never questioned it. But why, why hadn't I asked more, talked more to my mother, about her own mother? Had I assumed her to be private and distant, when I could have made more of an effort, could have shown interest? Would she have talked to me then, about what really mattered to her? The two faces constricted in front of my eyes when I thought of what this young, sepia-coloured girl would go on to do. Her baby gone. A whole life spent hiding it. What would it have been like for her, knowing every day that somewhere out there was a little girl growing up alongside us, a baby crawling, then toddling, then running, a girl nervous on her first day of school, her first day of uni, her first job, buying her first house? A whole other person who was missing in the photos along the stairs, who should have been next to me in every single picture.

I touched my mother's face through the glass, then Constance's, the curve of her mouth, her eyes squinting with suppressed but undeniably good humour, the tips of her fingers just visible at the base of her daughter's neck as she'd drawn her close for the picture. I willed myself to feel a connection with her, because I was part of Constance Holloway and she lived on in me, through my mother, like a chain. Our past and our present was right here in this picture and I wanted to feel that sense of belonging, of kinship, but the closer I looked, the further the two women seemed to slip out of reach, back into their soft-edged, sepia-coloured world, until all I could see of the grey eyes I knew so well was no more than two small dark dots in a neat, heart-shaped white face.

Chapter Eleven

I was so lost in thought that when the doorbell rang, I twitched, managing to drop the frame onto the edge of the bedside table where the glass shattered. I lunged for it anyway, fumbling at the empty air and cursing when the bell shrilled again. Hoisting my cardigan bundle higher, I carefully picked up the splintery frame and sandwiched it between the other photo and *Rebecca* so as not to cut my hand, then moved quietly to the top of the stairs to peer down into the front hall. In the yellow light coming in through the glass sides of the front door, I could make out a tall outline and was struck by a sudden sense of déjà vu. Had she followed me? No, she was thinner than that and, if I remembered correctly, not quite as tall. I saw the figure come closer, no doubt to escape the rain, and a face and a shock of sandy-blond hair squashed up against the frosted glass and the bell rang a third time.

'Oh, all right, all right.' I ran down the stairs and opened the door.

'Hi.' Andrew shook out his umbrella and wiped his feet on the doormat. 'I tried to call you but you weren't home and I figured you'd be here, checking on your dad. You seemed off this morning, I thought I'd better come check on you, bring you some dinner and—'

He stopped in mid-sentence, eyeing the bundle of clothes and balled-up socks over my shoulder, the broken frame in my hands and my hair, which was even bigger than usual with the mix of humidity and being untethered. His eyebrows rose slightly and he peered behind me into the dark and heavily silent house.

'What, exactly, *are* you doing here, Ads? Where's your dad?'

I swallowed and shook my head mutely and Andrew ran his hand through his hair, making it stick up in wet spikes. He held up a plastic bag.

'Fish and chips,' he explained, flapping the bag handles open and closed under my nose, then nudged me out of the way and stepped inside, closing the door behind him.

'You *could* occasionally answer your phone, you know? And why aren't you turning on the light?' With a practised move, he switched on the light, flung his umbrella into the wrought-iron stand and stretched out his hand to hang up his coat, then stopped in his tracks.

'What happened to the coat stand?' he asked incredulously.

'It broke.' I jabbed my chin in the direction of the jumble of wood and nails in the corner.

'But I loved that coat stand,' Andrew said mournfully, holding on to his jacket as if hanging it anywhere else would be an imposition. 'Your mum got it at that boot sale, remember, the one she dragged us to all the way out in Barnet? We went to the farm afterwards. Watched the pig race. That coat stand was practically an antique.'

'Probably why it broke.' I crossed the hall towards my familiar place on the bottom stair, sat down.

A second later, the stair creaked as Andrew sat down next to me.

'What's going on, Ads?' He crossed and folded his long legs so that his knees were resting against mine. His jeans were faded into a soft blue denim and his jumper was scratchy against my bare arm.

'How long have you got?' I said, setting the cardigan bundle and the photos between us.

'My shift doesn't start till nine a.m.'

'It's complicated.'

'I'm good with complicated.'

Andrew listened in silence, only now and again shaking his head slightly, and when I was done, he took the glassless frame from my lap and held it up so the light fell onto the black and white faces. 'A twin,' he said. 'If that is true, then that would be amazing, Addie. Truly and utterly amazing.'

I looked up, surprised, because I suddenly realised that no one in the last twenty-four hours, not least of all myself, had found anything remotely positive to say about the whole thing. It was only ever about lies and my father and the secrets my mother had kept, and might still be keeping, and how much everything had been changed by them.

'This is your grandmother? She's quite a dish! She looks like you.' Andrew gave me a quick once-over. 'It's the eyes, and the set of your chin.'

He looked back at the picture, prising a small glass shard off the frame with his fingers, which were capable and scarred, each knuckle familiar to me from years of cooking together. Andrew's sweater was pressed along the bare skin of my arm, the scent of fish and chips mingled with the slightly bitter smell of the soap he used to get the kitchen smell out of his clothes, and for a brief moment, the sensation of not belonging anywhere lessened, because that world of kitchen smells and Andrew and carbolic soap was one I did still and would always belong to.

Oblivious to my unexpected feelings for his scratchy sweater, Andrew put the frame back down and spread out the contents of the bag next to him, mopped up a bit of vinegar with a piece of fish, topped it with two chips dipped in ketchup and handed it to me.

'So your dad is okay, is he?'

'Yes, he is. Mrs Baxter rang earlier.' I shuddered. 'Venetia was unspeakable, carrying on because I wasn't getting in the ambulance with her.'

'Always is.' Andrew grimaced. 'She gets away with murder, your sister. You didn't go to hospital with them, then?'

'I wanted to. And then I couldn't,' I said, swallowing the memory along with a bit of fish. 'I think I had some sort of shock. I just couldn't move.' I chewed, concentrating on the crackling of the fried bread-crumbs and the tangy sweetness of the vinegar against the salty chips, then glanced at him to see if that sounded as weak as it felt to me.

'It'll do Venetia a world of good to be in charge for a change,' he said firmly. 'Not always you rushing off to do things for your dad.' He stuffed another hunk of fried fish between two enormous chips and held it out to me, watching closely to make sure it all went down. 'The way he was going, and how he looked last time I saw him, I'm fairly certain it would have happened either way. Here, last one.'

I inhaled the last two fish sandwiches almost in one swallow and realised I hadn't eaten very much since my stack of toast that morning.

'God, that was good. But you didn't eat anything at all,' I said ruefully.

'Made myself something earlier.' He handed me a napkin. 'This whole holiday lark is pretty awesome, I have to say. I don't think I've taken nearly enough days off in my life. Up early, get loads done, have time to come by and pester you at work.' He gave me a grin. 'Chef called me this morning, though, wanted me to come back in, but I fobbed him off. He got mad. And you know how Chef gets when he's mad.'

I most certainly did. I'd only met Andrew's erratic and foul-mouthed head chef one time in my life when I came to collect Andrew after his shift, and I'd vowed to never go near his restaurant again. I'd always hated big restaurant kitchens anyway, the few brief times I'd found myself working in one. Windowless, white-tiled worlds where everyone communicated in expletives and the temperature rose throughout the day until the kitchen was like a furnace, where dead pigs hung in the meat fridge and people gathered round to watch lobsters die in the pot, where the smell of scorched garlic and fish stock would hang in your clothes and cling to your hair and refuse to budge even if you drowned yourself in liquid bleach.

'He's getting worse, too. I'm desperate for a change, and I really, really want us to think seriously about Le Grand Bleu and . . . any-way . . . sorry . . . obviously not important right this minute. So what's happening now?'

He looked at me expectantly. I licked the last of the salt from my fingertips meditatively and looked over at my dad's study, then wiped my hands on the napkin. 'I think I'll have a poke around here,' I said. 'Who knows when I'll have another chance, alone and undisturbed, I mean. Or do you think that's—'

'A great idea,' he said bracingly.

'But obviously *you* don't have to stay, you're on holiday, with lots to do and—'

''Course I'm staying. Most exciting thing to happen in years. Let's get a move on.'

Inside my father's study, it was eerily half-dark, the yellow street light falling in pools across the bookshelves and the desk by the window.

Across the road, Mr Field's window was lit up by the blue glow of his television but otherwise the street was dark. Occasionally, a gust of wind shook the wisteria above the front door, flinging bursts of rain against the window.

We stood in front of the cabinet next to his desk. Everything else in his study was heavily masculine, the thick oak shelves, the enormous desk, the tartan sofa wedged into the bay window. The filing cabinet was functional rather than handsome, though, a simple metal four-drawer box with rows and rows of hanging folders. Little tabs showed the contents in my dad's spare, almost illegible handwriting.

'Finances. Mortgage. Pension,' Andrew muttered. 'There's got to be an important documents folder, don't you think?' He slid open the drawers one after the other, riffling through the folders. Insurance. Utilities.

'Down here?' I tugged at the bottom drawer, feeling less like a stranger in my own house and a whole lot more like a thief. I was almost relieved when the drawer wouldn't give and Andrew pushed me aside, levered his hand into the crack and pulled hard. There was a loud metallic clank and a grinding and it popped open.

'Andrew!' I hissed, appalled.

'Oops. So it *was* locked,' he said. 'Oh well, it's not like it was new. We can always blame it on Venetia. All right, so where – okay, aha! Like I said. "Important Documents". Surely, it's got to be . . . let's just have a look. Here are their birth certificates, and here's, ah, okay, yep . . .'

'What?' I said, falling to my knees next to him.

'Their marriage certificate,' Andrew said. 'Married in 1960. Three months after you were born, in May. So the May part is true in any case, it's just the year that doesn't match.'

He held out a grainy Xerox of a marriage certificate, which stated that Elizabeth Sophie Holloway and Graham Alexander Harington had got married in the Southwark Register Office on 9 May 1960.

I sat back on my heels, squinting at the Xerox in the torchlight, remembering, of all things, the speech that Uncle Fred had given at their Ruby Wedding party. He'd come up with all sorts of clever bits around the number forty and rubies and the *four* long decades passing. My parents had nodded and smiled as everyone else clapped, admiring, envying them their four decades of true love. Obviously, there was nothing more or less to admire about thirty-nine years of marriage instead of forty. Except the lying. And all the other things.

Andrew was still flicking through the papers inside the cabinet, taking everything out and studying it closely. 'Here's a copy of your birth certificate, all looking very respectable and – wait, what's this?'

I scooted over till I was right next to him and he pointed to the hanging folder that had held the sleeve with the Xeroxes, which looked exactly like all the other ones. 'See, there is something else here.' He pulled it out and apart so that it lay flat on the floor and now I could see it too. A piece of thin paper, which had been carefully cut to fit the folder almost exactly, taped close on all ends so that it was invisible until you'd pulled the whole folder fully apart. Andrew and I looked at each other. I reached for my dad's scissors on the desk, but my hands were shaking so much that Andrew took them from me, slipped the points in at the very edge and sliced open the top, finally extracting another piece of paper.

A birth certificate. Only this one had been registered just three days after my birth and a lot of the boxes had been left blank. The name, for one. The box next to it simply said: *Girl*. Mother: Elizabeth Sophie Holloway. Father: blank.

I sat back on my heels, gripping the two different birth certificates and the copy of the marriage certificate. So this was who I'd started out to be. Not Adele, not anyone, but *Girl*. And my father was nothing but a blank rectangle, an absence. Again, I floated, untethered, in a space that used to be familiar, a yesterday when I still knew who exactly I was supposed to be and what I was supposed to do, like buying a baby book for Venetia, reminding my father to go to his GP and trying to cry to make sure I was doing right by my mother's memory. Now, sitting here in the middle of the night, in almost exactly the same spot he'd taught me how to play chess and drunk scalding hot tea with me, *those silly Harington genes*, I was suspended in nothing, with no point of contact other than *Elizabeth Sophie Holloway* and *Blank*, two people who didn't even seem real, who weren't family at all, but complete strangers.

'I wish I could talk to my dad,' I said. 'I wish so, so much that I could talk to him.'

'He'll want to,' said Andrew, awkwardly putting his arm along the back of my neck and patting my shoulder. 'Maybe now's not quite the right moment, though.'

'Yes,' I said, sighing. And perhaps it was time I didn't need to have my dad to make sense of things, perhaps this one was mine to figure out on my own. I held out my hand to Andrew to help him up, grabbing his sweater sleeve for a second longer than necessary to push back against the sense of feeling untethered. Then I put the rest of the papers back into the drawer, only held on to the marriage and the original birth certificate, looked them over one last time until my eyes came to rest again on the blank spot where my biological father should have been. I shook my head and quickly shuffled the piece of paper underneath the others and closed the drawer. I couldn't have put it into words had anyone asked me, but for some reason I felt utterly incapable of squeezing this stranger into my new, free-floating life.

'I'm going to have another look through,' I said resolutely and turned back to the top of the filing cabinet.

Andrew jumped up and came to stand next to me, rubbing his hands together in anticipation. 'Okay, so what exactly are we looking for?'

'Anything on Phoebe's adoption or on my parents' lives before I was born. Anything on my mum before I was born, and then,' I took a breath to fortify myself, 'we'll go into her study. There's bound to be something there that will help me understand. And when I have something that actually makes sense, I have to call Phoebe Roberts.'

Chapter Twelve

Had anyone told me a week earlier that this was where I would be two days after the anniversary of my mother's death, standing on a stool in front of the shelves in my mother's study and pulling out her notebooks and folders, handing them down one after the other to Andrew, that at ten o' clock at night I would be picking up every one of her books and flicking through its pages, that I'd be reading her letters, her lists, her notes, that I was systematically dismantling her study when I hadn't been back in here properly for years – I would have said they were mad. I'd have laughed.

I wasn't laughing now. We finished looking through the filing cabinet without any further finds, then moved on to her study, working quickly inside the small space, occasionally holding up something for the other to see or stopping to have a closer look. My mother, unsentimental and pragmatic, had had her paperwork organised down to a tee. I found the old folder with birthday cards slotted into each month and my heart missed a quick, painful beat at the sight of June to December still bulging with cards because the woman planning to send them off hadn't been around to write them anymore. In another drawer was a stack of photos inside an envelope marked *Doubles* in my mother's looping handwriting. The originals would be in the family albums in the living room, so I took these, knowing that Venetia would probably want the albums at some point. In the back of the desk, I found the small box that had contained the Nokia, which she'd purchased at a shop on Tottenham Court Road, and later I came across the charger, neatly curled up on itself at the bottom of a drawer. Andrew started sorting through the papers and folders on the floor and I continued going through the rest of the cubicles in the big roll-top desk, looking underneath the surfaces for papers pinned in place, reaching behind drawers and around corners.

It was hard. Here, in this room, where she should have been most present, where I should have been reminded of all that she was, touching her things, submerged in her handwriting, her very thoughts – she was totally absent. She was simply a white space in my memory and the more I chased her, the vaguer she became until at around midnight I finally came to a stop in front of her noticeboard and didn't quite know where to go next. There wasn't much on the board, only an old ticket stub from a Munch exhibition she'd seen in February last year, a reminder to go to the dentist the day before she died, and a shopping list (organised by aisle and temperature). There was a list of emergency telephone numbers, including, I was glad to note, my own. A postcard of St Paul's shrouded in fog. I traced the outline of the perfectly round dome. What had this meant to her? She'd been incredibly tidy, my mother, and rarely kept anything lying around that wasn't strictly necessary, that didn't serve a purpose, almost as if her entire life was made to fit into her handbag, as if at any point she could up and go without leaving a trace behind. No old magazines, no old birth announcements or newspaper clippings, no letters, no 'to be filed' drawer, no 'miscellaneous' boxes. I'd made her a paperweight once, a big rock that I'd coloured with red nail varnish. Venetia was hopping mad when she discovered I'd used most of her Rimmel Cherry Red. It was still sitting on top of her desk, a garishly red lump without any papers to weigh down. So what had made her keep this postcard of St Paul's in the fog then, yellow and slightly curling at the edges? And why did I not know? How could I not know this simple fact about my mother? I stepped back from the notice-board and gave a noise of exasperation just as Andrew came to stand next to me, holding a white folder in his hand.

'I found – hey, everything all right?'

'I just can't seem to remember her,' I said, jabbing my thumb at St Paul's to illustrate my point. 'It's like she's not even there.'

He reached out to unpin the postcard, turning it over. It was blank.

'She isn't here anymore,' he said firmly, 'and nothing makes sense because nothing is what it was. But it will again. Trust me. This is difficult stuff, Ads, and you're doing really well.' He waved the post-card. 'You'll remember her eventually, I promise you. You'll figure out what happened to her, and to you and Phoebe Roberts. It'll all come together. You'll see.'

'It just doesn't feel like it will. It feels empty.' I heard my own voice sounding squeaky and feeble and automatically I squared my shoulders, blinked my eyes to hold back non-existent tears. *Chin up, darling.* I took the postcard of St Paul's from his hand and set it down on top of *Rebecca*.

'Empty is there to be filled,' Andrew said. 'And maybe this', he held up the white folder and smiled encouragingly, 'will help.'

Inside the folder were James Merck's bills, about six of them, paper-clipped together and tacked onto the inside of the folder, the first one dating back to November 1997. The expenses were methodically listed and painstakingly detailed, down to 'four books of first-class stamps, with two missing' and 'fifty sheets of paper, 4ppm, £1.99 at Ryman's'. A bulging thick wodge of paper followed the bills. Letters, at least a hundred of them if not more, from places like the Sussex Nursing School, the Medical Programme at Brighton General Hospital, Gloucester Home for Pensioners, and the United Kingdom Central Council for Nursing, Midwifery and Health Visiting. And people, too, Hugh Frameton, Lucy Jones. Patricia Hayworth. June Galloway. All writing in reply to her enquiry regarding 14 February 1960.

'So she really was looking for her,' I said. 'Look at all these letters, all that time she spent searching for Phoebe Roberts, who then shows up here, on her very own doorstep, a year after she died. It's too desperate, really, to think about.'

Andrew moved to stand right next to me, put his arm awkwardly around my shoulders and I leaned into him as we both looked down at the last thing in the folder, which was a yellow notepad, covered with pages and pages of notes and numbers and crossed-out bits and a lot of question marks. Someone called Dr Miller seemed to be at the centre of her search, because he was in the middle of various flowchart-type things in the notebook, and the stack of letters relating to him was the thickest, second only to a woman called Sarah Mason. The familiar swirls and loops of my mother's handwriting rushed across the lines until the very back where, inside a neatly pencilled grid, she had made a chart of every letter, the date it went out, the date a reply came back in. The first few letters were addressed to my mother herself at Rose Hill Road, but eventually they began to arrive at Merck Investigations, 35 Causeway, Shoreditch, as if she'd realised she was in over her head and needed help.

'She didn't seem to have much luck, though,' Andrew observed, holding up a letter from Molly Hayes who hadn't seen a certain Laura Remington for 'yonks'. 'All of these people are either dead or insane or otherwise gone.'

I flicked through the notepad again. Her handwriting was a bit erratic, starting out small at the top of each page, then bigger and more impatient halfway down until order was finally abandoned altogether at the bottom, where questions and numbers jabbed at the page in obvious frustration, arrows zigzagging up and down and occasionally sentences and words crossed out with angry strokes. *Dorset School of Nursing. Ask for Sarah Mason. Sussex council? UKCC. Paula Warren. Deceased? Call Hetty W again. Sarah Mason's sister?* I touched a deep groove left by her pen and imagined her sitting here, fingers tapping an impatient rhythm on the desktop, as she waited for someone to answer, calling directory enquiries to find Sarah Mason in Sussex, eyes fixed on a yellowing postcard of St Paul's.

'She started in March 1997,' I said. 'Why? Why look for her thirty-six years later? You're not looking for a baby any more, but for a grown-up, potentially with her own family. And it's no wonder these people were hard to find after all that time.'

'Didn't Jas have the twins around then, though?' Andrew pursed his lips and flicked through the folder. 'Maybe she was struck by being a grandmother, remembered the baby she gave away, that kind of thing. And this looks like an absolutely insane amount of work. Merck seems to have been even more organised than your mother, which is saying something. Clearly, a match made in heaven, God love her. Here, that fell out.'

He handed me a few clippings from newspapers. *Brighton's Beloved All Saints Hospital Makes 'Safeway' for Supermarket Chain* and *Charitable Sisters of Hope? A Difficult Time in Local History.* A small white card said

As promised, a few pieces of information, and I knew that somewhere in James Merck's bills, there would be an itemised expense: *Five A4 photocopies, 15p each.*

'What I don't quite understand –' Andrew frowned – 'is how she came to be in the home in the first place. They were supposedly pretty awful. My mum was watching a documentary once about some workhouse-type hostels in Ireland for unmarried mothers. It was just horrible. They made them work like slaves and just ripped away their bab—' He caught sight of my face and coughed before quickly adding, 'Er, well, I guess some were better than others so maybe . . . and this was England, anyhow. Lots nicer, probably.'

Wordlessly, I started reading the article on the Charitable Sisters of Hope. It had been a hostel for unmarried mothers on the outskirts of Brighton. Some of them were women, others just teenage girls, sixteen, seventeen years old. There was a fourteen-year-old girl who'd been raped by village boys. Her parents couldn't face the shame and sent her to the home for the duration of her pregnancy. Mothers went in for a few months or weeks before the birth of their baby and stayed on for six weeks afterwards to make sure the babies were healthy before they were given to an adoptive family. There was a bit on the day-to-day life at the home, the repetitive chores done by the women who were the ones responsible for the upkeep of the dilapidated house falling apart around them, the terrible food. There was a complete absence of birth preparation of any kind and the hassled moral welfare workers rarely had time to ease them into the adoption process. As homes went, the moral climate at the Sisters of Hope seemed to have been slightly less oppressive than at others, which were more like workhouses where the women were treated appallingly, their babies more or less sold for a donation. Here, the single mothers were occasionally able to go into town in small groups, or down to the pier or the cinema. There was a small reference to boxes or bundles of clothes that mothers were encouraged to assemble for their babies, a layette of sorts, and I thought of the little jumper, the bobble hat that my mother, who'd hated needlework of any kind, had knitted for an unborn baby.

I frowned at the pictures for a long time, black squarish blobs of a stately mansion that had bled across the Xerox machine, a row of beds in a dormitory, two women walking in a park-like area.

'Where were your grandparents, your mum's parents, I mean?' Andrew said, pointing to the line about the parents of the rape victim.

'They died when she was young,' I said, looking at one of the women. She had her back arched to carry the weight of her bump, faintly reminiscent of Venetia, albeit with an old-fashioned 1950s smock and a scarf tied around her head. 'She could have just gone into the home of her own accord, looking for a safe place to give birth when she was all alone.'

'Hmm,' Andrew said thoughtfully. 'Sure, or maybe it was . . .'

He paused delicately, but I just said bluntly, 'You mean, him? The father?' I jabbed my chin towards the birth certificate with its blank rectangles.

'Well, or *his* parents. And maybe they forced her to give up Phoebe?'

Looking at the picture of the dormitory beds in the article, I tried to picture my strong mother being forced to do something she didn't want to, being kept at this house and told, hour after hour, what to do, housework and needlework, both of which she was terrible at, in the cold months of December and January, which she loathed. And then giving birth and being ordered to give away her babies. The thought of her being forced rather than choosing, awful though that would have been for her, made my heart contract with a sudden, fierce squeeze of relief. It would mean that she hadn't done voluntarily what I thought she had, that she hadn't actually pointed her finger at two bundles to separate us. That she would have wanted us. Loved us. But all too quickly, reality asserted itself and, very reluctantly, I shook my head. 'I don't know. You knew my mother. Did she strike you as not being able to stand up for herself?'

We both gave an involuntary snort of laughter, which we quickly muffled because it wasn't remotely funny.

'And she *did* keep one of us, remember. If she was really forced, then we'd both have been gone, don't you think?'

We were both silent for a long time.

'Yes, she did,' Andrew finally said. 'And that's the great mystery.' He looked at the letters and the yellow notebook and the newspaper articles. 'Why one of you went and one of you stayed.'

'And why didn't she get Phoebe back when she could?'

He shook his head helplessly. 'I don't know. I suppose, she *was* only eighteen. That's so young. A teenager still, really. Very different to how we knew her, probably.'

'Yes.' I reached out to touch the picture of the young woman in the scarf, walking across the top of the Sisters of Hope article, and wished very hard that I could cry.

Chapter Thirteen

I was anxious to get going now, to put the study back together and escape, so I almost missed it in my haste to stuff the last few folders back on to the top-most shelf, and even then it was only because I stepped up on a chair to sort out a few stubborn papers that wouldn't line up with the rest that I saw it. A book, slim, slightly smaller than paperback-size, the jacket ripped at the bottom. I frowned, reached for it and turned it over in my hands, gently blowing the dust from the top of the pages. *Selected Poems* by Christina Rossetti.

Rossetti had been one of my mother's favourite poets, along with Edna St Vincent Millay and Louis MacNeice, and there was a beautiful first edition on the living-room shelf, an anniversary present from my father. This battered little book, however, I had never seen before. It seemed to have belonged to a set because on the side, in scratchy gilded lettering, was the number three. I stood on my tiptoes to scan the shelf again, but it was empty save for the white space in the grey dust that had collected behind the row of books where this one had lain.

'Andrew!' I jumped off the chair and sat down on it, setting the book on my lap. The pages were thin, like bible pages sometimes are, and right between two pages at the beginning, pressed almost completely flat, was a tiny sprig of a rose. Two blooms had been full and were now pressed into a flat fan of petals, with a few unfurled two-dimensional buds above. It looked brown and lifeless but when I brought it closer to the light, I saw that it was actually quite perfect, down to the little nubs of miniature thorns running up the stem.

Andrew came up to me and I held up the rose on the open book like an offering. He smiled, and then pointed to the name. *Constance Adele Holloway, 1949*, said the inscription on the flyleaf. I took in the old-fashioned neat writing, the year. Just a few days ago I'd been looking at the list of baby names in my mum's pregnancy booklet and had felt slighted because Venetia was in there and I hadn't been, and now here *I* actually was, tethered more firmly to my grandmother than I'd ever realised, anchored into my very own strand of history. I thought of the woman in the photo who was a stranger to me, a stranger with my mother's eyes and my dimple, I thought of this little rose which had been alive back then and was, in its own way, living on in my mother's love for roses out in her garden. As I leafed slowly through the book and poems flashed by, I wished I'd thought to ask my mother where my name had come from. *A Summer Wish, Another Spring, When I am Dead, my Dearest.* And then, right between *Dead Hope* and *A Daughter of Eve*, there were several small notecards. Andrew twitched next to me when he saw them and my fingers trembled. The first had only a few sentences, barely covering two thirds of the little card.

Hartland, 20 April 1960

There are several things I want to talk about and I very much hope that you'll be able to set my mind at ease. I'll be waiting for your letter.

Ever yours,

H

'Ever yours.' There was a vague familiarity there, a briskness, as if the writer was close enough to dispense with formalities, maybe picking up a conversation in mid-stream, something that had been started but not yet ended. I took a sharp breath. The second note was different – the same boxy writing as the first, but it looked hurried, more sprawling.

Hartland, 28 February 1960

Liz,

I know things must be very difficult for you right now, but if you can bear it, then I would like for us to meet and talk. I'm up in London now and again, so please send me a time and date that you're free and I'll see you then. Please let me know soon.

Harry

I checked the date above and saw that it was written two weeks after my birth, while the first one had come *after* this one, in April. My breath was making the little cards flutter in my hand and I stood up to lay them across the desk. Then:

Hartland, 15 July 1960

Dear Liz,
You haven't answered my letter, but I must talk to you urgently and will be coming up to London next Thursday. Can you meet me? I'm staying at the Langham and will wait for you in the bar at 7 pm. If you don't come, then I'll know you won't want to see me and I'll leave you alone, but I do hope that you'll be there. Just know, either way, that I am very sorry for what happened that night, and the way things turned out in the end. I hadn't meant for any of that to happen and I can't forget it, so I hope we can talk.
Harry

'H' was 'Harry.' And was there any way . . .

'Do you think Harry could possibly be – I mean, do you think it might be – *him*?' I asked Andrew, jabbing my chin at my birth certificate.

He was scanning the cards again. Finally, he pursed his lips and handed me back the notes. 'It could be anybody, really. But the dates . . . and "I'm very sorry for what happened that night"? At the very least it'll be someone who *knew* what had happened.'

'Harry wanted to meet her,' I said slowly, my breath stuck somewhere beneath the lump in my throat, 'but she didn't get back to him in February or April, and by May, she was married to my dad.'

Next to the notes, the dainty typeface of one of Rossetti's poems was visible.

My garden-plot I have not kept;
Faded and all-forsaken,
I weep as I have never wept.

How very sad to make this kind of discovery next to a garden poem when my mother had loved her garden so much and had been so happy there, and when someone, possibly Harry, whoever he was, had got her pregnant and not stood by her, had not taken care of her. I narrowed my eyes at the signature on the last card and felt an overriding surge of love for my father, who *had* stood by her in the end, baby and all.

But the other baby, *the other one—*

'I need to talk to Phoebe,' I said suddenly. I looked at the clock on the desk. Eleven forty p.m.

'It's not yet midnight. And she might not even be asleep,' Andrew said. 'She'd want you to call her, from the way she sounds.'

'But I don't have her number,' I said, panicked. What if I wasn't able to track her down again? What if I'd been so awful to her that she'd be gone now, actually gone, for a second time and forever?

'Let's call directory enquiries. Hello? I'm looking for a number in . . .' He looked at me questioningly.

'Birmingham, I think she said.' I held my breath.

'Yes, Phoebe Roberts in Birmingham. All right. Yes. Solihull? Sure. Thanks.'

He scribbled a number on to the back of his hand, then hung up.

It took me a few tries to work the unfamiliar rotary dial, but finally it was ringing. A voice answered on the second ring and from the breathless 'hello' it was clear that she hadn't been asleep yet. Andrew put his hand on my shoulder and squeezed it encouragingly.

'Phoebe? Er, it's . . .' I tried to force down the lumps rising in my throat, tried not to sound feeble. I was strangely keen to make a good impression.

An audible exhale hummed down the line, all the way from Birmingham and straight into my mother's study. She spoke quickly, stumbling a little. 'I'm so glad you called. So glad. I—'

'I'm so sorry for shouting at you, it was unforgivable, I know now that it's all true and I should never have—'

She quickly interrupted me. 'No, really, I'm the one who needs to apologise. I completely bulldozed you and I'm so sorry. Of course you need time to get used to it all. It's just, I don't have anyone to talk to about all this. But when you left I was so worried that now—'

'Me too,' I said and I could feel a smile break out on my face. Somehow, amidst the wreckage of what my family was and the dense fog of questions and doubts over my own place in this world, Phoebe's voice came through loud and clear, and even though we were two complete strangers, it was immensely comforting to know that we were not alone.

Chapter Fourteen

I was woken up the next morning by a noise and I shot up to stand dizzily, looking around me in confusion until I saw Andrew's head dangling from the side of the old armchair.

Rose Hill Road. My father in hospital. My mother's study. *I'm so glad you called*. After we'd put everything back, we'd come down here for a midnight snack, well, more of an early breakfast, really, considering it'd been closer to three a.m., and eventually had fallen asleep, me curled up on the old sofa covered by Andrew's jacket, and him on the armchair.

I rolled my head from side to side to work out the stiffness in my neck and was about to give into temptation and sink back on to the sofa for just a few more minutes when I heard another noise. And then, footsteps. Upstairs.

Quickly, I bent over Andrew to shake him. 'Wake up.'

Andrew grabbed hold of my arms and pulled me down towards his chair, but I tugged and pulled until he was finally vertical, muttering and swaying. Above us, the floorboards creaked as feet walked back and forth. The loo flushed. Then the front door opened again with a loud squeak.

'Morning, Mr Thomson.' Venetia's voice floated down crisply. 'You're about early today.'

Andrew raised his eyebrows at the ceiling.

'The postman,' I whispered.

'Yes, it's terrible. He's had to go to hospital. I've just come back to fetch a few things for him.'

I pictured myself coming up the stairs to greet Venetia, holding my mother's Hermès bag, bulging with stuff I'd taken from the house, a sleep-tousled Andrew in my wake, and I knew that after the night I'd had and the things I'd found out, I simply couldn't face it.

'Quick.'

I was across the room to grab the Hermès bag and my assorted plastic bags before Andrew had sat back down, grumbling, to put on his shoes. I tossed him his jacket and kicked the sofa cushions into shape, before pulling him out into the garden and, in one last fluid motion, sliding the French doors closed behind me. They wouldn't be locked but Mrs B would be in later. We quickly sidled down the left until we reached the rhododendron in the corner. Here, overgrown and barely visible, was the hole in the hedge that separated ours from his parents' garden on the other side and Andrew sped up of his own volition, clearly reluctant to run into his mum, who'd take one look at the two of us and start asking all sorts of excited questions.

We came to a stop in front of the Tube station, where Andrew inspected his muddy shoes and wet jumper with a frown.

'Seriously? Why couldn't we have just left the *normal* way, out the front door? Addie, you *must* stand up to Venetia at some point.'

He said it sternly but his face softened when he saw me sag back and nod gloomily, running my hands through my hair in an effort to prop myself up. In the muted grey of the morning, my square-shouldered determination from last night seemed to have fizzled out and instead of carving a new and different place for myself in this untethered, floating universe of mine, I'd slotted right back in where I'd always been, avoiding confrontation and pleasing people. The fact that I hadn't gone to keep vigil at my father's bedside seemed, in the light of day, no great feat of self-preservation or making my own decisions, but simply callous and heartless.

Suddenly, there were cool, rough fingers under my chin and Andrew tilted up my face, fishing in his pocket for a tissue. 'You look like you've been dragged through a hedge backwards. The hospital will want to keep you under observation.'

'I *have* been dragged through a hedge backwards.' I tried to squirm away, feeling unaccountably awkward and very close, but he took no notice, brushed a clump of moss off my shoulder, straightened my jacket and folded over the sleeve to hide the worst of the wetness. Drizzle hung white around the tops of the houses and the trees next to the Tube station, and all around us blurry shapes were trudging silently towards work. But the foggy morning draped its moist air around us like a gossamer blanket, muting all sound but our own breathing, pushing us closer together and closer still, until I could see the smudgy dark circles underneath Andrew's eyes and the graceful sweep of his mouth which was relaxed in a half-smile. He gently dabbed at my face and then smoothed my hair back with both his hands and, involuntarily, I felt myself relax into him and lean towards his smile, felt the rough wool of his sleeve against my cheek and the warmth of his breath on my half-closed eyes. His arm went around me and I had half-reached out to hold on to his shoulders, his face very close to mine, when I came to and pulled away with a backwards jerk. Andrew was my friend, my sparring partner and fellow cook. We weren't remotely – this. Whatever this was. We couldn't possibly be *this*, not after thirty years of bickering and bossing each other about and knowing all our ins and outs, warts and all. It would be too strange. Too much. It would never work.

I blushed fiercely and tried to twist out from underneath his arm, which was still looped around my shoulders, but he didn't let go until I dodged underneath his elbow, then, with a sigh, he finally released me.

'Have it your way,' he said, as I escaped quickly into the entrance area of the station and fumbled for my ticket. He caught up with me as we walked out on to the platform and I moved to the side to put some distance between me and that wool jumper that seemed to make me lose focus every time I came near it. But mercifully, Andrew made no other comment on what had just – *not* – happened and simply motioned for me to go further up the platform where it was less crowded.

'I wonder if your father is still around somewhere,' he said meditatively, suppressing a yawn. 'Harry. I mean, if Harry *is* actually *him*. If he was your mum's age, then he's still alive, I'm sure. I suppose you could find out, couldn't you?'

'Hmm,' I said, tucking my wallet into the side pocket of my bag, swerving to avoid a man with a large backpack.

'You don't want to?'

'His involvement can't have been very positive, considering what happened.'

'You don't know what actually happened,' Andrew pointed out.

'I know he didn't stand by her. I don't like that. And by extension, I don't really like him.'

'The way you described her, Phoebe will want to look for him.' Andrew came to a stop at the very end of the platform where we were all by ourselves.

'I know.' I pulled my denim jacket tightly against the damp May air and against Andrew's arm which was still too close to mine. 'It's so strange to think that we're twins. We don't really look alike. I can't quite get my head around it.'

'If you're fraternal twins you can look completely different.' Andrew stamped his feet. 'God, I hate the English weather. I'm beginning to rethink my Marseille plan.'

'Claudette would take you back in a heartbeat,' I offered with a forced little laugh.

He frowned at me, his eyes shadowy pools of blue in the murky morning light. Then he shook his head. 'Yeah, no, I'm past all that. Lots of new things to think about, and if we could get Le Grand Bleu off the ground . . .'

He lingered on the words 'things' and 'think' and I felt myself blush again, looked away quickly. Whatever *this* was, I wanted it to stop because I really, really couldn't cope with another big thing churning up my life.

'Anyway,' he continued, sounding reassuringly more like his normal self, 'I think people get overexcited by all this twin stuff when there's actually not much point romanticising it. You're two completely different babies, siblings really who just happened to be in the same womb for nine months instead of being born one after the other. You'll just have to get to know her, like anyone else, like you're meeting a new friend. And you should definitely call that guy, Merck, when he's back in town.'

'Yeah,' I said reluctantly. 'I'll have to come clean about pretending to be Mum.'

Andrew gave a sudden bark of laughter. 'I'd have given anything to be a fly on the wall for that conversation. Why didn't you just say, "She's dead. Can I help you?" You could stand to have a bit more gumption, honestly, Addie. The way you let Venetia push you around and let Grace run your kitchen. Just tell people what you want. They'll still love you in the end, you know.'

Starting with Le Grand Bleu, I thought. I stepped away from him under the pretence of checking for the train, but really thinking about all these things I was to everyone around me, what people expected me to do and how they wanted me to be, and it occurred to me that Phoebe was very different. She was an unknown quantity, as unknown to me as I was to her, away from everything I knew, and there she sat, waiting for me, like a completely clean slate. Somehow that thought was quite cheering, the fact that I could be someone new, that I could be *anyone*, free from who I'd always been, without pressure, without expectation.

'I think that's what I'm going to do.' I spotted the train's head-lights in the distance.

'What?' Andrew gave another huge yawn.

'Just get to know her. No pressure. That's great advice.'

'Gosh, that's a first.' He perked up, sounding pleased, as the train passed us and came to a screeching halt. 'So glad I could help. I'll come with you to hospital, if you like,' he offered. 'I'll even forsake my shower for you, old friendship's sake and all that.'

In the greyish damp early May morning, he met my eyes and smiled, a tired and friendly kind of smile that made me wonder whether I'd imagined whatever happened before.

'That's nice, but it's all right, really,' I said as the doors opened right by us. 'I'll manage, and Venetia will be there, too, didn't she say she'd be bringing stuff for him?'

'Call me later, though, all right? And don't let Venetia get to you. Always remember, she's only human, your sister,' he said. 'Although,' he took the carrier bag out of my hand, then prodded me into the carriage and towards a pair of free seats at the back, 'the jury may still be out on that one.'

Chapter Fifteen

On the train, Andrew promptly fell asleep, his head lolling heavily against my shoulder. As the train filled up, my bags had to make way for people who, unreasonably I felt, wanted seats, and by the time the train was held at a red signal, I had my stuff and the Hermès bag and Andrew's things, plus Andrew's head, draped all around me. Checking the watch on his arm lying across me, I saw *Rebecca* sticking out at the top of the bag, and as the conductor's voice came on to let us know that we'd be moving shortly, I fished it out and started leafing through it.

My mother had always made notes in her books, whether she read for pleasure or work, asking questions, trying to make connections. *Rebecca* had been one of her favourites and she often re-read sections and chapters when she couldn't sleep at night. Idly, I turned the pages, reading a sentence here and there, my eyes too heavy, really, to focus on the second Mrs de Winter's plight, swallowing occasionally at my mother's tiny notes and scribbles zipping by in a flash of blue ink. *Why?? Gothic markers. Maxim? Frustrating!* Right towards the end, my fingers suddenly flicked across a small piece of paper, stuck all the way inside the binding and held there by the unnatural open splay of the spine. I turned it over.

> Clean out front room
> Oxfam opening hours
> Speech for Dean's Commissioners Awards
> Finalise last para
> Fred's OP
> Addie's birthday
> Cake. Balloons. Confetti. Gifts. Tent.

I made a small sound and the woman sitting opposite me looked up suspiciously, her gaze travelling slowly over my dishevelled appearance and my unspeakable hair and all my bags and Andrew chortling in his sleep, before twitching her M&S carrier bag well out of my reach. I noticed her only dimly, staring instead at the inside of the Underground tunnel where craggy, mouldy growths on the walls were lit up, thinking of my tenth birthday.

My mother had hated winter and when January came around she usually either kept herself frenetically busy or became mute and shivery, snapping at us and disappearing into her study as soon as she could. I usually didn't have big birthday parties then, just a few girls over for games, but my tenth birthday in 1970 had fallen on a Saturday and my mother had told me to invite ten girls to mark my entrance into double digits with a bang. I was beyond excited at the unexpectedness of it all and for weeks before I went around polling people on what kind of things one did at a double-digit birthday party. But Mum seemed to have regretted her rash promise because when the week leading up to my actual birthday came around she was away for a seminar – the Dean's Commissioners Awards from the list maybe – with no party preparations or any plan in place for Saturday. By Friday, I'd started striking all sorts of deals with various karmic powers that the ten girls who were going to show up at three p.m. the following day expecting tea and games would actually have a party to come to.

So it wasn't until the early hours of Saturday morning that I had fallen into a leaden sleep, and when I woke up, the house was quiet. I poked my head out of the bedroom door, looking up and down the deserted corridor, listening hard. Nothing. Only the clock ticking downstairs. My chest contracted with a sudden panic and I looked back at the alarm clock: 10.30. Where was everyone?

'Mum?' I called. 'Vee?'

But my voice was so thin and reedy it made the silence even more pronounced and I closed my mouth quickly, my heart hammering. Slowly, I started walking and looked into Jas's room and Venetia's, then my parents' bedroom. All silent. I tiptoed down the stairs, suddenly terrified in the way that only a ten-year-old could be when waking up to an empty house after an anxious, sleepless night. Had everyone left, had they all disappeared? Moved? Been kidnapped? *Murdered?*

Downstairs, the hall was dark and empty, the living room locked.

I pressed down the handle gingerly but the loud rattling in the silent house scared me and I left it. Maybe they were all in the basement? Maybe the kitchen would be bright and cheerful and they were waiting to surprise me. Mrs Baxter might have made my favourite coconut cream cake, three-tiered, with ten candles; they'd have strung up bunting and balloons, and there would be music and light and noise. I was sure that's what it was, they were all waiting for me to come so I'd better go quickly. I took a deep breath, flipped on the light, walked downstairs, bracing myself for the shouting. *Surprise! Happy Birthday!*

I opened the door, just a crack at first, then all the way, disappointment and fear hitting me like a ton of bricks. The kitchen was dark and messy with breakfast dishes, a faint trace of bacon grease in the air, and it was as empty and deserted as the rest of the house. I started crying then, great, panicky, hiccuppy gulps. *Hello?* I shouted up the stairs, and *Anyone there?*

Suddenly, through tears and mounting hysteria, I spied a piece of paper on the table. It was a scrawled note in my dad's handwriting, which took me a moment to decipher. *'So very sorry, love, back soon, Happy Birthday!!'* It had red splotches on it, probably jam from their breakfast. It took me another few moments to stop crying. At least they *knew* it was my birthday. But why hadn't they woken me up? And where had they gone on this special day that marked my entrance into double digits?

I got dressed and stayed down in the kitchen for a while, cleaning up the dishes and trying to decide whether I could still bake a cake in the next hour and a half and where my mother might have put the party box so I could decorate the kitchen. Should I organise some games? Call Mrs Baxter to come and make us tea? I tried to think clearly but all I could see was the face of Dawn McCarthy, who was eleven already and vastly superior with her paint-your-own-pottery party and her pink party bags, and who'd be arriving with nine other girls in less than three hours.

There was a small clock above the range, which Mrs Baxter had stuck on to the side of the vent to use as a timer, and I sat at the kitchen table, clutching the note and watching the seconds and the minutes tick away. 12.15. 12.20. 12.30.

I couldn't stand it any longer. I turned over the note, wrote 'went to the park' in big angry letters, switched off the light and left the house. It was dark and cold, a February as grey and desolate as only an English February can be, trees and bushes and front gardens drooping with moisture, the streets a dirty brownish-grey, the yew hedges a muted dark green. Andrew wasn't at home either so I went to the park by myself, roaming the streets for a bit and then the playground, where a few intrepid parents had taken their toddlers for a well-wrapped-up play. I sat on the swing for as long as I could, faintly hoping that someone might actually come looking for me, and that the ten girls, if they didn't find me at home, might just turn around and leave again, but eventually the damp got to me and I trudged back, resigning myself to the inevitable. *Hello, Dawn. Nice to see you. Do come in.* I walked slower and slower until I was practically crawling, not daring to look up as I approached 42 Rose Hill Road.

But when I finally did look up, I almost didn't recognise it. All the other houses and front gardens had hunkered down into a melee of greys and browns, empty flower boxes on windowsills and bristly, leafless hedges. Number 42, however, was a riot of colours. There were balloons tacked onto the front door and streamers along the handrails. There was a huge banner and big fake flowers cut out of cardboard. It was so bright and so bouncy that after hanging around in the cold, grey park for an hour, it almost hurt my eyes. Quickly, I threw my bike behind the gate and ran up the steps. Through the kitchen window I could hear snatches of conversation and laughter and the radio that Mrs Baxter kept on the shelf next to the stove was blaring. The front door had been left ajar and I cautiously pushed it open. Inside, there were more streamers. No one was to be seen but I followed the trail of confetti down to the kitchen.

When I opened the kitchen door, I was almost thrown backwards by the impact of noise and colours. There were at least twenty people crammed there, milling about beneath streamers and balloons, which covered most of the ceiling. Children were chatting in the corner, and Mrs Baxter was pouring coffees, offering milk. The long-suffering Mr Baxter was eating a scone. Dawn was batting her eyelashes at

Andrew, who was scattering the last of the hundreds-and-thousands over a birthday cake and ignoring her. My dad and my Aunt Clara were carrying plates to the table.

I stood there for a few seconds, relief and exhilaration washing over me in great big waves, until I saw my mother in the middle of things, chatting and laughing animatedly, as if she hadn't even noticed that I wasn't there. It occurred to me that maybe she'd be cross now because I hadn't waited for them here, had not helped with getting things ready, when it was my party and it was all for me and, really, I should have been there to help. Uncertainly, not looking left or right, I made my way through to her, tapped her arm to get her attention, relieved when her face broke into a smile.

'Darling, happy birthday! Where on earth have you been? You're missing your own party!'

'I didn't think there was going to *be* a party,' I mumbled, the morning's abject misery welling up in my eyes again. I rubbed my hands down my dirty jeans and wished that I'd had the chance to put on my party frock, which had been hanging on the inside of my wardrobe for the last two weeks. 'I didn't know where you were.'

'But Dad left you a note,' she said, impatience creeping into her voice when she saw my tears, and she propelled me sideways until we were in front of the pantry doors. 'Addie, you really need to stop worrying so much. It was *meant* to be a surprise. Stop crying. Poor Venetia hurt herself, she was bleeding and we had to take her to A&E. You were still asleep, although how you didn't wake up with all that racket I don't know. And then we had to wait at the hospital for ages. Thank God for Mrs Baxter, as always. She organised all of this in the end. She's so much better at that stuff anyway.'

She said something else but my dad came up and was concerned: where had I been and was I all right, and he was so very sorry. And then people noticed me and surged forward with hugs and congratulations, the girls from my school trooping up dutifully to hand over presents. And there was Venetia, veering towards us, her bandaged hand carefully held aloft.

'Addie,' she shouted. 'I fell on the scissors! I have to wear this for two weeks!'

I looked back at my mother, who nodded. 'She thought she'd cut off her finger and went into hysterics looking for it everywhere, until she realised it was still attached.'

At this, I finally had to laugh, which was good because it kept those dreaded tears at bay. My mother was happy and I was ten and everyone was here and Andrew had made a cake and was grinning madly from the back as Dawn simpered next to him. All was well.

Chapter Sixteen

Slowly, I closed *Rebecca*, frowning at the Tube window. All hadn't really been well. Because always afterwards I had remembered going into double digits amidst panic and worry, vowing that if ever I had children I would never ever disappear just like that, that I would talk to them and include them and ban surprise parties altogether.

There was a sharp 'bing' from the loudspeakers and Andrew jerked upright.

'S'happening?' He peered about him in a drunk-looking way as the conductor informed us that we'd be moving in a minute. 'S'morning yet?' He stretched out his long legs, kicking the woman across from us in the shins, and she jerked them back.

'So sorry,' I said to her. 'Hey, wake up, Andrew. Andrew!'

'Yeaash.' He twitched but didn't open his eyes. 'I'm so tired, Addie.' He leaned his head against my shoulder. 'I think my eyelids may have grown shut together. Is that possible?'

The woman opposite looked disgusted.

'Do you remember my tenth birthday?' I asked him, flashing her another apologetic smile.

'Feb fourteen,' he mumbled obligingly.

'Yes, but my *tenth* birthday, we had a party downstairs in the kitchen?'

He didn't speak for so long that I thought he'd fallen asleep again. 'Three-tier chocolate sponge. Coconut frosting. Sprinkles. Red and yellow smarties. A beaut.'

'Not the cake. Do you remember the party?'

He yawned and the neon light shone on his closed eyes. Then he said, 'You mean when you got the tent? Camped in your garden. Made salt-crusted cod. And potatoes. Almost set the apricot tree on fire.' He turned sideways, snuggling into the upholstery of the Tube seat. 'Just five more minutes, Ads, please.'

'Sorry, sorry,' I whispered, offering him my shoulder, but he was already asleep and a moment later started snoring faintly but distinctly. I looked down at the list in my hand. *Cake. Balloons. Confetti. Gifts. Tent.*

The tent. Of course. How could I ever forget that tent? I'd wanted a variety of things in those years, in no particular order: a puppy, a mynah bird, a Mickey Mouse toaster and a gumball machine. But for my tenth birthday, my mother, for some reason unknown to my ten-year-old self, got me a tent, despite the fact that there was no place for us to go camping other than our back garden and that we weren't really a nature-loving, outdoorsy family to begin with. Maybe it had been the adventure part, the being free and on the move, or the idea of fitting your entire life on your back; maybe she'd been casting around for a gift and been inspired by listening to Dad read *Swallows and Amazons* to Venetia and me at night. Either way, at the very end, when the party hum had died down to a contented buzz, when we'd played games and won prizes and everyone was busy with their cake, my mum had materialised at my side.

'Come upstairs,' she murmured. 'I want to show you something.'

She pulled me out of the crowded kitchen and up the stairs, unlocked the lounge and stepped back.

'Look!' she said proudly.

And there, propped up by two chairs and weighted down on all four corners, stood my birthday present. A small canvas tent, just big enough for two people, and surprisingly, amazingly pretty. The original colour had been army green, I think, but someone had stuck on hundreds of flowers and stars all over the outside, in different colours, so that the dark grey-green of the tent almost disappeared beneath them. When I looked more closely, tentatively touching a big pink flower on the side, I realised that it had come from an old raincoat of mine. I could still make out the butterfly that had been on the sleeve. And there was a star cut from an old hat that Jas used to wear when he was little, and all throughout, circles of various shapes cut out of broken umbrellas and plastic tablecloths. On one side, there were a few splotchy pieces of fabric.

'Venetia's blood,' my mother said, rolling her eyes. 'We were a bit behind with everything, cutting out the last of the pieces, I just didn't have any time this week, and that's when it happened. Teaches me to give scissors to a six-year-old.'

'I'm sorry I wasn't here to help with the party,' I said, touching the raincoat flower.

'Have a look inside.' She pulled me forward, held open the flap and crawled in after me.

'It was my idea, and then everyone pitched in, helped with the flowers and things. Look, there's a pocket for a clock right here, see, and your book can go there.' She ran her hand over a series of pockets that had been added to the inside of the tent. 'Dad gave you a torch. And Venetia got you a pair of thick socks in case it gets cold in the night.' She pointed to another set of pockets near the entrance. 'And if you want to cook outside, Mrs B said this pot would probably be big enough but light, so it won't pull down the sides of the tent.' She pulled on a handle and a small pot slid out of another pocket. 'And a frying pan.' She unfastened a piece of fabric. 'Perfect for potatoes,' she said. 'And when you're done, you just pull out everything and put it in this canvas bag here. *I* made that for you. Look. Not well, obviously, but I managed to stitch your initials on it, see?'

I took in the inside of the tent, the neat row of spoons and forks slotted into little fasteners, thought of everyone going in on it together, planning together, just for me, and I felt stupid tears welling up again in my eyes.

'It's wonderful, Mum, I can't believe it. Thank you, thank you so much. I thought . . . I mean I was so stupid . . . I thought you'd forgotten my birthday.'

Downstairs I could hear the babble of people's voices, but inside the tent it was quiet and dimly lit, shapes of flowers hovering above. It was like sitting underwater, in a cool, mossy green pond. I was holding the canvas bag, which was a bit lopsided and had flowers on the side to match the tent. My mum had looked at me with a funny smile and her eyes were both soft and, I hadn't realised then, also a little sad. She scooted over and then she was sitting very close to me and I rested my head on her shoulder and felt her whisper right into my ear.

'I would never forget your birthday, Addie. Never.'

My eyes were clamped, unseeing, on a big greyish splotch of raggedy mould just outside my window, which started to blur as the train began to move again, slowly at first, then faster, speeding towards the light and my workday. I'd rarely if ever recalled that party all the way to the very end because it had been spoiled so much by the fear that had come before, and I don't know what happened to the tent at all. I'd used it a few times in the garden until Andrew and I did almost set the apricot tree on fire and were forbidden to cook al fresco ever again. And now, after a night grappling with my mother's ghost, my subconscious had proffered this very last moment of the birthday. Closeness and ease. Love. Just us two inside the underwater green of a tent that my mother had made especially for me.

Only, it hadn't been just the two of us, because unbeknownst to me the ghost of Phoebe Roberts had always been with us, wherever we were, and most particularly on the 14 February of every year.

I would never forget your birthday.

Hartland, 13 August 1958

It's my birthday today and I'm going to be seventeen! I'm writing this, my official birthday entry, at five o'clock in the morning. I left my curtains undrawn last night because I wanted to be woken up by the first rays of the sun shining into my window and the birds cheeping and cooing on the roof shingles of the dormer window right above my head. I haven't told anyone that it's my birthday because I didn't want them to feel like they had to do something special, but still, I wonder whether they do know. Either way, it's fine with me. Birthdays are not that important after all, and my whole stay here is a present in itself. Seventeen today. That's quite old, almost a grown woman, and grown women certainly don't run along and play like a good girl. Maybe Abel hadn't known that I was going to be seventeen.

Later

They did know! I came down to find a cake by my plate, a whole cake just for me, with candles and everything. There was another fat letter from Mum, which I quickly put away to read later. And Janet gave me the most lovely scarf, a big one, to drape over my head and my shoulders. An open-topped-car kind of scarf, she said, even though I've never ridden in a open-topped car in my life. And Harry and Beatrice and Felicity all came and congratulated me and Bert tried to hug me but Harry pulled him away because Bert always tries to press uncomfortably close against your front and squeezes your shoulders with his sweaty hands. Later, we all did drive up to Porthallow to have lunch in the garden of a tea room there, and I got to ride with Harry and John and draped my scarf across my head and the salty wind blew into my face and I felt like a queen.

But the most wonderful surprise of all was a telephone call from Mum! My mother, on the telephone to me on my birthday, it was like a whole other gift in itself. Janet had been all secretive when we got home and when I came down for dinner she pulled me into the study and pointed to the phone sitting on Abel's mahogany desk. 'I fixed it with your mum earlier,' she said. 'She can't wait to talk to you. Just sit tight right there and she'll call you in a bit.'

So I sat in the study, looking around at Abel's pictures of horses and all of his riding trophies and the big guns draped across one wall, and finally the phone rang and when I picked it up I almost couldn't speak because it was so good to hear her voice and I felt so terrible because I'd promised myself that I wouldn't enjoy all of this here, that I wouldn't be so very happy. But when she spoke she sounded good, perhaps even better than when I last saw her. And she asked me so excitedly about all the things I was doing and our excursions and adventures and was Harry still as nice as she remembered that I couldn't hold it all in. I told her about smelling the sea and about the beautiful rose garden and Harry teaching me how to swim and even a little bit about John and our rides out together because he's the only one I can't seem to write very much about in my letters.

And then it was strange, because I heard people in the background, two people talking, which is not at all like our silent house, and when I asked her about it, Mum just said that Sister Hammond was there. But so early, I said. Why so early? Are you in pain, Mum, please tell me?

She was fine, she said, absolutely fine and to keep the letters coming because she loved hearing about all the things I was doing. And that I was absolutely forbidden to worry about her. And maybe, when I got back, the two of us could go into London as a birthday treat. We could go to the circus, Lizzie. Or St Paul's, she said, if it's open. Have tea somewhere and walk by the river. Maybe buy you something nice and make a whole day of it.

Because of my own perfect time here I agreed with her, and I somehow allowed myself to believe that we would go to the circus or to St Paul's, just the two of us, just like old times – there goes stupid Hope again – and I started crying then. I'm not sure why, I wanted to not cry so badly because it was so lovely to talk to her and I missed her so much, but I couldn't help myself. So I didn't listen properly as she said a last goodbye and it was only after I hung up that I realised what she'd said. That she would always miss me. And now I'm left up here in my little attic room wondering and gnawing at my fingernails, beautifully manicured for the first time and in honour of my birthday by Bea, writing down the conversation word for word to see if there was anything I overlooked. For why would she miss me? And why always? I can't work it out but it has a threatening feel to it. They're ringing for dinner, though, and I haven't changed, so I better hurry up and go down. There is to be a party for me after dinner, drinks on the terrace and even dancing. I didn't want to say that I didn't really know how to dance either. I'll just have to play along.

Midnight (!!)

I'm writing this in the middle of the night, at just gone twelve, and not because I'm hiding, but because I'm only just now coming back from my very own birthday party!

Beatrice called the party an 'absolute smasher', and while I don't know nearly enough about parties to judge, it certainly was smashing to me and also perfectly lovely. We moved out to the terrace after dinner, listening to music and dancing. In my case, that meant mainly shuffling about trying to look like I knew what I was doing, which quickly got a bit trying because everyone wanted to dance a dance of honour with me. And I was having champagne, not one glass but two, and I don't think I will ever, ever taste anything more delicious than this first glass of champagne of my life, which I drank on the Hartland terrace, Harry and me watching John twirling silly Beatrice to Elvis, a velvety dark dusk falling over the garden, slowly, so agonisingly slowly, as if the day itself couldn't bear to come to a close, couldn't bear to give way to the full, fat moon hanging above the trees.

But the best part of it came much later, when it was fully dark. People were hanging about and languishing in the air, which was thick and almost syrupy with the day's heat, chatting and singing along and giggling, being silly. And then – I'm going to try to write properly about it, although I'm not sure, even if I want to hold on to it for Mum, that I can actually tell her about this very last bit. This last bit that was so wonderful that I just want to hug it to myself, all the tiny details of it. I want to not forget for as long as I live that there is no more romantic place, no more secretive, no more alive place, than the little orchard next to the gardens at Hartland. Through the trees, you can see the fairy lights strung up around the terrace and you can hear, ever so faintly, the sound of 'All I Do is Dream of You', you hear people laughing and little friendly creatures rustling all around. The air is cooler in here, playing around your flushed cheeks and your hair, but you're hidden really, the way you need to be when you're about to get your first kiss. A kiss isn't really a birthday present but it felt like one to me, like the most wonderful, exciting thing to finish off the day. I've read about love, between Jane Eyre and Mr Rochester and Prince Andrei and Natasha, but Mum and I have never talked about it much, and although Judy sometimes tried to tell me about her fumblings in the back row at the pictures, I never quite knew what exactly was waiting for me, didn't know anything about the undying love and passion and devotion that all the books and poets are always gushing about.

In the end, it didn't matter what I knew, because nothing on earth could have ever prepared me for what happened tonight, this rush that comes upon you and sweeps you away, an inexorable force that is at the same time giddy and light and aglow, making you forget all the things you were ever taught about propriety and sensibility, and instead pushes you up on your toes, lifts your arms to snake around someone's neck, tilts up your face to let go of where you used to be, to make you forget anything and everything else.

Chapter Seventeen

It was raining in earnest when I left the train after a couple of stations, ran up the stairs and stopped only briefly at the newsagent to buy *The Week* and a Curly Wurly, both of which my father loved. It took a little while to navigate the endless maze of corridors and white-clad people hurrying in different directions until I found the right ward. A nurse informed me that my father was sleeping. I was welcome to wait in the room, but under no circumstances was he to be disturbed or upset in any way. I nodded and elbowed the Hermès bag behind my back in an attempt to hide it, then opened the door.

My eyes fell on a narrow bed in which a figure rested, supine beneath a standard-issue NHS blanket. 'Hello,' I whispered furtively, but we were alone, my father and I, in this tiny room with just enough space for a bed, a stool and a lot of machinery draped around the headboard, blinking and occasionally emitting small buzzing sounds. In his sleep, his hands gripped the sides of the blanket. I forced myself to look at him, to really see him, all the deep crags and folds on his face, slack with sleep and a sort of greenish-grey hue, his hair, his broad shoulders that were almost too big for the bed, his long legs gracefully extended.

I thought of the man I'd discovered inside a hidden volume of Christina Rossetti's poems, who wanted to meet my mother at the Langham on 21 July. Harry. How had my father felt, raising another man's daughter? That I was a hand-me-down he'd had to put up with? Would I have been tainted for him somehow, spoiled, even if he never consciously acknowledged it? Or would *he* have felt second best himself; had he been the way he was, loving and supportive, because he somehow wanted to make up for the fact that he wasn't my real father?

I could feel the slideshow of memories start up again, good moments threatening to take on a fake quality, like the iridescent, metallic back of a fly's wing, like a prism breaking everything into a million distorted rainbow-coloured splinters. Knights wandering across a chessboard and blueberry scones with cream. The two of us in our old Volvo just after I'd got my licence, chatting about everything and anything as he helped me practise being out on London roads. *You're seeing that bicycle, yes? And the little boy there by the light? Wonderful.* The vaguely thrumming undercurrent of his anxiety whenever my mother was away and I was trying to help him with the cooking and Vee and Jasper's homework and getting them to bed, until it was just us two down in the kitchen, having a cup of hot milk at night. *I couldn't do it without you, Addie.*

Each memory was like a stab, but I let them all come because it seemed important somehow that I resolved this here and now, once and for all. Was I going to let it happen, let him become a stranger and my past with him a mockery? Or was I going to take him back for myself, to live my life as Adele Harington, my father's daughter? I sat on the side of the bed for a long time, watching his sleeping face, holding my mother's Hermès bag in my lap and picking *The Week* to shreds.

Suddenly, there was a small kerfuffle outside, then the door popped open and Venetia burst in, looking wet and uncustomarily bedraggled, laden with bags and a folded-up *Times* between her teeth. When she saw me perched on the end of the bed, her eyes widened above the newspaper.

'Gnhggng,' she growled, jabbing her chin at me, but I was obviously too slow because she spat the paper out on to the end of the bed, somehow managing to miss my father's legs, then started emptying her bag in loud silence, arranging a bunch of grapes on the side table and fanning out the *Telegraph* and the *Times*, a couple of paperbacks, a magazine and new pyjamas on the side of the bed. Pushing the Hermès bag underneath a fold in the blanket, I picked up my mangled copy of *The Week*, which had retreated before the onslaught of Venetia's many gifts, and put it on top. Venetia flicked it off with thumb and forefinger, raising her eyebrows at the shredded cover. I flicked it on top again. Nice, Adele. Very mature. With some effort, I left *The Week* where it was in order to take the high road.

'He seems all right, doesn't he?' I whispered.

'Really?' Venetia whispered back incredulously, giving a somewhat jerky gesture at my father's marble-like form on the bed, the orange NHS curtains, the blinking machine, which chose this moment to emit a hiss and a soft groan. Something was pumping and the blanket moved. I looked worriedly at Venetia, who snapped, 'They're monitoring his heart, of course. Jas said that there were some issues with the heart rhythm. Pull yourself together, for heaven's sake.'

Me? I looked at her annoyed face and quivering bump and all the things she'd spread out around his legs and suppressed the sudden urge to giggle.

'He needs absolute peace and quiet,' she hissed, still valiantly managing to keep her voice low. 'I can't believe you weren't here yesterday.'

She reached out and carefully straightened the edge of a tube hanging just above his face and I realised that Venetia, at her most venomous, her most disagreeable, was, in fact, terrified. All year, she'd been suspended between the two extremes of life, Mum's death on the one hand and the baby coming on the other, and now Dad's collapse had thrown her off once again. When she sat down on the stool, she slipped a bit and I reached out to steady her.

'Venetia,' I said softly, checking that Dad was still sleeping. 'I feel terrible that I upset him. You know that. But I spent the whole of last year trying to take care of him, every week, almost every day. I love him, just the same as you. But I had a shock myself yesterday. I just couldn't come to the hospital. I would have if I'd been able to. But I just couldn't. You simply have to accept that.'

'Addie, it was such a close shave.' Venetia, craning awkwardly around her stomach to retrieve her bag, pulled out another book and set it on to the nightstand. 'Apparently his heart has been compromised all along, and none of us noticed.'

'I did notice,' I said evenly. 'I've been taking him to the doctor. I made an appointment with the specialist, I put it in his calendar, I called him three times to remind him to go. I can't drag him there. He's still his own person. In a way, maybe this was a wake-up call for all of us.'

'A wake-up call? Because a woman says she's your twin and you had to burden him with it all, when we said we weren't going to?' Her face was a mottled red.

'Vee, it's all true. I know that now. I have a twin. And you have a sister. A half-sister. Aren't you at all – I mean, aren't you interested?'

'Addie, I just don't believe that Mum would do that kind of thing.' Venetia pressed her lips together. 'She's dead, I'm having a baby in two weeks and our father is ill. That's what I'm focussing on right now. And you have to shoulder some of this, I can't be expected to be here at all hours, honestly, I'm having a b—'

'A baby, yes, I think you mentioned it, once or twice maybe,' I hissed. 'But don't worry, you will not be inconvenienced in the slightest by our father needing help.'

'Which he wouldn't need if you had left him well alone,' she hissed back. 'I told you—'

She broke off and her eyes locked on to something at the bottom of the bed and when I followed her wide-eyed look, I saw to my dismay that the Hermès bag had emerged from hiding when Dad had moved his feet. It was now sitting on top of the blanket, in plain view of anyone, including my hawk-eyed sister.

'Is that – that's not – *Mum's* bag??'

She extended her hand towards it, but I was faster and had my hand on the handle and had picked it up before she could touch it.

'You took Mum's bag, Addie?' Her face was very white. 'You took it from the house? When?'

'Venetia, I was going to tell you,' I said, striving to keep my voice quiet, but she snatched at it and with surprising alacrity managed to grab hold of one of the handles. The Hermès bag splayed open, showing the maroon cover of *Rebecca* and the broken photo frame.

'Pictures and books?' The effort of being quiet seemed too much for her because she stopped in mid-sentence, frowned at the poetry book and the postcard of St Paul's in the fog peeping out from behind the envelope marked *Doubles* in my mother's handwriting.

'That's the picture from Mum's bedroom, that's been there for years. You can't just take stuff like that, not without asking, without *us*— It's hers, Addie, no one should touch it. And what if I or Jas want them? Or Jas's children. Or the baby? And when did you do all this, yesterday? After you drove our father into a heart attack, leaving me and Mrs Baxter to cope on our own? After that you went and ransacked the house for Mum's stuff?' She lifted her bump up and moved towards me. 'I want to see exactly what you took. And I want that bag.'

I didn't move, and she held out her hand impatiently, obviously expecting me to fold upon contact. 'Well?'

But I pushed the straps right up my arm. 'Venetia, the house is chock-full of the things that you and Mum did together. But I was the one who bought the Hermès bag with her; it's one of the few things that doesn't involve you at all. I'm going to keep it. And that's that. And you know what else? *I* think we were wrong to keep the house exactly the way it was, we should have each taken a few things to remember her by, then cleared her study, her bedroom.' My throat started to ache from having to talk in a hissed undertone, but I ploughed on. 'It would have helped Dad move on, us move on. Maybe he would never have got as bad as he did if he'd had a chance for a new start. And when he gets back, I'm going to talk to him about it. See what *he* says, rather than your precious Hamish McGree.'

I could hear her casting around for a retort of some kind because the few times I'd actually stood up to her were the stuff of family legend, and I wished fervently that Andrew could have been there to admire my gumption, but instead I just closed the bag, put the plastic bag with my dad's cardigan and socks on the bedside table. Then, remembering James Merck's promise to send the letter, the one that had started it all, I quickly flicked through the stack of post Venetia had set by her offerings.

'What're you doing now?' Venetia hissed.

'Nothing,' I said evenly and it was partly true because the letter hadn't yet arrived. 'I'm going to wait outside until you're done.'

'You can't leave now.' Venetia sounded panicked. 'You—'

Dad shifted again, groaned slightly, then opened his eyes. He looked around unseeingly for a moment, his eyes travelling over Venetia and all the stuff she'd spread out on the bed, before finally landing on me.

'Addie,' he croaked. 'You're here.'

His voice was barely recognisable it was so croaky, but the look in his eyes was unmistakable: glad and relieved and warm and happy. And in that one moment, it all ceased to be relevant, the memory slideshow and the secrets and the stupid tussle about my mother's handbag. The only thing that was important was that my dad was awake and he was motioning for me to come closer and that he was thrilled to see me. I cautiously perched next to him, watched him anxiously. He'd fallen back against the bed and his face was working slightly. 'I'm so sorry,' he croaked finally, pressing one hand against his chest. 'All this trouble, Addie, so sorry.'

He pushed against his chest and I could see that his hands were trembling. I felt my heart drop into my stomach and Venetia was already reaching for a button next to the bed.

'Addie, I think you should go. Clearly, you're upsetting him.'

My dad shook his head at her and opened his mouth, but when he drew a laboured breath, Venetia started jabbing at the emergency button.

'Dad, listen to me please,' I said urgently, 'there's nothing at all to be sorry about. Please don't talk right now; we have all the time in the world. We do, because you're going to be just fine. You'll come home, soon.' I paused a moment, then ploughed on. 'And we can talk about it all when you're better, there's no rush, just *get* better, okay? I'll make you blueberry scones as soon as you're out. With cream. So hurry and get better, all right? Nothing has changed, it's all still there.'

He didn't open his eyes again, but he seemed to understand this last bit and his hand moved away from his chest and found my fingers, squeezed them. 'Never meant to hurt you,' he croaked. A sweaty sheen had broken out on his face and I said urgently, 'I know, I *know* that, Dad. Please don't worry. I'm sorry about all the things I said. I didn't mean any of them. I just want you better, I want you to come home.'

'Addie, for heaven's sake, leave him alone,' Venetia said loudly, clearly relieved now not to have to whisper anymore, and a nurse materialised to check the monitors.

'I'm going to get a doctor,' she said.

More voices fluttered back and forth, the door opened, and then my dad suddenly opened his eyes again.

'I wasn't lying,' he croaked. 'Not in that way. He might have been your father, but you were always my daughter, you never belonged to him. My own daughter from the very beginning, and the most wonderful, lucky thing in the world.'

A breath caught in my throat and swelled there and I wanted to say something else but already the doctor was there and the nurse pushed me out of the way, another nurse opened the door and I pulled Venetia outside, keeping my eyes on my father's face until the door had closed behind us.

Chapter Eighteen

They wheeled him down the corridor and into another room for more tests, leaving us clinging to each other outside the door until the doctor came back to talk to us. If he'd wanted to give us a dressing down, then he clearly took pity when he saw us standing there looking terrified, and instead he launched into a state-of-affairs update, peppered with medical terms like *pericarditis* and *testing for pulmonary oedema* and *angina*, the finer points of which were completely wasted on us. Finally he said something we could understand.

'He'll be fine. Physically, he is as stable as can be expected after a heart attack, but he's quite weak and very tired. He needs rest and quiet.'

Venetia glowered at me but I ignored her.

'Can we stay?' I asked anxiously. 'Out here, I mean? I won't go back in and upset him, I promise.'

He relented slightly. 'Yes, of course, although he'll be in and out of tests, and he needs to be kept calm for a few days before he can come home. His heart needs a chance to heal.'

So I called Claire to say I wouldn't be coming in, said goodbye to a shell-shocked Venetia who had a prenatal appointment at the Portland she couldn't miss, and went back in to sit vigil outside my dad's room for a few hours until Jas arrived. I wanted to cancel Phoebe, but I knew I couldn't very well do that when she was coming all the way down from Birmingham; even so, I might not have gone if Uncle Fred hadn't suddenly rounded the corner, laden with grapes and more magazines, announcing that he was going to stay for a few days, not to worry, he was bunking down with an old mate, no trouble at all, and he'd make sure all was ticking along splendidly.

Phoebe was standing with her back to me when I arrived at the cemetery, looking at the wrought-iron gate between the stone pillars, peering through to the little gatehouse with its slate-grey mossy roof just to the left. She was wearing the same camel-coloured trench coat, belted tightly against the drizzle, cream trousers and high-heeled shoes. Her hair was down this time and hung, long and perfectly straight, like a glossy sheet down her back.

'Hello,' I said breathlessly and she whirled around, her face changing to an expression of relief.

'Hello.'

She moved towards me and I moved backwards, thinking wildly of the appropriate etiquette. Should I shake hands or just pat her upper arm the way you might do with a distant relative, or should we hug? I did a convulsive raising of both hands, moving my body backwards, and finally resorted to a regal-looking little wave.

'I didn't want to go in,' she said, appearing not to notice my strange dance. 'I thought maybe I'd miss you.' She smiled cautiously. Her voice had that melodic, mellow quality to it that I'd first noticed about her, and her lips curved to break up the symmetry of her face, giving her a faintly mischievous air. We stood close now and on a bit of an incline so that I almost matched her height. From here I could see right into her eyes, a luminous grey, set wide beneath her forehead, and – I felt a stab at the bottom of my throat – ever so slightly slanted. Made up beautifully, fringed by long black lashes that brought out the dark limbal ring of her iris; these eyes unmistakably belonged to a Holloway. My mother. My grandmother. Me.

I took a quick step back, unnerved by the sudden discovery, and pointed through the gate. 'It's quite small.'

For an awkward moment, we surveyed the empty gravelled rotunda, the small paths veering off to the left and right, the wider tree-lined avenue just ahead, framed by trees. There was a grinding noise at the back, the sound of wood being shredded, and a moment later, a burly man with a bald pate hidden rather unsuccessfully under a shabby, too-small trilby came into view from the left, pushing a wheelbarrow with wood shavings.

'Y'ello,' he grumbled when he saw us. 'In or out?'

'Excuse me?' Phoebe said politely through the swirls of iron, sneaking a sideways look at me.

'Are you coming in? Or not?' the caretaker said impatiently, then pointed to the sign. *Cemetery closes at dusk.* 'Closing soon.'

'We're coming in,' Phoebe said calmly. 'If that is quite all right with you?'

'Suit yourself,' he said darkly, giving an expansive wave across graves and yew hedges. 'No one here minds either way.'

When I glanced over, I saw Phoebe looking at the caretaker with a disbelieving expression and I bit back a sudden laugh, shouldered my bags and steered her through the gates. 'Come on. It's down here.'

'Closing *soon*!' the caretaker bellowed after us just before he pushed on and out of sight.

'O-*kay*,' Phoebe called back over her shoulder.

We walked slowly down one of the gravel paths, breathing in the damp smell of freshly mown grass and wet soil.

'Is the rest of your family here also?' Phoebe asked conversationally, as if we were at a christening party.

I stepped around a puddle. 'My mother didn't really have any family. She was an only child. My grandparents are buried down in Limpsfield. My father—' I stopped, suddenly aware of the grating stream of possessive pronouns and family attributes, but Phoebe was looking around interestedly and didn't seem to have taken offence.

'So she is alone. Until my dad – well. You know.'

The shredder was quiet now and the air grey and dewy. Droplets sat on the leaves of the rhododendron to the left and hung heavily on the underside of the elms as we zigzagged between gravestones and down grassy little paths, but mercifully the rain had stopped for the moment.

'She liked cemeteries,' I added quickly, 'reading what people wrote on the stones and how old they were when they died. Wherever we were, we looked up the cemetery. A bit of a gruesome obsession, but I read somewhere there's lots of people who like that. Just through there. I think in America there's even a name for them, something-philes.'

Phoebe nodded and I decided to stop talking until we reached the grave.

'So, er, well, here it is.' I awkwardly gestured to the rectangle below us, discreetly giving the headstone a little pat to let it know we were here.

We'd planted small boxwoods and they'd filled out over the past year, growing outwards into a sort of miniature hedge around the sides of the plot. Inside, wild grasses weaved through flowers, giving the impression of a tiny unlikely meadow. Only the space directly in front of the stone was empty and someone, Venetia I'd guess, had recently brought a big terracotta pot with a rosebush and set it off-kilter into the middle, obscuring the lettering on the headstone.

> Elizabeth Sophie Harington
> b. 13 August 1941, d. 15 May 1999
> I give, to him who gave himself for me;
> Who gives himself to me, and bids me sing
> A sweet new song.

When I glanced at Phoebe I saw that her face had constricted slightly, and her eyes were brilliant with tears. When she caught me staring, I quickly looked down, embarrassed and a bit envious, too, then made a small movement to take her hand or to put my arm around her shoulders, or any of the other kinds of things you do to comfort people. But she shook her head.

'I like the words,' she said.

'Yes, Christina Rossetti. She was my mother's favourite . . .'

I had a sudden vision of my grandmother reading Christina Rossetti to herself in 1949, reading it with her daughter later, passing on a love for words that had stayed with my mother and which she, in turn, had passed on to us, all avid readers, too. *A sweet new song*. Rossetti had always been a bit sombre for me but there was a bright note to these words my father had picked, ringing of beginnings and of hope. I smiled slightly to myself, liking this new sepia-coloured dimension to my mother, the way her life was linked with her mother's even beyond her death, the way mine was linked with the both of them, a small series of anchors tying us together.

Next to me, Phoebe was breathing evenly and when I looked over I saw her throat, white against the evening gloom, lifting ever so slightly with the movement. Finally, she pulled up the bag she was carrying and retrieved a small, squashed pot of flowers.

'It's had a bit of a journey, I'm afraid,' she said apologetically. 'I dug it up from my garden this morning. I wanted her to have this little primrose that I've been trying to grow.'

'At least we don't have to worry about watering it,' I said, jabbing a thumb at the grey skies. 'You like gardening?'

'Well, my green fingers are a bit of a work in progress, to be honest. And I'm away too much. But I do like it.'

She'd extracted a plastic bag with two gardening gloves and a small trowel, then dug a small hole in the muddy soil, right at the corner in front of the gravestone, squashed the primrose inside and shuffled the soil back around it. When she straightened I noticed that she, too, gave the stone a small stroke. Involuntarily, I opened my mouth to remark on it, this odd first quirk of patting our mother's gravestone at the cemetery, which we both seemed to share, but already she stood with her head bowed, a serene and graceful pose, and I shifted awkwardly.

'There's a bench over by the trees. I'm going to sit down. Take your time, all right?'

She smiled gratefully. 'I'll be over in a moment.'

Chapter Nineteen

It was curiously peaceful underneath the elm trees, the May smell of green things growing around me and the moisture, not quite so cold and clammy today but oscillating, moving and shifting lightly whenever the breeze came through the branches. There was nothing to jar the senses as I sat and hugged my mother's bag and, bit by bit, the hospital and my family receded, leaving behind only the floating sensation from last night, which, amidst the soothing greys and dark greens, had become less frightening, more of a simple, empty space. Maybe I needed to be completely untethered in order to rebuild my father, the same way I would have to find a way to rebuild my mother. Maybe I needed to start with *I will never forget your birthday* and *You were always my daughter*.

I took another lungful of damp elms and cool moisture as Phoebe appeared between the bushes.

'Phew,' she said, exhaling shakily. Her eyes were slightly red against the pallor of her face and she held a balled-up tissue in her hand, but otherwise her face was composed. 'It's still all so . . . so . . .'

'Crazy?' I said.

'Strange.' She cleared her throat, looked back at the grave.

'Difficult,' I offered.

'Sad.'

'Yes,' I agreed and she sighed, then carefully dabbed at her eyes so as not to smear her make-up. I smiled across the space dividing us on the bench, cautiously taking in her grey eyes. But the stab of recognition had already softened, because aside from the obvious similarity, Phoebe Roberts's eyes were expressive in entirely different ways to my mother's or even to mine and when she smiled and tucked the tissue away, her face was different again against the angles of her cheekbones.

'About the other day . . . Again, I'm really sorry,' I started, but she held up her hand.

'Honestly, Adele, I'm quite embarrassed to think how in-your-face I was. Can we just start afresh? Please? Before I stalked and bullied you, before you yelled at me and ran away?'

'Blank slate,' I said, nodding emphatically. I wasn't used to apologies being gracefully given or received. My mother had been the queen of the pursed-white-lip-lofty-eyebrow treatment, while Venetia's sulks lasted for days and were only reluctantly ended when I came back on bended knees.

Phoebe took a newspaper out of her bag, unfolded it and spread half on to the bench, put a plastic bag on top, then set the other half of the paper next to her and put her bag on top of it. She sat down on the plastic bag, taking care not to touch her trouser legs to the front of the bench. When she saw me watching, she shrugged.

'I hate my stuff getting dirty.'

'But what's with the paper *and* the bag?'

'Don't want to get newsprint on my trousers. And it's too mossy for just the bag,' she said.

Instantly, of course, I felt mossy moisture seeping into the seat of my jeans, realising at the same time that my knees had a neat muddy circle on them from kneeling in front of the grave. I stole an envious glance at her cream trousers, which despite her planting the primrose, practically glowed against the murky brown of the bench.

'You don't have kids, do you?' I asked.

'No,' she said. 'I'm on my own.'

She didn't offer any explanation and we both fell silent again. I had absolutely no idea what to say next. How do you talk to a stranger who is actually your twin sister? Or to a twin sister who, really, is a complete stranger? How can you forge a sisterly bond from absolutely nothing? Next to me, Phoebe sat, her shoulders hunched so that her head was the same height as mine, fiddling with the side of the newspaper beneath her bag. 'I imagined all this very differently. Maybe we shouldn't think too hard, just start talking about what we know. Maybe that'll lead us somewhere.'

To each other, she meant. 'Yes. You start,' I agreed.

She acknowledged my cowardice with a brief smile. 'My mum, my adoptive mother obviously, her name is Madeleine Roberts, she was pregnant, eight months. There was bleeding late in the pregnancy, quite heavy, and my dad drove her to hospital. She lives in Brimley, between Horsham and Haywards Heath, but All Saints Hospital in Brighton was where'd she been before because they had some special equipment. There was something wrong with the lining of her uterus and she'd had a string of miscarriages. This was her longest pregnancy and she still lost the baby at eight months. She was thirty-eight by that point and they were desperate for children, but when the doctor was done with her, it looked unlikely that she'd ever be able to even get pregnant again.'

I made a sympathetic noise and she nodded. 'Yeah, and in 1960, there wasn't much you could do about it, no matter how much special equipment you had. That night, there was a baby already, she said, just born, and the mother wanted it to go to a good family.' She paused for us both to digest the fact that 'the mother' was really 'our mother' and 'the baby' was herself.

'My parents had considered adoption before. But lots of people wanted babies and it was more difficult at their age. Plus, Brimley is the kind of small town where people talk constantly, poking their nose into any business that isn't theirs. You buy a pack of tampons at the chemist and next thing you know your neighbour is holding out a hot-water bottle as you pass their gate. I think people would have fallen over in shock if my parents had shown up with an adopted baby. But this was different, a private adoption, very discreet. No one would have to know and she'd be helping out another mother, it was a good thing. That's what she said.'

'And what happened when they came back to Brimley?' I asked.

'They never told anyone.' She grimaced. 'If you're ever in Brimley, you'll know why. And it was easy to do because she'd been so far along before the miscarriage. What with everything she'd gone through before, she just pretended I was their baby born a few weeks early, and I think over time that actually sort of became true for her.'

'Okay,' I said slowly. It was strange to think that, had my mother's finger pointed at Phoebe instead of me, this baby in Brimley might have had my life. I wondered if my mother had thought about Phoebe like that, as an unknown quantity she could imagine to be so very different from the worried, anxious-to-please daughter she ended up with. And I, would I have been happier in Brimley than at Rose Hill Road?

'I suppose they did it for me. They wanted me to grow up exactly like everyone else, without anything hanging over us. Things might be different today, although our town hasn't changed a bit since the fifties. The moment you set foot there, you can feel it putting a pinny on you and forcing you behind the hearth.'

'But you don't still live there?' I asked.

'God no,' she said, horrified. 'I left the first moment I could. Moved clear to the other side of London and up north. I live in Solihull; that's really nice and close to the airport.'

'Why the airport?' I asked. 'Are you a flight attendant?' That would explain a lot about her groomed, friendly glossiness.

'No, I'm a pilot,' she said.

'A pilot?' I echoed incredulously. Whatever I'd imagined her to be, *that* I hadn't expected.

'Yes.' She grinned. 'Commercial flight pilot.'

'You like travelling?'

'Adore it. Being up in the air, it's the best feeling in the world, and there's always a change of scene ahead of you.' She grinned. 'I've been everywhere. What is it that you do at the pastry shop?'

'Oh, gosh, well, obviously nothing nearly as exciting,' I said, thinking about how much my mother would have loved that, being up in the air, having been everywhere, always a new place ahead. 'I trained as a baker,' I added, because she seemed to be waiting for something.

Her eyes lit up. 'Oh, that sounds fab,' she said. 'I love cake. And that patisserie you work at looks so swishy.'

'I've been there forever. It's a good place, nice people.'

I listened to the sound of my voice, monotonous, apologetic even, and added almost defiantly, 'I love working in pastry, you know. It's a science. Hard to get right. I love it.'

'I love pastries, too,' she said enthusiastically, 'although I can't cook to save my life. And it's one of life's essential skills if you really think about it. I mean, if M&S didn't open early every day, I'd have long starved.'

'Your parents must be very proud,' I said. 'Gosh, a pilot. That's very cool.'

She bobbed her head modestly. 'They were. Not a very Brimley-esque career to embark on perhaps, but of course they were proud. I had to get loads of scholarships to pay for it all.'

'Was it okay for you, I mean, being with your parents? Growing up with them?' I asked, slightly reluctantly, because so far the ground we'd covered had been nicely safe — history, jobs, food.

But she didn't seem to feel the awkwardness, just considered the question, then said, 'You know, I've been thinking about that a lot, and the truth is it was fine. It really was. We got along well, and I'm still quite close to my mum. But they were older because they'd already spent so much time trying to have a baby. They were very set in their ways. When I finished school, my dad was almost sixty, and he was never a young-at-heart kind of person anyway. And growing up in Brimley — people there just go on as they always have, like nothing will ever change, or can ever change. No real possibilities, no one going beyond what they know. I guess I always wanted too much. And I was too tall.' She attempted a chuckle. 'Stood out like a sore thumb. So it was nice with them, but it was a bit lonely to be a tall and gawky child who wanted the moon and then some.'

'Do you have any other relatives?'

'Some cousins. One's younger than me, Chloe. She's a hairdresser in Brimley. She's quite nice, got three kids. All my other cousins are older and obviously I never had any siblings.' She hesitated, then added, flushing as she spoke, 'When I was in primary school and the other kids kept calling me "storky" and "teacher's pet" I always imagined I had a brother who'd stand up for me.' She gave a sudden snort of laughter and winked. 'His name was Charlie. He was taller than me and training to be a boxer. I'd even picked out his boxing kit. Black and yellow. For menace, I was thinking, like a wasp, you know.'

She gave me a nudge across the bench, and I had to laugh too, because she was so good at not being awkward that it was infectious.

'Things got a lot better when I left Brimley and went to the aviation academy. And the day I bought my own house was pretty amazing. It's an end of terrace in Solihull with a small garden, and I've put every penny I have into it. I've extended into the attic, converted the kitchen. I love it nearly as much as I love flying. It can be a bit lonely, I suppose. But you can do whatever you want whenever you want it, and no one comments.'

'God, I know the feeling,' I said fervently, because here, finally, was something I could unequivocally relate to. 'I spent the first few weeks in my kitchen baking till one in the morning. No one to complain about why you need fifteen bowls taking up cupboard space, no one to toss out your sourdough starter because it looks like a mouldy dishcloth.'

'Yes!' she exclaimed, although I couldn't imagine she'd ever seen a mouldy dishcloth in her life. 'And no one to take the TV remote from you.'

'And no one who messes up your fridge organisation with lots of beer bottles.'

'No one to watch you eat baked beans straight out of the tin, then put the tin back in the fridge and eat them again the next day.'

'No one barbecuing. I hate barbecues.'

'I do too. Especially if it means people trampling around my garden crushing everything underfoot.'

We were both laughing now and she was nudging me again, her eyes so bright and her face so open that if it hadn't been for the gravestones we might have been two friends catching up in the park.

'It would be different if you had a family, though.' She was serious now. 'I wouldn't mind any of the garden trampling and remote-stealing if I had two kids playing football on the lawn or watching a movie with me. A boy and a girl, that's what I'd love.'

'Do you have anyone? I mean, anyone to have them with?' I asked tentatively.

'Well, I do have a boyfriend, but he's a pilot too, so not around a whole lot. I went about this slightly the wrong way,' she said and I thought I could detect a tiny note of bitterness in her voice. 'I should have picked a different career, started looking for a dependable mate earlier. Flying is a microcosm and, let's face it, you can't have a family really if you're always flitting off to faraway places.'

I pondered this. 'I suppose you could teach flying or something?' I offered eventually.

'Yeah, maybe. But I'm not really sure if Craig – that's his name – is really the one I want Charlotte and Henry to grow up with.'

'Charlotte and Henry?' I raised my eyebrows.

'That's what I'd name them,' she said, almost defiantly. 'I thought calling the boy Charlie would be, well, a bit *weird* maybe, but . . . Anyway, what about you?'

'You mean do I have kids?'

'Well, we *are* forty. Not an unreasonable life choice to have made.'

'I haven't found anyone to have them with. Andrew used to say – he's a friend,' I added when she waggled her eyebrows suggestively. 'Works as a chef at a French restaurant. He always says that cooks can't have relationships. Maybe a bit like the pilot-microcosm thing. One-track mind, up hideously late all the time, smelling of onions and grease. Most of my boyfriends couldn't stand it because I always had to get up at four thirty to be at the bakery and when I came home, having been run off my feet all day, I was completely knackered. In the end, they always gave up on me.'

'But don't you *want* kids?' She sounded so incredulous that I felt almost embarrassed not to join in with her enthusiasm.

'Not burningly, no,' I said cautiously. 'I sort of always assumed that I'd have them eventually, but it's just not fallen into place the way it has with other people. So far I've preferred being on my own to whatever other option there was. I do really like it, my mouldy sourdough starters and my fridge organisation,' I added to lighten the mood, and she smiled slightly.

'Then that's what you should do. I'm a big believer in going for what you want to go for. And you could always be cool Aunt Adele to Henry and Charlotte.'

I laughed. 'Auntie Addie, with highly unsuitable presents, and taking them out on the town and feeding them lots of cake. So hurry up and get started, will you?'

'Forty is the new thirty,' she said wisely. 'There's still loads of time.'

But she sounded a little sad when she said the last bit and I reached out across the space dividing us and cautiously patted her arm.

'So what happened then?'

'I found the bundle and the diary and it all got slightly out of hand. My mum was crying a lot, and I was, I don't know, I was just angry. Stupid, I know, but all I could think of was me as a child, trudging back from Brimley Primary, having imaginary conversations with Charlie and hating Brimley, always feeling out of place and picked on. And suddenly, so much turned out to make sense, in a slightly awful way, but then, the more I thought about it, the more it *didn't* make sense at all, and my mum couldn't really remember anything properly. She didn't know about the other baby, you I mean, even though it was right there in the little booklet, and she couldn't recall anything about the process of the adoption because she's always been a bit hopeless with paperwork and stuff. She was holding on to me and begging me not to leave and generally bemoaning the fact that I'd found out in the first place. It really was pretty awful. I don't know – did you feel any of that when, I mean, after I came to see you?'

'I, er, yes.' I avoided her eyes, feeling slightly ashamed that my own emotional Celestial Cyclone had somehow eclipsed the larger implications of her appearance. Mercifully, the caretaker chose this moment to start up a wood grinder, filling the air with an ear-splitting rattle, and when that stopped, there was the sound of a bell from up front, accompanied by shouting. This didn't seem a very peaceful place for a final rest, what with all the shredding and shouting and bell ringing.

'I did go back to All Saints Hospital,' Phoebe said when it was quiet at last. 'But it's gone. And so is the women's home. I thought maybe I could have got someone's name, that someone might remember her.'

I held up my bag. 'Like mother, like daughter. She wrote hundreds of letters to try and find *you*.'

* * *

162

She took such a long time to read Harry's notes that I started fidgeting and when she looked up, I saw that her eyes were full of tears again. She held a finger below her lashes to stop the tears from falling on to them and I scrabbled around for a tissue, but all I could find was a couple of paper towels, crumby with broken biscuits that I'd brought home from Grace's the other day.

'Sorry,' she said shakily, refusing the paper towels in favour of her own crisp new packet of tissues. 'But do you think that this could be *him*?' She leafed through the folder, straightened a few bent edges. 'We could start with Hartland and take it from there.'

'Well . . . I mean, are you sure you want to find out about him and – everything?' I asked back tentatively.

'How can I possibly not?' She looked surprised. 'Our father is out there somewhere, we were all supposed to be together. Don't you want to know what happened? Don't you want to meet him?'

I looked at her, her face tilted towards me, her eyes beckoning me, wanting me to be there with her, to be a part of her, and for a moment, I felt paralysed in the face of so much expectation, such a determined demand on my ability to give. Automatically, I felt my mouth open to reassure her, to bow to her needs, as I would have done any other day. But then I closed it again, because I had to be sure what it was that *I* wanted to do.

'I might not,' I eventually said. 'But I think I'm going to take it one day at a time.'

She accepted that. 'It's still almost absurd, isn't it, us being together, like this? Exciting.'

Her eyes were still red-rimmed and a bit swollen but the rest of her face was settling back into its creamy white pallor and when she touched my hand, she was smiling. She was a toucher, a reacher-out, not at all like me or any of my family, but it didn't feel quite so awkward this time and I couldn't help but return her smile and feel a frisson of elation at having an 'us'.

'Yes. Very,' I said emphatically.

'There you are!' The caretaker popped out of the bushes next to us amidst a shower of raindrops, his face a picture of wrath. Phoebe gave a squeak, holding up the folder like a shield.

'Didn't you hear the bell?' he demanded. 'Closing time.'

'We didn't know what it meant,' Phoebe said apologetically from behind the file.

'We're sorry,' I added.

The caretaker glowered at us and lifted his rake and we both cowered, but he merely pointed it towards the little path, waited for us to get up and pack our things, then walked behind us so closely we caught his muttered threats and mulchy smell. Then he bundled us unceremoniously out on to the other side of the gates and locked them noisily behind us.

'Oh well, it was getting late anyway,' I said, frowning at his retreating backside. 'And, wait, yep, it's starting to rain again.'

I opened my umbrella, held it over both our heads and we looked back into the shadowy interior of the cemetery.

'London's a funny place,' Phoebe observed. 'Here, could I take the notes and all these letters with me? I'll do a bit more research at the library. Maybe I'll come up with something that the worthy Mr Merck has overlooked.'

I wouldn't put it past her. I'd only known her for a few hours but already it was very clear that Phoebe was not much in favour of uselessly shilly-shallying, not when you could be getting things done yourself, solving world hunger and the fate of baby seals in the process. I smiled, forcibly reminded of the one other woman I'd known who believed in solutions over problems and who considered the library the only place where life could be persuaded to make sense.

'Can I take the pregnancy booklet thingy to look at then?'

She reached into her bag and brought it out. She'd put it into a clear plastic bag with a sturdy seam at the top.

'Don't lose it, okay?'

'I won't.'

Juggling the umbrella and the Hermès bag, I tucked it carefully away, taking longer than necessary because I wasn't quite sure how to say goodbye. Suddenly, without warning, she put her arms around me, umbrella and all, and pulled me close. I felt my body instinctively push back against the onslaught of unwarranted intimacy, but then forced myself to relax, to rest my head against her cheek for a second.

'It was good to see you,' I said awkwardly.

'Yes,' she said. When I met her eyes, I saw that her face was flushed. 'Do you want to, I mean, do you want to meet up again, maybe soon? I'm off work this entire week, flying out to the Virgin Islands next Tuesday. So I'm free and easy for a few days. We could have dinner, talk some more?'

'You could come to my flat,' I said, surprising myself, but before the invitation was even fully out of my mouth it felt like too much too soon, and I started back-pedalling. 'Or, let's go out somewhere. Or, well, whatever is better.'

'A neutral place might be better.' She smiled. 'Are you going to be able to talk to your dad soon? I mean, when will he be a bit better, do you think?'

'It'll be days. He's still recovering.'

'Could I maybe come and meet him some time? Not now, obviously. But when he's fully better, I mean? Oh sorry, is that too forward again? You know, anything is good with me. Really.'

'Let's see how he is getting on,' I said quickly. 'When we get together, then . . .'

There was a pause and I was trying to think of something else I could offer her to distract her from my father when she suddenly said, 'Would you be up for meeting my mother with me?'

I gaped at her. I may have been unsure about a lot of things in life, but I really, *really* did not want to meet Mrs Roberts. I had enough to do to sort out the new roles of my current mother and father in this scenario, not to mention *Father: Blank*. Who might or might not be Harry. Not remotely did I want to introduce yet another player into the mix.

'But why on earth would she want to talk to *me*?'

'She might have less of a problem, be less emotional, I mean, about talking through the night of our birth with you,' Phoebe said eagerly. 'And I think it's important that we're all out in the open, talking to each other, so that everyone gets used to the idea. So maybe while we wait for your dad to get better—'

'Phoebe, I . . . I don't think . . . it would probably be . . .'

Awkward. *Weird*. On the other hand, Mrs Roberts was the only immediately available first-hand witness who might have met Dr Miller and Sarah Mason, who might be able to connect some of the dots. Who might have seen my mother there, might have seen me. I shook rain off the top of the umbrella, undecided.

'Okay, sure. Just let me know if there's a good time in the next few weeks and—'

'How about tomorrow? I was supposed to go and see her. I could bring her up to London instead.'

Tomorrow? Dear god.

'I don't get out till five,' I said. 'That's probably too late, isn't it, so let's just—'

'Five would be great,' she said enthusiastically. 'Oh I'm so glad. Thanks for agreeing to do it. She'll really like you, I think.'

Chapter Twenty

*What if*s came in all shapes and sizes, and as sizes went, Phoebe Roberts (and not me) ending up with Mrs Roberts was a fairly substantial one in the great karmic unfolding of my life.

I was exhausted and still I lay awake for a long time that night, trying to picture the sliding door that opened up on the life I might have led in Brimley. Would I be married with children, living in a small mid-terrace and working in the bakery down the road? Would I have felt secure in the narrowness of it all, or hemmed in by the claustrophobic small-town ways Phoebe had talked about? Would I have rebelled and gone on to do big things, like Phoebe had?

The next day passed like a flash, leaving me little room to ponder the Brimley reincarnation of myself, or any of the other questions thrown up by recent developments. Despite my short night, I got up early to sort out the breads and pastries at Grace's, then went to the Royal Free and sat for a couple of hours reading to my father, who was groggy and tired. Back at Grace's, I spent most of the rest of the day trying to get an electrician on the line for a faulty electrical outlet in the kitchen and monitoring one of the shop girls who insisted on coming to work with a carpal-tunnel-syndrome arm in a sling because she couldn't afford to miss work. Following her slow progress restocking the glass display case, I listened to my messages.

Andrew had called to talk about a variety of things ranging from Dad's health and Phoebe Roberts to estate agents and restaurant options. I watched the shop girl manoeuvring a petit four into a box with one arm and pondered the way this whole Grand Bleu thing seemed to have taken on a life of its own. Andrew was almost pathologically stubborn when he got his teeth into something, but surely he'd have to see sense soon, at the latest when it came to signing an enormous mortgage with all the trimmings that neither of us was really able to shoulder. And who'd oversee all the renovating, the hiring of staff, the day-to-day managing? And then, working along-side Andrew. I chewed at the inside of my mouth when I contemplated that prospect with rather mixed feelings and only snapped to when Andrew's message wound up by asking if I wanted to meet up for a drink that night. His voice sounded uncharacteristically unsure at that last bit and I cringed, thinking about the almost-thing in front of the Tube station.

All in all, I was relieved when he didn't pick up the phone, and I left him a rambling message before settling down for a chat with Mrs Baxter, who said that she'd found the back door open and should she get in touch with the police? And how was I doing? Was I going to come and see her soon?

Venetia, on the other hand, had been deafeningly silent since the episode at the hospital yesterday, which, I reflected as I checked on the one-armed shop girl one last time, was not a bad thing as I certainly had enough to be going on with at the moment, most pressing of all my impending meeting with Mrs Roberts at the Stanhope Café.

I'd been so preoccupied with my end of the *what if* scenario that it came as something of a surprise to me when I stepped up to 'our' Formica-topped table and almost immediately realised that Mrs Roberts was not there to 'really like' me at all, but solely and entirely to please her daughter. As Phoebe jumped up to introduce us and I stuck out my hand, taking a deep inward breath, Mrs Roberts's brown button-like eyes scanned me for a moment and she withdrew her own hand almost before I could shake it to sit back down and smile quickly and determinedly at her daughter.

'So, Addie is a pastry chef just down the road, Mum, isn't that amazing?' Phoebe burbled. 'Did you have a long day, Addie? Here, have some tea.'

On cue, the little waitress bustled over, greeting me as if I was a long-lost friend, clearly looking forward to another exciting afternoon in our company. Mrs Roberts motioned for her to fill Phoebe's cup first, then her own, then mine, and as chairs scraped and milk and sugar were being exchanged, I surreptitiously studied Phoebe's adoptive mother, who was nothing like I'd imagined her to be. I'd thought she was going to be brisk and sensible and solid, someone good at coping and making do, but instead she seemed nervy, brittle almost, the muted colours and coarse textures of her clothes bulky on her birdlike frame, her face flushing easily underneath her powdery make-up.

Initially she said very little, engaged mostly in making sure her daughter was supplied with all necessary accoutrements for her tea, and I certainly wasn't putting forward any sparkling conversational gambits, but Phoebe steered us safely through the initial awkward moments until, coaxed and prompted by her daughter, Mrs Roberts started talking.

A lot of the things she said I'd already heard from Phoebe, which was just as well because Mrs Roberts veered erratically across the storyline, doubling back and forth, straining to remember a bit, leaving it, only to pick it back up later, stopping continuously to throw questioning or anxious looks in the direction of her daughter. There was much about the agony of the miscarriage and the abject horror of giving birth to a dead baby, then, on that same night, the doctor coming in with the baby girl and the elation when she got to hold her so soon after losing her own, the good turn of fate, the blessing. *Fourteenth of February, a Valentine's baby*, she'd said several times, her voice rising whenever she came to that point in the story. Phoebe, it was clear, had been urgently wanted and happily received and, as far as she was concerned, *I* should have stayed under the bed along with the old winter jacket, because, her button eyes narrowed at me occasionally, I seemed to be causing her daughter no end of trouble.

I watched her, as she talked, unable to take my eyes off this woman who might have been my own mother. I swallowed against the lump which had taken up its usual residence at the bottom of my throat, and pictured Mrs Roberts waving me off on my first day of school instead of my mum fussing over a stain on my school uniform; Mrs Roberts making me a white-bread sandwich with the crusts cut off for tea instead of Mrs Baxter's spag bol; imagined her waiting for me every day, enquiring after homework and whether I'd eaten enough for lunch; pictured that flush that might have spread across her cheeks when she had to explain things like periods and sex and armpit hair.

As if she'd read my thoughts, Mrs Roberts gave a nervous laugh at something Phoebe said, the wispy curls next to her ears bouncing up and down, and suddenly, awfully, I felt an overriding sense of relief at the turn of fate that had nudged me towards my life at Rose Hill Road, with its limitless possibilities that I didn't avail myself of and my mother, who'd never made a sandwich in her life and left periods and armpit hair to Mrs Baxter, but who'd been anything but nervous or wispy, who'd been someone to aspire to, however tiring it had often been.

It took a moment for me to realise that both Phoebe and Mrs Roberts had stopped speaking and were regarding me rather strangely.

'So, then, you, erm, went home with the baby?' I squeaked.

Mrs Roberts looked at me slightly incredulously and raised her eyebrows at Phoebe as if to question her enthusiasm for a newfound relation as dim as myself.

'Yes,' she said, exaggeratedly slowly. 'I took her *home*.' She said the last word loudly in an obvious attempt to penetrate my limited understanding. 'I was still quite weak at the time but I thought we'd be better off in a familiar environment, get used to things, so we went home a couple of days later.' She coughed and pulled out a handkerchief.

'But wasn't it customary for mothers and babies to stay for a while?' I said. 'A "lying in" or something like that?'

Mrs Roberts's eyes came to rest somewhere above my left shoulder.

'Yes, I suppose,' she said vaguely. 'A lot of women stayed well over a week. But the baby was fine, healthy, taking the bottle well. I didn't want to linger. I don't like hospitals much.' She reached for the salt shaker that was sitting once again in the middle of the table, moved it around. 'I'd seen a lot of them by then. I had three miscarriages before Phoebe came along; two of them ended in that same hospital.'

She slid her eyes towards my face and finally locked them fully on to mine. There was something challenging in there, defiant. I frowned back at her.

'And did you see her . . . our mother . . . there?' I asked slowly, not taking my eyes off hers. 'Or did you . . . see me?'

Another long moment passed and Mrs Roberts was the first to look away.

'No, the doctor brought the baby *to me*, like I said before.'

'But we were just a day old, right, wouldn't she have been there somewhere?' Phoebe said.

'I'm not sure,' Mrs Roberts said guardedly. 'I only know what *I* was doing. He just said the mother was young and wanted it handled discreetly. I only saw him very briefly. His name was Miller, I remember that for sure, because my sister married a Miller, she's now Arabella Miller.'

Mrs Roberts leaned back, clearly pleased that she had remembered something, and missed the look Phoebe and I exchanged as we both thought of the yellow notepad.

'Dr Miller, of course.' I started tapping the table with my fingertips. 'Do you know if he's still alive?'

'Alive?' Mrs Roberts looked nonplussed, but gamely considered the question. Out of the corner of my eye, I saw Phoebe's finger start tapping the table alongside mine. 'I can't imagine. He was very helpful, a lovely chap, but he *was* getting on a bit, even back then. He was fifty, fifty-five maybe?' She seemed to warm to the theme. 'But so proper, a true gentleman, very polite. Spoke with authority, too, and had all the nurses hurrying around to do what he said.'

She gave the salt shaker a gentle spin and for a moment we all mulled it over.

'And how was the adoption done exactly?' I was beginning to feel a bit like an interrogator, not helped by the fact that Mrs Roberts flinched in an exaggerated way every time I asked a question, and then answered in a quivering voice as if I was offering up torture instruments for her to choose from.

'Matthew took care of all that,' she said. 'The paperwork and things. He always did; he looked after everything.' She paused to dab her eyes.

Suddenly, a teapot appeared next to me. 'Just me,' the little waitress said cheerfully. 'Thought you might need a refill. Fancy some sandwiches?'

'Ham and cheese, please,' Mrs Roberts said quickly. 'You have to eat, love,' she overrode Phoebe's protests, reaching to pick a piece of fluff off her daughter's cardigan. 'You're too thin as it is. You really should—'

'So this paperwork your husband took care of . . .' I was thinking out loud and they fell silent. 'Was that the actual adoption papers? And did any other people sign them, any of the staff at the hospital? The, er, the mother maybe?'

The waitress bustled back with cutlery and napkins.

'Oh, no.' Mrs Roberts looked scandalised. 'Things like that were very strictly handled back then, the mother's identity was to be protected at all costs, you see, because their reputation might be ruined. Well, in this case, I suppose—'

'It was already ruined?' I finished for her.

'Well, I mean, you know,' Mrs Roberts said quickly. 'It was before the pill and there were a lot of pregnancies that young mothers never wanted anyone to know about afterwards. That's why there were the women's homes. Dr Miller was most helpful explaining it all.'

Phoebe looked down at the table and her fingers stopped tapping. 'Actually, we'll know more about the adoption fairly soon, because I've applied to view the records.'

'You have?' Mrs Roberts said, startled, and not entirely pleased. 'But you have your birth certificate. What else do you need?'

'You can apply for the original records at the General Register Office. You have to meet with an adoption advisor beforehand, and then he can give you more information on the adoption. It takes a while, so I thought I'd start things moving.' Phoebe straightened her napkin, lined up her silverware, not looking at her mother.

'I thought you said you didn't want to . . .' Mrs Roberts frowned. 'You said *having* her name was all you needed. Why do you need more papers?'

'If she'd been alive, I wouldn't have needed the papers. But I want to know who my father was.'

Mrs Roberts frowned. 'Your father was your father,' she said firmly. 'No one could have been a better father than Matthew.'

'Yes,' Phoebe said, gently now, and she looked up to smile at her mother, reached out to hold her hand. 'He'll always be, I know that, Mum. He was wonderful. And finding this other man, it doesn't take anything at all away from him. But you understand that I'd like to know? That I need to?'

It was very clear that Mrs Roberts didn't understand that at all. She picked up the salt shaker again, spinning it round and round, frowning to herself. Each time it spun too far it released a burst of salt until the area in front of her was gritty with small white grains. 'Well, I'm not really sure, love,' she finally said. 'I knew all this would stir up such trouble if it ever came to light.'

The waitress came hurrying towards us with three hastily assembled sandwiches and a couple of bags of crisps, and Mrs Roberts turned towards her, clearly relieved at the excuse for a break in the conversation.

'Let's leave the sandwiches for a bit, Mum,' Phoebe said. 'This is important to me. I wanted you two to meet, I wanted us all to talk about things, to get everything out in the open so we can start looking for . . . I don't know, something. Addie found a list of names her mum made, maybe of other people on the ward that night. Do you remember anyone in particular?'

'I'm not sure.' Mrs Roberts pushed Phoebe's sandwich close to her. 'Big ward, it was, with all those women always squawking about and carrying on. Matron was awfully strict. But the only person I remember was that young nurse. She was from the West Indies or Jamaica or somewhere. Had just started her training. She was on duty on the ward, came and made me cups of tea. You won't believe how thirsty you get. Anyway, on the second night, she had the bundle with her, I told you about that already, Phoebe. The clothes were folded together very small and those pregnancy papers were tucked right inside the little hat. She was most insistent that we should have the clothes. Apparently the mother had been preparing them for the baby to take with her, for later, you know. I wasn't sure how *that* was correct procedure, given that the birth mother's name ended up being in there clear as day, but the nurse was very firm and I promised to hold on to it. I didn't really think about it at the time anyway, to be honest, and I only opened it once, when we got home, then never thought about it after.' She frowned, clearly unable to forgive herself for not just chucking it out and saving her beleaguered Phoebe all this trouble.

'Do you remember *her* name, the nurse's?' I asked. 'Edith Cuthbert, maybe, or Laura Remington? Sarah Mason?' I offered.

'I'm not sure. Possibly,' Mrs Roberts said guardedly. 'All I know is that she was young, because she got in trouble with one of the sisters for spilling tea on my bed. And I was very weak from my own birth, so you must forgive me for not really remembering anything properly.'

'But if you were that weak, why did they let you leave the hospital so quickly, and with a baby to boot?' I asked. 'I'm sorry, Mrs Roberts, but that just doesn't quite . . . make sense.'

'All right, all right.' Madeleine Roberts threw her sandwich on to the plate but narrowly missed so that ham and bread ricocheted off the rim. 'I was worried, all right? I had Phoebe, I wanted to be gone from that place. I didn't want anyone to come back and take her away again.' She shivered. 'I was worried and I've been worried every single day for forty years that someone would come and want my daughter back. Surely that's understandable? It's not a crime, you know.' She narrowed her eyes at me. 'We could give that baby a safe place to grow up. If we didn't take her, the doctor said, she'd just be adopted by someone else. Or else go to a children's home, and wait there to be adopted. I mean, honestly.' She shook her head angrily. 'We'd been trying so hard to have a baby. I'd lost three babies. *Three babies!*'

Her voice rose to a sob-like choke and from across the room the waitress stared at her with wide-open eyes.

'Can you imagine what it was like? To come in for a check-up happy as Larry, and to hear the doctor say that my baby was dead?' She took several quick breaths to calm herself. 'It'd been my longest pregnancy, eight months gone, and it was unbearable, utterly unbearable to me, the thought that I'd been walking around in Brimley, excited and happy, when all along I was carrying a dead baby inside me. Dead just like all the others, who just kept on dying and dying and dying.'

She locked eyes with me. 'And do you know what they did with stillborn babies in those days? Do you?'

I shook my head mutely, feeling my cheeks go hot.

'They took it from you without you even seeing it, but not before they make you give birth to it, like a proper mum, only you're not a proper mum, are you, you're not a mum at all, and then they put it in a bucket and burn it along with all the amputated legs and arms. If they're being particularly kind, they toss it into someone else's coffin so at least it gets a decent burial. I never got a chance to say goodbye to any of my dead babies; only that last time did I even know whether it was a little boy or girl.' She clapped her hands in front of her mouth and her shoulders were shaking. Phoebe put her arm around her and when she looked at me I saw that her eyes were shining with tears.

'And there, right in front of us, was this beautiful little girl.' Mrs Roberts leaned into Phoebe. 'Of course we took her, and gladly, and I would do it again, a thousand times over. You were lying in your little crib and I could just see your hair peeking out of the blanket, your eyes were closed and your hand was so tiny, up by your cheek, your fingers all scrunched up in a ball. So a couple of days later, I left with my beautiful healthy baby girl.'

She met my eyes, as if daring me to challenge the possessive pronoun, but my heart went out to her and I wanted to say something, anything, that might make her feel better. Already, though, she was looking away as she exhaled a long shaky breath and reached for a napkin to wipe her hands. 'Now if we're quite done here, I must go and catch my train.'

'But you haven't even eaten your sandwich,' Phoebe said quickly. 'Mum, do please stay. We don't have to talk about it anymore if it's so painful. Let me get you another cup of tea.'

But Mrs Roberts made a show of checking her watch, getting out a little pamphlet of train times, and silence fell over the table. Then I suddenly *knew*; I was so certain that I bent forward and reached out my hand, touched her arm, made her look at me.

'You did see her there, then, didn't you?' I said softly. 'And that's what frightened you? That she'd come and take Phoebe back?'

'What do you mean?' Mrs Roberts said, her eyes still on the train times, but her hands were trembling and she was gripping the paper very hard. 'All right,' she said then, letting the timetable drop back on to the table and throwing up her hands. 'Fine. Yes, I saw her. Or at least I think I did.'

'You did?' Phoebe leaned forward in her seat. 'Why didn't you tell me?'

Mrs Roberts's shoulders slumped as if all the fight had gone out of her.

'We were on our way out, Matthew and I, and that's when I passed the bed at the very end. They'd kept screens around it for most of the time.'

She took off her glasses, rubbing her eyes, taking most of her mascara with it. She looked tired and old, with large dark circles underneath her eyes.

'Just as I passed, a nurse went in. It was the little black nurse I told you about, the one who'd brought the baby clothes. She saw me, and then she gave a start, and she tried to adjust the screen to cover the bed, and then I put two and two together. They didn't want the unmarried mothers mingling with the others, you see, so Matron must have put her out of sight behind the screen, and I knew then that this had to be her.' Mrs Roberts's eyes were filled with tears as she looked across at her daughter and me.

'I only saw her for a moment. She was lying in bed, sleeping. On her side. She had curly hair, dark and short. It was pulled back so you could see her face and she was pale, and she looked small and very young. It was her. I can't explain it, but I knew.'

A moment. I focussed on my tea, now cold, adding sugar and reaching for another packet to add more, forcing myself to sip it slowly, moving the sickly-sweet liquid down my throat with my tongue, like medicine, until I could feel it settle in my stomach, spreading out towards that one moment when the life of this woman across from me had connected with that of my eighteen-year-old mother.

'But where was I, Mrs Roberts, didn't you see me?' I held my breath.

'No, you weren't there . . . but I—' Mrs Roberts's face was working again, but she pressed her lips together as if to make herself concentrate. 'I'd seen you before.'

A chill ran across my sweaty skin, a strange tightening that spread from my scalp down towards the pit of my stomach.

'I . . . I, yes.' Mrs Roberts sounded strangely strangled. 'Because . . . you see, when the doctor came to talk to us about Phoebe . . .'

Phoebe was gripping my arm and I was glad that she was holding on to me as Mrs Roberts spoke again, sounding firm, defensive almost. 'He'd offered for us to have both of you.'

There was an identical, incredulous noise from Phoebe and me. Mrs Roberts leaned forward, looking at her daughter.

'And I would have taken both of you in a heartbeat,' she said, 'but Matthew didn't want to. We had to go back to Brimley, we weren't prepared. He didn't think we could manage, he didn't think *I* could manage.' Mrs Roberts spoke faster. There were tears in her eyes, but she forced them back.

'When he took the second baby away, I wanted to run after him, take her too, but Matthew was quite insistent. And then he was worried that there would be trouble, that the mother would wake up and want you back. I didn't think I'd have survived that.' She swallowed. 'So as soon as I could walk, we left. And I never saw her again.'

'*Trouble?*' I said incredulously, and Phoebe whispered, 'Oh Mum, why?'

Mrs Roberts reached out to touch Phoebe's arm. 'Listen to me,' she said urgently, 'I'm sorry that this is causing you so much upset. I wish to God you had never found out. We could have all gone on the way we were. But I'm not going to apologise for taking you and keeping you as mine, not when I was able to give you a good life and all our love to boot. You were the best thing that happened to us. We were a family, we *are* a family. And no matter what happens from here on, we will continue to be a family. No one can take that away from us. She was giving you up, she wasn't able to cope. I'm sorrier for that and for her than I can ever say because she didn't have you and I did.'

'But twins are meant to be together. It's damaging to separate them,' Phoebe said in a choked voice.

'You didn't ever know,' Mrs Roberts said. 'It can't be damaging if you grow up as if you weren't a twin. You didn't even know her.'

'She should have, though.' I'd finally found my voice, albeit a raspy version of it.

'And how could you never have told me?' Phoebe said. 'All these years, I could have known Addie, could have spent time with her, could have had a sister. But you waited forty years, when half my life is over? And even now you wouldn't have told me if I hadn't found out, if I hadn't bullied you into doing it.'

Mrs Roberts sounded defiant more than contrite when she said, 'God knows, it wasn't easy. Every time the doorbell rang, or the phone, every school trip you took, every stranger you'd meet, every single time, the worry that you would one day run into your sister, or that the girl in the bed would come to take you back.' She increased her grip on Phoebe's arm. 'And I would never have let that happen. And the irony is that . . .' She hesitated, dragging her sleeve across her eyes and shaking her head.

'What?' Phoebe said. 'What?'

'That she did almost find you, in the end.'

'What do you mean?' I said cautiously.

'I received a letter. About eight months ago. A man was asking if I'd been on the ward that night. If I knew anything about an adoption. He was looking on behalf of a woman who'd lost her daughter. A woman called Elizabeth Holloway.'

'And what did you do?' I whispered. 'What—'

'I ignored him. Burned the letter.'

There was a moment's shocked silence, then Phoebe got up, pushing back her chair. The waitress stood not too far away, her eyes going from one to the other, and Mrs Roberts still sat, looking down at the table.

'I cannot believe you didn't tell me,' Phoebe said to the back of her mother's head, then she pushed her arm into her sleeve of her coat so quickly that there was a faint ripping sound.

'But, Phoebe, I didn't ever *want* you to find out!' Mrs Roberts sounded strangled and she was crying again. 'Please listen, please sit back down, because, you see . . .'

But Phoebe had already turned on her heel and left, and, grabbing my stuff, I jumped up and followed her.

Limpsfield, 14 August 1958

Today is the first day of life without my mother. She died yesterday, on the night of my seventeenth birthday, and it's turning the whole of my birthday and every single day of these last four weeks bitter and terrible, because while I was living the life of Riley on the Hartland terrace, my mum was hurtling towards death without me there to comfort her. Was it when I was drinking my first glass of champagne or when I was laughing with Harry at Bea's antics? Was it when I slipped off among the orchard trees or was it when I stood on my tiptoes and felt that heavenly roaring in my ears as I was being kissed for the first time? Did she breathe her last breath right then, while I was falling in love?

It doesn't matter now whether I fell in love or whether I was kissed or whether I dare to write it in here for my father or anyone else to come across. Nothing matters, except that I wasn't here to say goodbye to Mum, that I wasn't here when I should have been. I should have been reading to her, should have been talking about our outing to St Paul's. I should never have been made to leave her.

The morning after my birthday party, very early, there was a phone call and Janet came and fetched me. The maid helped me pack and Janet herself drove me to the train station before anyone else was up. I sat on the train in a daze of shock, because my father had called from hospital, not from home. As it turned out, while I was imagining my mother in her own bed or in her armchair, being at peace and looking out on to her garden and possibly – how could I have been so stupid as to fool myself into believing this – possibly getting better, she hadn't been there at all, but had been transferred to hospital the very day that I left for Hartland. To die in hospital, that's why she'd gone, that's why I was sent away.

Sister Hammond told me about it, she did it quickly without wasting many words. Mum had known that it wouldn't be long; it was her choice, Sister Hammond said, gently but firmly, because she could see me looking at Father, angry and unable to forgive him for putting her into hospital when she couldn't have wanted to go, and for not ringing me earlier when the end had been near. But my mother had not, under any circumstances, wanted me to have to see her in hospital like that, Sister Hammond said, not lying on a ward and diminishing by the day. She hadn't wanted me not being able to visit or sit with her except during the short visiting times. Sister Hammond talked about it for a long while, told me that Mum had been comfortable at the hospital, that she'd been on a small ward with a nice other lady who was so impressed with all the letters Mum had got from her beautiful daughter, all the stories I had told, how proud she'd been to talk about me. I'd made all my mother's years – but especially her last few months – a joy, and now I had to be strong, stay strong for my father. Sister Hammond is very kind so I didn't want to tell her that she was wrong, that Father had been wrong and Mum, too, for keeping me away. Mum had hated the hospital when she'd first gone in, when they couldn't find out what was wrong with her and she needed help. She'd hated it so much that she'd come home, especially after it was clear they couldn't do anything more and Sister Hammond had kindly agreed to tend to her pain for as long as it would take.

I now understand her euphoria, the swell of her memories, her fat, overflowing letters, her excitement for me. It doesn't make it any better, it simply explains it and it leaves an awful, ashy grey taste in my mouth. I'm in her room now, sitting in her armchair and looking out over the garden as I write. My father is downstairs, and I've slipped down the corridor one last time, to say my final goodbye.

Her bed is made and someone has thrown out the last bunches of flowers because the vases are gone, and for the first time in a long time there is no fire burning and no kettle boiling. But other than that, the room is exactly the way I left it four weeks ago.

Christina Rossetti's poems are on the side table, a postcard of St Paul's marking the place we'd last been reading. The *Radio Times* is where I left it, right next to the old wooden Pilot radio, which we'd never moved from its place on top of the dresser because Mum was afraid that it would fall apart. The little stool I sat on to talk to her is still by the armchair where I left it. They haven't taken the tiny potted rose by the window, which I brought up from the garden for her in April, and when I put my nose right into it and smell it, that heavenly smell of roses in bloom, it makes me so sad that I want to die. I found Mum's pruning shears and cut off one sprig, the little blooms so tiny and so perfect, and put it between the pages from which I'd read to her just a few short weeks ago, trying to make it sound good for her, to tide her over till I got back home.

The last light of the first day without her gathers in the mirror on the wall, it catches the edge of a silver picture frame, it lingers on the bottles of perfume clustered on her dresser, but already, there is more shadow than light in the room, and the evening stretches ahead, like the days and the weeks and the months to come, bare and empty and alone. I'll tuck the potted rose back on to the windowsill before I leave so it can scent the room for just a little longer while my mother's spirit still lingers. I'm tracing the outline of St Paul's Cathedral on my mother's bookmark and will her to stay close, to pause, just for a moment, on the threshold between life and death. The room remembers her still, the mattress retains the shape of her body, the pillow that of her head. Tiny particles of her skin are still where her hand last touched the curtains, the pages of the book whisper close above the postcard, which she held in her hands just a few weeks ago. The very air in the room congregates and flows around the memory of this one beloved person, who was here only a short while ago and is now forever gone.

But it'll start to go soon, that memory, I know it will. The air will shift and finally become still, dust motes will drive away the last lingering aliveness in the room. Her smell will go, and then the touch of her hand, the brilliance of her eyes; the sound of her laughter will start to fade. Who will remember Constance Adele Holloway, who will say her name again, ever? Who will remember her if not me?

I know I should write about her, that writing might keep her alive, might keep her inside me and around me, but the words are hard to find now. They've come in such a rush these last few weeks at Hartland, all those thoughts and feelings soaked up by those thirsty pages, to preserve my elation, my joy, my freedom for my mother who was waiting for me here in this very room. But they mock me now, those words and my eagerness to write them. There will be no need for me to capture my days anymore, because she's not here to hear about them. There is no way these pages can hold all the things that are going around in my mind, not when I can't even bear to look at the previous pages, bulging with all this happiness. I simply cannot bear it, and so I'm going to hide them away until a time when I can think about life again.

Chapter Twenty-One

Outside the café, it took me a moment to get my bearings, but I spotted Phoebe immediately, looking up and down the road. I took her by the elbow and, as I steered her down the heaving street, oncoming pedestrians quickly snapped their umbrellas out of our way. We clopped down the stairs of the Tube station and when the train came, packed to the hilt with grumpy and sodden commuters, we squeezed ourselves into the far corner by the door. My hair was smothering me and I was sweating in the warm carriage. Phoebe, in contrast, seemed almost eerily calm. She was studying the Tube map but I could see that her eyes weren't completely focussed, and when the train swerved just after Gloucester Road, she fell against me and I was glad I hadn't let go of her arm.

'Come home with me, Phoebe, okay?' I said urgently, propping her up as best as I could. There was a fearful scuffle as the other passengers struggled to move away from us. The train started to slow down for the next station and I felt her hair falling across my shoulder and, pressed between me and the glass barrier, she relaxed against me and closed her eyes.

In front of my house, Phoebe leaned against the low wall next to the two rubbish bins while I fumbled for my keys. When I pushed open the door, a small cat suddenly shot through the opening, made for the gate, and vanished. A second later, another cat zipped through, but this time Phoebe, with amazing presence of mind, dived and managed to snatch it up before it, too, could disappear. She straightened, cupping her hands around the little squirming body so that only a pair of eyes blinked out from between her thumbs. The door opened all the way and Mrs Emmet, my downstairs neighbour, emerged. Looking pleased to find at least one of her charges still on the premises, she shook her finger at the kitten.

'You silly thing. Now I'll have to be up half the night waiting for your brother. Oh well, he won't go far. He hates the rain. Hello, Addie. You brought a friend?'

Mrs Emmet was the nicest neighbour in all of London. She brought me cups of tea when I was sick and kept me all the gossip mags she was addicted to, turning down pages she felt were crucial for my shockingly underdeveloped knowledge of celebrity affairs.

'This is Mrs Emmet. She lives downstairs,' I said to Phoebe, who seemed to have been jolted out of her stupor by the cat rescue and now opened her hands a tiny bit so that the little kitten's head popped out.

'An honest-to-god cat lady,' Mrs Emmet confirmed as the kitten wriggled out of the confines of Phoebe's hands, clambered up her neck and sat on her shoulder.

'And this is Phoebe. She's actually—'

I paused. Phoebe studied her shoes, looking lost, and in the half-light, my heart went out to her.

'She's my sister,' I said warmly and took her arm, pulled her close. It was the first time I'd said it out loud and I meant it, without a doubt, without any question, with pride almost and it made things between us oddly concrete, gave our connection a lovely, definable shape. 'She's my *twin* sister,' I added. 'We're twins. And we just met a couple of days ago.'

'Gosh.' Mrs Emmet seemed taken aback but then she nodded enthusiastically. This kind of thing was just up her alley. 'That's ever so nice for the two of you. Wow.' She paused to think, then said, 'Met Venetia, have you?' She raised her eyebrows, pressing her lips together to hide a grin of delight.

'I most certainly have,' Phoebe said darkly and at this Mrs Emmet laughed out loud. 'Her bark's worse than her bite,' she advised. 'At least I think so. Well, really good to meet you, Phoebe, I'm sure. This is Potts.'

Mrs Emmet pointed to the furry bundle on Phoebe's shoulder. The little cat pawed at my keys and I moved them up and down, watching it swipe the air. Phoebe held it back out to Mrs Emmet, who waved her away.

'On loan for the evening,' she said, pushing open the door to her flat. 'Best therapy there is. But make sure to share, you two. And, for the love of god, don't give him any more food.'

'I'm fine, Addie, really.'

I had forced Phoebe to lie down on my sofa, which was too short for her, so that her feet were hanging over the edge and my rug barely came to her ankles. I'd laid a cool cloth sprinkled with lavender oil on her forehead, covering her eyes, because that was Mrs Baxter's fallback for any ailment from sore throat to broken toes, then tucked the kitten into the crook of her arm, found a cool cloth for my own face, emptied half the bottle of lavender oil on it and slumped into the chair opposite her, closing my eyes against the image of my mother curled up in a hospital bed and Mrs Roberts's look of defiance and guilt when we left her. And now the new and terrifying *what if*. My mother had never wanted to keep me at all. I, too, had been meant to be given away.

I wondered what Phoebe was thinking, whether she was also scrabbling at ground that seemed to be constantly shifting beneath our feet. But I supposed she'd already been through all that a few weeks ago, when she found out that Elizabeth Holloway had given her away. I, on the other hand, because I had stayed with my mother, had somehow, stupidly, assumed that I'd been *chosen* to stay, only to find out now that it was nothing more than a glitch of fate.

At some point, I heard the kitten hit the ground with a soft plop, then the sound of claws clicking against the coffee table. An ominous rustling ensued and we both started struggling upright at the same time. Clutching the wet rags, our eyes searched out the kitten playing with a plastic bag next to the counter, then met across the coffee table. Pushing wet strands of hair out of our faces, we grimaced at each other, identically straggly haired, splotchy faced and exhausted looking.

'I can't believe it all,' I said hoarsely, forcing back the lump at the bottom of my throat. 'I keep thinking I'm going to be immune to it all soon but it just keeps on coming.'

'Oh hell.' Phoebe hunched over her knees. Her hair was all over the place, there was a dusty patch on one of her trouser legs and her eyes were bruised and smudged. The sight of her, the nape of her neck that seemed so exposed and vulnerable, made me sit up and pull myself together. We couldn't both fall to pieces at the same time, someone had to keep their chin up.

'Something to eat, that's what we need,' I said briskly, availing myself of the only thing I knew that had the power to improve any desperate situation. 'I'll fix us something. And a stiff drink sounds pretty good, too.'

Phoebe hesitated. 'Do you think we could make some tea, maybe?'

''Course we can.' I got up, stiff-legged. 'If you want the loo, it's just there.'

When she came back, Phoebe had pulled her hair back again and cleaned up her face, buttoned her cardigan properly and found her glasses. But when she pulled herself on to one of the stools at the island and rested her chin on her folded hands, she looked, despite her long legs almost reaching the ground, absurdly like a child.

'What do you feel like? I have goat's cheese here and some bread. Or I could make a quiche?'

She looked like she wanted to decline, but then she changed her mind. 'That sounds delicious. Really, though, don't go to too much trouble.'

I was already reaching for the flour on the top shelf above the stove. Pastry, flaky, warm, delicious. Just the thing to make when you've had a shock and to eat when you're feeling grim. I cut up the butter, got ice cubes for the water. We didn't talk but it was a comfortable, familiar silence, between two people who acknowledged it but didn't feel compelled to fill it. I briefly thought of Venetia's chatter and the way I always braced myself, ever so slightly, for assault, and I smiled to myself because Phoebe was a very restful sort of person in comparison. She just sat quietly, tapping her legs against the stool and sipping her tea, watching me roll out the pastry dough into a small tin, just big enough for the two of us, and put it into the fridge to rest. I set her to chopping two sprigs of asparagus into tiny pieces, which she did with a concentrated crease between her eyebrows, gripping the knife in a way that would have made Andrew faint on the spot.

'I did tell you I wasn't much of a cook,' she said apologetically when she noticed me twitch every time the blade came down two millimetres from her thumbnail. She pushed the mutilated asparagus shards towards me, then lapsed into silence again and, her hands folded, watched the kitten gambol around the room until it came back towards the plastic bags next to the counter and started toying with the crinkly material.

When I saw that it had discovered the broken frame, I quickly knelt and scooped it out. Somehow, after all that we'd heard today, I couldn't quite cope with those two faces. Maybe later, another day, when we'd had time to process it all. I gave the cat a pat on the rump to send it skidding off towards the sofa and reached for the handles of the bag, intending to casually fold the top in on itself. Just then there was a barely discernible intake of breath above me, though, and when I looked up I saw that Phoebe was looking straight down at me, that she had seen me hiding my mother's picture from her. She didn't say anything, just looked up and away as I slowly straightened and awkwardness bloomed all around us.

'Sometimes,' she said softly, still looking away, 'mostly at night when everything is so quiet, I feel this enormous sense of regret, about this entire life that I didn't get to lead. All the things I've missed.' Her eyes followed the cat now skittering around the room. 'It sits right here.' She tapped her throat and I nodded knowingly. 'It makes me panic, that feeling. Like I need to race back in time to find everything all at once, to make up for it, quickly, right this minute. I think that's why I barrelled into your life the way I did, why I came to your house, to the pastry shop, why I want to meet your father, your sister, almost as if to squeeze it all in now. But always, I come back to the question of why you got to stay and I didn't.'

She fell silent again, her eyes, those beautiful grey eyes that were so like my mother's, so like mine, never leaving the cat, who'd jumped back on to the counter, pawing at the pots of chives and rosemary, making the plant stalks rustle softly.

'I think we should talk to your mother again,' I said. 'Maybe she'll remember something else that'll help us . . .' I paused, thinking, then said, settling on something that seemed reasonably in reach, 'Understand.'

'Yes.' Phoebe's face softened for a moment. 'She's had it so hard, and I . . . I shouldn't have run out on her. Got so cross with her.' Then she frowned. 'But she never said any of this stuff before, not in all the conversations we've been having since I found out. She only ever said it was a private adoption arranged at the hospital. But what really happened is that she took me and ran, Addie. She separated us, and even when Merck got in touch with her last year, she lied to him. And to me. Just think, I could have met Elizabeth before she died.'

'I don't think you would have,' I said as gently as I could. 'She died a year ago. Merck must have sent the letter after she died. He did say they hadn't been in touch in a while. And your mum didn't do it all alone, don't forget. It was the doctor, mostly.' I was trying hard to hide my dislike of Mrs Roberts, for Phoebe's sake more than anything else. 'I think she did what she thought was best.'

She looked at me with a bitter expression. 'Easy for you to say. You *had* her in the end, our real mother, and I . . . I was left behind.'

'But Phoebe,' I said pleadingly, 'you weren't left behind. Your mother did what she did out of love, nothing else. That was very clear. She loved – loves – you very much.'

Phoebe leaned back along the counter, widening the space between us. 'But why did she – Elizabeth – take so long to try and find me? Why didn't she turn right back around, bring me back into this whole other family that I should have belonged to. Where *you* got to be.'

'Phoebe, it was a fluke,' I burst out, running my hands through my hair. 'Don't you get it? It was a complete accident that I stayed. I was meant to be go but there were no takers.' I fished a rubber band out of a dish on the counter and pulled my hair back so hard that Phoebe winced. 'Would you rather grow up with an adoptive mother who wanted you, wanted you so badly she was prepared to fight tooth and nail for you, including take you and run for it? Or your very own, your *real* mother, who had already given you up for adoption and then had to make do with you after all when there was no one around to take you off her hands? Yeah? You tell me. Please do.'

She glared back at me with smudgy eyes, and then her shoulders sagged and slumped backwards. 'I'm sorry, Addie. You're right.' She gave a sudden, shaky laugh. 'Let's maybe not fight about who has more cause to feel abandoned right this minute.'

I, too, exhaled and attempted a smile. The cat came back up to me, pawing my leg and mewling softly, so I picked it up and tucked it under my chin, feeling a tiny burr against my throat. From under my lashes I gave Phoebe a long look, took in her face, which still seemed new and yet already familiar with its angles and grey eyes, her ponytail swinging behind her when she moved.

'You were always there,' I said, 'all those years, in everything I did, all my birthdays, all my days, all *her* days, they were touched by your absence. I know it now, I can see it so clearly looking back at all she did and said. Whatever happened when we were born, whether she was the one who chose what to do or whether she was forced to do it and never went back to undo it, she had to live with it all her life and I think she saw it in *me* every single day. So you were never left behind, because for her, I was only ever half of a whole.'

Silence fell and deepened, and the rainy evening, my stainless-steel counter gleaming in the last murky light, my sense of floating among constantly moving signposts, the scent of pastry baking in the oven and the tiny cat purring against my throat, it all shrank down to this very small space between Phoebe and me standing next to each other in my kitchen. And then, inexplicably, there was a connection between us, deep and raw, like a twang on a string linking us, both beautiful and discordant: we *were* two halves of a whole, two pairs of identical cloud-grey eyes looking at each other, two hearts beating close, feeling the depth of what we'd lost and what might have been and all the things we could still be, and it was both amazing and desperate at the same time. Phoebe must have felt something, too, because she moved, in a gesture that was both a recoil and a reaching out.

'You would have been my Charlie,' she said, and tears filled her eyes. 'All that hair clashing with the yellow and black stripes.' She half-laughed, a choked, teary gurgle. I looked down, the pressure behind my eyes almost unbearable.

'I'd have loved to have been Charlie,' I said, with some effort. 'He sounds *much* nicer than Venetia.'

She gave another shaky laugh, mopped her eyes and put the towel down to brace herself on the worktop. I bent down, picked up the plastic bag and handed it to her. 'Here, these are some things I took from the house. Pictures mostly. I would love for you to have them.'

She reached to unpick the knotted plastic handles but I put my hand over hers.

'Just take it home. One of the frames is broken, so make sure you open it carefully.'

'But don't you want to put them up here?' She frowned, looked around my apartment.

I shook my head, unable to explain that I wasn't ready for Elizabeth and Constance Adele Holloway, not until I truly understood my mother, until I finally knew what had actually happened on 14 February 1960.

Chapter Twenty-Two

We sat at the worktop next to each other and drank tea. We ate the quiche and a salad, then some beautiful strawberries I'd brought home from the market the day before, floating in thick, vanilla-scented cream, and, when we were still hungry, I pulled out two chocolate brownies from the freezer, stuck them into the still-warm oven and we ate those with the rest of the cream and another big pot of tea.

'Amazing,' Phoebe said, assiduously picking up a last crumb with her fingers and popping it into her mouth. 'I never eat this much. I can't believe you whipped that up in less than an hour. Even your cream tastes better than anything I'd have in my fridge at any given moment. Couldn't you do a mail-order business to Solihull?'

'Teacakes, gingerbread, lemon cake,' I mused, stacking the plates. 'Shortbread, of course.' I was warming to the theme. 'And I could definitely send through chocolate. Lots of chocolate. And—'

The sound of a phone ringing interrupted me, and the little cat, which had been surreptitiously sniffing round Phoebe's empty plate, scampered away.

Predictably, Phoebe's phone was where it should be, in a zippered side pocket, and she held it up. 'Not me. Must be yours.'

The ringtone kept jangling and the little cat was fidgeting until I fished out my two Nokias. Mine was silent. It was my mother's.

'James Merck,' I said, looking up at Phoebe. 'He's back.'

'Just answer it,' Phoebe said and when I didn't move, she reached over and clicked the green button.

'Mrs Harington!' The hoarse voice suggested he was thrilled to have caught me. 'James Merck here. I just wanted to check that you received my letter?'

'Not yet, I'm afraid. But the post sometimes takes a few days.' I cleared my throat and Phoebe flapped her hands encouragingly. *Tell him*, she mouthed.

'Let me know what you'd like to do. And I found another NHS records archive that could be worth a try. I'd sent an enquiry a year ago but I could also go up in person. Although that would incur certain costs, which brings me to the other point – my fee, which, really, Mrs Harington, I must insist on resolving. Has your father's account been closed?'

'Er, my father's account?' I asked. 'Well, he's in hospital – wait, I mean – what, exactly, do *you* mean?'

'Well, I thought that's where the quarterly bill is being paid from. Is there another way you could transfer the money? Or send me a cheque?'

'Yes, certainly, but, Mr Merck, now, before we talk further, and this may sound strange . . .' I paused.

'Strange? If you've been in my profession for forty years, you cease to be surprised.' He huffed in what seemed be a humorous way and I looked imploringly at Phoebe. *You can do it,* she hissed.

'Mr Merck.' I took a deep breath. 'My mother died a year ago.'

'I don't think I understand. Are you quite all right, Mrs Harington? I did think you sounded off, to be honest. Are you sure you've recovered properly?' He sounded concerned and, squirming a little, I said, very quickly, 'My mother, Mrs Elizabeth Harington, she has actually passed away. I'm Adele Harington, her daughter. I was the one you spoke to the other day at home, and I also found her mobile.'

I paused, held my breath, and when there was no immediate answer, I ploughed on. 'I'm very sorry about not telling you right away, but there didn't seem to be a good moment to clear up this, er, small misunderstanding the last time.'

Phoebe nodded approvingly, mouthed, *Well done.* There was a brief, merciful lull in the conversation, but it didn't take James Merck long to grasp the development and I had to hold the phone away from my ear, which had the added advantage that Phoebe was able to hear every single word.

'I simply cannot believe it. You impersonated your dead mother? Never in a million years . . .'

'I thought he'd seen it all.' Phoebe rolled her eyes and I suppressed a choke of laughter, before putting the phone back against my ear.

'Mr Merck,' I said firmly. 'Why did my mother hire you?'

'Because I'm the best in the field,' he barked.

'Who found absolutely nothing,' Phoebe whispered next to me and I elbowed her sharply.

On the other end, there was a moment's silence, then: 'I'm afraid I can't help you further. Please accept my condolences on her death. Your mother . . .'

I looked at Phoebe, made a worried gesture. She brought her head close to mine, listened in.

'. . . was absolutely adamant that the whole search would be discreet. Under no circumstances was I to compromise that. I suppose whenever the time was right, *she* wanted to be the one to tell the story. She didn't want her husband, or any of her family, to be involved. I think that's partly why she brought me in, to outsource the incoming information. So you must understand, I cannot be the one to breach that confidence. I have a reputation to uphold and I have very strict guidelines. I'm sorry to say that I am not prepared to violate them, especially not to someone who—'

'I'm her daughter!' I interrupted, indignantly. 'This is *about* me, for heaven's sake. Surely, now that I've found out all this stuff, that I've found you, it would be fine for you to talk to me?'

'You only found out this *stuff*,' his voice was cold, 'because you pretended to be your dead mother. That doesn't sound particularly trustworthy to me.'

'I am sorry for that,' I said. 'Truly, but Mrs Roberts said she'd got a letter. How—'

'Look, Mrs – I mean *Ms* Harington, do send me your mother's death certificate and I might be able to forgo my confidentiality agreement. But I would very much like to resolve the payment issues. I take it you won't need my services from here on?'

'But—'

'Let's speak again when you've had a chance to send it all through. Goodbye.'

* * *

'God,' I said, tossing the phone back into the bag. 'I'm sorry, Phoebe. If I wasn't so completely useless we'd be getting the entire story from Merck right now.'

'You're not useless! And you were good on the phone; he just dug in his heels. He sounds like a right stickler. Let's send him the death certificate and an official-sounding letter. And let's pay him. That'll certainly make him come around.'

'Yes, although – wait.' I stopped. 'Talking of paying him. What was that he said at the beginning. "Your father's account". Isn't that what he said? But if he was assuming that I was her, then that would have been—'

'Yes. Oh—'

'*Her* father.'

We stared at each other.

'But you said he was dead,' Phoebe said, confused.

'He died when she was young,' I said. 'Both my grandparents did.'

'But when *exactly*?' Phoebe pushed her hands over her hair, her cheeks flushed with excitement.

I thought back to the scant conversations I had had with my mother about her upbringing, Phoebe looking at me expectantly.

'No one ever talked about them,' I said. 'Mum only occasionally mentioned how hard it'd been for her once they were gone, working several jobs, how cold she always was, how you'd have to boil water for your bath, feed the heater with coins, patch up your shoes. That kind of thing. They were living in Limpsfield, that's where she grew up. Venetia did a family tree for school once and was embarrassed because my dad's side is like some big, shrubby bush of all these relatives and distant cousins. Honestly, you wouldn't believe it if you saw it: everyone marrying like mad and producing loads of children. And Mum's side was pretty much bare, with almost everyone dead by the time we came on to the scene, except some distant cousin or other, who then promptly died the following year.'

Phoebe reached for the pen. 'Okay, so what were their names?'

'Constance Holloway obviously.' I jabbed my chin towards the photo now in Phoebe's bag. 'And . . .'

I tried to visualise Venetia's shrubby family tree poster. She'd painstakingly drawn all the branches in different colours using the new set of scented pens she got for her birthday and that I'd been insanely jealous of.

Across from me, Phoebe made a disbelieving noise at the back of her throat. 'I could name you every single relative I have in the greater Brimley area,' she said. 'Down to my cousin Chester, who seriously is the most tedious man alive. I can't believe you can't remember your grandfather's name.'

'George,' I said quickly.

'And so you think they definitely died *before* we were born?'

'Yes, when she was—'

'Oh my god, Addie, if you say *young* one more time I will set fire to your precious Hermès bag, go home and never come back. Nineteen is young. Even twenty is bloody young for your mum to die. All I'm asking is whether you're positive that they weren't still there on February the fourteenth 1960, because if they were, then it would explain a whole lot.'

'If you put it like that, obviously, I'm not one hundred per cent positive,' I said defensively, 'but if her father *was* alive all along, he'd have been there for at least some of my parents' married life, which I was too. It'd have been impossible to keep it a secret. We'd have heard of him in some way.'

'With the way your family handles family relations, I'm not so sure,' she said drily. 'I'll look up their death dates.' She pulled out a notebook, scribbled something down, then chewed the end of the pen, thinking.

'Could the account even be still active, even though he is dead?' I wondered. 'Could she have had power of attorney to use it or something? Because having Merck's retainer come out of that account, rather than my parents', would certainly have made sense if she'd wanted to keep it all secret from Dad. Okay, so here's a thought.' I put my hands together. 'Maybe Merck was hired by him, by George Holloway?'

'Most of these scenarios would require him to be alive.' Phoebe brought out Merck's file and the yellow notepad and flicked through it. It was a curious mixture of organised text and chaotic scribbles, doodled sunflowers and numbers, which my mother had obviously jotted while on the phone, because names from the letters were dancing across the pages, amidst various almost illegible notes to herself. *Call back on Mon. Wrong Emily! Nurse not on staff. New address for J Smith — 4 Love Lane. Petersfield. HANTS.*

'Dr Miller was her main target,' I said. 'The only other person who has as much space is Sarah Mason.'

'Well, if she's the young nurse from the West Indies, then she transferred the bundle so she'd have been a certain link between us. And Dr Miller was at the administrative centre of things.' Phoebe ran her finger down the numbers. 'He executed the adoption; he was the only other one who knew where I'd gone. If I was looking for me, those two are what I'd start with.' She gave a sudden half-giggle and I had to laugh, too.

'This is so weird. And I have no clue what any of these numbers here mean.'

We looked at the jumble of numbers underneath the notes on Dr Miller's whereabouts.

'This one's got to be a phone number, here, this one starting with 01883. And she wrote Frog right next to it. Or Throg? What the hell is a Throg?'

'It's a who,' Phoebe said absentmindedly, raking her eyes across the numbers.

'I do hope not because I truly pity the person whose name is Throg,' I said with some spirit and reached for my Nokia. 'Now that I've cleared things up with Merck, shall I continue with my newfound gumption?' I waggled the phone.

'At nine thirty at night?' she said. 'You can't call anyone at nine thirty. That's when Brimley lowers the blackout curtains and prepares for the Messerschmitts.'

'Nine thirty is perfectly respectable.' I was already dialling the number, my thumb fumbling across the keypad. It rang a few times. 'Maybe Throg's busy with the blackout curtains,' I whispered to Phoebe. 'No one's picking up.'

But just as I was about to hang up, a bright little voice chirped into the phone. 'You have reached Throgmorton, Russell and Crowe

Solicitors in Oxted. The office is currently closed. Please leave your name and a detailed message and—'

I hung up, looked at Phoebe.

'Aha! Throggie is actually Throgmorton, and he's a solicitor in Oxted!'

I rooted through Phoebe's stuff for the map I'd seen. There was Oxted, on the A25, just below the motorway, surrounded by places called Chalkpit Woods and Godstone and Crockham Hill. Brimley was about halfway between Oxted and Brighton, both of which she'd marked with little red Xs. I moved my finger across the map to connect the various dots, then stopped. Just next to Oxted, almost part of it, was Limpsfield, where my mother had grown up. It looked like it had started out as its own village, and then slowly reached out towards Oxted and attached itself to it. Above the map, our eyes met.

'Throg is connected to George Holloway. I know it is. And I'm going to find out tomorrow.' I tapped the map. 'I wonder what Limpsfield is like. It looks like a tiny village, really.'

'Did your mum never take you?' Phoebe started gathering her things to put them into her bag.

'No. There was never any reason, really,' I said. 'I suppose I should have questioned it at the time.' There were so many things I should have questioned at the time.

'It's a lovely place, actually, on the North Downs,' Phoebe said. 'Very villagey, and all around the countryside is wonderful. She must have missed it, being stuck in London and all.'

Limpsfield, 7 November 1958

I've come back here, I'm back to writing. I bunched the previous pages together with two big paper clips because even now I can't bear to read about me being silly at the beach and horseback riding and laughing while Mum was lying in hospital. But life is so dreary here in Limpsfield, the November days so cold and dark, that I've been craving the release of sharing things with someone, even if it's only a page. And after all that's said and done, it's a forgiving little thing, this grey notebook, always listening to me, and I feel marginally less desolate knowing that it is waiting for me in the vase with the dried flowers or tied behind the desk with pieces of string.

I do need a friendly thing in my life. School is long over and any dreams Mum and I might have had about me going all the way through A Levels and on to university have faded because Father doesn't see the point of it. My English teacher, Miss Steele, even got in touch with him to ask him to reconsider but he ignored her. In his world, which is stuck somewhere around the time Queen Victoria was at the helm, women get married, preferably sooner rather than later. They keep house, bear children, go to church on Sundays and generally fade into domesticity without any nonsense like careers or achievement or free will or causing any kind of unnecessary trouble. I was shockingly bad at Domestic Science at school, I think they still talk about my burned sponge cake and the wobbly egg custard they had us make, which dried up against the side of the bowl like phlegm, so I do hope whoever is in store for me won't expect anything sophisticated. Or else that he'll be content with listening to me decline Latin nouns and reciting the history of the Napoleonic Wars. Either way, I am not entirely sure where Father thinks I would ever meet this paragon of Victorian virtue, since other than secretarial school, which is where he's sending me so I can do something useful for a change, I am generally kept out of the way until I get married. He's not allowing me to go out and about much at all, let alone to any places where young men might be found.

So on the outside, my days have not changed much at all. I still get up every day and board the bus with the strict instruction to be back home as soon as I finish. I sit behind my typewriter and then come back to sit behind the window to watch Mrs Peckitt and Mrs Smith tend to their families across the street, only I don't have Miss Steele's English lessons at school or my mother at home anymore. I just have my shorthand notepads with 'Dear Sir, with reference to ... most sincerely, Yours' looking like chickens walking across the page, and my mute, friendly diary. Chilly meals with my father bookend the day, lasting almost exactly seventeen minutes and thirty seconds, sixteen minutes if I eat fast.

On the bus today, having waited interminably for it and then stood for most of the way back, I was suddenly struck by the fact that I will either die in this house, alone and husbandless and imprisoned forever, as a sort of spinsterish companion for my father, or I'll be foisted on someone he dredges up at church or at the bank, and will eventually die, no doubt, in a similar place to this one. Neither version is particularly appealing; both involve dying and neither sounds happy at all. Is it possible that this is now my life? That this is all I'm ever going to be? Putting Mum's death behind me and preparing for a long, lonely life as a wife that will eventually lead only to yet more death, namely my own? We had big plans, Mum and I. I was going to read English Literature at university, the way Mum didn't get to do during the war, or I was to become a teacher at the very least. Being a teacher had been a nod towards respectability, mostly for my father's sake, really, but she'd always said that once I was qualified to do something, I could do anything.

The house is so quiet, and it's cold now that winter is almost here. Wind and draught seep in from beneath the doors and the other day, ice was on the inside of my windows when I woke. Fog is starting to roll in tonight, although it's never quite as bad in our village as what we read about in London, but when it does come, the green-brown oily mist settles everywhere so you can barely even see the street lights or the bus when it comes around the corner. Mum used to hate the fog and would anxiously wait for me to come home from school because she worried the bus would lose its way.

Everything brings back memories: the cold, the bus, the fog, the house, every single thing I do or think or touch is tinged with the heart-squeeze of nostalgia and desolation. Our capacity to remember is so strange; when you only have such a short time with someone before they die, then your recollection becomes condensed somehow, vivid and alive all around you, maybe because your time with that person wasn't stretched thin over a whole lifetime but round and dense and compact over the few years you did have. Mum waiting for me after school to unwrap me from layers of school clothes and asking about my day. Sliding my feet into the cold bottom of my bed to find that she had tucked a hot-water bottle in to warm it hours before. Sitting on her lap as a little girl to have my hair brushed in front of the fire after my bath, slowly and gently, the strokes so hypnotically repetitive they'd almost lull me to sleep, my curls rising under her hands like down. We'd laugh at the funny shadows they would throw on the walls; she would make it wild and raging or else pulled right down by my ears from where it would spring back up in a tangle, and eventually she'd tidy it away with a ribbon because Father always felt that so much hair was somehow not quite normal.

I don't think about the big things too much, how we sometimes sneaked into the cinema when Father was busy or took the train over to Knole House to poke around or went to the theatre on my birthday, and I rarely think about the few times we argued or rowed. Instead, she is simply there, in all the ordinary, everyday things I do, like brushing my hair and sitting by the fire, and finding new books and writing about them and listening to *Mrs Dale's Diary* on the radio and wondering whether it will get any easier at all.

Tonight, I came right out and asked Father about the bed freeing up in the lodging house where Ellen, another girl from the college, lives, lucky thing. It's right close to where the secretarial course is, and it's so respectable, almost more respectable than my own home, because the landlady won't stand for any funny business at all. 'Funny business' is one of Father's favourite expressions, along with 'saving for the future' and 'a good marriage'. I tried to tell him that this is the 1950s not the dark ages, and that I have to be outside somewhere in order to meet anyone, that for saving to make sense, there has to be a future. Then I threw all caution overboard and said that other girls my age are all out there working and learning and going to the pictures with their girlfriends (and going dancing at the town hall drenched in Coty perfume and meeting boys at the hop and eating knickerbocker glories in coffee houses, although I didn't mention any of that, obviously), and that maybe it was time I did the same. But Father feels very strongly that the world is not improving these days, what with all this jazz music churning up people's minds and young men trashing cinemas in the throes of rock 'n' roll and Doris Day looking like a (rather cheerful, I think) scarlet woman in every one of her films.

I watched him slice his pork cutlet into eight little squares of exactly the same size, each of which he puts in his mouth and chews for several seconds before laboriously swallowing it down. I followed the movement of his Adam's apple up and down and remembered how Mum ate, impatiently and with too much enthusiasm for Father's liking. When butter was still rationed, my father would only take a tiny knife-edge amount for his toast, scraping a gossamer layer across it that disappeared into the grey surface of the mealy bread almost instantly. My mother, on the other hand, who adored butter, always had her whole weekly ration on the table and ceremoniously spread a layer of creamy, buttery hills and valleys on one big piece of bread, then ate the whole lot all at once, giving me a secret wink before she handed me the best piece, where a butter wavelet had crested into a peak. Father would lecture her on being sensible and fastidious and filling my head with nonsense, but I don't think either my mother or I ever paid the slightest attention to him, our mouths full of buttery bread; the glorious taste a memory that lasted the exact same seven days as Father's scraped-thin layer of nothingness.

I must have smiled to myself at the memory, at least a bit, because Father cut our supper short by an unheard-of three minutes, got up and left.

Sitting by the window now, wrapped up in my blanket against the chill, my legs curled under so that every inch of me is covered in blanket except for my hands, I peer down into the street below, which is dark and cold and wet and so miserable that anyone with their wits about them is staying indoors, huddling around TVs or fireplaces or radios. I could try and sit by the radio for company, but it is still in Mum's room. I avoid her room if I can and particularly tonight, when it's so unbearably cold, I can't face sitting in her chair, listening to our programmes. I've taken out a whole load of new books from the library, *Room at the Top* and *1984* and a new novel called *Saturday Night and Sunday Morning*, angry books, difficult to read and hard to get through. But even reading reminds me too much of everything and I can feel myself becoming like those books, bleak and wrapped up in myself, and I don't want to be, not really. What I am is aching to be free of this life, of this house where I'm reminded every minute of my mother, where I'm still listening for her cough, where I am sitting through seventeen and a half minutes of conversation in a cold room downstairs, before coming back up to sit in my bedroom, practising chicken squiggles and preparing for a future of exactly the same forever more. I'm aching to be some-thing. Anything.

Chapter Twenty-Three

Phoebe had wanted to take the last train home, but I'd persuaded her to stay on the sofa bed in my spare room. It was comforting to know that she was downstairs, as if she kept watch over us, and up in my attic bedroom, the rain drummed on the roof and the cat and I slept like the dead. Too soon, however, I heard the sound of claws against the windowsill and hungry meowing and when I opened my eyes, the cat was scaling the curtains towards the rail.

Catching sight of the clock, I sat up and the cat dropped back on to the bed where it sat on its haunches to watch me, making no protest when I took it and a change of clothes downstairs to the bathroom. There was no sound from the spare room and I got ready as quietly as I could, grabbed my bag, jacket and the various phones, scribbled a note to Phoebe and left it on the little console table by the phone, scooped up the cat and posted it through Mrs Emmet's cat flap downstairs.

Outside, the streets were dark and quiet; it was foggy and an early morning drizzle pearled in my hair as I walked to the station. At the restaurant across from Grace's, a sleepy-looking man was retrieving a handful of dead rabbits from a delivery van, swinging them by the ears to give me a wave as he disappeared through the doors.

Most people disliked getting up early but these first few hours alone in the shop were always my favourite because they were so calm and everything was clean and tidy. Quickly, almost automatically, I sorted the bread and pastry delivery and shoved six trays of pre-made rolls from Maxwell Corner into the big ovens in the back, before very happily settling down to make a batch of small fairy cakes for the Kensington Women's Group spring tea that morning. Grace preferred me ordering everything ahead from Maxwell Corner, but it was six a.m., the morning was dark and the kitchen all mine. Nothing and no one to come between me and my fairy—

There was a sharp rap on the back door. I jerked backwards in surprise and the large metal measuring cup slipped from my hand and landed on a palette of eggs, punching a neat cup-shaped circle into the white shells as it rained sugar in a wide arc across the worktop, the floor and down my front. For a second, I stood and stared at the heap of broken eggshells oozing glutinous whites and yolks on to the sugar-covered worktop, then turned to the door, wincing at the loud crunch underneath my feet. Whoever it was that had come between me and my fairy cakes had a lot to answer for. Before I could move again, though, there was another sharp knock, followed by the rattle of the door handle.

'Addie, hey,' a voice came from outside. 'Are you in there? C'mon, open up. It's raining.'

Crunching my sugar-sprinkled way towards the door, I wrenched it open.

'Double espresso with half water, half milk, a squirt of chocolate syrup at the bottom and a big dollop of whipped cream on top. Organically sourced cocoa sprinkles. Full-fat milk. Boiling hot, just the way you like it.'

Filling the entire doorframe, grinning happily and buzzing with insufferable cheerfulness, Andrew held out a large takeaway coffee.

'What on earth are you doing here?' I demanded.

'Came to see you.' The drizzle glistened on his shoulders and his damp hair was pushed back from his forehead. 'I've been up for ages, wanted to talk to you. I'll even force down one of your dry Maxwell Corner rolls if I have to. Although you should really check on them, Ads; that leavening agent they use is rubbish, puffs up the dough without any substance, gives it a dusty feel in the mouth and—'

'Oh my god, just get in here before you wake up the entire neighbourhood.' I pulled him across the threshold and closed the door.

'Did you notice that I came in the *back door* way?' he said, pushing the coffee cup into my hands, then producing another one from a paper bag and tipping it against mine in a toast. 'Shame Grace wasn't here to see me, eh? Bowing deeply as befits us lowly serv—'

He had been about to take a swig from his cup when he saw the egg-sugar mess behind me. 'What in god's name have you been doing in here?' he said, scandalised. 'Exfoliating the floor?'

'I was trying to bake in peace and quiet,' I said defiantly. 'When you arrived and started banging on the door.'

'Wow,' Andrew said. He took a few crunchy steps towards the worktop, then stopped and looked around him, impressed. 'Grace will pitch an absolute fit.' He set down his coffee cup. 'We better clean it up before she comes in, otherwise she'll find a way to blame me for it, I'm sure. You can fill me in on your famous twin sister as we go. And I want to talk to you about Le Grand Bleu—'

'Don't worry about it,' I said quickly. The prospect of a tall, over-caffeinated Andrew bouncing across my formerly quiet six a.m. kitchen and talking about our joint restaurant was daunting, to say the least. 'I have to get those cakes done for the women's club this morning. Thanks for the coffee, though, I'll just call you—'

But Andrew was already looking around for an apron, found a broom and a mop, ran water into a bucket from the cleaning closet. 'Come on, we better get cracking.'

In between numerous coffee breaks – my coffee *was* indeed perfect – I filled Andrew in on what had happened with Phoebe and Mrs Roberts. He was an appreciative audience, listening attentively and nodding at all the right moments as we swept eggs and sugar into the bin, scraped glued-on egg yolk off the stainless-steel worktop, dug gritty granules out of the grouting before Grace's eagle eye could spot them.

'God, that's hard,' he finally said, manoeuvring the mop across the floor for a third time. 'Even if you grew up happily, finding out that you aren't at all who you thought you were, and not even in some small fashion but in such a basic, straight-to-the-gut kind of way. That's bloody hard. And it's not something you can properly articulate either, because most of it is happening so deep inside you.' He thumped his chest. 'Where all that stuff sits that makes you *you*.'

'I hope Phoebe can patch things up with her mum.' I brushed down the worktop again.

'She has to.' Andrew was full of sympathy for the prickly Mrs

Roberts. 'Poor woman made the best of a complicated situation, by the sounds of it.'

'She should have told Phoebe.' I ran a hand over the worktop, felt for any last granules.

'Sure. But she didn't do it out of spite. She did it out of love. Can't argue with love, Ads.'

He saw my moue of disbelief and laughed. 'What, just because I'm not in Marseille making up to Claudette's *maman*, I can't appreciate the finer points of love, family and everything in between? You'd be surprised, Addie, at all the things I can do.' He pushed the mop across the floor one last time. 'It's so nice, though, the way you two are becoming close. *She* sounds nice. Maybe we can get together some time? I would love to meet her.' He disappeared with the mop before I could answer and I dropped a handful of old towels on the floor, started to dry it in a rudimentary fashion.

'She's not looking for a job in the hospitality industry by any chance, is she?' Andrew asked when he came back into the kitchen. 'We could bring her into the fold, one big happy family.'

Underneath the worktop, I bit back a laugh, thinking of us, a cosy threesome among the floor-to-ceiling mental-hospital tiles, Phoebe chopping asparagus and me walking around with the staff schedule tattooed on my forehead.

'She's a pilot,' I said proudly as I straightened up and tossed the dirty towels in a bucket. 'She's really quite cool, Phoebe.'

'A pilot? Man, the amazing things people do. That *is* very cool,' Andrew said, then he paused and threw me a glance. 'You know, it's actually quite curious, how much she is . . . you know. Your mother, I mean. She'd have—'

'Yes, I know,' I said flatly. 'I know she would have.' I turned away from him to face the mixer, fiddling with the whisk attachment and frowning when I thought about my mother and pointing fingers at white bundles in a crib and the *Sliding Doors* lives that Phoebe and I might have lived and what my mother might have preferred, although it was getting increasingly difficult to fathom what my mother had thought at all. Andrew came to stand next to me, nudged my fumbling fingers out of the way and fixed the whisk attachment to the mixer with quick, sure movements, then reached for the flour, the baking powder, pushed the palette of unharmed eggs towards me.

'It's in the past, Ads,' he said softly. 'Don't think about it anymore. *She's* in the past. I'm sorry I brought it up. All that matters is what you make of things *now*. And I'd say you're doing pretty well, both of you.'

He gave me another little nudge and I leaned into his arm, feeling his breath on my cheek, then I straightened resolutely and reached for the butter, and we were quiet, falling into step at the worktop the way we'd done for years. Creaming butter and sugar, adding eggs, sieving large quantities of flour, we passed ingredients and implements back and forth. Murmuring thank-you's and occasional questions, our hands moved in perfect unison as the butter rose fluffily against the sides of the bowl and flour filled the air with a fine white fog.

'Thank you,' I finally said.

'For what?'

I swept my hands across the sixty dainty fairy cakes standing in their little red and white cardboard shells in front of us and the clean floor and the remains of my perfect coffee, brought to my doorstep at six a.m. The way he listened and talked and was always there, with food and endless supplies of gumption and good cheer.

'You know. Everything . . .' I said, rather inadequately, but I think he understood because he nodded and smiled to himself as he manhandled the big trays into the oven. And because it was still early and we were by ourselves, we stood and watched our cakes for a moment, the melting sheen spreading across the little heaped tops, the surfaces flattening slowly and glistening in the heat.

'So, speaking of Le Grand Bleu.' Andrew broke the silence. 'I think I found it.'

'You found Le Grand Bleu?' I said, confused. I turned to look at him. 'But it doesn't exist.'

'It will, though, because I found the perfect space for it. Yesterday and quite by chance. Saw an ad, called the seller, went by to see it. It really is perfect, Addie, I mean it. So totally *us*.' He leaned forward and in the yellow light from the oven, his eyes were shining. 'Not too big, not too small, lots of exposed brick and a wonderful location – yes, it's in Kensington, which I know you don't like –' he held up his hands even though I hadn't opened my mouth, 'but if you see it, you'll love it. I know you will. Lots of foot traffic but still a cosy area. We could start small, expand later, bring people on board if we want to.'

He reached out and grabbed my hands, held on to them. 'I was there for an hour with the seller and I've walked by it like five times since then, each time loving it more. It's got a flat above, we could live there—'

'Live there?' I finally found my voice, albeit a squeaky version of it. 'I have a flat, Andrew.'

Not to mention a job and no inclination to leave it. I tried to pull my hands back but he held on to them and I felt the heat from the oven bake the hairnet against my hair, making my scalp itchy and hot.

'Yes, of course,' Andrew said soothingly. 'Not the flat then. But the restaurant, Addie. Just think of it, think of *us* . . .'

He let go of my hands, fumbled for his bag on the worktop and brought out something I hadn't seen in years. Our battered Grand Bleu scrapbook. He opened it at a photo of us at twelve or thirteen, wearing home-made toques out of white paper. 'We've been dreaming for three decades,' he declared in a hushed voice, turning the book and holding it out for me as if that made it all clear. 'It's time, Addie. It's finally time.'

I opened my mouth again, this time to say, very firmly, that I didn't want to, that I couldn't be part of this, but across the photo his eyes were so brilliantly blue and open and so full of the particular brand of optimism that only Andrew could muster, that I couldn't quite find the words to shatter his dream. I closed my mouth again and looked down at the picture for several long minutes, until even Andrew finally recognised my recalcitrance for what it was.

'You really don't want to do it, do you,' he said, sounding slightly surprised and immeasurably disappointed at the same time, and when I looked over I saw that the happy gleam had gone from his eyes. 'I really thought we could do this, the two of us. Just like it was this morning, being in the kitchen together. It makes me happy. Doesn't it make you happy? I think it's what we were always meant to be, but I suppose . . .'

He turned away. A shock of sandy blond hair fell across the side of his face so I couldn't see his eyes but a flush had spread across his cheeks and then he fumbled for the zipper on his backpack and started slotting in the scrapbook, handling it roughly, not at all as carefully as he had earlier, and I thought I saw his hands tremble. All of a sudden, I couldn't bear it.

'No, it's not that.' I put a hand on his arm to hold him back. 'I'm sorry . . . yes, let's look at the space together, okay? Saturday morning. I can do Saturday morning.'

Oh god.

Andrew looked up quickly. 'You mean it?' He smiled uncertainly. 'I don't want to steamroll you, you know. It's no use if we're not both totally on board. But we've been planning it for so long and you have so much going on with Phoebe and things, I thought if I took the lead in finding the space, you don't enjoy that stuff so much anyway, and then—'

'Sure,' I said quickly, feeling hot and awkward and anxious. 'No problem. Let me know when you've made the appointment.'

'Yes,' Andrew said, nodding happily as he gathered up his things. 'Right, I'm off then. I was going to pop by the hospital later to see your dad, maybe I'll catch you there? And watch the cakes, Ads, they go from underdone to over in a fraction of a second. And, Addie.' He patted my shoulder. 'It'll be wonderful. You'll see.'

Chapter Twenty-Four

Throgmorton took a bit of back and forth to get in touch with, the receptionist first informing me that Mr Throgmorton wouldn't be in till ten (the life of some), Mr Throgmorton then calling back sounding all of eighteen years old and eventually managing to clear up the misunderstanding that I was after the *old* Mr Throgmorton, who wouldn't be in till noon (the life of *some!*) and could I ring back at 12.30.

Taking an early lunch break (at 10.30), I left Claire in charge and rushed down to take the Tube up to the hospital to check on Dad. Looking at my watch to calculate how much time I had before 12.30, I rounded the corner at a good clip and barrelled straight into the belly of an elegant pregnant woman with a mobile clamped to her ear.

'Addie!' Venetia gave a screech. 'Watch the baby, for heaven's sake.'

'So sorry,' I panted, coming to a stop in front of my dad's room. 'Didn't see you there.'

'Obviously.' Putting down her phone, she took in my tattered appearance, the flour in my eyebrows and raspberry sauce staining my nails, although she generously refrained from commenting. 'I called you earlier. I wanted to talk to you. Although I'm still mad at you, you know.'

'You behaved abominably last time I saw you.' I put my ear on Dad's closed door to listen for any noise within.

Venetia looked around. 'God, I don't like hospitals. All the germs floating around and waiting to latch on to you.' She hugged her stomach protectively, then rested it on a small ledge on the wall. Eventually, she gave a martyred sigh. 'Okay, so I'm sorry for shouting at you. And you can keep the Hermès bag. Happy now? I spoke to the doctor earlier and he said Dad is definitely on the mend. He's resting a lot, and he's supposed to be *very* calm.' She managed not to sound threatening on that last bit and I quietly opened the door and peeked in, taking in the now-familiar single bed and machinery around the headboard and my dad's still form beneath the blanket. His chest was moving up and down evenly and I carefully withdrew, keeping my hand on the closed door for a second after.

'The nurses are all aflutter around *Mr Harington*,' Venetia mimicked, leaning cautiously against the wall and reaching into her bag for a small bottle of antiseptic gel. 'Hopefully, he'll be home soon. I can't keep coming here.' She looked around her as if expecting an immediate assault by the four horsemen of the apocalypse. Another long pause fell as she looked at me expectantly. 'Don't you have something to say, too,' she prompted.

'You're a pain,' I said, sagging against the wall next to her. 'All right, I'm sorry too.'

'For going back to the house and rummaging through our mother's things without me?' she asked, squirting a big dollop of antiseptic gel onto her hands, rubbing them together.

'For taking a few bits and pieces, unimportant to anyone but me,' I said. *And Phoebe*, I thought.

Venetia looked down at her gleaming ballerinas and didn't say anything for a minute. Finally, she gave me a sideways look.

'It's just so hard.' She was still rubbing her hands methodically up and down, interlacing her fingers.

I thought back to our conversation with Mrs Roberts yesterday afternoon. What, exactly, was so hard for Venetia? Coping with the anniversary of Mum's death? It wasn't as if *her* entire life had turned out to be a complete sham, that she'd been destined for either adoption or a children's home, that she'd missed out on forty years of growing up with a soulmate.

'My first baby. And Mum not here,' she mumbled. 'I just miss her so much.'

I eyed her exasperatedly and opened my mouth to say something along the lines of wishing I had her problems, but when I saw the rigid set of her shoulders and her clenched jaw, I didn't have the heart to say anything at all, because it *was* hard when you were about to have a baby and your mum wasn't there.

'I'm really sorry,' I said softly and slid my arm through hers, put my head on to her shoulder. 'I promise I'll be the best auntie ever, to make up for not having any grandparents, well, grandma.'

She didn't say anything but against the side of my head I felt her jaw relax into a smile.

'Speaking of grandparents, Vee, I wanted to ask you something. Did Mum ever talk to you about our grandparents?'

'Our grandparents?' She seemed to realise that her body was actually touching the hospital and stood up straight, looking back at the wall and pulling her pashmina close around her. 'They're dead. We went to their funerals. Remember, Aunt Clara had that hysterical fit and dropped her smelling salts into the grave? I mean, who even has smelling salts anymore?'

'No, not them, George and Constance, Mum's parents.'

'Why?' Her eyes narrowed. 'Is this about that woman? Addie, I'm telling you, be careful. You know nothing at all about her, and remember, if it hadn't been for her, Dad would not be in the hospital right now; *we* would not have to be here.' She looked around her in disgust, then crossed her arms on top of her belly and frowned.

'So do you? Remember anything about George and Constance?' I said.

'They died when she was young.'

I suppressed the urge to laugh and Venetia eyed me sceptically. 'It's not really funny. Did you know that her mother died on Mum's seventeenth birthday? Pretty terrible way to be reminded of it forever after.'

I hadn't known that. I had opened my mouth to ask a question when Venetia unexpectedly added, 'They're buried in Limpsfield. I went there once, with Mum.'

'You did? You two drove down there? When?' My bag slipped and I bent quickly to pick it back up.

'You should disinfect that right away,' Venetia said. 'Here.' She produced the little bottle again and squirted some on a tissue. 'I think I was ten, twelve maybe? I came into the kitchen one morning and Mum was crying. And then she just bundled me into the car and we went down to see the grave.'

I gave the bottom of my bag a few cursory wipes, more to keep her talking than anything else, and tried to process the fact that my mum, *my mother*, had been crying. I hadn't ever seen her cry. I'd heard the keening from behind the study door, but it had been unearthly, unreal.

'We drove down there in the old Volvo and I needed the loo for most of the way, but she didn't stop, she just drove and drove, and then she made me go behind a tree outside the village. I didn't want to, but . . . you know how she was sometimes.

'Well, anyway, we got there, and the cemetery was a bit barren, it was in the churchyard. And it was hot. God, it was so hot. She was tense, I think, and she snapped at me because I was whining about one thing or another.' Venetia paused and her sharply beautiful face was unusually relaxed in the memory. 'She was pointing out the ages of people, and the small children who died, and there were war memorials and soldiers' graves and I was feeling quite spooked by it all. We walked through the entire cemetery and I was just thinking that maybe she didn't know where to go when she told me to sit on a bench beneath a tree in the shade. And then she went and knelt by a grave off to the side. I remember thinking that it was a bit funny, you know how careful she was about her clothes and things, but she just dropped to her knees right next to it, right by the headstone and sat there for ages.

'I was terribly upset by that, I remember it like it was yesterday. So I went to sit with her, but she didn't really pay any attention to me, she just cried and cried. Then we heard someone coming and Mum was up quickly and pulling me away from the grave. We almost ran out of the cemetery, taking a bit of a roundabout route. We stopped in a pub on the way home and she went into the Ladies and when she came back out she was back to normal. She never told me not to say anything, but I wouldn't have, because it was so strange and upsetting. The heat and the little cemetery and her kneeling.'

'So why is Mum not buried there?' I asked.

'I'm not sure.' Venetia shrugged. 'It's far away, she lived here, Dad made the decision.'

She paused, lost in thought, then she opened the antiseptic bottle again. 'You know how she never said much about her childhood, but when I was doing that genealogy thing for school she did talk a bit, about her own mum, that is. And although I could never get her to be specific, I got a strange feeling.' She squirted out the last of the liquid, rubbed her hands together and gave me a wry smile. 'Could be just family stuff. God knows, families can take it out of you. But the way she talked, reluctantly and in circles, it was, well . . . it was almost as if somewhere something had gone very wrong.'

Chapter Twenty-Five

Venetia couldn't remember any more than that but I was glad we were back on speaking terms. Things really were changing, I reflected, as we slipped into the room and sat with Dad for a while, not talking, just sitting side by side next to his bed. Venetia was changing – becoming human, by god – and *I* was changing and it was about time too. I needed to stop apologising for who I was and why I did things the way I did them. Maybe there was some value in the way my mother had always urged me to leave London, to see something else, to leave my comfort zone. Because how else could you ever fill your blank slate with meaning, if you simply continued to chug your pre-dictable orbit around the way things had always been?

Eventually a nurse came and shooed us out. I helped Venetia up from the little stool and we made our way along the corridor, Venetia throwing suspicious glances at the doors we passed and muttering things about campaigning for cleaner NHS hospitals. We'd just come to a stop in front of the lifts and Venetia was rummaging around in her bag for a tissue to press the button with, when the door opened with a ping and Andrew came out.

'Twice in a day, lucky me,' he said, smiling when he saw me. 'Brought this for your dad.' He held up a parcel. 'It's a dressing gown. All those nurses popping in at all hours, all that bedpan indignity. Terrible, really. Man'll need some privacy. And,' he pulled a Curly Wurly from his pocket with a flourish and slid it under the ribbon, 'something to stick to the old ribs. Hospital food is such garbage. I would have brought him a nice lamb chop but I thought the smell would give it away.'

'That's lovely! He'll be so happy to see you.' There was a lump in my throat when I looked at the Curly Wurly and suddenly I gave Andrew a quick, fierce hug. It was a bit awkward and completely unexpected. When I drew away I saw that he'd flushed with pleasure.

He was about to open his mouth when Venetia emerged from her bag and pointed accusingly at the Curly Wurly.

'He's not supposed to have that, you know.'

Andrew clearly hadn't seen her and jumped when she popped up next to him, but he managed to incline his head frostily in greeting.

'Venetia.'

'Andrew.'

Andrew and Venetia had disliked each other since the day Venetia had accidentally-on-purpose let the air out of his precious Raleigh Chopper tyres when she was trying to pump them up and Andrew had accidentally-on-purpose dropped her favourite butterfly hair clip into the drain outside our house where it twinkled for weeks, clearly visible among the slush but unreachable through the grate. Open hostilities had properly commenced when Venetia told everyone that Andrew still slept under his Mickey Mouse duvet and Andrew retaliated by kidnapping one of her Barbies (complete with a very nasty ransom note, which she still had and was apt to produce at key moments). For the past two decades, they'd tolerated each other, the way grown-ups are forced to do in polite company, but their longing to go back to the days of doll stealing and bike mutilating always hung heavily in the air.

'I'll take that choccy then.' Venetia reached around me.

'Oh no, you won't.' Andrew twisted away round my other side and for a moment I was caught in a very undignified body sandwich.

'For heaven's sake.' I rolled my eyes. 'This is a hospital.'

'Then tell him not to give our father a cheap chocolate bar when he's at death's door,' Venetia hissed.

'He's not at death's door,' I said indignantly.

'Tell her a man's got to eat.' Andrew shook his head.

'Tell him if it's from the newsagent downstairs then every infected orderly has probably touched it. It's dripping in germs, it's got to be,' Venetia said heatedly.

'Don't touch it, then,' Andrew shrugged.

'I won't.'

'Good.'

'Good.'

Venetia lunged for it anyway, as I knew she would, and I took a quick step sideways so she ran straight at Andrew who, ever the gentleman, caught her in a strange sort of embrace from which they both leaped back, making a big show of wiping their hands.

'Dad's down that way,' I said, grinning. 'Turn right twice. It's so nice you're coming to see him, Andrew, and on your day off, too. I'll see you later, yeah?'

I reached out to press the button for the lift (Venetia gasped and shoved the tissue at me), but Andrew held me back.

'I made an appointment at that restaurant space, Addie. Saturday at ten thirty. I talked us way up; the seller is really looking forward to meeting you.'

'Seller? Restaurant?' Venetia perked up.

'Addie and I are going into business together.' Andrew beamed happily.

'What?' Venetia was so taken aback that she forgot to add an insult.

'Well,' I said, swallowing quickly. 'Not quite yet, we're just looking, really, and nothing's been decided—'

'It'll be called Le Grand Bleu. We're looking at it on Saturday, just off Cranley Gardens,' he said. 'I'll send you the address, Ads.'

'When did this happen? And why am I the last to hear about it?' Venetia demanded.

'Because not everything needs your seal of approval,' Andrew said loftily just as I said, 'Because it hasn't bloody *happened* yet.'

The lift doors pinged open next to me but Venetia stood rooted to the spot and seemed to be warming to the idea. 'You know, Addie, much as I deplore your choice of partner – is there *any* way I could talk you out of aligning yourself with Satan incarnate? – I've got to give it to you, that's a *great* idea. I always knew you had it in you.' She gave me an admiring glance as the lift doors started to close. 'Wow. And in such a swish neighbourhood. You know . . .' She swallowed and her voice got croaky and a bit choked. 'Mum would be so pleased. Oh Addie.' She clasped her hands above her bump and smiled mistily.

I threw Andrew a look and sighed, then pressed the lift button for what seemed like the hundredth time and the doors opened again.

'Maybe,' I said as I stepped in, although more to myself than anyone else because Venetia still stood out on the landing, nodding happily. 'But who knows what she ever thought of anything.'

When I got back to the shop, it was quiet, and in the kitchen Claire was kicking her heels, cleaning out the back cupboard and singing old opera tunes, so I retreated to the office, ostensibly to deal with some paperwork, but really to finally get hold of Mr Throgmorton. The display glowed greenly in the dim light of the little room as I dialled the Oxted number for the fifth time, spoke to the receptionist who told me that Mr Throgmorton would take my call 'in just a mo', then settled down more comfortably on the chair, resting my back against the wall and my feet on the little rubbish bin opposite, and waited.

After less than a minute, a voice came on. 'Hello?' An older man, rather pleasant sounding. 'Mrs Harington?'

This time, I was ready. 'No, it's Adele Harington, actually,' I said. 'I'm Elizabeth Harington's daughter. My mother passed away a year ago.'

'Oh. Well, I am truly sorry to hear that.'

'Did you know her? I mean, did you know her personally?'

'Well, yes.' Mr Throgmorton sounded surprised. 'Not well, of course, but I met her several times after her father's death.'

'So, back in the fifties, you mean?' I asked cautiously. 'When she was seventeen?'

I held my breath because this seemed almost too easy, but Mr Throgmorton clearly wasn't a fool.

'Miss Harington, might I first ask what this is about?'

He didn't sound unkind, but still I sagged against the cubicle wall. I was getting quite tired of having to work so hard for a simple bit of information. In very few words, I told him about Phoebe's appearance and what we knew.

He was silent for a moment, then he said, 'Well, Miss Harington, sadly, I don't think I can help you substantially, not because of confidentiality necessarily, but because I don't really know anything about the story you just told me. All I know is that Mr Holloway and I set up a will, which left everything to his daughter. After his death, I tracked her down and we met a few times to sort out the particulars and dismantle the contents of Mr Holloway's house in Limpsfield. She struck me as a very smart, very capable woman and I'm truly sorry to hear that—'

'So when was this?' I asked breathlessly, because the next few minutes would be crucial, could change every single thing I had assumed about my mother for the last few days. 'I mean, when did he die?'

'Oh, this was just a few years ago, let me see, mid-nineties I think? If you bear with me, I'll look it up for you.'

He left me then, with the tinny sounds of piano muzak and the stunned realisation that George Holloway had been alive, he'd been alive until recently! For my mother's pregnancy, for the actual day of our birth, and then, unbelievably, for decades afterwards, living in a house in Limpsfield, while my mother and I were rubbing along in Hampstead like curdled vanilla custard and she pretended that both her parents had died young.

'Miss Harington? Yes, I'd remembered correctly, he died in April 1996. It didn't take very long to find his daughter. I have it in the records here that I spoke to her on April the twentieth to notify her and we met for the first time just after his funeral. What took quite a while was to dispose of the house and the contents, that sort of thing.' He paused. 'It wasn't any of my business and I certainly didn't know there was this kind of a history, but for what it's worth, I can tell you that she was very reluctant to come back for his funeral and to sort out the house. It was almost impossible to pin her down on deciding any of the details. She told me to just do whatever was necessary, to sell the house as it was; she didn't want anything to do with it. Unfortunately, for various reasons, tax purposes and such, some of that had to be done in person. Later, when I talked to her, she said she'd been to the house after all and had organised for a company to sort out the contents. I was instructed to sell it and everything else, depositing the money in her father's account, which I did. It was no problem, it sold easily. Miss Harington? Are you still there?'

I was very much still there, my mind working so fast to slot the new bits of information into place that I was bunching up the yellow lined paper of the notepad inside my fist.

'So, did you know – I mean, did you know what had happened to them? Why they were estranged?'

'I don't, I'm really sorry.' He did sound it and I could tell he was trying to think of any other information he could share with me. 'George Holloway never mentioned it at all. He'd already made all the funeral arrangements ahead of time and was buried with his wife in the Limpsfield churchyard, and the will itself was so straightforward, there being no other descendants, no contestants or anything, that there was no occasion to ask any questions or for him to have to volunteer extra information. Mrs Harington only said they hadn't been in touch for a long time. That was it.'

'Nothing about babies, twins, Brighton, Hartland? Any of those ring a bell?'

'Not at all, I'm very sorry.'

Outside I could hear a babble of cheerful voices and Grace's high-pitched laughter.

'Mr Throgmorton, I think I'll have to go, but thank you very much. Maybe, if you don't mind, I'll think about all of this and if I have another question—'

'You give me a ring,' he said encouragingly. 'I'll have a think, too, and maybe something else will occur to me. I can see your number on my phone right here, so I'll be able to get in touch. And if you ever come down to Oxted, I'd be very glad to see you at the office for a cup of tea. Just let me know. Not a whole lot of casework anymore.' He chuckled affectionately. 'My son is too efficient.'

'Actually,' I said, 'I do have one last question. My grandfather, since you met him, I was just wondering, I mean, what he was like.'

There was a pause and then he said, all traces of laughter gone, 'I didn't know him very well, but I don't think anyone did. He came across as an austere man, very conservative, a churchwarden. He spent little on himself, kept to himself.' He paused. 'He lived alone in a big house, his wife had died decades before, and his daughter, you're now telling me, had cut off all contact. If I had to hazard a guess, I'd say that he was probably very, very lonely.' He sighed. 'Families are hard work. On all fronts. I wish you the best of luck, Miss Harington. And I do hope we speak again.'

I hung up, gazing unseeingly at the top of my desk. Austere, conservative George Holloway could not have wanted his eighteen-year-old daughter to have a baby outside marriage, and so he'd driven her to the home for unmarried mothers six months before we were born, he'd been at the hospital after we were born. He must have been the one to instruct the doctor to offer Madeleine Roberts both babies.

I felt something open up inside me, something that had hardened when I first started imagining my mother choosing between two baby bundles; that had solidified when I realised that my parents had both been lying to me for forty years; and even further when I'd heard, yesterday, that my mother had meant for us both to go. Forever, Throgmorton would have a special place in my heart, because listening to him describe George Holloway I could feel that hardness inside me start to crack, that place where my mother's culpability, her rejection of us, her straining towards freedom at any cost, met my own difficult grief, my distorted, fragmented memories of her. I thought of that dispassionately pointing finger and, with relief and a great internal wrench, I let it go, thinking instead of the underwater green inside a small canvas tent. *I will never forget your birthday.*

Limpsfield, 8 January 1959

I had a visitor today. I saw him from the window at the college and I didn't recognise him at first because he looked so unfamiliar in his dark suit with his hair pulled back from his face, because the last time I saw him, that same hair had fallen across his forehead, his eyes burning down into mine just before he kissed me on my birthday, hidden in the Hartland woods.

I have stabbing pains all inside me when I think about that night last summer, horrible darts of guilt and regret, and like the dry, racking cough that started the beginning of her death, that kiss has, in my mind, become a messenger of the end, a kiss of death, and the memory of it is lodged inside me like a hard, bitter pill.

I watched him wait outside, his collar pulled up against the January rain and sleet. I didn't go out to see him and, finally, he left.

Limpsfield, 9 January 1959

He was back today. I waited for him to leave and then missed the bus. Father was so cross when I came in late for supper.

Limpsfield, 12 January 1959

Back again today; he talked to Ellen. She pointed to a window and I moved back, hoping he hadn't seen me.

Limpsfield, 15 January 1959

Today he waited right inside the entrance, so I couldn't see him from the window above and, thinking he wasn't there, practically ran him over when I came through the door, anxious not to miss my bus this time.

He smiled a little, but his eyes weren't really laughing, I could see. He'd come to see how I was; they'd not heard from me and he was worried. Had I received their flowers and was I all right? I smiled, involuntarily, because it reminded me so much of how they all used to ask me whether I was all right at Hartland, but then it felt strange, too, for why should he be worried? One kiss doesn't mean a thing, especially not a kiss that brought in death the way it did. But he held out his umbrella and walked me to the bus stop and talked to me, about nothing in particular, until I had to board my bus.

Limpsfield, 23 January 1959

Almost every day this week, he's been waiting for me after work, walking me to the bus station. I tell him that my father wouldn't approve, not of the secrecy or the vaguely improper air clinging to these meetings. But he says that walking to the bus is nothing to be ashamed of at all. It's just putting one foot in front of the other, to get yourself from one point to the next in order to be home in time for supper. That's all it is.

And that's what we do, we walk. It's 325 steps to the bus stop, 285 for him, because his legs are so long. We walk them slowly, all those 325 steps, and we don't always talk, sometimes we're just silent. He might bring me a sweet, a chocolate bar or a pastry, and one time a book, which we'd been talking about. I'm not entirely sure why he keeps on coming, honestly, because I'm only a girl, a seventeen-year-old girl, who's seen absolutely nothing of this world, who has little to offer and not very much to give. And I'm different now; things are different now. I'm not who I was last summer, giddy with possibility, infectious with my stupid enthusiasm for their world of fun and glamour and sunshine. It's winter now and I'm empty of all those things, a shell who's still thinking about her mum or else pondering how to escape from life with her father, with few real prospects at all. In his world, which even in winter must be full of glamorous, interesting things like soirées and dances and the pictures and opening nights at the theatre, I'm nothing really.

I'm not bothered about it, because in a way what I had with him wasn't real at all, it was a summer fantasy, it couldn't even be called a fling. I tell him some of that, but it's not true, he says. And he says other things, too, that he's been thinking about me all the time, that he can't get me out of his head, that I'm different from any other girl he's met. It seems absurd to me because in his world, a grown-up world where people work and live on their own and can take the train anywhere they want, not just ride the bus along the well-travelled road between home and college, surely, there must be more interesting girls, well, women, really, who are sophisticated and know what love is all about?

Maybe it's not love he's after, maybe he likes coming to talk to me. I'm not sure. We talk about books and what's happening in the world, he tells me about work sometimes, and I tell him about my classes. He's been to a film I read about in the papers, *Ben Hur* with Charlton Heston, and I was jealous, because Mum and I would have loved to see it. He offered to take me, right there and then. Skip class, he said. Instead of walking from the bus stop to the college, just take a few different turns and go down the road to the Odeon. It would be the most natural thing in the world. I had to laugh and shake my head because his definition of 'natural' and mine − or indeed Father's − do not match at all.

We never talk about the kiss or about the days at Hartland or indeed much about any of the other people there. Hartland in my mind has become a Technicolor film of the past, like *The Wizard of Oz*, which we saw once on a school trip. A swirl of garish colours, of orchard greens and ocean blues, and the blinding white of the pebbles beneath my window. It isn't real anymore; even my memory of it isn't real but two-dimensional and separate, as if I was only ever a spectator on the sidelines of a grand whirlwind of things and have now simply slipped back to the wings from where I can see the flat, two-dimensional cardboard stage decorations of a rose garden and a terrace and coloured lanterns on trees. And in any case, it really is the deepest, greyest winter now and time has narrowed down to these 325 steps across a dark, icy square on a January night. Sometimes, just as I climb up into the bus and turn one last time, I think I can see the kiss there, twinkling in his laughing eyes when he looks up at me and gives me a wave, and I'm reminded for a brief moment of the Hartland magic and the warmth of a summer's night.

I keep my distance, though, or I try to, because I'm not sure what this is, because in my mind, he and Hartland are interlinked with death, with the end. But little by little, I can feel myself warming up. It's so cold everywhere. The college is freezing because the building is so old and decrepit that we have to sit at our typewriters with gloves that have the fingertips cut off. My father's house is always cold and dark because it doesn't seem worth lighting all the fires and turning on all the lights for just the two of us rattling around on our own. The roads are cold to walk on and the bus is so cold that I can barely get off when my stop comes up, and waiting by the bus station is so cold I have to jump up and down not to freeze. But those few moments of talking and chatting and looking into those laughing eyes, those are somehow never as cold.

Limpsfield, 5 February 1959

I did it, today, I actually did it. I told Father there was a special additional lecture I needed to attend and that I would be a little late. At the college, I was going to pretend I had a doctor's appointment and needed to leave early, but then, by a great stroke of luck, Mrs Phelps was off sick and so I didn't have to risk being found out in my lie.

I met him early and instead of walking our usual 325 steps, we ran, to make the most of our time and because it was so cold, around the corner and down to the Odeon, just like he'd suggested.

I had to swallow down my memories a bit because I was reminded of coming here with Mum, not only the coming, but also the feeling of illicit pleasure, of knowing you were not supposed to be here. Mum never lied outright to Father but by an unspoken agreement we always kept our cinema trips to ourselves, knowing that at the very least he'd spoil them with lectures and rants on the frivolous, degenerating state of the English youth, when all we wanted was to fall in love with Cary Grant and Deborah Kerr.

But if you're on borrowed time, if you're risking a lot for something, then you feel it that bit more keenly and you've got to make every moment count, enjoy every second. So once I got over my fear and stopped looking over my shoulder and pushed away all the eagerly squirming memories of my mother, I was prepared to be frivolous. I sat in the back stalls of the warm theatre as the screen lit up and felt the familiar thrill of watching the curtains part, the orchestra music accompanying the news, watched the young queen cut a ribbon somewhere and felt for her in this cold, then waited for the lion to roar up on the screen and for it all to start.

Maybe he had different expectations; in fact it is very likely that he must have. A kiss and a cuddle and little whispers like the couple sitting just ahead, maybe even more, although I'm not entirely sure what more he could expect. Whatever his hopes were, I fulfilled none of them, because the moment the screen lit up, I sat and watched, unable to resist the sweep of the story, the rising curve of the music and the romance between Esther and Judah. I was like a sun-starved animal, turning my face towards warmth and colours and brightness, the taste of popcorn sugary-sweet in my mouth.

Something made me turn, though, right towards the end, and I realised that he was watching me in the half-darkness, had perhaps been watching me all along while I smiled and cried and agonised over the lepers' colony, and I was suddenly embarrassed because I must have looked so silly, like a child, dangling my feet in my seat and eating popcorn. His face was strangely alive because the moving pictures flickered across his cheeks and eyelids, and when he slid his hand into mine, it felt almost like it was part of the film, like it wasn't me and him sitting on the fold-out chairs, but that we, too, were part of the foreign world of death and passion and revenge in the desert. For the rest of the film, I dared not move at all, feeling his hand in mine and his arm pressing against my shoulder, and for the first time since last August, it seemed utterly right to be where I was, to be doing what I was doing.

I was so reckless that I agreed to stay out for a bit and we ran back up to the square to the corner tea shop from where we would see my bus rounding the corner in time for me to get home. I asked for tea and a bun, because I didn't have much money, but he ordered a Knickerbocker Glory for us to share and we sat and ate it from both ends with two spoons. Around us, people were talking about poor Buddy Holly dying in a plane crash and Fidel Castro freeing Cuba, but my face was glowing with happiness and I couldn't help smiling because somehow *Ben Hur* had taken away the memory of Mum's death that had been between us and the tea shop was now doing the rest. It was so deliciously warm and smelled of buns fresh out of the oven, someone put music on the Wurlitzer, and the caramel sauce from the Knickerbocker Glory slid down my throat so easily. We stayed for far too long, eating ice creams and buns and getting another pot of tea, and I didn't let go of his hand until I almost missed my bus home.

To think that only a month ago, the college had seemed to be just an extension of the prison of my life here, and a reminder that all the plans Mum and I had would never happen. And now it's my ticket to freedom. Not only the 325 steps, but also the promise of him and of what we might come to be. Because, surely, no one would keep coming in the darkest, wettest months of the year just to walk and talk if they didn't mean there to be more? We don't talk about the future much, just as we haven't talked about the recent past, but he talks about me, and what he likes and thinks about me when he's not with me. There's an urgency there, a desperation, I can feel it, and I can only think that it means he wants more, more of my time and of me. If only I could give him that, because I do want to and every time I try to convince myself that it's not possible to have someone like him, that he couldn't think of me with any real intent, that he couldn't think of me for forever, he does something or says something or simply smiles, and I begin to hope again, that maybe he'll take me away with him, that maybe he might be my forever. Stupid, wonderful, irrepressible Hope, which has come back to haunt me even though I thought I'd managed to banish her for good.

Now I'm in bed, trying to work up the courage to push my toes down into the damp cold at the bottom of the bed, writing by the light of the moon coming into the window. I'm going to close the diary soon, and I'll hide it more carefully than usual, because if my father ever, ever finds out about all of this, then my days at the college are over. I've opened up the paper-clipped pages about Hartland and brought out the pictures Felicity gave me from our day on the sea. There's one in there that I love, one of us laughing on the pier, and although I've vowed not to think of Hartland again, although Hartland is Wizard-of-Oz-green and strangely remote, that picture is not remote at all. It's alive and happy and I want to feel it right underneath my pillow as I lie back and try and remember every second of that hour in the tea shop, smell the buns and taste the caramel sauce and the warmth of the tea, I want to feel his fingers interlacing with mine and even remember the censorious glare of the lady working behind the counter, who clearly thought it entirely inappropriate that a young girl like me should be sitting there holding hands with a young man in public.

Chapter Twenty-Six

'Addie, your sister's here.' One of the shop girls stuck her head into the kitchen just as I'd rushed in from the office, feeling very guilty at having taken the longest lunch break I ever had.

'My sister?' I said cautiously, pushing back my hair and ignoring the phone buzzing in my pocket, which was probably Andrew, who had tried to call me earlier.

'Dunno, tall, expensive-looking? She's ordered a box to go and wanted to see if you had a minute.'

Claire, who loved Venetia's visits, brightened. 'Ooh, ask her whether she'll be freezing her placenta,' she begged. 'And if she's planning on eating it in a year and what recipe she'll use. My cousin says—'

But when I came out on to the shop floor, it wasn't Venetia at all, but Phoebe, who was in the process of ordering a cappuccino with her box of pastries. Her face broke into a huge smile when she saw me come out from behind the counter.

'Addie! You won't believe . . .' She shrugged off her trench coat and tossed it on to the counter in a very un-Phoebe-like gesture. 'I know,' she said, beaming. 'I *know* about George Holloway. I found them at the General Register Office. The register said he died aged ninety-five. I can't believe it. She *lied* about him being dead.'

'And Throgmorton said he was a sad, lonely man,' I said happily.

'And, you won't *believe* what *else* I found.'

I pulled Phoebe towards the little bar on the side where people could have a quick coffee with their pastries. I wasn't really supposed to be hanging out with the customers for extended periods of time, especially not if my apron and jacket were still hanging behind the door in the office, but it would have to do for now.

'It was a house. Hartland, I mean.' Her face was flushed and excited and she took a big, steadying sip of coffee. 'Took a while to find, big fire there in the seventies, everything burned to the ground, family dispersed.' She pulled out a map. 'Look here. It's close to another place called Porthallow, a few miles from the coast.'

'Did Harry own the house?'

'Couldn't find Harry unfortunately, just a family called Shaw, Janet and Abel and John Shaw. But I found something else. Oh Addie!' She took a deep breath, her eyes glowing. 'You know that broken frame with the picture? I took it out to change the frame and right behind . . .'

She held it up for me to see. Another photo, of three people, two young women and a man in front of a stretch of water. In the middle was my young mother, linking arms with the other two, pulling them backwards, away from the camera, laughing, like a child waiting to be swung into the air. The man was tall, maybe a bit older than her, with dark hair. The other woman was round and rosy looking, peeking out from beneath a large sun hat. I couldn't make out their features very well, the snapshot was slightly blurred with so much movement, but the woman seemed nice and sensible in a flowery dress, holding a wicker basket. Her mouth was a small dark 'o' and she looked like she was about to say something, steadying them perhaps, or simply laughing. The whole picture breathed sea and sun and vitality. I looked at the tall man and then homed in on my mother's smile, drowning in its giddiness, feeling the wind and salty air, hearing the splashing of water behind them.

Hesitantly I turned it over. *Tideford Cross, Summer '58.* My mother's girlish handwriting.

'Here.' Phoebe wrestled with the map. 'Look.'

I followed her finger southwards from London, crossing the M25, past Crawley, then the little specks of Pease Pottage and Sayers Common, then down towards Lewes, and along the coast on a smaller yellow road. Somewhere past Lewes was Porthallow and then, down towards the Channel, there was a tiny 'x' in smudgy red ballpoint. She tapped the 'x'. 'This is Hartland.'

And a little way below it, perched right on the edge of the bright blue stretch that marked the English Channel, a mere speck on the map, was a teeny-tiny dot called Tideford Cross. I looked at the picture again, all that sea and wind and laughter, and then at the map, then back up at Phoebe. She was nodding vigorously at the picture, ponytail flying around her face, her eyes bright.

'Don't you see,' she said. 'The note was written right *there*,' she jabbed the picture, 'in Hartland in early 1960, and she and this man were in Tideford Cross, *there*, in the summer of 1958. This has got to have something to do with us. And don't you think that *that* might be Harry?'

Harry? I'd been so busy looking at my mother, happily grinning between the woman with the sun hat and the tall man, that I hadn't immediately made the connection. 'I don't know, Phoebe, this was two years before we were born. It could be anyone.'

Phoebe looked at me, slightly disappointed, and took the photo back. 'Why are you so against Harry? I just have this feeling it could be him. Don't you think he looks a bit like me?'

I studied the fuzzy round shape of the man's head. 'Well, he's tall, I suppose,' I said reluctantly. 'But I'm not sure, Phoebe, honestly.'

'We should go,' Phoebe cut in without listening to me. 'I'm off till Tuesday. We could go tomorrow, first thing, just take the train down to the coast like she did forty years ago.'

'Oh, I can't, Phoebe,' I said, stricken. 'My dad, I can't really leave him right now.'

'It's a chance to find out more.' Phoebe tapped the photo thought-fully. 'There's a train to Porthallow tomorrow, I looked, at eight seventeen from Victoria and then a bus to Tideford Cross.'

When I bit my lip indecisively, Phoebe pressed the photo into my hand. 'Why don't I go down there for a reconnoitre and we can talk when I'm back, okay?' She smiled, picked up her box and vanished through the door, ponytail swinging in her wake.

Back in the kitchen, I stood at the counter for a long time, looking at the photo that I'd propped up against a stack of bowls, of my mother laughing with two strangers on a beautiful, sunny day by the sea. Resting my palms on the worktop, I felt the cool stainless steel spread through my fingertips and up my arms into my shoulders, calming my flushed cheeks. Her photo-face was almost luminous in the shadow of the bowl behind it, so very young, and so unaware of what lay ahead. And then austere, old-school George Holloway had turned that happy, excited woman against us. I imagined him bundling his newly pregnant daughter into an old-fashioned car and handing her over to a starchy Sister of Hope. I thought of him walking the hospital corridors in search of Dr Miller so they could find an appropriate set of parents for each of us. She'd blamed him for that, for all of it, blamed him so determinedly and wholeheartedly that she cut him out of her life completely.

And then, bit by bit, some of my earlier elation started draining away, because the one thing I couldn't understand was why she'd blamed *me*, too. Why had she not gone back for Phoebe, and why hadn't she loved me when I was all that was left? Why hadn't she held on to me and supported me and cherished me every one of the forty years we'd had together? Why had she been so impatient with me, irritated that I wasn't making enough of myself, that I wasn't strong enough, determined enough, good enough?

Because I hadn't been. I'd only been half, and that half had come at too high a price for our relationship to ever be anything other than fraught, fractious, bitter. I rubbed my throat to ease the air into my lungs because it all made sense now, every moment on that stupid rollercoaster, every time she closed the door to leave us, straining to be free, every impatient mouth twitch. She *had* strained to be free, from the memories and, in turn, from me, because I was only ever a reminder of those memories. Somehow, my strong, capable mother had not been strong enough to fight against the past, to fight *for* her love for me.

I looked back down at that happy, laughing woman who wasn't yet that person and wished with a desperation that almost choked me that I could talk to *her*, that I could connect with her before things went so terribly wrong.

'Lovey! There you are! Were you out earlier?'

I looked up to see Grace materialise in the kitchen entrance, holding a tray of miniature sablés in little red-and-white boxes.

'I was out for lunch and then, er, quickly up front.' I slipped the photo into my back pocket.

'Looking like that?' Grace wagged her finger. 'Do me a favour, dearie-dear, and do come in the back way when you're not in your uniform. It's not the most confidence-inspiring thing to have the head pastry chef come in from the street.'

'I'm not much of a pastry chef these days, am I?' I muttered, feeling quite fed up with things all of a sudden. 'And where else would I come in? I do have to travel here.'

'Yes, of course, of course,' she said soothingly. 'But,' she offered, 'perhaps not so very far in your lunch break and not coming through the shop floor in your street clothes?'

'I'll go put my uniform on,' I said wearily.

'That'd be wonderful,' Grace said cheerfully. 'Oh, and your friend Andrew called just now. The office, I mean. I think he was trying to reach you. He doesn't seem to be able to keep away from this place; maybe we should offer him a job?'

She set down the sablés, then reached for one of the little boxes and held it up for me to inspect. 'I think this one didn't survive the journey, look. I really have to talk to the driver, he needs to be more careful.'

'You know this wouldn't happen if *we* made all these here,' I said. 'Every time I turn around, more things come in from the head kitchen. Pretty soon we won't be making anything here at all, just pre-baked rolls and breads and things. What would Claire and I do then?'

'Eat all the broken bits,' Grace said philosophically. 'I did want to talk to you about that, actually, Addie.'

'The broken bits?' I tried not to look as annoyed as I felt.

'No, the deliveries. And a letter was dropped off for you earlier. Let's go look for your uniform and I'll give it to you.'

Grace gently pushed me out of the kitchen, across the little hallway and into the office. It was dark and cramped and the airless space wrapped itself around me like a too-warm blanket.

'It was just here.' Grace sat down behind the desk and started rummaging in the in-tray. 'Now, lovey, do listen. I know you still want to keep a hand in with the production of everything like we used to, but it just doesn't make sense to keep doing them here. I'm sorry. Even the cakes to decorate – they can make them in huge batches at the head kitchen in half the time, and we'll just personalise them this end if we need to. Even considering deliveries, the cost of making them here doesn't add up.'

'Grace,' I said, alarmed. 'Please—'

But Grace had finally found what she'd been looking for and handed me a brown envelope. 'And we'll have to think seriously about . . .' She inclined her head meaningfully towards the kitchen, where Claire could now be heard singing 'Fantine's Death' from *Les Misérables*.

'You're letting her go?' I took the letter without looking at it, stuffed it into the pocket of my jacket.

'The business is changing,' she said briskly. 'We're getting bigger. Batching at Maxwell Corner is the only way to go. She's not really needed, she doesn't have enough to do. You do see that, don't you?'

'And me?' I asked carefully. 'Will I—'

'Take on the other stores,' Grace said simply.

Or leave. Shut the door on Grace's. Do something else, not Le Grand Bleu, not another job, but something of my own. Oddly enough, the thought didn't fill me with nearly as much panic as it would have done only a few days ago when Andrew was waving around his estate agent brochures. It wouldn't have to be all big mortgages and perfect premises and bank managers nipping at my heels. It could be small and I could do what *I* always wanted to, what I'd loved about Grace's from the beginning. Exposed brick, a worn wooden counter and a big coffee maker gurgling away. There'd be fluffy lemon poppy seed cake and high-domed muffins glittering with coarse sugar, little knots of challah bread, fresh out of the oven and dripping with salted butter, smelling like little buttery cloud puffs.

Grace had been watching me, smiling expectantly for me to join her enthusiasm for a mechanised, depersonalised kitchen where 'batching' was the way to go, but I knew then without a shadow of a doubt that if that was really what was going to happen, the batching and no Claire to chivvy me along when I spent too much time on the meringue nests, no smell of my own bread greeting me when I came back in from whatever length lunch break I wanted to take – then the time had come for me to go my own way. I remembered myself at twenty-five years old, fired up by Grace's optimism and her drive, how pleased she was when I'd taken over the Kensington shop, had brought in champagne and toasted not her, but *our* success, and I remembered, above all, how Grace's had got me through the first few months after my mother's death. She'd always been there, offering hope and encouragement and security, and for that I would be forever grateful. But things were different now and although I might never go and get the moon, the new me could sure as hell muster enough gumption to stand up for what I really wanted.

'Grace,' I said gently. 'The years here have been amazing, you're amazing, but I think it's time I went my own way.'

'Oh, no, don't say that.' Grace half rose from her seat but I reached out across the desk and put my hand over hers.

'I would never leave you hanging. I'll stay until you find someone else.'

'Addie, please,' she begged. 'You've had a lot on lately, so take a couple of days off. I'll get one of the other girls to cover for you. And we'll talk again next week.'

I shook my head and opened my mouth to protest, but she got up and opened the door, handed me my bag, my umbrella. 'You'll come around to it, I know. Change is a good thing, Addie. You'll see. I'll talk to you in a few days.'

I stood on the other side of the street, looking across to Grace's as the late afternoon traffic droned along the road, commuters weaving around me and mums pulling small children through the puddles, carrying shopping bags and school satchels and umbrellas. Clouds hung so low to the ground that they obscured the top of the building and Grace's emerged from the fog like a fairy cave, lamps twinkling through the tall windows, the neat blue and white paintwork and the window boxes planted with lavender. Resisting the urge to run right back across the street and into Grace's office to undo what I'd just done, I shoved my hands into my pockets to pull my jacket closer against the chill and felt something rustle. It was the brown envelope Grace had given me. *Addie, I think you'll want this. Give us a bell soon! xx* was scrawled across the top in Mrs Baxter's handwriting. The letter itself was not addressed to me but, in James Merck's crabbed handwriting, to my mother.

Slipping my thumb under the flap, I pulled out several A4 sheets of paper. An itemised bill, similar to the ones I'd seen in the folder. A reply from a West Sussex archive company asking him to pay them a visit if needed. And finally, a letter, opened but still in its original envelope, sent a couple of months ago by a certain Madeleine Roberts, 4 Crabtree Lane, Brimley.

Dear Mr Merck,
Thank you for your second letter dated 28 January and I apologise for not being in touch when you first wrote. In answer to your question – yes, I was a patient at All Saints Hospital on 14 February 1960, although I am not sure I will be of much help as I stayed only very briefly and kept very much to myself. I do not recall anyone's name there but would be willing to talk to your client if that's what she'd like to do.
All best wishes,
Madeleine Roberts

Chapter Twenty-Seven

The train was already waiting when I ran up the stairs from the Tube, scanned the big board above the shops for the platform of the 8.17 to Porthallow, raising my hand in greeting at the tall, thin figure hovering just in front of the turnstiles. There was a shout and then a whistle. Doors began to close with a clap that started all the way at the front of the train. I accelerated, clutching my bag, my eyes fixed on Phoebe's hand hurrying me along. She shoved our tickets into the turnstile, tearing along the train, jumped on to the very first carriage and I grabbed her hand, let myself be pulled up. Behind me, the conductor slammed the door and the handle hit the back of my thighs, pushing me forwards.

In the dirty neon light, Phoebe's eyes disappeared into the shadows of her face.

'Don't get me wrong, Addie, I'm really glad you came, but when I suggested you take a day off, I didn't mean quit your job altogether.'

'It's all right,' I panted, bending over and clutching the stitch in my side. 'Let's find a seat before I die.'

The train chugged slowly out of the station as we picked our way along the corridor, past the grimy doors of the loos and mismatched luggage piled into the racks. The train was less crowded than I'd thought it would be, probably because the weather didn't encourage weekend jaunts into the country, so we found a carriage at the front that was mostly empty. A sudden acceleration pitched us forward, then we came out of the tunnel and slowly chuntered through the cityscape of South London towards Clapham Junction and Croydon. Rain lashed against the train windows as back gardens and unfamiliar streets flew by. We fell into seats opposite each other and Phoebe set a slightly squashed brown bag with two lidded cups on to the table.

'My mum always says that no decent work gets done without at least three cups of coffee,' she said, still eyeing me with some concern. 'If we get started now, we can get another two in before hitting Porthallow.'

I wrapped my fingers gratefully around the hot paper cup she handed me and Phoebe got out a plastic box. She inspected the table-top and brushed a crumb off it before setting down the box.

'I tried very hard to finish your pastries last night because they were so delicious, but at some point I was defeated,' she said. 'Not to mention being up half the night with sugar shock. So I brought some for our trip.' She smiled at me, cocked her eyebrows at the box. 'Under the circumstances, I didn't want to bring them in the original packaging. I thought it might invoke post-traumatic stress disorder.'

She leaned forward, opened the box, cast a professional eye over the selection and sat back with a small apricot Danish in her hand, watching me.

'Very funny.' I took a sip of coffee and cautiously relaxed into the seat. 'I've been with Grace for fifteen years.' I kept my eyes on the moving landscape outside. 'I didn't think I'd ever leave, even though Andrew's been on at me about it for most of that time. I didn't ever *want* to leave. But this whole thing with Mum, seeing that photo yesterday, it made me so – sad, and angry. She'd always talk about making something of yourself and being strong, and then whatever happened that night took over her life and our entire relationship, all forty years of it. And she just let that happen. It's so stupidly futile. Such a waste. So when I was talking to Grace, much as I love her, I realised that I need to do what I want. Not what Grace or Mum or Andrew want me to do.'

'And what is it you want?' Phoebe selected another piece of pastry.

'Something simple,' I said. 'A little bakery off Islington High Street. Nothing fancy, and, please god, nothing French. Just me and the kitchen. By the way, here's the photo back. I thought you'd want it.'

'I had a copy made.' She patted her bag and grinned. 'I figured maybe we'd both like to have one. I also made a copy of your mum's photo and there was that little envelope with all those others. I made copies of everything.' Phoebe reached out and held my hand, squeezed it. 'I think you can do anything you want, Addie. You live on your own, you're your own person. You're a pastry goddess.' She held up the rest of her palmier. 'I'll help you, if you like. I'm really good at figuring things out.'

I had to smile. Somehow that didn't surprise me.

'There's also something else,' I said. 'I finally found the letter that Merck sent to Rose Hill Road.'

'Really?' Phoebe was digging through her bag for a sleeve of papers but now she sat up. 'Anything new?'

'Yes,' I said. 'It's for you.'

I handed her the letter, watched her start at the return address on the envelope, read the few lines of lined paper. Finally, she looked up at me.

'God, Addie, she did it in the end, she wrote back. But didn't she *say* she'd burned the letter?'

'She must have changed her mind when he wrote a second time. We did run out on her, didn't we, more or less in mid-sentence.'

'Still, she should have told me back then. I could have . . .' Phoebe put the backs of her hands underneath her eyes, blinked away tears.

'It's not her fault,' I said firmly. 'It's George Holloway and the doctor's fault. The whole of the nineteen fifties' fault for being narrow-minded and old-fashioned. But not your mum's.'

She was quiet for a moment, then re-read the letter.

'But you know, there *was* something very strange at the register office yesterday,' she said, frowning. 'Constance and George took me a while to find. She died aged forty-four, so indeed *very young*.' She threw me a brief smile, then looked down at the letter again. 'And when I looked for myself in the birth register . . . well, it turns out I don't exist.'

'You don't?' I'd been stuffing my coffee cup in the little rubbish bin but now I looked up. 'What do you mean?'

'"Phoebe Roberts" exists, fair and square in the register, born in the first quarter of 1960 in Brighton. But "Holloway Girl Number Two" doesn't exist, there's just one and that has to be you because you have the birth certificate to match. And then, what's really fishy is my birth certificate, you know the one I showed you that first day, with my parents' names on it and everything? Well, I shouldn't have that at all. I spoke to a woman at the council about it when I was researching what I had to do to view my adoption papers, and she said as an adopted child I should have an adoption certificate and no birth certificate at all. Adopted children usually get a shortened certificate, which doesn't reference the adoption but just states the child's adopted surname and the various birth details. You can use it for everything, but no one, including you, would ever know you were adopted unless you came across the full-length adoption certificate.' She gave me a wry smile. 'Or strange bundles of baby clothes with pregnancy booklets. But the fact that I have a normal birth certificate, like any normally born baby, looks like my parents simply registered me as their own child, as if my mum had actually given birth to me; as if I was theirs. That's not technically supposed to be possible with an adopted child.'

'Maybe she has the original at home somewhere,' I suggested. 'After all, I also had two certificates, the original one, which was hidden, and then the official one that has both my parents' names on it.'

'Your hidden version doesn't exist for me. If it's not in the register, then there isn't a certificate to match. The register is like the table of contents for all the certificates. And the fact that you have two certificates, well, that's a bit fishy too. You were first registered as her baby and then your dad's name must have been added to the birth certificate soon after. It's not usually done that way, because, really, you can only change your name by deed poll. It did occasionally happen, but only in cases where the father came forward quickly after the birth and owned up to being the father.'

'Except he wasn't.'

'No.' She shook her head. 'And my mother wasn't my mother, and yet she's on my birth certificate as if she was my natural-born parent. It's—'

'Fishy indeed,' I said, frowning. 'It must have been different for private adoptions. Different channels, that's all.'

'Maybe. But officially, all adoptions, including private ones, were supposed to be done through the courts or the council. The fishy birth certificates certainly explain why Merck didn't find anything to link us, because in terms of official paperwork there's absolutely no connection between you and me at all, anywhere. Except what the nurse and the doctor might know.'

She paused, tracing her mum's name on the envelope.

'You don't think . . . well, maybe, that she stole me?'

'Your *mum*? No!' I was so taken aback that I didn't say anything for a good few minutes. 'Phoebe,' I finally managed. 'Your mum was a bit . . .' Frantic. Desperate. Obsessed. But a baby thief? 'No,' I said again, but less certainly this time. 'God, no.'

But she looked as troubled as I felt. She brought out the photo of the three people by the water.

'Do you think someone might recognise these people?' she asked.

Looking at the fuzzy faces I thought you'd be hard-pressed to recognise a man who'd been there forty years ago and possibly not been back since. But I was tired and a bit weary and so I didn't say anything else, just settled back into my seat, watching the train stations come and go and wondering whether my mother had taken this very same route when she travelled down to Hartland all those years ago, a small suitcase in the racks above, her hat hung up carefully, a boxy handbag on her knees. Maybe she'd have read or slept, her face pressed against the window, to wake up with a mark on her cheek from the window frame. Would she have travelled with her father, sitting opposite each other, like Phoebe and I were doing? And what had brought her to Tideford Cross, to Hartland, in the first place. A holiday?

'Do you have a picture of Hartland?' I asked.

'Yes, I found one at the library.'

She handed me a colour photocopy of a picture spread over two pages of a book, a mix of watercolours and fine black pen, showing a honey-coloured country house set amidst gardens. The house was lovely, but whoever had drawn the picture had clearly loved the gardens most, because the building practically disappeared amidst an undulating green sea of lawns and trees and bushes. Drawn with swift, almost careless watercolour brushstrokes in all hues of emerald, mint and teal, the gardens burst from the page, so lush and so vivid that all you wanted was to fall into the picture and wander down the little grassy path leading past the wing on the right towards the horizon.

I imagined my mother stepping off the train in Porthallow, as we would in just a moment, then arriving at Hartland later and walking down the lane towards that house. I thought of all the lives lived and wasted and what it was that *I* wanted to find in Tideford Cross. Understanding, maybe, of what it was that she hadn't been able to escape. And acceptance, that she wasn't as strong as she always appeared to be, as she urged me to be. I wanted a connection with her, with that young, happy, excited version of my mother, and I wanted to be able to forgive the woman she would later turn out to be. For not fighting for me and for Phoebe; for not trying a little bit harder to love us. Forgiveness, I think, would be the only thing that would let me leave all this behind.

An hour later, we got off the train at Porthallow and ran across the station to catch the little bus going down to Tideford Cross. Remnants of a greyish morning hung in the air and I thought I could detect the faint tang of salt water, or perhaps it was just the sound of the gulls, swooping and squawking, that suggested proximity to the sea.

The bus driver, whose life's dearest ambitions clearly didn't include ferrying old ladies in an oversized vehicle along the coastline, drove like a maniac, picking up and depositing people at top speed, waving them in impatiently and shutting the door on them on their way out, so that some only just managed to stumble off the bottom step before he pulled away with a roar. The bus was packed too, with people and bags and all sorts of things, and it wasn't until we were almost there that we were able to sink, sticky and slightly nauseous, into seats next to each other in the front.

'Next stop Tideford Cross,' the bus driver shouted from the front and whipped around the corner. I swallowed a small surge of bile but Phoebe suddenly sat up and gripped my arm. 'There,' she breathed. 'Addie, look, the sea.'

And then, as if in slow motion, the bus crested the hill and for a moment we seemed poised to take off straight into the clear morning air. There was a faint echo of my mum's laughter at the top of Celestial Cyclone, but none of the terror or the claustrophobia, only possibility and chance and bright, sunny skies. The clouds had ripped apart to reveal slivers of sky, turning the water a sparkly blue against the grey-green of the coastline. If this had been a film, the music would have accelerated in a crescendo to indicate a moment of complete and utter perfection. I felt a huge smile break out on my face and when I looked at Phoebe, I could see that she, too, was smiling. Then the front wheels connected with the road again, I clutched my stomach, and we hurtled down, faster and faster, whipping round bends and curves towards the sea below. The coastline bowed towards the water here, to create a huge natural harbour, then gathered its skirts and spread them out in a tidy fan of weathered grey roofs, granite walls and a patchwork of streets. The driver negotiated the last few bends with one hand, ringing the bell with the other, and I gripped Phoebe's arm right back, bouncing up and down in my seat, as we belted towards Tideford Cross.

Limpsfield, 24 April 1959

I'm a fallen woman! I am ruined. Damaged goods, scarlet to the bone. And I've never been happier in my life. Surely, something can't be so wrong, so shameful, if it's so very lovely?

We'd been planning it for a while, we both wanted to so badly. Holding hands for 325 steps and sneaking off to the tea shop and talking fast to make every minute count – I was getting so sick of it. And greedy. I wanted more. I wanted to be alone with him, have whole hours, a whole day, somewhere warm and safe. It was getting to be an obsession of mine during that long February and a cold March that followed; an obsession with him and with being warm and I sometimes didn't know which I wanted more, until I realised I wanted to be warm and together both, and not kissing urgently at the pictures while images moved fast across our faces or holding hands across the table in a tea shop where the lady looked at me like I was no better than I should be.

I'd been nervous even thinking about it because I know it's wrong, and not only because my father says so, but because I know that that's not what you do, not without a ring and a promise of forever. He talks like forever, though, we both do, holding on to each other and talking and smiling, knowing each other's thoughts and sensing our moods. That, to me, says forever. Seeing him every week for months on end, even if it's only for stolen hours and 325 steps, that says forever. And I wanted to turn that into something real, I wanted to have something more solid, even though at first I was too frightened to do anything about it. It's too fast, too tenuous. And I'm not quite sure Mum would like it.

But now it's suddenly spring out there, an early spring that puts a definitive end to winter and scatters crocuses and daffodils and tiny little white flowers across the green as we walk to the bus stop. It's the kind of spring that bursts forth in order to finally have a proper revenge on winter, that won't hold back but thrusts upwards and shoots outwards and pushes roots down into the ground, because it is so full of life and full of intoxicating newness that it simply won't stand for being held back a minute more.

I've been to St Peter's churchyard a lot these last two weeks. There are war graves here along with the parish graves and spring is not quite as daring, I think, keeping the surfaces in between the gravestones respectfully simple. Secretly, I would have preferred Mum to be somewhere else, somewhere with more life, so I bring bunches of early flowers from her garden, where spring has carpeted the ground with daffodils, tulips and bluebells, and set them by her stone almost every other day.

Father doesn't want her grave to be untidy, though, and I noticed that he's taken away one of the bunches I brought earlier in the week and has thrown it on the compost heap. But maybe spring's recklessness has rubbed off on me, because the very next day I took the tiny potted rose that was still hidden behind her curtain and buried it right into the ground where he cannot remove it without creating a mess. It's an inconspicuous spot, nestling next to the gravestone where the late morning sun finds it, but I know that she'd like it very much. I've tried to talk to her about the tea shop—bus stop illicitness, tried to find the words that explain my craving for warmth and freedom. That part, she would understand, I know for certain, but she might not understand some of the other yearnings I have, for love and passion and the kinds of things you only occasionally read about in the sort of books my father would ban immediately, and that you shouldn't even be thinking about, not without a firm promise, without things being done properly. She doesn't know that there is promise, that the very air between us is full of promise, and she's not here, after all, to tell me not to do what I want to do, so very much.

It took me a little while, though, walking around in a permanent state of anticipation and anxiety, feeling almost as if I'd already done it, that I had already committed the crime and was cringing for punishment. Sitting through seventeen and a half minutes of supper at night and going to secretarial college was agony because I'm so sure people can read it in my eyes, all that craving for warmth and love and newness.

But in the end, he made it all happen, and he made it sound so easy, so normal. I suppose that's how it is out there in his world. It's easy to be in love. The plan was for me to pretend to be too sick for class, forging my father's signature on a note, and he was going to pretend to have been sick at work. I'd asked him how he was able to come and see me so often as it was, but he said he just comes down on the train after work, it was easy. His parents have gone overseas for a bit and he's living at Hartland now, and he just takes the train back there in the evening, finds his car by the train station and drives home. How I envy him that easy train-taking and car-driving. Anywhere you wanted to go, and I was fairly certain that the train, at least, was warm. I have started thinking about Hartland again, too, as a real place, not this strange, dream-like part of my past. I've been imagining the house waking up to this wonderful, intoxicating spring every day, the honey-stone walls glowing in the sun, the doves on the roof. In my mind, I'm slipping down the garden paths to see the rose garden come back to life after the winter and the ground beneath the trees covered in blue-bells, an ocean of brilliant bluebell-blue shimmering beneath the trees where I spent my last evening. But here I draw the line, because I don't want to go back there. Instead, I think about the future, the most imminent future, which is going to happen in Purley.

He was the one who knew of a place for us to go, this sweet little hotel in Purley where I was supposed to check in and say I was Mrs Smith, coming in to visit her cousin. I didn't think I could possibly look less like a Mrs Smith coming in to visit my cousin if I tried, but I didn't want to say that in case he thought I was being feeble. I was feeble, though, very feeble indeed, sitting across from my father at the supper table and looking down at the stew so that he wouldn't be able to discover all those Purley secrets in my eyes. And then, ten days after we'd first talked about the plans, I was ready. I was so very tired of being sad and lonely and cold in my father's house in Limpsfield. I wanted to be Mrs Smith in a hotel room in Purley.

And now that it's done and I'm a scarlet, fallen woman, who's had champagne and been kissed and made love to, I feel, for the first time since Mum died, that the future holds something for me, that there is something worth sticking around for.

Chapter Twenty-Eight

'Good god, will you look at all these people?'

Tideford Cross was positively heaving. People as far as we could see, streaming along the high street to look at stalls set up on every available surface, spilling over into the little side streets. My legs were trembling slightly when I got off the bus and I breathed deeply to get rid of the nausea rolling round in my stomach.

'Market day,' a lady said behind us. 'First one of the season so it'll be a bit crowded today. But best fishcakes around.'

'Brilliant,' Phoebe breathed happily. She gripped her bag more tightly and turned to me and I registered, with some alarm, that she was looking quite ferocious now. 'Okay. This is what we do. We work our way down the road, asking at the stalls. But, I was thinking, maybe we don't want to scare anyone. Let's not show the photo until we meet someone promising. And should we say that we're working on a research project about the rise and fall of the upper classes in a world fraught with post-war realities and are trying to follow up on a lead?'

I felt my eyebrows disappear into my hairline. Post-war realities?

'Well?' she said impatiently. 'It's reasonably obscure and not scandalous in any way. It is a real book, I saw it in the library, and we can always add to the story as we go along. That way, if someone does know Harry it doesn't raise any immediate red flags. I'm a bit worried now that he might not want to talk to us. I don't want to put him off before he even knows the whole story and sees that we're normal and sane.'

She was tapping her shiny boot on the cobblestones, her eyes scanning the stalls selling produce, baskets and plants, looking anything but sane, and I had to laugh.

'Post-war realities it is. Let's go.'

Then Phoebe was off, skipping between stalls, parting the crowd like Moses parted the Red Sea. My arm clamped firmly under hers, she steered me towards the first stall and from there further along into the village, perusing the goods, scrutinising the faces of the vendors. Again and again, she stopped to buy food or little trinkets, chatting to the stall owners, her hair flying in the breeze, her face animated and flushed. *Wonderful day today, isn't it? This is pretty! This is delicious! Are you from around here?* But despite the friendliness and the general buzz in the air, people were intent on selling as much as they possibly could and few of them could afford to hang around chatting. I started feeling vaguely hassled by all the noise and the shouting, and a scone and two admittedly delicious fishcakes later I'd had enough.

'Phoebe, this place is packed.' I pulled her into the entryway of a small cottage and shoved the apple fritter she'd just pressed into my hands back at her. 'We need to be more systematic. Let's finish this side and then I think I saw a shop down that lane, let's ask there. And Phoebe?' She took a bite out of the fritter, held it out again. 'Calm down a bit, okay? You're frightening people.'

She tossed the rest of the fritter into a rubbish bin, patted my arm reassuringly and was just about to steer me back into the throng when the door of the cottage opened and a woman appeared, staggering backwards underneath a big basket, which wriggled and twitched uncontrollably in her arms. Seeing a paw shoot out of the top, I leaped backwards into Phoebe, who grabbed the pole of the seafood stall. The woman lost her balance and the basket shot through the air. Automatically, my arms reached up to grab it, then there was a crunch as we crashed down in a heap of arms and legs and furiously swiping claws.

It took us several minutes to disentangle ourselves and when we did, I wanted to immediately lie back down. The damage seemed inordinate, given the one small moment of the actual collision. Half the stall had collapsed, oysters, paper plates and napkins strewn about.

When the cat finally managed to free itself from the basket, it sank its claws into both my forearms and I winced, stepping straight into the embrace of the cat owner. Giving me an involuntary hug, she started to laugh and, still laughing, took control of the situation.

'Oh, do be quiet, Hughie,' she said to the stall owner. 'And you too.' She bundled the cat back into the basket, spitting and hissing, and tied the handle at the top.

'Should have done that earlier. So sorry about the scratches. I'll get you fixed up in a mo. It's all my fault really, Hughie, so stop being so cross.' She gave the irate man a smile and Phoebe, her face red and smudgy with the dust from the road, hurriedly bent down to retrieve the scattered oyster shells. 'I'm so sorry,' she said. 'Of course, I'll pay for the damage.'

'Nonsense,' said the woman firmly, 'this isn't even an official slot, right here in front of my door. Hughie was just trying to make a few quid with the morning's catch.'

She collected the two spindly posts that had held up the awning and together we manhandled them back into place. The canopy was beyond repair, but Phoebe unearthed a few safety pins to patch up the worst holes, and then tied it to the posts with the seashell necklaces she'd purchased on our way here.

'I like it.' The woman stepped back to survey the repair work. 'A maritime theme, Hughie. Come on.' She gave us a wave over her shoulder. As Phoebe disappeared after her, I stopped to press a twenty-pound note into Hughie's hand, then followed them, holding up my bloodied forearms.

At the end of the main street where it met the harbour, we came to a stop. Here, as everywhere, people were milling about, and the woman pulled me behind a flower stall where a teenager was hopping in place. 'Finally,' she said accusingly. 'I need the loo.' She dashed off.

'Thanks, Kate,' the woman shouted after her, then smiled at two customers bent over the lavender pots. 'Hello, there. Let me know if you need any help.'

She held up my forearms. 'Ouch. And it's not even my cat, it belongs to my mother, but it has taken an unfortunate liking to me and keeps appearing in my kitchen, eating anything it can put its paws on. Now, let's have a look.'

She briskly dabbed at the cuts on my left arm, cleaning off the blood, then wrapping a handkerchief around the worst part. Across the wooden table, one of the customers held up a pot of lavender. 'How much for this?'

'Five pounds for the medium ones, ten for the big one with the bow. Twenty for the ones on the floor,' she rattled off with another encouraging smile. The customer drew in a scandalised breath and put the pot down, picking up a tiny sheaf of wheat bound together with twine, examining it closely. The woman gave her a dark look, then rolled her eyes at me. 'Tourists,' she mouthed. 'I'm Fiona Hawker, by the way.' She was small and neat looking, with a round face, short curly hair and red cheeks, like a Russian doll. I smiled back, patting my wrapped-up forearm.

'Thanks so much. I'm Addie Harington, and this is—'

'Phoebe Roberts. So nice to meet you,' Phoebe chimed in. 'I'm sorry about the oyster stall. If there's any way we can help *Hughie*? Or was it *Harry*?'

'Excuse me, miss, how much for this?'

Fiona turned her smile on the woman still examining the tiny bundle of wheat. 'This one is two fifty, but there are other, smaller pots of lavender I could give you for three.' She bustled around the stand, retrieving a smaller pot, then wrapped a strawberry plant for a man with a huge backpack bulging with vegetables.

Phoebe busied herself behind the table, tidying away some wet wrapping, sweeping up a few dead plants, until Fiona came back around the counter. 'Have you lived here long, Fiona?' she asked, reaching for a brush to sweep some dirt from the table.

Fiona, counting her change into a box, looked taken aback at Phoebe's activity behind her stall, but then said, 'Twenty-five years, maybe? My dad moved here when I was five. But my mum was born here. She's really my stepmum, you know, and—' but before she could continue, there was another angry mewl, followed by the sound of the basket moving across the ground.

'Blasted cat,' Fiona muttered. 'Listen, could I ask you a huge favour? My mum has a stall down by the harbour. I'll just drop Trixie off with her and be right back. Change is in there, not a ton but should be enough. Fantastic. Help yourself to a drink and make sure you have a bun.' She gestured to a basket underneath the trestle table, not unlike the one hopping on the spot next to us, then picked up her irate charge and disappeared down the small lane leading to the harbour.

When she was gone, I rounded upon Phoebe. 'Honestly, you're practically moving in. I didn't know where to look.'

Phoebe wasn't remotely contrite. 'Well, now we're here. You were the one going on and on about being systematic. She is the perfect person to help us with Harry. Her mother's *from* the village, not just from around, that's promising.' She smiled happily. 'Maybe we can treat her to a coffee or something. Make up for the commotion, eh?' She dug me in the ribs cheerfully and I had to smile. She turned to another woman holding out a bunch of marigolds.

'Those are lovely. And how about one of these pots of lavender? I can give you both for six.'

When Fiona came back, Phoebe had sold five bunches of flowers, two of the little fiddly baskets and a big parcel of dried lavender, and Fiona beamed with pleasure.

'Gosh, you're doing infinitely better than me.'

There was a momentary lull in the steady stream of customers and Fiona bustled around the stall, putting out more flowers, rearranging the baskets. Moving around the counter, I spied her herbs.

'You've got a lot of sage,' I said.

'Yes, we're against the side of the hill, nice and dry. It doesn't like being soggy.'

'I know,' I said. 'My mum grew it in our back garden.'

I had a brief, piercing vision of my mother's grey eyes gleaming under her sun hat as she surveyed her herb garden, kneeling forward to crush a verbena leaf, stroking the silvery velvet leaves of her little sage bush to encourage it to hang in there, holding out her hands for me to smell. *Remind me, Addie, which one do you use for that green sauce Dad likes so much?* For an entire summer, I'd made that salsa verde almost every week until her supply of parsley and cress had run out. *And which do you think we'll need more, chervil or sorrel? I can never remember which is which. Here, give me a hand with the brush over there, will you, darling?*

I pushed my nose right into the sage plant and smiled to myself at the little memory, then, when I saw Fiona looking at me curiously, I said, 'I'll take one. Take it back for Andrew. He likes useful gifts.'

Fiona wrapped it for me in cheerful yellow paper with red dots. 'Make sure you don't overwater it. What brings you to my doorway anyway? You're not from around here, are you?'

'We're actually here to do a bit of research,' I said quickly before Phoebe had a chance to speak. Meeting Fiona's expectant gaze, I faltered slightly, 'For a book on academic families, a biography on—'

Phoebe graciously stepped in. 'On the rise and fall of upper class families after the war. One of our research objects is a family called Holloway, and our research shows that Elizabeth Sophie Holloway spent some time here in the fifties, possibly in relation with the Shaw family and a man called Harry. We have some correspondence that we wanted to fact-check.' She sounded so expert that I had to fight the urge to clap.

'Elizabeth Holloway? Hmm.' Fiona thought for a moment, then shook her head. 'But I wasn't born then, so there's no reason I should know anything about it, which isn't to say that someone else wouldn't remember her. Depends on how long she was here.'

Phoebe brought out the photo. 'That's her in the middle. And this is a man called Harry. Do you recognise any of them? They'd be much older now obviously.'

I could practically feel her holding her breath.

Fiona studied the photo, then handed it back to Phoebe, her regret obviously genuine. 'No, sorry. I wish I could help you.'

'And the Shaws, the family that lived at Hartland before it burned down, do you know anything about them?'

'Gosh, that was so long ago. I heard about the fire, sure, when I was little, but no one's lived there in decades. I tell you what, though, things are going to be slowing down in a bit and Kate is supposed to be back and finish off here while I sort out Mum's stall. I'll take you round to meet Pat. He runs the Ship Inn down by the jetty. He knows everyone. And if you need a room for tonight, he'd be your man.'

'Well, I think we're taking the last train back up tonight,' I started.

'But the pub sounds great,' Phoebe said firmly. 'Shall we meet there at, say, five?'

Chapter Twenty-Nine

It was quiet out, and dawn was only just starting to steal underneath the curtains when I woke, my arms wrapped around me against the cold. I pulled on the blanket but it wouldn't give and when I reached for my alarm on the right, my hand groped emptiness.

Dawn. Gulls. The sound of water. The Ship Inn.

I groaned and forced my eyes open. In the grey morning light, the hump next to me in the narrow bed was completely still. I eased my feet out from underneath the blanket we'd been sharing and found my clothes from last night. Creeping across the room, I stole out into the corridor and darted into the loo on the landing.

There weren't any signs of other guests when I came downstairs a couple of minutes later. The pub was dark and quiet. In the back, light and movement indicated that breakfast was under way, but I didn't want to linger. A lone raincoat hung on the pegs by the door and I eyed it doubtfully for a second, but it looked female and reasonably clean, so I pulled it on and opened the door.

Outside, dawn hung close to the ground and the lead-grey sky almost touched the surface of the water so that above and below blurred into a soft muted grey. The damp was cool but not unpleasantly so and the brighter light towards the east promised sun later on in the morning. Pat's marquee and beer benches stood slightly desolately amidst the debris from last night's post-market-day celebration. Leaving behind the Ship Inn and the houses shrouded in fog, I walked out on the breakwater jetty. It jutted straight out towards the Channel at a right angle, before turning sharply to cradle the harbour, facing another breakwater arm across the open water, this one with a lighthouse at the end. I took my time, skirting puddles swimming with gills and other fishy debris, picking my way between piles of rope and pollards. The closer I got to the open water, the windier it was and I huddled gratefully into my borrowed raincoat, jumping when a gull squawked and took off right next to me.

Images of last night flickered through my mind. Phoebe helping Pat in the beer tent, flashing me a smile as she handed out drinks, chatting animatedly to anyone within reach. The crowd of villagers, happy with the afterglow of a successful market day. The last rays of the sun sparkling on the waters of the harbour. The most delicious fried fish I've ever had, consumed on a step at the end of the street, listening to someone playing the guitar. Phoebe buying Fiona a drink in the pub. Buying me a drink when I suggested not going home after all but staying the night. Buying Pat a drink (in his own pub, for heaven's sake) when he made space for us in the tiniest maid's bedroom in the attic. Pushing my imminent future, my father's health and my mother's past to the very back of my mind and simply sitting back to watch my beautiful, tall twin sister be the life and soul of the party, buying drinks for everyone and waving to me occasionally as she talked about post-war realities with a happy, drunken gleam in her grey eyes. I hadn't had that much fun in a long time.

Out on the breakwater, I leaned against the wall. Light had started seeping through the clouds to illuminate the clear, glassy surface of the water, which moved and rippled around the boats protected inside the embrace of the harbour. Outside of it, the sea churned and gurgled restlessly, small bursts of wind throwing greyish-green masses of water and dirty foam across boulders and rocks nestling against the breakwater. I watched the water surging up towards me, then receding in a brief moment of calm, before rising again to break, hissing and spitting, below my feet. When the heave of the water started to reverberate slightly inside my stomach I turned away and sat down against the wall.

Not a single person had recognised my mother's name yesterday, despite Phoebe's insistent though increasingly incoherent questioning. At some point, the post-war reality story had been abandoned and she was quizzing people about the Shaws and any Harry in a radius of twenty miles and then the village's male population in general. Most people knew Hartland obviously, but like Fiona only as a distant part of village lore, the name of a house that had burned down thirty years ago, rather than any specific memories. People had nodded knowingly at the name 'Shaw', and one or two older men had commented on Abel's horses and told us about a grandmother who had worked there in the 1920s or a young girl sent to help during the war. But the Shaws' remote location coupled with their social status meant that even the older villagers couldn't dredge up much more than what we already knew from Phoebe's research.

'I knew you'd be out here,' a voice rasped next to me. Phoebe's face had a green tinge and her mascara had run into all the fine lines beneath her eyes, giving her a faint famine-victim look. She cleared her throat, tucking her hair back behind her ears, and gave me a wry smile. 'Clearing out the cobwebs?'

Her melodic voice was rusty and thick and surveying her I bit back a laugh. 'Speak for yourself.'

When I'd finally got her to go to bed last night, propping her up against the wall while I pulled back the thin floral bedspread, she'd fallen forward and sprawled across the bed still in her clothes, and even when I came back from the loo a few minutes later and tried to heave her over to make room for myself, she never woke up.

'God, I never drink this much. Don't know what came over me.'

'Uh huh,' I said, trying not to laugh.

She scrutinised the ground, then gave a hopeless look at the state of her trousers before sinking down, her back against the wall, looking towards the village. After a moment, I sat down next to her, my borrowed raincoat bunching up beneath my legs. I must have been out here for a while already because back on the quay the morning activity was already well under way. There were lights in the pub and people had started pulling covers off small boats. One man was scrubbing the side of his trawler. But out here, it was still quiet, the brightening skies punctuated by gusts of cool wind and the sound of gulls swooping along.

'Breakfast will be put out in a sec.' Phoebe broke the silence again. 'I suppose we should think about catching a train back up to London after that.'

She sounded subdued and when I looked at her she shrugged. 'I guess it was a silly plan trying to find him or to think that Harry is even him or that the man in the picture is Harry. It was all so long ago. Let's just wait for your dad to get better, then we'll maybe know more.'

'Oh, Phoebe.' I couldn't bear the disappointment in her voice. 'Let's at least ask around some more this morning before the train goes. We haven't spoken to the vicar, for example. Who knows, he might be ancient and remember the good old days when the peasants still paid their tithe up at the big house. And we did have fun last night, didn't we?'

She laughed croakily and nodded. 'What a party.' Then she groaned and held her head.

A gull was perched on the mast of a small boat bobbing right in front of us. Across the harbour, a window in the pub was thrown open, the glass catching the glint of the sun. I leaned back against the wall and turned my face upwards. In London, it had rained for so long that I'd practically forgotten what the sun looked like. Next to me, I heard Phoebe shift and groan at the cracking in her neck. There was the sound of a zipper opening and I heard her rustle around in her bag.

'Is aviation guy, what's his name, Greg, not a partygoer?' I asked.

She was silent for a while and eventually I opened my eyes. She was holding the copy of my mother's photo in her hand, looking at it.

'His name is Craig. And we broke up.'

'You did?' I sat up further, stared at her. 'But when we talked about him, wait, that was only a few days ago, weren't you still going out with him then?'

She looked up from the photo and scanned the harbour. 'He's not what I want,' she said. 'This . . .' she waggled her hand between me and her and the photo, 'made me realise that I don't want a guy who already has two kids from a previous marriage and doesn't want to start another family.' She paused. 'I want Charlotte and Henry and I want them now.'

'Oh-kay,' I said slowly.

'That day, after we talked at the cemetery, my telling you about Charlie and things, when I was sitting on the train back home I realised that I actually did want someone to steal my remote. Very much so. I went by his house and told him.'

'Just like that?'

'It wasn't easy.' She moved a bit, then leaned back against the wall. 'We all want to be settled, to have something to hold on to. But it's that panic of us having lost all that time together and with her. Like you said yesterday, of the years going by and just being towed along. I want to have a family of my own. I want what we, you and I, could have had growing up.'

I nodded, digesting this. 'But you don't have anyone to have these children with.' I sat up and looked at her. 'Or do you?' I wouldn't have put it past her to have got herself pregnant in the span of twenty-four hours.

'Oh, please.' She kicked at a pebble and it bounced towards the edge of the quay. 'It's so hard to find any half decent man, let alone a prospective family father. But if I can't find a man, like, literally, next week, I'll have to go for it alone. Test tube, one-night stand.'

'You've gone stark staring mad.' I shook my head. 'I'll be a test-tube auntie? Good god. I better start making home-made vegetable stock for the swede purées. Venetia is always going on about things like swedes and freezing breast milk. No nephew of mine is growing up on M&S ready meals.'

She laughed and tossed her hair back. 'I'm not doing so badly on M&S ready meals. But you hold on to your Andrew, let me tell you.'

'He's not "my Andrew", and I told you, I'm fine the way I am. With my sourdough starters. And I have other plans to make now, to open my café. It'll be a whole new era.'

'Sure. *I'll just get this little plant for Andrew,*' she mimicked. 'Could I meet him some time soon? Something tells me he's going to be around for a long time.'

'And something tells *me* that you two would get along great,' I said resignedly. 'I guess we could go for a drink together.'

She made a gagging noise. 'Please do not talk about drinking ever again. Come on, I need some coffee.'

She handed me the photo to hold as she heaved herself to her feet and shouldered her bag. I looked down at the water behind the three people, looked up, turned on my heels, looked back down.

'Phoebe!'

'What?' She was brushing at a stain on her trousers, muttering crossly to herself.

I was slowly looking around, then stopped, held up the photo.

'I think she was here,' I said. 'Look, Phoebe, I think the photo was taken right here!'

She frowned, turned, framed the air. 'Yes. And this could be that rusty bollard thing over there,' she said excitedly, gesturing out to the harbour.

'And that ring might be this reddish patch here? And those posts, don't they look like the ones there, next to the wall?'

Keeping her back to the sea, Phoebe moved up and down the wall, framing the scenery again and again, checking it against the picture until, arms aloft, she said, 'The sun would have been right behind the camera because they're squinting so much.'

Suddenly, I felt fully awake. 'Maybe it was even early morning like now because look, the sun is coming in from the water, behind the wall.'

We looked at each other.

'She was here,' I said in wonder. 'In 1958, she stood *right here*, right where we're standing now.'

I felt emotion welling in my throat and I blinked and took Phoebe's hand and held it very tight. As leads went, it wasn't spectacular; after all, we had been working off a picture labelled Tideford Cross, so it shouldn't have come as a great surprise to find the spot in Tideford Cross where the picture was taken. But after days of searching for a new understanding of her, on the heels of an entire year trying to remember her properly, the fact that she had stood here forty-two years ago, on these cobblestones beneath our very feet, gave me an odd sense of timelessness, as if all *three* of us were together right here, on a white-washed, sparkly, sunny morning by the sea; as if I'd only have to look a little harder, listen a little more closely, and I might see her there, hear her laughing, her beautiful hair tumbling across her face.

Limpsfield, 4 August 1959

I can hardly write with excitement and fear and nerves, and I haven't been able to for days now, fearful that it might not be true, that it might be something else entirely when it would be so very wonderful. And then I'm terrified, at what I did and what I know deep down is happening to me and will continue to happen for another six months.

When I first realised what it was, I didn't pay any attention to it. Everything has been so up and down, between Mum's death and discovering all this magic, it hasn't really been a regular monthly occurrence, but when I began to feel sick a few weeks ago, a constant, nagging nausea that came on the moment I opened my eyes in the morning, and when I almost fainted after class once, it started me thinking, until I came to the only obvious explanation. Even then, I wasn't sure at first because he'd said he would take care of everything.

Up until Purley, my understanding of 'everything' was rather naive and quite hazy, based purely on what Judy had told me and reading between the lines of Elizabeth Jane Howard, and, truth be told, I'm still not entirely sure what's gone wrong. Mum went too early for her to tell me what exactly 'everything' entailed, except for a most general (and rather unsatisfying) explanation. And then I found out exactly what it was in Purley and I was glad I did so, at least the lovely end of it, and it was so exciting and nerve-racking that I'd gladly relinquished control of all the other 'everything' to him.

Either way, even with my limited understanding I'm fairly sure what this must be, and because we haven't been together that often, what with him so busy lately, it is not hard to pinpoint the dates. I don't know what you do in a situation like this and I don't have anyone to ask, except Ellen, who seems knowledgeable about these kinds of things and might be a reliable source. What I do know is that I have to be absolutely certain before I tell him the news. There is really only one thing for him to do, but nonetheless I have to be sure.

I know, though, deep down I *am* absolutely sure, and I'm walking around once again in a permanent state of excitement and fear, because it is both wonderful and terrifying to think that I might be – a mother. I hope I'll know how to do that, be a mother. I don't have much experience of being close to someone in the first place because of the only two people I ever felt close to, one is dead and the other is – well, the other is lovely. So there is nothing to worry about. Nothing at all.

9 August 1959

Now that I know, it's suddenly completely obvious to me, the way my blouse fits differently each week – the buttons gape horribly in the middle – and my skirt seems to have become a bit uncomfortable. I started wearing a corset, which is horrid on any given day, but especially so now because it's difficult to breathe properly and it makes me sit up unnaturally straight so it won't dig into the small, hard, rounded bulge that's started showing around my navel. But I can't do it for that much longer because soon it won't fit anymore. Already, I worry that you can see it, that Father's eyes will soon fix on my waistline when we sit down for supper, with a horrible understanding dawning. Before then, long before then, I'll have to come to him with a promise and an engagement. I don't see John as often these days as I did in the winter and the spring, but I understand, he's very busy at work these days and Hartland takes up a lot of his time, so I've been carrying my secret – our secret! – around with me for some time now, waiting for the right moment to tell him.

10 August 1959

I pretended to be sick halfway through my day today. Mrs Phelps said she had thought I was looking a little peaky and to take care of myself, she really is ever so nice, and I went out to the train station, bought myself a ticket and went up to London – on the train! – to see a practitioner that Ellen had told me about in great secrecy. If I was married I could go to the clinic in Oxted, I'd be given vitamins and orange juice and the company of other women like me. But being who I am – at least who I am for the moment – I'm going to a doctor who isn't on Harley Street, she said, where the fancy doctors are, but a place near St Paul's Cathedral. No one would know who I was or ask too many questions, she said.

It wasn't so very bad, really. You had to go in the back door, and his hands were cold and he wasn't overly friendly, but I didn't care at all because seeing him and having him confirm it makes it all the more true! I asked him whether I needed to wait for a test of some kind, but he gave me a bit of a condescending smile that seemed to imply I wasn't the sort of woman to ask for a proper test, then said it was clear as day, that with the dates given I could assume to be about four and a half months along, maybe five. Congratulations, Mrs Smith. The woman who'd opened the door gave me a strange look when I left, but I gave her my brightest smile because it is warm and cheerful out there and I'm going to have a baby.

Out on the street I walked for a while, feeling somewhat adrift because everyone was hurrying in every direction and seemed to know what they were doing, all these secretaries and workers and typists, while I was here in my loose blouse and my skirt digging into my corseted waist and a long cardigan to cover it all up, trying very hard not to look like I'd stolen away for the day to confirm a surprise pregnancy at a back-street doctor's practice. I hadn't much liked the way his receptionist had looked at me. It was so knowing somehow, and disdainful and a bit haughty, and as I was standing there on the side of the road, watching the red buses trundle down the Strand, with people jumping off and on and a man hanging off the pole at the end and lifting his hat to me, I was squirming with anxiety because I knew, I did know, of course I did, even if I didn't know 'everything', that this wasn't quite how it was supposed to go. That I should be at the Oxted clinic, as me, not Mrs Smith who'd been secretly visiting hotels in Purley.

There was a phone booth just down the way on the corner, and I was looking at it for a long time as people hurried all around me to the places they knew they had to be. I wanted to talk to him, quite urgently now, just to hear his voice and be reassured. But it occurred to me that I had never before tried to reach him. He'd just always been there. I walked down to the phone box and stood behind the man waiting for the person inside to finish the conversation. More people came up behind me and I dug very reluctantly for some old pennies in my purse because I didn't much relish the thought of having to tell him, while a small queue might be forming outside the telephone box, that I was carrying his baby.

In the end, I left without doing anything at all. The man who was waiting gave me a curious glance and I knew I was blushing, that I was looking guilty almost, and I was convinced that he, too, saw me for what I was. I had to give myself a severe talking-to as I walked down towards St Paul's. It was fine, it would be fine. I just needed to wait for him, tomorrow or the next day. I had already carried the baby for weeks and months. Surely, I could wait another day or so to tell him, for him to make it all right?

I knew I probably should have gone home, that I was risking being found out by Father, but the dome of St Paul's was so close it was impossible to resist. St Paul's had stood when London was burning during the war. It had been a sign of hope, of a future for us all, Mum had said. She'd shown me a picture she'd cut out of the paper the year before I was born, which showed the great dome of the cathedral rising proudly through fire and smoke while all of London was devastated and frightened by the Blitz.

I walked up the steps, suppressing every single memory of going there with Mum just a few years ago, of her plans for a birthday outing that had never come to pass. I simply emptied my mind and went into the church as if I belonged, as if I wasn't a harlot at all but just any other mother who was looking ahead to a life with a baby. I dropped my old pennies into the collection box and walked right down the nave.

There I stood, under that beautiful cupola that Mum had always said was a gateway to heaven, finally allowing all the happiness and the excitement and this bright, bright future that would include my very own husband and my very own family to feel real.

Chapter Thirty

There was no way Phoebe and I could go back to London now. After a hasty breakfast, we collected our bags and my sage plant and I returned the coat to the peg by the door and then we made our way up to the village shop to enquire about the vicar and any other possible sources of information.

The shop was small and crowded with people getting their Saturday papers, and I decided to let Phoebe go ahead. She seemed to take up a lot of room inside, towering over the rickety shelves crammed with cereal boxes and chocolate bars. I watched her talking to a young man behind the counter, waving her hands around and sending the bar of neon light swinging from a particularly emphatic gesture. The young man gave a series of small nods, then shook his head and pointed to a fellow shopper, an older woman with a paisley scarf clutching a small box of teabags. I noticed the slightly forced smile on Phoebe's face as the older woman motioned for her to speak up, then flapped her hand impatiently for her to repeat it. Phoebe pulled out the photo and the woman bent to peer at it short-sightedly. I laughed to myself, because even from here, Phoebe was practically thrumming with impatience and hangover, then I scooted to the side until every inch of me was in the sun.

In this fresh, sunny place that smelled so deliciously of the sea and that had seen my mother walk out into the harbour forty-two years ago, being untethered wasn't actually all that intimidating. Without Grace waiting for me back home I could float away, anywhere, do anything, I could *be* anything. And without my mother's constant focus on me making something of myself it might be quite easy to do that very thing, because in the end, nothing about my mother had been the way I'd always assumed it was.

Suddenly, with an adrenaline surge that hit me like a brick wall, I remembered something else, oh god, something I'd blanked completely, something that meant – oh no – that my good friend, who didn't remotely deserve to be blanked, was now waiting for me in front of the 'perfect premises' with the seller. How on earth could I have forgotten that? I scrabbled for my phone, my face fiery-red and itchy-hot with guilt when I saw all the missed calls, because the last twenty-four hours had somehow slipped away from me and I'd meant to call him, I *should* have called him, and I was such a stupid shilly-shallier and—

'Addie!' I could hear traffic noise on his end and Andrew's voice, raised to be heard over the din, spilled into the fragrant morning air. 'Are you almost here? The seller has another person coming at eleven thirty and we're waiting for you.'

'Er, Andrew, so, you know – I'm really, really sorry,' I started.

'Can you speak up a bit? I can't really hear you,' he shouted into the phone.

'Well, that's – I'm so sorry, Andrew. I'm not in London. I can't come.'

'What? Can we just talk when you get here?'

'I'm not in London,' I said very loudly. 'I'm really sorry, Andrew, please don't hate me. I'm not coming.'

There was a pause and then Andrew gave a growl of irritation.

'Man, Addie. I thought we – where are you, then? Shall I make a new appointment?'

I could picture him standing on a Kensington side street, pushing his hands through his hair in that irritated snap he had when he was trying to keep calm. I slid off the wall, feeling another wave of guilt wash over me.

'I should have told you,' I said desperately, then, quickly, before I could chicken out, 'I quit Grace's.'

'Already? Wow, that's great. So then hurry up and—'

'But I can't go into business with you, Andrew. I'm really sorry.'

'Come on, Addie, it's all organised and I thought—'

'I'll explain everything tomorrow, okay? You'll understand. And, Andrew, I *am* really *sorry*.'

'Never bloody mind.'

He hung up without another word and I sagged against the wall and hung my head in shame, the loveliness of this sunny morning completely lost to me. Why on earth had I not taken a stand, told him right away? Instead, I'd dithered and stalled and just agreed to it all, the way I always did, hoping it would somehow go away.

In the shop, Phoebe was still talking. A woman wearing a big red hat with a wide brim that flapped over her nose squeezed by her to leave. She juggled her bags as she tried to open the door and I jumped forward to reach for the handle, but the young man was ahead of me.

'Goodbye, Mrs Sinclair.' He pushed open the door and bowed. 'See you tomorrow.'

The woman he'd addressed as Mrs Sinclair lifted her head, hat flopping in the breeze, and smiled in thanks. Her face was a mass of tiny weathered wrinkles but her eyes were a dark clear blue and her step was brisk as she walked down the street.

'Can I help you?' the shop assistant asked me, eyeing my red face and my wild hair slightly suspiciously.

'Just waiting.' I shoved my phone back into my pocket.

The bright red hat came back into view further along the street leading to the cliffs, floated up the stairs to the top and bobbed along towards the coast path. Behind me, the shop door pinged again and Phoebe came out, clutching a bag of scones and two bottles of Coke, and she didn't look happy at all.

'And?' I took the scones off her.

'Nothing,' she said, unscrewing the top of a Coke bottle.

'Had enough caffeine for the morning?' I said, watching her drain half the bottle in one go.

'Why?' She rubbed her cheeks and slapped them, then pulled back her hair more securely to fix a few stray strands into her ponytail.

I pointedly looked at the tremor in her hand, but she was already scanning the street, clutching a piece of paper.

'No one knew anything new in that useless shop. The lady drew this for me, though, look, here's the church, she said the vicar would be doing the flowers about now, and apparently, there is a Mr McEllen, who covers some of the stuff for the *South Coastal Observer* but he's out of town today. No one here seems to know anything at all, to be honest. We'll just go back home, don't you think?'

'We're here now,' I said firmly. 'Let's go and check in with the vicar at least. And find Fiona's mum, she might know something and—'

But the rest of my words were drowned out by excited yipping and yapping and by a sudden crow of delight from Phoebe, who had let go of my arm and dropped down to crouch over a tiny dachshund.

'Oh, how precious, how sweet,' she crooned.

Following the dog was the woman with the big hat who'd been at the shop earlier, Mrs Sinclair. The shopping bags were gone now, replaced by a worn dog lead attached to the dachshund, who was excitedly sniffing the bottom of the wall in front of the shop, then Phoebe's outstretched hands. Woofing happily, it allowed Phoebe to pat its head.

'What's its name?' Phoebe asked, scooping the little dog up on to her knees to bring its nose right up to hers, then turning to the woman, who gave her a long look before she answered. 'Scully. It's a she.'

Attached to the dog by the leash, the woman had to stand right next to Phoebe, but looking at her, I realised that she was actually straining away from her, tilting her upper body back in the direction she had come, with a strange expression on her face.

'Phoebe,' I said, watching her fluff up the dog's ears and tickle her under the nose. 'We should probably let – Mrs Sinclair, is it? I heard the shopkeeper say it earlier – be on her way.'

The dog gave a series of short joyful barks and rubbed her head against Phoebe's hand. The woman tugged on the leash, her eyes still on Phoebe's face.

'I just love dogs,' Phoebe said, rather unnecessarily. 'I always wanted one myself but I'm away too much. '

As if in answer, the dog offered Phoebe a tiny paw to shake.

'And she already knows tricks?' Phoebe said delightedly. 'What a smart doggie you are, yes, I mean you, you gorgeous fluff ball.'

Feeling that things were getting distinctly out of hand I raised my eyebrows at Mrs Sinclair, who made a face. 'She's a bit overenthusiastic sometimes.'

I was trying to decide whether she meant the dog or Phoebe, when she spoke again. 'I heard you ask about the Shaws?'

'Yes?' I said quickly.

'What exactly is it that you're looking for?'

Phoebe straightened, much to the dog's chagrin, and took a deep breath, but before she could launch into one of her wild speeches, I put my hand on her arm.

'We're doing some research on upper class families after the war. We're looking for information on the Shaws and, specifically, we're trying to track down a woman who was here, possibly visiting them between 1958 and 1960.'

'A woman?' Mrs Sinclair repeated. The little dog was snuffling softly round our feet.

'Her name was Elizabeth Holloway,' I said. She had her head down, pulling Scully away from Phoebe's shoes so I couldn't see her eyes, but at my mother's name she twitched, a tiny but unmissable movement, and there was something around her mouth, a tightening that made me take a step towards her. 'Do you happen to remember her being here?'

Mrs Sinclair bent to scoop up the dog. 'No, I'm sorry, I don't know her,' she said. 'It's just, I haven't heard the Shaws mentioned in years and it seemed strange that someone would come looking for them, after they'd been gone for so long. They didn't mix much with—'

'The village, yes, we know,' Phoebe said quickly. 'But anything you remember—'

'I'm sorry, I don't think I can help you. Good luck, though.'

She gently spilled the little dog back on to the floor and started moving on, up the road.

She hadn't reckoned with Phoebe, however.

'I'm so sorry to be persistent.' She hurried after the woman, not sounding remotely sorry at all. 'But did you know the Shaws personally? We've been trying to find someone who did. All we're looking for is a bit of information.'

'I'm sorry.'

The woman picked up her pace, clearly regretting having stopped to talk to us at all, and quickly disappeared up a steep staircase and around a corner, bumping the little dog up the steps on its hindquarters. Scully barked, looking back imploringly at Phoebe, who was gaining on them. I threw myself up the hill after her, clutching my bag and the sage plant. We'd almost reached the last of the houses when the woman stopped in front of a small, grey cottage. Scully ran into the back of her brown lace-up shoes, then flopped on to her belly, her tongue hanging out. Phoebe stopped outside the front gate, her hand reaching for the handle. The woman looked rather forbidding now, unsmiling, and Phoebe pulled back her hand quickly. I crossed the last few metres, stopping next to Phoebe.

'We're really sorry to bother you,' I said breathlessly, 'we're just trying to connect a few dots. Elizabeth Holloway visited here in 1958. She died last year and, you see, she left a few, er, questions unanswered—'

Suddenly, despite the gate separating us, the woman's face was very close to mine, so close that I had to lean back. She spoke, slowly.

'Liz is dead?'

Chapter Thirty-One

I took a step back and the woman leaned towards me, her body half-way across the gate. Then she reached out for Phoebe, who was right next to me, took hold of her arm.

'Is it true? Liz, she's gone?'

Phoebe seemed completely dumbfounded. 'Yes, she is, but what—'

'I have to go,' the woman said faintly. She turned, scrabbled in her pocket. I saw the gleam of a key as she fumbled with the lock, heard the click of the handle.

'No, please,' I said, panting from both effort and surprise, and I touched her sleeve. 'If you know anything, it would mean so much to us. We're not looking for anything terrible, I'm so sorry about this book palaver. The truth is, well—'

Phoebe had caught up with me and I could feel her breath on the side of my face. The woman had her back to us, one foot poised to step through the door. The dog, clearly excited to be home, threw herself on to a water bowl off to the side to lap noisily.

'You see, Elizabeth was my mother.' There was a soft exhalation from Phoebe. 'Our mother.'

The moment seemed to stretch endlessly. The morning sun had burned off the last of the fog and only a few wisps of cloud were racing along a blue sky. An old brick wall to the side of the little front garden sheltered clumps of flowers. The woman had her hand on the doorknob. Eventually, her shoulders slumped, and she stepped into the house, turning to hold the door open.

'You should come in, I suppose.'

Inside, we hovered uncertainly as Mrs Sinclair hung up her jacket and disappeared through a door at the back. After the brilliance of the sun, it was dark in here and I shivered. Sticking her head back out, the woman motioned to the small sitting area off to the right.

'Make yourselves comfortable.'

I looked at Phoebe. She still had a dazed look on her face and meekly sat down on one of the stiff-backed sofas. Craning my neck, I could see the woman moving around in what seemed to be the kitchen, then the sound of the back door opening and the clink of bottles. Phoebe had scooped up Scully and was stroking her, mechanically pulling the soft ears through her hands over and over again.

The cottage wasn't large. It seemed to have been two small sitting rooms once, but the walls had been knocked down to create more space. The sofas were tucked next to one of the small, deep windows and beams of sun were funnelled sharply on to the glass coffee table, picking out the chestnut hue in Phoebe's hair and the white skin on her hand stroking the dog. To the left of the door was a dining table and a few ornate-looking chairs, wedged so firmly underneath that it didn't look like they were used much.

I set down my plant and bag, then prowled around the room, from the sofas to the shelves to the table, until I forced myself to stop by the large fireplace against the back wall. I noticed only one other heater and briefly wondered how on earth the woman could heat this place when gale-force winds were buffeting the coast. Paintings were scattered on the walls but there were only a few photos. Two children. A small family in front of a log cabin. A black and white shot of a family in front of a big house, in which I recognised a younger-looking version of Mrs Sinclair standing in front of a man who had to be her father. None of the other faces meant anything to me, not that they should, but I studied them nonetheless, hoping for a random spark of recognition. Then I went on, trailing my fingers over the book spines, peering up at the heavy oil paintings on the low-slung walls, the knick-knacks and figurines littering the surfaces. I wasn't an expert, but I reckoned that most of the paintings were fairly valuable. There was a beautiful silver bowl holding a small selection of shells and rocks pounded smooth by surf and sand, and an ancient china cabinet crammed with delicate plates and old platters.

I had just picked up a set of silver brushes on the small desk in the far left corner when a quiet cough from Phoebe made me drop them and spring forward, relieving Mrs Sinclair of the tray. She spent a minute laying out the tea things, straightening the silver spoons, fussing over the big pot, turning it until the worst of the tarnishes were pointing away from us.

'I very rarely have guests,' she said apologetically, pushing the jug of milk and the sugar bowl towards us. 'Please help yourselves to a rock cake.'

Eyeing the small, greyish lumps I decided to decline but gratefully accepted a cup of tea. For a moment, we kept busy with milk and sugar and I was forcibly reminded of our afternoon with Mrs Roberts. Next to me, Phoebe sat with her eyes fixed on the woman and when I looked down I saw Scully vibrate slightly beneath her trembling hands, which the little dog seemed to enjoy because she'd gone to sleep, only occasionally moving her ear.

Following my gaze, the woman said, 'You're welcome to put her back down. She does have a bed, even if she ignores it most of the time.'

'It's fine,' Phoebe said, clutching the dog closer. The woman looked at both of us in turn, studying our faces.

'You're Liz's daughters.' It wasn't a question. Her face was set in tense lines that ran along her forehead and dug deep groves around her mouth.

'I'm Adele, and this is Phoebe,' I said.

She nodded. Now that her hat was gone, I noticed her eyes, dark blue and unblinking. She was really rather handsome, but in a statuesque, no-nonsense way, with square limbs, a robust face. The web of fine wrinkles was more pronounced in the subdued light but you could tell that her skin must have once been wonderful and even though her clothes were old and faded, they were cut well and suited her frame.

'When is your birthday? Your birthdays, I mean?' She spoke very slowly and, I got the impression, with some effort. When I said 'the fourteenth of February 1960', I heard her inhale, almost as if she'd known the answer before I gave it.

'We're twins,' I added.

She breathed back out then and all the tension left her face, making it sag and crumple.

'Twins?' she said somewhat shakily, picking up her cup and holding on to it, her eyes resting once more on Phoebe. 'I can't believe it. So that's – oh god.'

Mrs Sinclair listened to my account of what had happened without a word.

'But when we found the notes and the photo, we put two and two together and decided to come and look for her here.'

'Notes?' Mrs Sinclair finally spoke. She sat straight in her seat, grasping her elbows with each hand.

'Yes, from someone called Harry to my mother, asking her to meet up.'

I reached for my cup. The teaspoon clanged against the saucer and Scully lifted her head. The sun had moved a tiny bit, throwing a shadow over Mrs Sinclair's mouth and chin.

'The notes,' she said. 'Do you have them? Here?' Her voice was tight and she pressed out the last word with some effort. Phoebe frowned, pulled up her bag, found her notebook and carefully extracted the notes. She was about to read the few sentences when the woman held out her hand.

'May I?' she said. 'Please?' Phoebe hesitated slightly but then handed them over and Mrs Sinclair reached across to the side table for her glasses.

It couldn't have taken her long to read the notes but she held on to them for a moment until she finally shuffled the little cards back together then put them down on the table. When she took off her glasses, the guarded expression on her face had given way to something else entirely. I scooted uneasily into my seat.

'What is it that you want to know?' she said.

'Phoebe thinks, and well, I do too, that there is a possibility that Harry is our father.'

Mrs Sinclair's head snapped up. 'Your *father*?'

'Yes, well, that's what we think,' I said defensively.

'Why on earth do you think that Harry is your father?'

Next to me Phoebe leaned forward in her chair, spilling the dog on to the ground and opening her mouth for the first time since we entered the cottage.

'Do you know him? How do you know he's not—'

'I know,' she said flatly. 'Because *I* am Harry.'

Limpsfield, 13 August 1959

On this day last year, my mother died. It's also my birthday and once again I woke on the morning of my birthday too full of possibility for the world to tolerate, once again I was feeling things I clearly should not be feeling, not today, not when my mother died 365 days ago.

By the day's end, however, it was all over. It shouldn't have come as a surprise maybe, but still I marvel that it is possible, once again, to fall so far in such a short time. To go from St Paul's and that beautiful cupola with its swirling, bright paintwork and the sun coming in through the little windows, feeling on top of the world with thrill and possibility. And then to hear, with a certainty as absolute as my mother being dead and gone, that that future was never going to happen.

Because he's married, he was engaged to be married even before he first came to see me, and he got married this summer, and I never knew, never had an inkling because if I had, I would never have done what I did. I would never have allowed myself to feel the way I did.

When I met him and told him about the baby, I knew that my eyes were shining and my whole body was waiting for him to take me into his arms and push a ring on my finger, and whisk me off to Hartland, or somewhere far away from Limpsfield, any place, I didn't care, as long as it was warm and sunny, and we'd play with our baby and take the train anywhere we wanted and live happily ever after.

How could I have been so stupid, so unbelievably naive, not to question him more about his life outside our 325 steps across the square and our furtive hours at the Purley hotel. How had I not seen our relationship for what it was, tiny fragments that to me meant everything because I didn't have much else, and to him were only that, fragments on the outskirts of a whole other life, a life full of a grown-up relationship, a commitment to wife and family and Hartland.

It wasn't easy for him to tell me, I could see that at least, and he looked wretched when he did, guilty and wretched and helpless and even a bit pathetic. I had never seen him helpless, only ever smiling and confident, everything coming to him quickly, falling into place with obliging ease. But when he spoke of Hartland and family money troubles and his marriage of convenience that had saved the house and his parents, that had given the Shaws a future, he was mumbling and squirming. He was ashamed.

I can never give the Shaws a future. Not when I am not even really part of their present but an interloper in this glamorous, expensive, grown-up world, where married men take seventeen-year-old girls to hotels in Purley, say they have 'everything' in hand and then leave them stranded with a baby.

So in the span of just a few days, I have become a danger to him, a threat to his convenient marriage, because for him there is no way out of it, not even with me wanting him nor a baby on the way needing him. He says he's loved me ever since last summer, that I was so different from the carefully dolled-up and artificial women around him all day. I was real and alive, I felt things so much more than they did, I understood how things really were. He says he was helpless against it, even when his father told him to stop, that he finally had to come and see me, that he loves me even now in spite of it all.

I don't know what I believe. Maybe he did feel all those things and maybe on the other end of that love, there was me: eager to escape, so desperate for that small ray of light piercing my sadness after Mum died that I would have believed anything. I was hungry to be loved at any cost.

Looking back now, I wonder if the signs weren't obvious all along if you knew where and whether to look, from overhearing Abel's voice in the stables that day, all the way to realising I had never once phoned him, had never written to him, had hidden him away between the pages of my diary in the back of an old vase with dried flowers. Had my need for secrecy and illicitness conveniently masked his need for discretion, had it all suited him just fine? Either way, it doesn't matter whether he did love me then or does now, because he is not prepared to take on me or the baby. He wants me to get rid of it. He's afraid someone will find out and that it would be the end of his marriage and the end of Hartland. He told me there were ways to do it, even now at this late stage. Take hot baths with mustard powder and drink gin or shower yourself with a special soap. Everyone did it, he said, so much so that there were women out there who helped women like me. He was red in the face and guilty, because those knitting-needle women are criminals and he knows it perfectly well. And how dare he say that, 'women like me', how can he stand there and belittle what we had, to take no responsibility whatsoever? It made me happy, in an awful, bitter way, to tell him that I wouldn't. I could never do that, regardless of whether it's a crime, regardless of what my life is going to be from here on. How could I possibly come out from last year's cloud of dying and illness and death, to get rid of this new life, something that's all mine? I may not have much reason to believe in God's wisdom these days, but the part of me that does believe and that has grown up for eighteen years believing, that part knows that I cannot and will not do this. Mum wouldn't approve of what I'd done in the hotel in Purley and my face burns when I think about what she would make of my situation now. But I do know, in my heart of hearts and with absolutely certainty, that she would never have wanted me to get rid of this baby.

And then I went up the steps to the bus and sat down behind the driver and drove off into the night, feeling like something had broken inside me. When Mum died, there was a constant ache that never went away, a fine thread of yearning and grief and remembering, aching nostalgia like an insistent high-pitched whine you cannot escape from. When I heard the word 'married', it was altogether different. It was like a punch in the stomach, deep and leaving me dizzy with its impact and disoriented with shock. Sitting on the bus and for the very first time not looking back as it pulled away, I felt like my insides had torn clear apart, leaving jagged edges that pushed the pain even deeper, past the baby, until I was doubled over, willing the bus ride to go on forever, because at the other end of it I would have to get out, walk home and find a way to tell my father in the span of seventeen and a half minutes that I was pregnant with a married man's baby.

Chapter Thirty-Two

'*You* wrote these?' I said incredulously. Harry, to me, was a tall man falling backwards on the breakwater, not this square woman with brownish-grey hair and very red hands.

'I used to be Harriet Shaw, although I don't think anyone here knows that because I took my maiden name back when my husband died and I moved here. When I was young, I went by "Harry", one of those silly hockey-sticks abbreviations from boarding school that stuck like glue. I quite liked it, actually, it made me seem a lot more jolly than I was.'

She opened her mouth again, but Phoebe stopped her. She had the photo in her hand, held it out and shook it.

'But look at this, here, this man. Who is this man?'

Harriet Sinclair took the photo and looked at it for a long moment. Scully went back to sleep and outside, a group of ramblers walked by on their way to the coast path. What I'd seen in Harriet's face a minute earlier was back and had shifted slightly, a combination of anguish and uncertainty and reluctance. But even as I watched, she was pulling herself together, smoothing out her expression, and when she spoke again, her voice was low and controlled.

'I haven't seen this in a long time. Yes, he's your father. You're right. But his name isn't Harry, it's John, John Shaw, my husband. And this,' her finger pointed to the sensible-looking girl on the left, her face shadowed by a giant sun hat, 'this, believe it or not, is me. I always liked wearing hats.'

Harriet Sinclair reached for the tea, poured Phoebe another cup and, without asking, added sugar.

'Hartland belonged to John's parents. I didn't live there for very long, less than a year. I had a flat up in London but then, well . . . I'd known John for ages before we got married. I'm from Somerset originally, I went to school in the Chilterns, close to John's school, and we knew many of the same people, spent weekends in various country houses or in London. I didn't ever think we'd be a couple, although I was quite smitten with him for most of what I can remember. You couldn't not be, he was incredibly easy to fall in love with – charismatic, vivacious, sure of himself, and when he looked at you, you always felt like he'd singled you out among all others. The Shaws had had a hard time during the war and took a long time to pick themselves back up after Christopher, John's older brother, died in forty-five. He'd only been nineteen.'

Next to me Phoebe rustled and when I took a sideways look, I saw that she had sat forward.

'But that summer,' Harriet tapped the picture, 'the summer of 1958 was absolutely glorious. I was working in my father's business, he was a wool merchant; John had just come back from Cambridge, was due to start at his uncle's bank in London in the autumn. The Shaws had a big house party staying at Hartland for the summer. My mum, who was a good friend of Janet Shaw's, took my sister Beatrice and me to stay, and friends of John's from school would join in too. Janet loved having the house full; she loved young people. I think she found it a bit quiet down there in the summer, too much time to think about Christopher, too many memories. And here was one of those summers that you'd remember forever, where you couldn't possibly stay sad. The skies were blue and even if there was the occasional foggy morning, you'd simply sleep it away. Golden days, an endless string of them, to be filled with activity or laziness. There was a real sense, that summer, that we were all on the cusp of things, that after this things would change, we girls would work and eventually marry and the boys would become terribly serious in their jobs and we'd all be too grown-up to just hang around and play. But for this one summer, we didn't have to think about the future and the evenings were warm and we were sitting on the Hartland terrace, watching dusk fall on their beautiful garden, and knew that another perfect day was waiting for us tomorrow.'

Her eyes shone with the memory and for a split second she looked young and happy. But when she saw our expectant faces, she seemed to remember why we were there and just as quickly the vitality and illusion of youth faded, until she was once again a handsome, square-shouldered woman with greyish-brown hair.

'Of course, nothing that good will ever last. I didn't know much about it until my father came and talked to me, but the Shaws were already deep in financial trouble. Abel's horses were expensive to keep and Janet was addicted to clothes, jewellery and parties. Hartland was costly to run and they still maintained a London flat, too. Janet was lovely, she really was, but she was too generous, spent money faster than it came in, was up in London, running up huge amounts with her glitzy friends. So,' she smiled slightly, 'when my mother arrived that summer, she and Janet Shaw started talking about the possibility of my marrying John.'

She saw my surprise and gave me a wry grin. 'Hard to believe that this was only forty years ago, I know, but it wasn't so very odd back then. Parents wouldn't necessarily force you to marry but they'd be quite happy for their children to be strategically aligned if it suited all round. They didn't say anything to me straight away, but they were laying plans in the background and when I first heard of them a few months later, I certainly didn't mind at all, because being married to John seemed to me then the most wonderful and exciting thing. I would have loved for it to have been his idea, I suppose, I didn't much like it being tied to our money, but there were worse things and if I got John in the bargain, so much the better.' She shrugged, played with the handle of her teacup.

'Then, one day, about a week or so into our stay, Liz arrived. Constance was my godmother. She and my mother had been good friends, although we hadn't seen her in ages because she was very ill with cancer, had been in and out of hospital for a while, and finally had to be readmitted to hospital when it was clear that she was going to die before too long. Liz had had a very hard time with her mother's long illness and Constance didn't want her there in those final weeks, so she'd spoken to my mother and asked if Liz could join me for the summer.

'Janet and Abel were very generous, and hospitable to a fault. Of course she could stay. The more the merrier. And I think Janet, having lost her son, could relate to Liz more than the rest of us could. So there she was, fresh out of school and a lot younger than us all.' She gave me a half-smile. 'I'd met her once before, when she was twelve, maybe, quite lovely then and very clever and completely unselfconscious. She was a funny thing, really. George Holloway was very strict with her. She was an only child and she must have spent so much time with only her mother for company that she was quite grown-up in her manner. She had none of the awkward silliness that girls often get in puberty. You could tell that she was changed by her mother's illness, because she was a lot quieter than when I'd last seen her. Not shy necessarily, but – wary, I think. Waiting for life to deliver the ultimate blow. Janet was worried because Liz was by herself so much, always slipping off to walk alone in the garden or in the library picking out books. We all had instructions to draw her out, to make sure she had company and wouldn't be left to be sad about her mother. I went for walks with her sometimes, because my mother knew her mum so well, but I didn't force myself on her. I think things at home were very hard for her and I could understand that she needed time to recharge.'

I frowned. That did not quite match what I remembered of my mother at all, her quickness, her impatience. But it also didn't sound so totally different from the way she guarded her privacy and her freedom, only that Harriet saw her solitude as a need to recharge, rather than straining away from domestic burdens as I'd always assumed. I felt a bit ashamed to have grudged her that solitude, because, after all, that overriding need to be alone was almost exactly how I felt, after any busy weekday in the kitchen.

'Constance was wonderful. She was an old school friend of my mother's, who'd always said she couldn't fathom how on earth dry-as-bones George Holloway had managed to get Constance up the aisle because they were so very different. She was well educated, funny, warm, clever. He was terribly old-fashioned – about women and girls in particular – wouldn't let her work, didn't want Liz to go to university, kept them rattling around in that house in Limpsfield. And he certainly can't have had the first idea of how to deal with a young girl who was about to lose a beloved mother because Liz was devastated and hadn't wanted to come to Hartland at all. She told

Janet once that she worried all the time that something would change at home, and it would happen too quickly for her to go back and say goodbye. "A change at home", that's what she always called it. I think George didn't like her talking about dying, because . . . well, I haven't the faintest idea why but George *was* a bit strange.'

I shook my head, feeling the lump in my throat expand and my eyes sting. 'It sounds awful,' I said. '*He* sounds awful.'

'Yes,' Harriet said. 'But the stay at Hartland seemed good for her. She came out of her shell as the days went on, and she was so excited by all the things that we completely took for granted, like going out on the boat, the gardens, the abbey ruins. It was quite sweet. You'd think she was never let out of the house back at home. This was a really nice day.' She tapped the photo. 'A few of us had gone out on the little boat they kept down here in the harbour. Felicity had brought a camera and we were goofing around with it, just down along the end of the harbour wall. Bea almost fell into the water, she was such a klutz.

'They were all very taken with Liz. John and my sister Beatrice, and John's friends, my parents, and Janet, because she was so small and pretty and she seemed so sad at first and then so obviously charmed by Hartland and all that we did. People fell over themselves to take her under their wing. John was no exception. I was jealous, of course I was, even though John and I were only friends at that stage. Liz and I couldn't have been more different. I was more of a serious person, terribly sensible. She was so self-contained and alert and not precocious at all. She drew people to her even if it was clear that she wanted to be by herself. I was just too dull and pondering.'

I made a sympathetic noise because I knew what she was talking about when it came to measuring up to my mother, but Harriet shrugged philosophically. 'I'm way too old to worry about being interesting these days. Anyway, I did tell myself that it was only for the summer, that we were all going to go back to London eventually. Liz was just a teenager, barely seventeen. We were in our mid-twenties, living a whole different life. I didn't think it would be an issue at all.'

She raised her eyebrows at me and I looked over at Phoebe, who hadn't made a sound since Harriet started talking.

'Then it was her birthday and Janet had planned a surprise party in her honour. We'd put on all Bea's records and were dancing and drinking, smoking those little French cigarettes we were all mad about. One moment John was there, and the next he wasn't. I was walking around and trying to dodge John's cousin Bert, who was just this awful creep we had to put up with for the summer. Afterwards, I sometimes wonder whether he was actually following them, because he really quite liked Liz. Either way, he was the one to see them first and held me back to make sure I saw them too. And there they were, among the trees.' She stopped. 'I saw John kissing Liz and she was kissing him right back, reaching up to put her arms around his neck. She was small, you see, and he was tall. Like you,' she nodded at Phoebe with a tight smile. 'You're so like your father, it's quite shocking. Except for the eyes. John had the bluest eyes, dark blue, almost black. But the rest of you – when I saw you in the shop earlier, heard you asking about Liz, I just *knew. You're* more your mother.' She smiled at me somewhat shakily, dragging her hand below her eyes. 'How could I ever forget that hair?

'They didn't notice me; they were looking at each other, focussed only on each other, to the exclusion of everything else. Bert was keen to spy on them, but I was mortified. Nothing had been spelled out about John and me, so no one would have known, but John certainly knew what our mothers were cooking up. I pulled Bert back with me before he could say anything and let them know we'd seen them, which would have been beyond humiliating. We ran back and I fell and cut myself on a branch – here, I still have a scar.' She held out her hand and we both bobbed our heads mutely to acknowledge the thin silver line on the side of her palm.

'Next morning, Liz wasn't there. It turned out there'd been a message from her father early that morning. Her mother had taken a very sudden turn for the worse and passed away in the night.'

Phoebe and I gasped in unison.

'So it did happen,' I said bleakly. 'She didn't get the chance to say goodbye.' A sob caught in my throat and got stuck there as Harriet continued.

'I didn't see her again. It got to be winter, and at some point I heard that she was doing a secretarial course. She was still living with George obviously, that's what girls did till they got married.'

She paused, took a sip of tea. 'And I didn't really care, because over Christmas, John and I became engaged, and so I had something so lovely to look forward to that I didn't give her another thought, really. The wedding was to be that very summer, June 1959. It was not quite the long engagement I'd wanted for planning the wedding and getting ready to move in together, but Janet and Abel had decided to move to South Africa for a few years and wanted us to live at Hartland in the interim. Janet and I really liked each other, but I don't know that she wanted to continue on as she always had at Hartland, paid for by our money. Anyway, John wanted to live there, so I moved out of the place I was sharing with Felicity after we got married—'

'But Liz,' I interrupted her. 'My mother, I mean. What happened to her?'

It felt odd to call her 'Liz' when she'd only ever been Elizabeth to us all or 'Lizzie' to my father, who'd pronounced her name with a slow, affectionate lilt. Somehow, I couldn't quite superimpose this sober, lost 'Liz' that Harriet was describing on the 'Elizabeth' or the 'Lizzie' I remembered. Outside, I could hear voices, children laughing, but across from us Harriet had paused and a long silence had fallen. Abruptly, she got up and went into the kitchen. I looked at Phoebe and she looked back at me.

'I'm almost afraid now—' I said.

'Me too,' she said, looking down at her hands. 'It's like watching a person walk into an oncoming train.'

Brighton, 18 November 1959

They seem to think that they've broken me: my father, the Charitable Sisters of Hope, who have very little inclination to be charitable or to give any hope to anyone at all; the horrible back-street doctor who my father dragged me to in order to see whether it would still be possible to undo what I'd done. The doctor, without ever spelling it out, hinted that it was uncertain because it was already too far gone, not to mention a crime punishable by law and, in any case, my father was too worried about the vicar, God and the state of his mortal soul to have something like this on his hands. So he's shipped me off to this place instead, which is meant for women like me, who're black with sin and are not allowed to be part of normal society again until they've duly repented and cleared themselves of the stains on their soul.

Am I broken? I don't know. I often still feel as if I am, like I did that day on the bus, reeling from a punch. But the jagged edges of my insides have solidified into more of a compact numbness, as if I'm moving slowly through a dense fog pressing down on me from all sides, exhaustion mingling with fear and hopelessness. I know I need to find the will to stand up to them before too long, that I need to put myself back together in order to know what I'm going to do.

I've blocked out most of the weeks and months after I caught the bus home and found my father and told him what had happened. I came right out with it before anything else happened or I could change my mind, because even after that steep plunge from happiness to the punch of betrayal I wasn't ashamed of it. I'm sorry for the way it's turned out but I'm not sorry for having wanted a small sliver of happiness. I'm not sorry about wanting to be loved and falling for the first thing that seemed real.

Father took the week off work and paced the house, alternately towering over me in a rage and trying to decide what best to do with me, how to punish me adequately and still keep it all secret; decide how and where I could have the baby and then come back here and be married off quickly and quietly without anyone knowing that somewhere out in the world, a secret Holloway child was walking off to a different family. I almost had to pity my father, because if he didn't know what to do with me while I was still whole and ready to be settled in respectability, then he certainly didn't know what to do with me when I was ruined. I think it was the vicar who suggested the Sisters of Hope, who were god-fearing and down by the coast and would know how to 'sort me out'. It was too early for me to go, though, they wouldn't take me till later, so I was sent to another woman, an acquaintance of the vicar's wife, where I sat in my room and waited, for weeks. It was there, in the middle of nowhere, with nothing to do and nothing to read, that that big, black, acid-bitter fog of desolation descended. Before Mum died I was sad and innocent and after Mum died I was heartbroken and yearning. But always, a part of me continued to believe in Hope, part of me was still able to move, even if it was aching and forever waiting for something else that life might have in store for me. When I finally left the woman to be transferred to the Sisters of Hope, I came out of my fog different again, bitter and disillusioned and hard.

The Sisters of Hope are housed in a big falling-apart Edwardian place, on the outskirts of Brighton, and if you are outside, you can smell the sea coming in on the wet autumn breeze. We're not allowed out much, though, so I haven't seen it, only heard the gulls and felt the wind on my face when I was standing by the window for a brief moment at the top of the stairs. The salty gusts bring back memories, unwanted and sharp, of a summer wind smelling of the sea, and although I push them away I secretly long for them too. Oh, the irony, that Father sent me here, so close to where it all began, so close to Hartland. He pestered me endlessly about who the baby's father was, intending no doubt to force him to do the honourable thing, which I already knew wasn't possible, so I refused to tell him, thinking of his uncomfortable twitching at the Hartland gates the day we arrived and not wanting to give him the satisfaction of blaming Mum for any of this.

There are maybe fifteen women here, but it changes, too, as they come and go after they've had their babies. We sleep six to a room, which are more like wards with narrow beds lined up on both sides and bedside lockers you cannot lock and a lumpy blanket that's no protection at all against the November chill. There are no curtains on the windows and at full moon the ward is lit with a ghostly blueish light that picks out the cracks in the cold stone floor, the empty fireplace, pregnant bellies pushing up beneath the blankets and one or two flaccid empty ones of those who have just returned from hospital.

Our days are all the same. We get up and do the chores we're assigned, then we have breakfast, a meal so terrible that it makes me almost long for my seventeen and a half minutes at Limpsfield, even if it means conversation with my father, simply to have warm porridge and sugar and the cream from the top of the milk. Here, we have cereal and sometimes toast, the crusts of which are given to the women who've just had their babies. And then, all day, every day, we do whatever they tell us to, which is cleaning and mending and working in the house to keep it from falling down around us. I've been assigned to clean the front stairs, all thirty-seven steps of the staircase that swings up from the entrance hall in a graceful wide arc towards the first floor, from where I sometimes imagine the daughters of the big house descending, amidst the bustling of Edwardian crinoline. 'You use the back stairs,' Matron told me in no uncertain terms. Because of who we are, a disgrace to the rest of society, a bedraggled heap of degraded and morally frail sinners, we're not allowed to walk up those front stairs. We use the back stairs, as befits us. Someone else cleans those back stairs, too, a girl from somewhere north of Bristol, who was made pregnant by an uncle during a family gathering, and has been sent down here by her parents. Then there's a woman, Rosie I think she's called, who was going to get married until she fell for a baby and her fiancé didn't stand by her, she's on laundry duty, and a girl who they whisper is carrying a mixed-black baby, the ultimate sin, is in the kitchen. They're not all girls, of course. A few are younger than me, then there are some nineteen-year-olds, even a twenty-four-year-old woman. But we're all called 'girls', maybe to show us that we're not women, only naughty girls who should have known better. The Sisters of Hope don't take any second offenders, so these are our first babies and none of us really knows what's in store for us. The girl from Bristol told me babies come out of your belly button and that she's worried about what happens to the hole in your stomach after.

I start the stairs at the very first step in the hall, scraping out dust and grime from every crevice with a metal pick, hunched awkwardly over my belly, which seems absurdly big given the sparse meals I get. I dust and wash each step, up and down, wipe each inch of bannister, up and down, then take the polish off each step, up and down, then re-polish each step. Up and down. Every day. It takes me all morning and some of the afternoon, because if it's any shorter one of the sisters comes and makes me start again. There are worse jobs, like the laundry, which smells of other people's sweat and carbolic soap and is overseen by a truly awful woman with small, mean eyes. I'd love to be assigned to the garden, just so I could smell that salty air, but I try not to let on how much because if they know you like something they won't ever let you do it. It's not meant to be enjoyable. It's a chance to work off the stain of our shame.

As places to be when your married lover has left you in trouble, I could have done worse. There is space to breathe and there are other women the same as me. Secretly, I actually think it is quite nice to be surrounded by people, to have someone to sit with and eat meals with, even though no one is terribly talkative. Almost anything is better than home, where Father would be relentlessly bearing down on me and my shame, where people would talk and whisper. Here, I'm just one of a ragtag bunch from different walks of life and different situations. We don't care all that much about each other, to be truthful, but we all still share this one thing, this enormous reality at the centre of our lives, and although you don't like every girl here and you don't bond with anyone, not truly, not lastingly, we treat each other reasonably well. We're all in the same boat, after all, a sisterhood of sinners united in the half-shadows of normal society from where we're expected to return and start over again, leave behind our mistake and move on. Because that's what you really do here: you finish breeding your baby, you deliver it at the hospital across town, then you come back and tend to it for six weeks before handing it over to a social worker or the family who've come out specially to pick up the new addition to their lives. That's how the world works: you're not told anything about 'every-thing', instead, you're let loose on a world of married men and hotels in Purley without any armour whatsoever, and then they make you give away your baby to another family, who take it in exchange for a donation to this falling-apart, crumbling house with its thirty-seven beautifully polished front stairs.

My father has only ever spoken of the baby in a roundabout, cryptic way, when he did speak to me at all, and in the miasma of despair I paid scant attention to what the doctor or the vicar or the social worker might have told me about what would happen. But only three days after I arrived, we were all herded into a room and instructed not to show ourselves at the window. We stood in the middle of the room in an awkward group and most of the younger girls had obediently turned their backs to the window while others studied the ceiling or the floor. No one talked. Something made me look over my shoulder, though. It wasn't a big room and I was clos-est to the window and stupid enough to want to look. I saw a car drive up, a nice, big, black family car. There was the sound of the front door creaking open. I'd only polished the stairs twice, but I'd already come to hate that creak. Then the sound of voices, foot-steps on the stairs. And, finally, a wail from somewhere, a loud piercing scream of utter heartbreak that shot into our room like an electric current, making the cluster of women shift and mutter, avoiding each other's eyes. The sobbing above seemed to go on and on as the footsteps came back down the front stairs, the door squeaked again and the car came into view, driving back out and on to the road. Above us, there were more words and the sobbing changed, and then I didn't hear it anymore through the roaring in my ears, because I suddenly realised exactly what had just happened above me. I felt myself stagger and one of the women put out her arm to steady me, an older woman, Edith, who took me with her when we left the room to resume our chores, who came to collect me later when we stopped for tea. As I went on polishing the stairs where just minutes before a happy couple had walked out with their brand-new baby, I listened for the sounds of the woman who'd been crying above us. But we never saw her again.

In the weeks since I arrived I've ceased to rail at my own naivety. It's a waste of time. Instead, I wonder how many more times this year I'll have to lose a piece of my innocence, how many more things I will learn about the world that will make me not want to be a part of it. Sometimes, when we walk in the garden and I steal off on my own, I allow myself to think of the rose garden at Hartland and of the funny little slip of a girl who was walking around there, self-importantly reciting Christina Rossetti to herself because her mother was dying. Now that I'm here and my belly is growing huge, now that I am going to be a mother, my life before all this is starting to feel so distant, foreign almost, and I can't seem to remember that girl very well at all, only that I can't bear thinking about her, or about Hartland or the 325 steps across the square or about whatever will happen to me after the Charitable Sisters. Which doesn't leave me with much I can bear to think about, so as I lug my metal pail up and down the stairs I try to keep my mind carefully blank.

They have us make baby clothes at night. There are patterns and lots of horrible scratchy green wool that comes from other people's clothes and army blankets, and there's some stiff fabric to sew with. Some of the other women have bought stuff or brought clothes in from home to make up their layette. Some of it is sweet and quite fancy, but I don't want to spend what little money I have brought. So I took the wool they gave us and, trying to remember my patchy domestic science lessons from school, started a jumper and a bed jacket and little trousers and socks. And I'm planning on making a blanket if I can manage because I'm determined that no baby of mine will ever be cold. It might itch itself to death because the wool is quite horrid, but at least it'll be warm.

Some of the women think it's the final humiliation, having to make clothes for the baby's new family, but I don't mind, because I know, with an icy calm that deadens all doubt, that when the time comes, I will find a way not to let them break me and I will not give my baby away.

Brighton, 31 December 1959

I'm worried now. I started feeling worried after Angela came back from hospital pale and heavy-eyed and very silent. The same way that Gwen did last week, and Charlotte before her. Some of them seem to recover more quickly, others have family to return to, and some of them seem to be almost relieved to pick up the pieces of their lives. But all are lost, in one way or another, and now that the year is closing and February is looming near, I'm starting to dread it, not so much the birth but what happens after. I can't help myself, even the strongest resolve not to do what I'm supposed to weakens after six weeks of polishing the staircase. Six weeks of walking in a line, two by two, to church on Sundays, mornings and evenings, past all the disapproving eyes of upstanding housewives who whisk their children and their skirts out of the way as we pass and cram into the last pew where we can hear, more clearly than our own laboured breaths, all the whispers and snickering coming from behind hymn books. Six weeks of chilly nights listening to other women cry. There's always someone crying here, and I'm reminded of the nights lying awake listening to Mum coughing. Now I lie awake listening to sobs and moans and muffled wails into pillows, an eerie and desolate cacophony of sound that's begun to chip away at whatever it is that has wrapped itself around my heart and made me numb against all the longing and the sadness, and that has given me this steely determination to keep my baby.

Edith Cuthbert, who has become something of a friend, she is so cheerful and no nonsense, was marvelling at first at how calm I was, how steadfast, until she realised that it was because I don't count myself among these women. That I'm going to be free. That I'm going to make a life for myself and my baby, somehow, even though I am not yet quite sure how. And then she sat me down and told me exactly what was happening, about doctors forcing women's hands to sign adoption papers, threatening them with mental institutions if they don't, about nurses taking your babies away, literally prising them off your breast and handing them to adoptive families who are lining up to accept these babies, donations in hand. Edith talked for a very long time and when she was done, I wasn't calm anymore, but very, very frightened.

Brighton, I January 1960

There must be a way out of this, there must be something I can do. I'm allowing myself to think back to Hartland, not as it must be now, rain-sodden and grey and cold, but the way it was back then, open and free and bright with sunshine and possibilities, and I'm absolutely sure that if John knew what went on here, he wouldn't want this to happen. After all the things he said, after all that we talked about, after the life and the love that was buzzing between us for so many months, surely he couldn't possibly want this baby – his baby – to be ripped off my breast and handed over to strangers to disappear. I cannot reconcile his laughing eyes, his face so warm over buns and tea, with going along with what is about to happen to his baby. And I want to see him. For the first time since we parted by the bus stop, I long to see him again. He must be so close, just down the coast from here, and even with a wife there, he might be able to think of something, might somehow be persuaded to take care of me, tuck me away in a room somewhere in London, where his child could grow up. I'd be ever so quiet and wouldn't make any trouble at all.

I felt so restless after I left Edith that I stole out to the garden, even though it was cold and very dark and I would have been in trouble if anyone had spotted me, but I need to be outside to think clearly. Other than Hartland, what are my options? Edith paints a very brutal and very real picture of the life of a single mother out in the world. How she'll be shunned by all, how she is the lowest of the low and won't be given a job where she can keep her baby or a place to live on her own with her baby; how no one ever forgives a single mother for what she's done if she keeps the baby as evidence; no one will want to touch her, not the state, not the charities, not even the church will help her or make any effort to understand her unless she is prepared to start over again, unless she puts her baby before herself and gives it the future they think it deserves.

I'm too young to pretend to be anything other than what I am, a stupid girl who fell for a baby and doesn't have the decency to allow it to have a better life away from its degraded mother, amidst a good and respectable family. Father has only come to see me once, mostly to reassure himself that the baby will disappear quickly and efficiently, that I will come home as soon as possible. People at Limpsfield have been asking about me, and the longer I stay away, the more firmly the whiff of gossip and scandal will take hold. He's troubled by that and tried to impress upon me the need to keep up the facade. When I told him that I won't be giving up my baby without a fight it clearly worried him and he went and talked to Matron for a long time.

If only Mum was here, if only she was still alive to protect me. But I am going to be a mother now, I'm going to have to do all the protecting. It's hard, though, and it's so cold out there and I feel quite small myself.

Brighton, 15 January 1960

I can't shake the thought that Hartland is my only hope. I will be twenty-one in two and a half years' time and if I can manage to cling on until then, find a safe place where I can hide until Father has no control over me ... but what then? And what before then?

Sometimes, in the middle of the night when I listen to the crying from the other beds, I catch myself thinking of just giving in, of letting the baby go to a better life, letting it be packed up in a big black family car and driven out on to the road and to a nice house where it'll be doted upon and cherished by strangers. Maybe that would be the best thing to do. But somehow I can't, I can't let this baby go. Between my Hartland summer and Mum's death and the Purley hotel, this baby seems to be the only good thing that's come of all the misery, the only decent, innocent thing in this world. Moving about in my belly, this little hub of warmth and love and possibility is Hope, really, as if something of Mum and me has returned, in a different form, but still there. I can't give it away, I simply can't. I need to run away. I need to go to Hartland and, failing that, I need to have a plan. Find somewhere to hide. And there is not much time now, so I must do it soon.

Brighton, I February 1960

I've had news, today, news that went through me like an electric current, that's been keeping me on the edge of my seat, fidgeting and flitting about until Sister Mary Claire threatened me with isolation. There's a very real possibility that I'm carrying not one but two babies! The midwife came today and she took longer to measure me and listen with her funny tube and asked me all sorts of questions, and she finally brought Matron in and told her that she was fairly certain I was carrying twins. Twins! I was smiling, because it's exciting, isn't it, but already I could see Matron's mind whirring away, two babies to sort out, two babies to find families for, two babies to receive donations for. The midwife marked some of the details down in my little booklet and she frowned when she saw the list of baby names I'd made there. Before she left, she took a last dubious look at my scrawny hips and my body which has become so thin on crustless toast and worry, and she pronounced that I most certainly will have to come to hospital to give birth, as I'd surely be trouble, and then she left.

Time's ticking now, and if I do this, if I slip away to save these babies, then I need to do it now. I can hardly sleep anymore. I'm nervous and afraid, driven only by the thought of escaping here, escaping my father and Matron and the housewives on Sundays, of taking myself to a place where I can finally be warm and come to rest.

I'm gathering what I need. Before, during my early days of drifting about Number Seven Bough Road, locked in and away from prying eyes, before Father sent me away and the fog of numbness descended, I'd made all kinds of wild plans to run away. So I took my birth certificate from the box where I knew it was kept and I took the picture of Mum and myself from my bedside table and the photo taken at Tideford Cross, which I slipped right behind it, because my baby might at some point in the future want to know who its father is. I took all the money I had collected over the years and the couple of pounds Father has had to give me for the layette, which Matron had told him we were expected to provide for the adoptive family. The clothes I made look lumpy and awkward but warm, and now that I'm supposedly having twins, I can make more clothes without it being conspicuous. So I made a third hat but bigger, to fit my own head, and blamed it on my staggering ineptitude at housewifery. And I made longer socks, so they'll fit my own feet and legs. I'm keeping all of this in my handbag all the time and I stole a sewing needle and some thread and sewed my birth certificate and some of my money into the lining of my winter coat. I've almost finished knitting my very last piece, a large baby blanket. Perfect for two, I told the sister, but I'm going to use it over my coat because it'll be cold out there. A dark, icy, February kind of cold.

Brighton, 6 February 1960

I managed to steal a train timetable from one of the women in the kitchen when I went to empty my pails. I've worked out how to get to Hartland, although I will have to walk some of the way, and beyond that I've memorised trains to as many places as I possibly can. At church, when they think I'm on my knees praying for deliverance from all my sins, I'm reciting the different routes I might need: from Brighton to Crawley, from Brighton to Haywards Heath and from Haywards Heath to Redhill; from Brighton to Lewes and Lewes to Croydon and from Croydon to Victoria. 10 a.m. 3.15 p.m. 5.10 p.m. 6.20 p.m. 7.10 p.m. 8.05 p.m. Over and over and over again.

I've checked on buses, too, and, carefully, because I don't want anyone to try to deter me, I've asked around for places in London where a girl like me might have a chance to disappear: Salvation Army homes and charitable mission houses for women in trouble. I've memorised an address and the exact bus routes to go there from the station, although a place like Dulwich seems absurdly far away and I worry that I won't be able to do it, without a pram and without help. But I feel very sure now that Hartland holds hope. That once he sees me, he'll help me. It's a tiny sliver of hope, a very desperate echo of Hope, but it is better than nothing, and certainly better than sitting here, watching that family car come up the drive to take my babies away.

Brighton, 8 February 1960

I'm still waiting for the perfect time. I thought it might be tonight but a girl came in crying and carrying on and we had Sister Mary Claire upon us most of the night.

Brighton, 11 February 1960

I'm looking for my chance. Every minute of the day I'm ready, tightly sprung, waiting to launch, but something must be radiating from me because I can see Sister Mary Claire's gaze on me a lot. I'm even more careful to hide my diary and I always keep my eyes down when she's near, on the wood polish or the stairs or my prayer book, so that she can't see me straining to go.

Brighton, 12 February 1960

Not much time now, not much time at all. I can feel the babies getting restless, maybe because I am so restless, but I'm begging them to stay where they are, safe for just a bit longer, until I make it to Hartland. I was about to slip away today but I ran into one of the workmen and didn't manage it. My courage is starting to fray with each day. I'm not sure how much longer I can stand the fear.

Brighton, 13 February 1960

It will have to be today. A group of us is allowed to go into town and I'll slip away. Oh god, give me courage.

Chapter Thirty-Three

It wasn't until Harriet returned, a loaf of bread in one hand, a plate with cheese and meats in the other, that I realised it was past lunch-time. She poured water from a jug, sliced the bread.

'I don't have anything else,' she said, almost apologetically.

I wasn't really hungry, despite the fact that breakfast had been ages ago, but I took a piece of bread and some cheese, glad of something to busy my hands with.

Harriet downed two glasses of water in quick succession. Then she said. 'That summer, a few weeks after our wedding, Liz was back in our lives.'

I had been half-standing to reach for the water jug but immediately sat back down, leaving my bread untouched.

'And then I understood why John had been so keen for us to live at Hartland, and for years I couldn't think of those few months with-out burning with embarrassment because I'd been so unaware of it, so blind.' She paused, then went on. 'John was very hard to resist, it was something about him, he was so gregarious, always optimistic, even if he'd lost his brother, even if Hartland was on the verge of col-lapse, he just went on blithely, pretending all was fine. And Liz was reeling from losing her mother and George was so god awful to be with. So it's not all that hard to see how it had happened between Liz and John, although I've tried not to dwell on it too much, because it was so painful to me. That he went to see her, just after we got engaged, and that all through planning the wedding, which was meant to save him and his heritage, while I was sending out invita-tions and choosing flowers and going to fittings for my dress, he was sneaking off to see Liz, funny, sad little Liz. He only told me about it later, how for months on end, he was waiting for her after her secre-tarial classes, sometimes once a week, sometimes several times. It was easy, he said, she had to be home at a certain time anyway, and I was busy and we were still living apart. He didn't see her quite as often once we moved down to Hartland. And then, of course, I found them out. These things always come out. Not reaching him at work when he said he'd be staying behind late, a receipt for some treat or other in his pocket. The oldest story in the book. There I was, newly married, trying for a baby, and I found out that my husband had been cheating on me ever since we got engaged.

'I confronted him and threatened to leave him. Predictably, he panicked. Family finances were in a bad shape, the house was mortgaged to the hilt and Janet and Abel had disappeared to South Africa. He needed me and my family's money to hang on to Hartland, even to pay the on-going bills. He literally couldn't afford to lose me. So he swore that he would break things off with Liz if I gave him another chance. What was I supposed to do? Divorce was technically possible, of course, but in 1959 it wasn't really an option, not for someone like me, and the humiliation was beyond unbearable. And I loved John, despite everything else. I might never be a girl you kissed among the trees with the sort of determination it made your throat ache to watch, but I was a good wife, a good partner. John and I were well suited, we came from the same background, knew each other well.

'So I gave it another try. For a few weeks, it all seemed fine, John was home on time, we got along well. But when I found a bill for a hotel in Purley, where a "Mr and Mrs Smith" had stayed, I went down a different route. I got in touch with George. This was, oh, July, August, I think? I didn't really want to, I didn't like him much, but I told him to keep his daughter away from my husband. He was his usual stern self but oddly enough he didn't seem overly surprised. I later realised that he had just found out about it himself. Anyway, when I asked John a few weeks later, he said that Liz had left London.'

She paused and poured herself some more water. Her hair had escaped the butterfly clasp. It was curling around her drawn face and the dark smudges under her eyes and I wanted to reach out and pat her arm.

'It was about six months later that it happened. I was pregnant, about five and a half months along, and I was thrilled, because here it was at last, the family life we wanted. Everything was going to settle down. I was just putting the kettle on and pottering around the kitchen, waiting for John to come home, when I heard a knock on the front door. Hartland was quite remote and John would have come in the back entrance through the kitchen, so I wasn't sure at first whether to open the door. It was eerie out there, dark and cold and the house was very big and silent after the housekeeper left in the evenings. There was another knock and I did open it. It was Liz. I almost didn't recognise her. Her hair was a lot shorter, and she was draped in this woollen blanket, and she looked terrible, chattering with cold in a thin coat. The bottom of her dress was soaked with water and slush and her stomach was absolutely huge. I cannot tell you how shocked I was. It was as if my brain just stopped processing things for several moments and I stared at her without understanding. It took me only a moment, though, to put two and two together.'

She looked away and I saw her throat working but she didn't speak for so long that I finally said, 'Harriet?'

But she didn't look up and I lapsed into silence until she finally spoke again, her words coming haltingly.

'It was terrible. I behaved terribly and all these years after, I still remember it. I was so angry. It's hard to describe it properly, but it was – like I snapped. I told her to go away and leave us alone. She seemed just as shocked as I was to see *me* standing there, and I think John hadn't told her that it was me he'd married. She just stood there. I shouted at her, tried to close the door in her face. She was crying.

'"I need to see him," she said, and that she was so sorry, she wasn't going to bother us or come between us, she just needed help getting on her feet after the birth, she didn't know where else to go. And then she saw that I was pregnant, too, early days but you could probably see it, and I think it must have hit her then, I could see it in her face. All of a sudden all that misery of the previous year and my husband's betrayal and the two of them playing me for a fool and me being stuck down here while she got pregnant up there – it all came out and I pushed her backwards, off the step and away from the door. She didn't fall far, but she suddenly doubled over and held her stomach.

'"I think it's starting," she said. "You have to help me," or something like that. She looked so scared. I didn't believe her at first, and I think I said something scathing, but when she was clutching my arm and doubling over in pain, I got scared too. I wasn't sure where she'd even come from, all the way from Limpsfield? And what would I do with her now? I thought about ringing the midwife but I hadn't really got myself acquainted with the locals and the last thing I wanted going round was that the local midwife had brought John's illegitimate child into the world ahead of mine. And Liz didn't want me to either, she kept begging me not to because they would take her away. I knew there was a cottage hospital in Porthallow, the midwife had told me about it. It was very small but the bigger hospitals were right across in Brighton. In the end, I did the only thing I could think of, I called George. But their help answered the phone and said that he'd left to go to Brighton earlier.'

'To the women's home,' I said.

'I suppose they'd rung him as soon as they'd discovered that she was missing. I told the maid that it was urgent, that Liz was here at Hartland, and that I needed George to ring me immediately because she had to go to hospital. Liz was in agony, she was walking up and down the front hall, so I decided to take her to the cottage hospital in Porthallow. Then George called back. He was in Brighton and wanted me to take her to All Saints Hospital and he would meet us there. I thought it was too far to go now, that I should call the midwife after all because Liz looked like she was about to give birth right there in my front hall. He wanted her there, though, it was the hospital associated with the women's home, so they'd be able to take over. So I bundled Liz into our jeep. But it wasn't long before I bitterly regretted driving all the way to Brighton, because it was freezing in the car and Liz was in so much pain, crying next to me, and I had to stop several times for her to be sick. Anything could have happened. Anything.'

She paused. I was cold all over, then too hot, the panic and fear from the story sloshing around in the pit of my stomach. I hated thinking of my mother like that, scared and in pain. She was meant to be strong, she was meant to be able to stand up to her father, and hold on to us, but I could see where the story was going and I almost couldn't bear it.

'There was a nurse waiting for us at the hospital, and she took Liz away. George was there, too, looking very angry. "I'm so sorry about all of this," he said.' Harriet gave a bitter laugh. 'And I remember thinking "Sorry for what? That your daughter was about to have my husband's baby all over my car?"'

There was a sob and I realised that Phoebe was crying.

'I'm sorry,' Harriet said, but her voice had an edge to it, 'but there are some things you don't forget.'

'Of course not,' I said. 'Please, just go on.'

'He was keen to leave, though, because he wanted to speak to the doctor, and I made him promise to ring me later to tell me the . . . well . . . the outcome. It was getting dark as I drove back to Hartland. I knew John would be home soon, and that drive was one of the most anxious, most nerve-racking I ever did. Pushing Liz out the door, all her pain, John's baby about to be born. What if she'd given birth in the car? Us all alone? When I got home, I sat by the phone because I had to know that she was alive and, well, I had to know what would happen to the baby, because after all – this was John's baby – would it be around to haunt us forever or . . . ?'

She paused. Her eyes were on Phoebe. 'Finally he did call. He said that there'd been complications and that she'd gone straight to the theatre for a Caesarean, but would be fine. Thanks to me.'

I shook my head, images crowding inside my head. My mother in a hospital bed. And—

'And the babies?' I asked.

'The babies?' Harriet said, almost reluctantly, as if she'd been hoping we wouldn't ask. 'He never said that there were *two* babies. He told me I needn't worry about Elizabeth anymore, that the problem had taken care of itself. There *had* been a baby girl, one baby, but she'd been born dead.'

Brighton, 16 February 1960

For the past two days, the pain has taken over everything and has refused to let me go. I've been moving and turning in the hospital bed to escape it and other times I tried to lie completely still, hoping it would overlook me, hoping it might move on to one of the other women who are murmuring and sighing in their sleep. But it has always found me, and I now think my body has reached the end of it all, that place at the end of the road where I relinquish any and all link to the world and simply lay myself down, drop all my burdens, and close my eyes and die.

But even that is denied me, because I'm held here on this ward, where people come and look at me with cool, discerning eyes, too indifferent to comfort me beyond the basic needs, instead watching me trapped inside this shell of a body, which is numb and leaden and racked with pain all at the same time. I think this is what hell must feel like, like being buried alive in your own body, wrapped in a cloud of pain that squeezes and pulses and contracts all around you, leaving your mind feverish and ill with worry and grief, clawing to get out, to find relief, and all the while knowing that relief will never be possible again.

I've asked to see my surviving baby, which I think is in a nursery down the corridor, and I asked to see the body of the dead baby. I asked to see the midwife or the doctor or anyone who might tell me at least what she looked like. It was a she, that much they said, but as for the rest, I'm not to know, I'm not allowed to hold her body or even to look at her. That's not what they do when babies die, they say, it's better that way, and I cannot get up to fight that fight. Father has come and gone and I would give anything never to see him again. He was there when I came into the hospital, but then

I don't really remember him after that because everything is shrouded in this enormous, enveloping cloud of gut-wrenching pain. They said the baby was already dead inside me and they had to cut it out of my belly, along with its sister who was barely alive herself. They said it was my fault, too, for foolishly running away, that I killed my own baby. I don't remember much of it all, not the operating theatre or the hours after, when I eventually awoke, but these words I remember and I will forever remember them, because already, my mind has started turning them over and over. My fault, my fault, my fault, until I'm groaning with the pain and the guilt of it all and Sister Marianna comes and tells me not to be a nuisance.

It's been three days now and I still haven't seen the baby that survived. My milk has come in and adds yet another layer of pain, my breasts throbbing and tingling when I hear babies coming in from the nursery and on to the ward, where the other, normal women hold them and feed them and fuss over them and show them off to their families during visiting hours. I'm not allowed to feed my baby yet. Matron and the ward sister consider me too weak for it or maybe they don't care or want to punish me. I worry that they're letting it starve just because Matron doesn't like me being on her respectable ward, carrying on when I brought it all on myself and was no better than I should be. They can't quite decide where they want me, right under their eyes where they can see me at all times, or hidden away so I don't offend the normal mothers. For a bit I was in a sort of side room, off the ward, but someone else needed it and so they moved me to the very end of the ward and put a screen around me. This way, I can't see or be seen, can't be part of the normal, homely routines of eating and feeding and being taken care of, but I still hear what is happening on the other side of the screen and am constantly reminded of what I have brought on myself.

There's only one nurse, very young and herself quite frightened of Matron and the ward sister. She is kind where everyone else is dismissive and I think it's because she's young, and soft looking despite her starched uniform. She brings me food and water and cups of tea, even though the ward sister reprimands her for neglecting her real duties. I beg her for news of my baby and she's kind enough to slip off and check on her when the ward sister isn't looking, and comes back to say that the little girl is well and healthy, so at least I know that they feed her. I want to see her, so desperately, but I'm not allowed out of bed and, in any case, I can't move very well yet, and won't be able to do much for myself for another few days at least. Ten days we stay here, the normal mothers and I. From what I hear of the chatter amongst the others, they are almost relieved not to have to re-join the real world too soon and instead have help with the babies and to ease into their respectable lives with husbands and little ones. To me, however, ten days are interminable, because at the end of them I'm supposed to take the baby back to the Sisters of Hope and wait there with her until another car comes down the drive and I hand over my baby, and then go back home to life in my father's house.

And that's where hell starts all over again, the thoughts and the guilt and the pain. It's worst at night, when there's enough light from the night nurse's station to make out the eerie shapes in the folds of the screen around my bed, when the steam steriliser hisses and draughts from the windows make the curtains move, throwing shadows on the polished floors. The other women sigh and snuffle in their sleep and I lie in my bed with my fist stuffed into my mouth so as not to scream.

I've asked the kind little nurse about my bag and my coat and she's brought them and put them right by the bed in a metal locker where I can reach them. I've given her the bundle to bury with the baby and she's taken it, but I see from her shifting eyes that the baby is already gone, that I will never know where she's been buried. As soon as she left, I felt for my papers and my money, which thankfully are still where I've hidden them, as is my little diary. I'm going to hide it under my pillow as soon as I've finished writing, because if Sister took it away its loss would be devastating. Somewhere in the graphite-grey collection of pages which has seen this silly sixteen-year-old girl leave school and run home to her mum with a marked-up *Radio Times* and plans for the summer, who was then swept away by Hartland and first love, who's seen death and been exiled and run away and given birth, somewhere in there, there must be something of me left and if I have any hope at all, I need to find it again.

Brighton, 22 February 1960

The day of my return to the home is close now and I cannot avoid thinking about it any longer. I'm so tired, though, and growing more so every day. It's almost as if the pain kept me alive in those first few awful days and now that my body is healing and the pain is receding, my mind is left alone with it all and just wants to slip away into the oblivion of sleep, somewhere I can forget about what has happened and what lies ahead. It's a strange half-sleep, a grey haze where nothing can touch me, nothing comes close, where I drift along in the twilight, weightless and almost free. But in my clearer moments I know I have to be strong for the baby. I cannot allow myself the luxury of the grey-haze oblivion, because even after all this, even after all that's happened, I cannot let that baby go, not when I've already lost the other one through my own carelessness and selfishness. I'm going to be accountable for the death of that baby for the rest of my life, and I know that I couldn't forgive myself for letting the other one go.

It's a simple plan, really, so simple that it probably doesn't have much chance of working, but it's all I can think of so it'll have to do. Tomorrow I'm meant to bring the baby back to the home. Instead of making my way there, though, I'm going to find the train station and take the train up to London. I remember the address of the place in Dulwich that the woman at the home had given me, I still know the bus and train schedules by heart, and by the time I'm in London, they won't be able to find me. It's my last chance and I pray that someone at the mission house in Dulwich will be able to help me. I've asked the young nurse, Sarah is her name, for an extra sheet. I don't dare tell her what it's for, for fear that she'll tell Matron or someone else about it, and she doesn't ask, but she must have guessed because she's just brought me not only the sheet but also a small parcel with a few nappies and two glass bottles filled with water and milk powder to mix it with. Once more I have to pack my bag, although I hardly have anything to take by now. My diary, Mum's photo, my birth certificate, the money. I've packed the second bundle of baby clothes, wrapping the bottles into the nappies so they won't clink together or break. I'm going to turn the sheet into a sling for the baby, which I'll tuck inside my dress tomorrow and pull my coat on over the whole thing as I leave. I've grown so thin this past year, and my coat is so big, she'll fit right in there and hopefully won't look too conspicuous.

I'm so tired, so, so tired all the time. I can feel myself constantly sliding into greyness and my body seems too heavy for this world. It doesn't want to defy gravity, it doesn't even want to stay upright, it wants to slip and slide and drift, pushing me to let it go into the grey where nothing seems to matter, where everything is blurry and free. Maybe it's my body's way to heal and I need to try harder to look into the future, to be in the present. How much I want to be able to do that. To shake off the night of the birth. The knowledge that my baby is dead because of me. If I hadn't left the home, she'd be alive now, but because I walked through the snow to see my lover, who was another woman's husband, my baby had to die.

And now I have this one baby left and I must fight for her, even though deep down I know that I have forfeited my right to be a mother. It's time to leave the dead baby behind now, time to meet the one that survived, time to take her and run. I wish I'd had a gentler beginning with her but what's done is done.

I feel myself weakening again and I fight it, even though it takes an inordinate amount of will not to succumb to the pull of the haze that's beckoning me, but I must stay alert, I must focus. I've failed one baby and now I owe it to the other one to save it.

Chapter Thirty-Four

'Dead?' I said incredulously and I could hear my own voice rising, 'Dead?' I looked at Phoebe, my eyes wide. *'That's* why she didn't come right back for you, Phoebe. She must have been told the same thing – that you were dead!'

'But who would do that?' Phoebe whispered, her face ashen. 'Who'd do that to their own daughter?'

And to you, I thought desperately. *George Holloway did that to you, just to save his daughter's reputation.*

'I don't understand, Harriet, I just don't understand,' I said, pushing out the words with some effort. 'What happened to her?'

'She disappeared.'

'She disappeared?' Phoebe said and at the same time I said, 'Where on earth to?'

Harriet shifted, picked up the notes that were on the table and looked at them. 'I have no idea.' She held up two of the notes. 'I wrote to her a couple of times, and I wrote to George,' she held up the third note, 'because the weeks after that day were terrible. I was relieved somehow that the baby was dead, and guilty at the same time, and then guilty at being relieved; and it all became about the baby, John's dead baby, which haunted me and which had died because of me.' She folded her hands in her lap, interlacing her fingers tightly. 'I never heard from Liz, which I guess was fair enough, but George did write back, asked me to come and see him.' She put the notes down very gently. 'I went up just before I gave birth myself and he told me that Elizabeth had taken the news of the baby's death badly, that she'd left the hospital at the end of her stay and – vanished. I didn't believe him at first, thought he'd put her away somewhere himself, had locked her up in a mental asylum or something. You heard the most awful stories back then. But he looked pretty terrible, rattling around in that house of theirs, haggard and tired, and I knew he was telling the truth, at least about Liz. I didn't know about the second baby then, obviously, didn't know until you told me today that there were two of you, so to me, she had left by herself. She was still underage so she'd have be discreet for a while, but with a bit of money and luck she could have started a new life, found herself a room somewhere, a job. But leaving with a baby, now that puts a different spin on things altogether. She would have had a very hard time with it.'

'But how could that have happened?' I said, still stunned. 'Wouldn't she have asked to see the body at the hospital? Or see the grave? Some paperwork? Surely they couldn't just get away with something like that? It's a crime.'

'It is,' Harriet said, 'but unmarried mothers were treated appallingly back then, and doctors had a lot of power, they were god-like, almost. If he'd orchestrated it cleverly, no one would have dared doubt the doctor's word or rushed to protect the single mum. It's hard to imagine now,' she shook her head, 'with all the counselling and antenatal care and women's right to choose. But back then her father deciding what happened to her would have been perfectly normal, expected even.' She thought for a moment. 'All I can think is that she was supposed to give up the baby for adoption at the women's home, but that an opportunity presented itself at the hospital and they gave one of the babies away right then and there. Maybe George was caught off-guard, maybe he hadn't expected twins and wanted to act fast. I think the fact that I was involved made things more complicated from his point of view. He had to tell me something and he would have wanted to avoid a scandal at all costs, so he just told me the baby died and probably thought he could sort out the rest. How would I ever find out different? If the doctor certified the baby's death and authorised the handover, it would have been a private adoption and the baby would have simply disappeared without ever being traced back to John or myself.'

Phoebc's face still had a slightly frozen look to it. The dog had woken up and was threading through our legs, whining slightly at the tension in the room.

'Dr Miller,' I said, thinking out loud, 'that's why she tried so hard to find him. She must have realised what he'd done, maybe found something in the house after George Holloway died that made her think he'd lied to her.'

I put my arm around Phoebe's hunched shoulders.

'She was looking for you so very hard, she must have been desperate to find you.' I thought of the correspondence snaking back and forth, the years of her painstaking, painful search. 'Oh Phoebe, I'm so sorry. I'm so sorry that it came too late. It's—'

Abruptly, she stood up. Harriet said very gently, 'Why don't you go out into the garden for a bit? It's lovely and quiet out there.'

When Phoebe went, the dog skittering in her wake, I stood up too but Harriet put her hand on my arm. 'Leave her be,' she said. 'It's a lot to take in all at once.'

I sank back down on the sofa and took a sip of my cold tea. 'Did you ever see George Holloway again?'

'Just that one time.' She paused. 'Because one other thing he told me was that John had rung, asking after Liz. That's when I knew that it had to stop. I told John I really would leave him this time, him and his bankrupt parents, taking all my money with me and letting Hartland and his family go, if he didn't agree to a new start after our own baby was born. So eventually we shut up the house and moved to America in December of 1960. I had an uncle there and John was able to get a job in his company. We started over again.' She smiled wryly. 'Janet and Abel came back to Hartland at some point but it all ended with the fire in the seventies. And life does go on, doesn't it, despite all its dramas. John and I had another stab at being married. It wasn't the most idyllic arrangement, but we muddled along fine, lived in Buffalo, New York. It wasn't until John passed away a few years ago that I came back to England for good. Our daughter, Caroline, got a job in London and I decided to come with her. Be close to my grandchildren. I changed my name back to Sinclair and,' she smiled wryly, 'don't ask me why but I decided to move down here.'

'So John is dead,' I said slowly, processing this last and very important information. Part of me was relieved that I didn't have to give *Father: Blank* another thought. 'We're going to have to tell Phoebe.'

'I'll do it,' Harriet said, 'although I hope she won't dwell on him too much. I don't know what kind of a father he could have ever been to the two of you, given the situation, and he certainly wouldn't have been any better or worse than what you both grew up with believing it was the real thing.'

'Did my mother ever get back in touch with you or John?' I asked.

'We never heard from her again,' Harriet said. 'I sometimes wondered what had become of her.'

The sun had started to go down behind the thatched roof and shadows began to pool around the low wall and behind the bushes by the time I went out to check on Phoebe. Harriet's back garden was overgrown and fragrant, a small green square of grass bordered by crumbly stone walls, a few trees and a bench, withered in the sunlight. Against the shelter of the back wall, wild flowers grew, splashes of colour against the more orderly rows of herbs and carrots. A garden my mother would have loved.

Phoebe wanted to stay for the weekend. I offered, half-heartedly at first, then more insistently, to take her back with me, but she was firm. She wanted to be on her own for a while and maybe, if Harriet wanted to and if she, Phoebe, wanted to, they'd talk some more.

So I took the bus back to the train station and sat by the window as we trundled away from the sea. I smiled involuntarily, thinking of Phoebe's happy shout when we'd first seen the sea. As I waited for the next train to London I tried to call Andrew but he didn't pick up and I reflected that it served me right for having taken his cheerfulness and pragmatism and all his gumption so much for granted that I'd probably used it all up now. I left a mumbled and confused message about taking the train to Victoria and seeing him soon and how sorry I was. Then, when the train came, I sat by myself, my eyes tracking the blurry shapes moving past the window.

I replayed Harriet's account over and over in my mind, but I didn't think about my grandfather or John Shaw or Harriet or even Phoebe; there'd be enough time to think about everyone else later. Instead, I imagined Liz Holloway, a seventeen-year-old girl, breathless on a dusky evening in the Hartland orchards, a young woman slipping into a hotel in Purley, an expectant mother knitting a clumsy baby jacket, stumbling through the snowy night towards her lover's house, sick and helpless in a hospital bed, and then gone with her baby, eventually finding my father and somewhere along the line turning into the mother that *I* knew, this difficult, demanding, private person, who was always straining to better herself, always straining to be free. And now I knew why, because by the time I knew her, this whole other life had already been lived, grief for a dead baby, recovery from a trauma, an estranged father.

It all went round and round in my head, things clicking into place, only to disengage again and flow back into the maelstrom of questions and answers, remembering scenes and moments and conversations with my mother, all different now and terribly poignant, things I'd never understood now becoming clear. Had she read the newspaper, hoping and fearing for news of her father? Had she looked at cemeteries everywhere she went, searching for a dead baby's gravestone? Had she bought clothes and scarves and coats and thick socks because she'd spent the winter that would change her life being cold to the bone and, forty years later, was still trying to warm up? Had her mouth twitched impatiently when I told her I was going to be a baker because to a girl growing up in a claustrophobic house with a small-minded, old-fashioned father, not taking the freedom and adventure and possibility when it was handed to you on a silver platter would have been tantamount to a crime?

I sat on that train and raged at George Holloway and at fate and at life itself for turning on this one young girl who'd made a few bad choices and paid for them so dearly. I raged a bit at my mother for doggedly continuing to pay that price, even when she ended up with a good life, a loving husband, a full career, three children. She could have made our relationship work differently, could have let Phoebe's ghost go and brought me close instead. But more than that, I squirmed with remorse and guilt when I realised how very quick I'd been only a week ago to judge her for wilfully separating us, for selfishly abandoning a baby, just so that she might be free.

If I'd gone to Tideford Cross wanting understanding and acceptance and forgiveness, I didn't know which of those I'd got in the end, because now most of all I was sad. Bitterly, bone-crushingly sad. For her and for us, and for the fact that she'd never felt she could tell me what had happened. And the knowledge that I might have understood her and loved her differently. I wished desperately that I could see her again, just one more time, to be with her, to rail at her and, perhaps, to get a second chance to talk her properly, like I'd been meant to, like she had deserved.

In the half-darkness of the carriage, I felt something behind my eyes sting and burn. And when I stopped fighting it, stopped thinking altogether and just opened up to everything that had been and could still be, the tears finally came, blissful and clean, and I found that I couldn't stop crying for the rest of the journey.

I stepped off the train at Victoria feeling completely drained. Just putting one foot in front of the other seemed to require a massive effort and by the time I finally made it to the end of the platform, most of the passengers had already dispersed. A familiar lanky shape stepped towards the turnstiles, pulled me through, held a hand out for my bag. Andrew was still in his chef's whites and was carrying a squishy-looking parcel.

'Hey, stranger,' he said, smiling down at me. 'Travelling with plants these days?'

'For you. I'm sorry,' I said, held out the now distinctly scruffy-looking pot and promptly burst into tears again.

'Dear lord!' he said, and set down the bags. 'You're crying! Amazing! That's the first step, Ads, you've made a big leap. There, there.'

He patted my back consolingly and I cried into his jacket for a while until finally he pushed me away and crouched to look into my face. His eyes were warm and blue as he dabbed at my cheeks and my eyes with a crumpled-up tissue, smoothing down my hair and tucking it behind my ears, before finally offering me the tissue to blow my nose.

'I'm really sorry, Andrew. I should have told you about Le Grand Bleu,' I said hoarsely, crying and blowing my nose at the same time, so loudly that one of the ticket collectors looked over.

'Addie, it's fine.'

'It is?' I stuffed the tissue into my pocket.

He picked up my bag. 'You should have said immediately that you didn't want to do it.'

'I tried. And then I thought you'd be cross,' I said disconsolately.

Andrew snorted in disdain. 'Addie, we've known each other for thirty years. I might be disappointed, but I won't be forever. Although I'm somewhat incensed you didn't keep me posted on Phoebe and all that exciting stuff.'

'Yes,' I said. 'It all happened so fast.'

'Of course, we'd have been great together,' he said matter-of-factly. 'You know that. But all I want is for you to be happy,' he said firmly. 'Really, that's all I ever wanted. And now, I'd like to go home with you and have a drink and hear about your seaside adventures. Come on.'

And with that, he put his arm around my shoulder and pulled me down the stairs to the underground.

Chapter Thirty-Five

'Addie, did you put the lemonade in the fridge? And are you sure there are enough chairs out there for people to sit? Could you move that brown chair to the back? That way there's space. Hi, Jas, it's me. Are you on your way? What? What do you mean you're not supposed to use your phone in the hospital? No, that one, Addie, there, the brown one on the left. Oh my god, Adele Harington, are you really going to make me get up, nine and a half months pregnant, and move that chair myself? All right, all right, Jas, I'm still here, keep your hair on. When will you be here? Thirty minutes? Is he okay? Great. Good. Okay. Bye. Now, where are the balloons?'

It was two days later and a lot had happened since I'd left Tideford Cross.

First of all, summer had burst upon London with the unashamed vehemence that only English weather can muster in late May, just when everyone had started to despair. The birds were singing, the skies were the brightest baby blue and the sun only sank reluctantly at the very end of the evening, surfacing with almost indecent haste the next morning to shine brightly into my attic window.

Coming back from Victoria Station to my flat that night, Andrew and I were greeted by Mrs Emmet's cat, which was waiting in front of my door and seemed intent on adopting me for good. Andrew and I then sat and ate some squashed but very tasty lamp chops with potatoes au gratin and I cried quite a bit and we talked for a long time, mostly about Tideford Cross and Harriet, some about my father and Phoebe, but also quite a bit about what the future would bring. Eventually I keeled over in mid-sentence and went to sleep and when I woke up it was the middle of the next day and Andrew had gone.

The entire next day, I hid in my apartment. It was good that I'd stored up sixteen hours of sleep because I spent a lot of the following night in my kitchen, the kitten curled up against the sage plant which

Andrew had forgotten to take back with him, alternately polishing the worktop or baking cake or else sitting over the slim volume of Christina Rossetti's *Collected Poems*, trying to remember my mother and to absorb the new revelations about her past. I cried a lot, but I abandoned myself to every tear with gusto, glad that my Niagara Falls had returned and feeling like I was being washed clean from the inside.

Phoebe had stayed overnight in Tideford Cross and we'd talked on the phone several times – long, free-fall conversations about everything and anything that left me exhausted but happy.

I'd wanted to go and see my father in hospital almost immediately, but because I woke up so late the following day and he was going to be discharged to come home the day after, I'd decided to postpone our conversation until we could find a quiet moment to talk. My mother's secret had been around for so long, it could be left in peace for a little while longer.

Venetia had not changed at all in the twenty-four hours that had seen my own life turned upside down. She rang me the following day demanding to know where on earth I'd been, had I been to see Dad, telling me that I really needed to shoulder some of the burden, that the baby had dropped and she had to pee every thirty seconds, and should we put on a tea and cakes party to welcome Dad home? Have some of the family round, make him feel part of things again, what did I think, nothing big, maybe twelve to fifteen people? I stopped listening when Hamish McGree's name came up and started to cry when she'd finished, which surprised her so much that she was, for once, lost for words. I then invited Mrs Baxter, Uncle Fred, Jas and Andrew to Rose Hill Road for the following afternoon, gathered all the cake I'd baked and arrived at Number 42 well before my dad was due home.

Now, leaving Mrs Baxter to sneak out for a cigarette, Uncle Fred moving chairs and Venetia sitting at the table telling everyone what to do, I'd been dispatched upstairs to find some balloons in my mother's party box, which Venetia thought we could string around the hall and the kitchen to lend some additional cheer to his return.

'Addie, see if you can find mostly blues and yellows. Those are meant to be refreshing and uplifting, Hamish says. No green, please. Do you hear me? NO. GREEN.'

'All right, all right,' I muttered to myself, rolling my eyes. 'Green only, it is.'

Upstairs was very different to the last time I'd been here, bright and airy, the breeze coming in through the open windows scented by lavender and lemon balm from the window boxes newly planted by Mrs Baxter. As I passed my parents' room, I threw a quick look over my shoulder before darting through the half-open door. The room was much the same, the blanket undisturbed, the wardrobe closed, but here, too, the window had been left open to let in the sun and it smelt fresh and clean. Listening to the noise downstairs, I reached into my bag and extracted a picture frame decorated with seashells and glitter that I'd made when I was ten. I'd chosen a photo of the five of us, dressed up for my parents' Ruby Wedding, Venetia in a dark red silk dress and me in the trusty purple Diane Furstenberg wraparound that had served me well for over two decades, my mother and father in the middle. We'd had just enough of the Pomegranate Martinis to grin into the camera with a happy flush, our faces close, my hair rising to frame the shot. Gently, I set the frame down, not on my mother's side, which I left empty, but on my dad's, tucked behind his alarm clock where he'd see it when he turned to switch off the lamp at night. I brushed some glitter off the surface of the nightstand, ran a hand down the length of the blanket and left the room as quietly as I'd come in.

The balloons were in a box labelled 'Party Things', which lived in one of the wardrobes up in the attic. I carefully picked every green one out of the jumble, smiling at old streamers we'd made and the bunting and a wodge of half-burned candles which my mother had always brought out for birthday cakes until they'd burned down to little nubs. My heart skipped a beat when I came upon a party hat and, right next to it, a tiara with the words 'Fabulous Forties' emblazoned on it. I held them in my hands for a moment, then tucked them back underneath the red and blue bunting.

Lost in thought, I made my way back to the first floor. Downstairs,

I could hear the doorbell and, faintly, Venetia's commanding voice from the kitchen, but it was too early for my dad, so I lingered in a pool of sunlight that flooded across the bottom of the attic stairs, idling along the bookshelves which housed most of my mother's books, stopping occasionally when I came to a piece of paper sticking out, half an empty envelope marking her place, a piece of toilet tissue wedged between the pages, thin and feathery with age. *Pamela. Vanity Fair. Frenchman's Creek.* Vera Brittain. But also, more recent ones. Margaret Atwood. Maeve Binchy. *The Shell Seekers. I Capture the Castle.* Anita Shreve. Joyce Carol Oates. Georgette Heyer.

Venetia, my mother and I, united in unusual harmony, had all been obsessed with Georgette Heyer and at least half a bookshelf was crammed with her collection of books. It was all the way at the end, tucked right below the stairs to the attic, rows of newly reprinted and colourful paperback editions next to older hardbacks, which we weren't allowed to touch because they were so fragile; their bindings brittle, spines faded to a universal brown-grey. I looked for the purple-gowned spine of the new *Frederica* paperback, which had been my favourite, and its faded first-edition counterpart just below. I hadn't read Heyer in a long time and it made me sad to think that these books would now sit here for years to come, unread and unloved, this whole treasure trove of memories and afternoon chats about which phaeton we'd choose if we'd had to promenade in Hyde Park and who we'd marry if we had the choice. Maybe, if Venetia had a girl, she should take them all, pass them on to her daughter. Or maybe Phoebe should, for little Charlotte. Or me? Who knew what was still in store for us?

'Addie!' a voice shouted.

'Coming!' I shouted back. I said a silent farewell to *Frederica* and was just about to step away when suddenly my eyes caught something that looked different. It was right at the very end, hidden from sight by the shadow of the shelf's side and the faded spine of *Faro's Daughter* protruding next to it. If you were walking by and looking from above you'd never have noticed it, but now that the late afternoon sun was beaming sideways from the alcove window and I was half-crouched to rekindle my special friendship with *Frederica*, a silver-edged corner popped out in a way I'd not noticed before. Curiously, I touched it, taking care out of automatic deference to my mother's instructions not to disturb the cracked cover of *Faro's Daughter*, and when I'd finally prised it away from its companion I opened it carefully, turned the first page, then sat up so quickly that I almost hit my head on the side of the bookshelf.

It was a diary.

Chapter Thirty-Six

It was dark grey, very simple, sombre almost, and I opened it to my young mother's handwriting, careful and girlish across the pages.

'Hello? Anyone up here? Adele?'

I snapped the diary shut and shoved it back into the shelf, my heart hammering. I could hear steps coming down the corridor and, looking a lot better than when I'd last seen him, my father rounded the corner.

'Dad!' I said, jumping up quickly and forcing my eyes away from the shelf. Was there another? Were there several? 'I didn't hear you come in.'

'Venetia said you'd got lost up here. Everything all right?'

'Balloons,' I said, 'I came to find balloons.' I held up the handful of balled-up green balloon shells. 'They should have been up when you arrived, I'm really sorry.'

He smiled. 'The house looks wonderful as it is.'

'It's so great to see you. You look – good.'

It was true. He looked rested and there was some healthy colour in his face, but, more importantly, he'd lost that strained look that I'd become so accustomed to over the last twelve months. He was moving cautiously, now and again reaching for his chest as if to reassure himself that all was well in there, but his eyes were clear and he was looking at me, actually *looking at me*, when he spoke.

'Andrew is here, too. And Fred. What a nice homecoming.'

My dad was talking in full sentences! And several sentences, too, so that they actually amounted to a whole *conversation*.

'Dad,' I started, 'I'm . . . I'm so sorry. About what I said. And—'

He interrupted me. 'I owe you an explanation.' Some of the tranquillity had gone from his face. 'I told the others to go ahead and start on the cake and booze. Not much of that for me anymore anyway, I'm afraid. And it'll keep them busy for a bit.'

He lowered himself on to the stairs leading up to the attic and motioned for me to sit next to him.

'I had a lot of time to think while I was in hospital, where, by the way, I don't ever want to end up again. All that fussing and all that resting. Enough to finish a man off.'

'You had a heart attack,' I said sternly. 'You were supposed to be fussed over and to rest.'

He waved the words away, then took a deep breath. 'All that you said was true. Well, almost. Lizzie, she'd met this man down in Sussex, and—'

'Yes, I know,' I interrupted. 'John Shaw. I met his, well, his wife, in Tideford Cross and she told us everything up until the birth.'

'Wife?' His eyebrows rose. 'Tideford Cross?'

'Yes. Listen, maybe you can just tell me what happened right after the birth, when I was a week or so old, and then I can fill you in on the rest later. It's just, I don't think we have that much time and Venetia—'

Thankfully, this kind of verbal economy was one of my dad's strengths.

'Well, all right, a week old, that's in fact when I first met you. I was studying at the LSE, you know, I had a bursary, and I was living with my aunt in East Dulwich. She was on her own and glad of my help around the house, and I was relieved to have a place to stay. Housing was still very tight in London and I didn't have a whole lot of money.

'So there I am, sitting in my room, and when I happened to glance down into the street I saw someone walking along, a woman, although she was so wrapped up it was hard to tell. It'd been a cold day and it was getting dark already and there weren't many people about, so I was watching her make her way past my house. There was something about her that seemed odd, then, just past the front door, she stumbled and fell. I waited for her to get up, but she didn't, she just lay there, curled up, on the cobbles. I ran down and out on to the street. It was freezing cold and it had been snowing off and on all week, and I tried to help her up quickly before the snow soaked through her clothes. But she was so weak and couldn't stand, so I made her sit on the step for a moment. And that's when I saw you. She'd been carrying you in a sling tied to her body, a piece of fabric, but it had started to come undone when she fell and she'd only just managed to keep you from hitting the street. Lots of hair, already at two days,' he smiled, 'and the smallest little round face, peeking out of the shawl. Not a peep out of you, either. You were always such a good girl.'

His smile faded. 'Your mother wasn't really with it, though, and I was worried she might faint again if I let her go. So I brought her into the kitchen and I wanted to call a doctor but when she'd come round a bit, she was adamant that I was not to. She was trying to get to a place she knew, a mission house for women in trouble, but she couldn't find it and she didn't know where to turn. I wasn't sure I'd done the right thing, picking her up off the street like that, and I was worried about what my aunt would say when she came home, but your mum was so young and so sad-looking and she was holding you like she didn't really know what to do with you, so I couldn't but let her stay by the range in the kitchen to warm up. When my aunt came home we tried to decide what to do. My aunt – you never knew her, but she was much like your grandmother, very practical and, really, just a good person with a big heart – she made up a spare bed and helped your mum undress and feed the baby and filled a box with blankets for it to sleep and said we'd talk about it in the morning. The next morning she didn't have the heart to send her away, and so she let her stay another night, and helped her with the baby, and with one thing and another it was a few days before we got the story out of her, about the dead baby and the one she was able to save from the women's home and the adoption, and when we tried to determine where her family was and whether they were looking for her, she completely shut down, she was so traumatised and bruised and frightened, and we couldn't bring our-selves to turn her out on the street. She was ill, physically partly, but more than that, mentally. Today, she'd get all sorts of counselling and grief therapy, but back then, that wasn't really readily available. My Aunt Lavinia took her under her wing and fed her and fussed over her and bounced the baby about and when Lizzie was better, she worked around the house, following my aunt like a shadow. We made up a whole story about her being a distant cousin coming to visit with the baby so that she could go out and not be embarrassed in front of the neighbours, but Lizzie didn't want to see anyone, didn't even want to leave the house, because she was absolutely terrified that her father would appear and take her away. I sat with her a lot and talked to her when she felt like it, and I played with you and took you for turns in the pram around the small neighbourhood park because Aunt Lavinia was quite adamant you needed fresh air.'

His face was sad. 'It took her a long time to get better. It was hard for her, because she'd been so badly hurt and she was still young, had lost her mother, had lost a baby, but I could tell that she wanted to get better, and she really tried. The four of us, we became a unit, and you were a wonderful baby. So content and quiet. It was almost as if you were anxious not to give your mother any trouble. Taking the bottle eagerly and going to sleep when you needed to and otherwise gurgling in your bed. And you were so bright. You know, you rolled over much earlier than other babies, and you were so happy to be read to and entertained. I'll never forget those early days. I loved Lizzie, from the very beginning really, and even if she didn't love me back in quite the same way, she was working hard to be part of a world again where love would at least be possible, and that was enough for me. I loved you, too,' his voice was matter-of-fact, but he blinked, 'and I think she was grateful that I did because she didn't have much left in her to give you at all.'

I swallowed awkwardly. 'That sounds, well – complicated.'

He sighed. 'It wasn't easy. But it was very special.'

'But didn't you mind that I . . . that I belonged to him?'

He didn't say anything for a long moment and I started fidgeting, hoping Venetia's nine and a half months would keep her from climbing the stairs. Miraculously, though, save for murmuring and laughter floating up, it sounded like we weren't yet missed.

'I didn't mind as such, but that was because you never did belong to him. It's partly why I insisted on adding my name to the birth certificate. I didn't want there to be any second thoughts, any complications once we were married.' His voice was harder now. 'He was taken and he wasn't a decent person to start with, not if he got involved with a seventeen-year-old girl while he had a wife at home. Poor Lizzie was fighting on so many fronts, trying not to lose her mind, really, trying to get better. He was out of the picture and that's where I felt he should stay.' His face was set. 'When I asked her to marry me, I could tell that maybe she wasn't ready for it yet. But she wanted to, very much, because I think she needed a resting place, a home. She was still so young, you see, only eighteen. So we made a deal. She would leave him behind, mentally, emotionally, and she would commit to our life together. Fully and completely. No looking back. In return I would take you as my own and we would be a family. We would never speak of the past and we'd raise you together as if you were mine.'

I looked down the corridor, remembering how few personal things she had held on to, her tidiness, the absence of sentimental mementos, of emotional clutter. Clearly, she had more than abided by that stipulation. Had she secretly wanted to put up more pictures, keep old letters, gather mementos? Or had she been too sad and hadn't wanted to be reminded of the past and fell in with her husband's condition easily, perhaps even with some relief, until it had become part of her personality altogether?

'And George Holloway?' I asked.

He paused, looking sad. 'She never saw him again. We got married a few months later, just the two of us at the Southwark Register Office while Aunt Lavinia was watching you at home. We continued living with her after that, for while, and you had to hand it to your mother, she went out the next day to find herself a job and she worked very hard at making something of herself, eventually going on to university and earning her degree. All of that seems easy to do today, but it wasn't remotely easy back then. She worked for every one of those things and she never took them for granted. It was hard, of course, but I won't ever forget those early years. You tripped off to school and we both worked, and then you came home, always full of stories, always interested, such a bright, cheerful little thing. We might have done it in a bit of a roundabout way, first the marriage, then the love, but in those early years, we made our family and the love came with it eventually. Her father wasn't part of that and the other man would certainly never be part of it if I had anything to do with it. And you were my daughter, Addie, my child, from the day I first saw you. I was the one who saved her, and you. I would never have let anything take that away from me.'

I shivered, remembering those exact same words spoken by Mrs Roberts. The things we do to keep our families safe.

'You lied about your Ruby Wedding,' I said, frowning.

'Yes,' he agreed. 'And about Elizabeth's age. She should have been twenty-one to get married. But it was easy because in those days you just told the registrar your age and with a bit of luck he didn't question it. We went and got me added to your birth certificate the day after we married, told them I was your biological father and was prepared to honour the birth.'

'And how did you explain to your family that I was suddenly there?'

'We fudged it, told only my parents and Fred that we'd had a baby, an accident really, had to get married quickly. My mother was fairly philosophical about it all and my aunt supported us, so the issue passed until it wasn't one anymore.'

Knowing Granny Harington, that made sense.

'And Phoebe? Did Mum ever tell you what had happened?'

'At the very beginning, yes,' he said. 'Lizzie talked about the dead baby incessantly, how it was her fault, how she had killed her. It was terrible, really. Terrible the way they made her feel at the hospital. That could never be undone, really.'

'But I don't understand *why* they told her that Phoebe was dead; why didn't George Holloway just give the baby up for adoption and tell her that's what he'd done?' I blinked against the sun, which shone through the dormer window too brightly and too happily for all this misery.

My dad shook his head. 'I'm not sure. All I can think is that he was in a rush because he knew that she wasn't going to give in to the adoption process easily. He must have been very worried that the problem wouldn't go away quietly and acted quickly, while she was incapacitated. Only you were left.'

'Because Mrs Roberts only took one.' I sighed. 'And Mum never talked to her father again. Did you know that he died, that she went to the funeral?'

'Yes,' he said. 'I knew. It was the first time she'd brought him up in years, but I went down with her to the cemetery. It was a bleak affair.' He shuddered. 'He was buried next to his wife, even though Lizzie didn't want that, in the churchyard there in the village. The solicitor was talking to Lizzie about the house, too, but she didn't want to go at first, didn't even want to look at it.'

'And did you know that she hired Merck to look for Phoebe? He was looking for her for a good three years. Sorry, Dad, all these questions, but so much happened, I'm still trying to put it all together.'

'That's quite all right. No, I didn't know that she hired an investigator,' he said and he sounded very sad. 'I wish she'd told me. I would have helped her. I would have wanted to be there for her.'

His voice was thick with emotion and I said quickly, 'I just can't get over it, how you can live with such a huge trauma and simply go on with your life.'

'Once we got married she stopped talking about it altogether.' He cleared his throat. 'It was like she had decided to put that part of her life behind her.' He saw my frown and said firmly, 'Not only because I *made* her do it. I think at that point, she had finally accepted it. She *wanted* to look ahead. She never mentioned the dead baby again. And, to be honest, we had enough to be going on with – young and married and penniless, with a little girl to take care of, working several jobs. Not much time to think about things. And then later, yes, sometimes I could tell she wasn't right but—'

'Mrs Baxter thought she had depression,' I said.

He nodded thoughtfully. 'I occasionally tried to get her to go and talk to someone, even persuaded her to see a doctor once. But you know how she was about keeping to herself.'

'Poor Mum. She was so strong and so not strong at the same time.'

I started crying, but he didn't seem unduly agitated by it, just patted my back and murmured soothingly, which is probably exactly what he did forty years ago when my mother had wept over her dead baby, and, amidst all that I'd heard, I found myself glad that instead of whoever in London she'd come to find, it was my father she had found, who had been by her side for forty years. *I give, to him who gave himself for me; Who gives himself to me, and bids me sing a sweet new song.* That's what he'd done, my dad, he'd given her hope, a new beginning, and that's what he put on her gravestone at the very end. *A sweet new song.*

I could hear noises from below and voices and tried to pull myself together.

'Will you meet her, Dad, Phoebe, I mean? Can she be part of us, part of being here? If she wants to, that is, and Jas and Venetia are all right with it?' I fished for a tissue, pressed it against my eyes.

He was silent for so long that I looked up to see whether he was all right. Then he said. 'Yes. Yes, of course. It's what Lizzie would have wanted more than anything, to have you two be together. Bring her soon. I would love to meet her.'

I leaned against him, dabbing at my eyes and sliding my toes along the worn runner. It was warm from the sun and bright and we watched dust motes and little grains of lint dance in the sunlight.

'I wish she'd told me,' I said quietly. 'I wish I'd known all of this. It would have made it easier, I think.'

'Made what easier?' His voice was gentle.

'Mum and I. She was so different to me. Expected things to be so different with me.'

'You always had to be twice as much as you could possibly be,' he agreed. 'That's hard for a child. Your relationship was, well, let's just be kind and call it complicated, shall we?'

'If I could only talk to her again,' I said. 'There'd be so much I would say.'

'I know.' His voice was very quiet. 'More than anything I wish she was still here. I always thought we'd grow old together. I miss her so much.'

'And sometimes she's so hard to remember, sometimes it's like she's already slipped away.'

'We should talk about her more,' he said. 'We should talk about her all the time. It's the only way to remember people, to talk about them. I think the others really will be waiting now.' He got to his feet.

'You go ahead, then, Dad.' I blew my nose, wiped my eyes.

'Are you sure?' He hovered solicitously.

'I just want to be on my own for a bit.'

'Of course. I'll square it with Venetia.' He bent and patted my shoulder clumsily, then walked away and I watched him go, still stooped, still a hint of a shuffle in his steps, but much calmer, more present now. No matter what else happened, Phoebe's appearance had at the very least jolted him out of his grief-induced trance. She had brought him back to us.

London, 9 May 1960

I'm getting married tomorrow. I'm eighteen years old and I'm going to be married on a beautiful spring day at Southwark Register Office. I'm marrying a good man, a very kind man, whom I know I can come to love eventually. Soon. I know that I will, because in a small way, I already do. He is everything that neither John nor my father could ever be and that is a very good thing. I try not to think of that kiss in the Hartland orchards now or of the afternoons in the Purley hotel, because that reckless thrill and intense passion isn't really designed for a future to be built on. Lovely, yes, but also fleeting and unpredictable and unstable and not at all the 'love that made us one' that Mum sometimes talked about. I'm a little sad for her, because I couldn't imagine that that's how things turned out for her with my father, given the kind of person he is, but Graham is different. He is warm and steady and strong, all in a quiet, reliable way that feels to me more real and more substantial than anything I ever felt for John. It's the kind of life where I'm going to be able to write in my diary without any fear of him reading it, I can be silent if I choose and talk if I want to and he'll be there to be silent or to listen. I can close my door and be alone and yet know that I'll never be alone while I'm with him and that in itself is a wonderful thought.

There isn't a door to close at the moment and our future looks quite sparse because I own little more than the bag I came away with, the clothes I wore when I left the hospital. The baby has very few things to her name and she's growing so quickly, but once I'm Mrs Graham Harington I can go out and find work and raise a family and be safe in all my respectability. Aunt Lavinia was the one who made that all happen, and she's been kind in ways I can never repay, so solid and unshakeable and down-to-earth, just like Graham. I've grown so attached to her that I'm almost afraid now to become part of a whole new, different unit with Graham. But it's good to be married when you're eighteen and the past holds only dark and cold things, because it means moving on, leaving it all behind.

Graham has been very kind today, leaving me to myself for most of the day, and I've been thinking of Mum. I wish she was here, on a day when any mum would want to help her daughter get ready on the eve of her wedding. We'd be laughing over my hair the way we used to, and she would have fussed with my dress and taken out her set of pearl earrings and necklace for me to look the part, made me a hot cup of Horlicks and sat talking with me when I got nervous.

None of what happened to me would have done so if Mum had been around, but I've ceased railing against whatever it was that took her away because it makes me so tired to always be angry with the world. She would have liked Graham, very much, but I wonder what she would have made of this new, harder, quieter me, the one that has stopped being surprised by anything life has the power to do. When I look at Adele, even though she is just a baby, I sometimes catch a glimpse of something I remember from my years with Mum, warmth and affection, unconditional and uncomplicated, a simple giving, a joy. But it's hard for me to let it come anywhere close to that space inside me that once had the capacity to grasp any of those concepts.

In a way, in leaving Limpsfield and my father, in leaving John and Hartland and the silly, impressionable, excitable young me behind, I'm going to have to shut a door on my mother and my memories of her. I won't be going to tend to her grave any time soon, I won't return to Bough Road where she was so very present. I'm old now and away from all that, I have to be my own person, I must be a mother myself. I owe it to Mum to make a go of myself, of this new life, to find a way forward, even if it means being separate from all my memories of her, even if it means leaving her behind.

And I want to move on. I don't want to think about the dead baby anymore, or about any of the things I should have done differently. I don't want to see my father again or think about John and the 325 steps across the square. I don't want to measure my life in poems about love and death and sin. I want to live.

Chapter Thirty-Seven

My dad had barely turned the corner before I was on my knees in front of the lower bookshelf, scrabbling at the little grey book, pulling it back out. *Faro's Daughter*, unsupported, sagged to the right, and other books followed, expanding into the space freed up by the diary. I frowned, ticking off the titles on my fingers. *The Reluctant Widow. Black Sheep. Cotillion. Bath Tangle. Arabella.* Then, a blank spine. Another blank spine. Five more diaries, which, bearing the full brunt of the sun, had faded into a uniform hue of yellowish grey, looking almost exactly like the rest of the Georgette Heyers next to them minus the gilded title letters. I scanned the other shelves, just to make sure there were no more, then, hardly daring to take a breath, I opened the one I'd found when my dad had come up the stairs, this time starting with the first page.

Limpsfield, 17 July 1958

I bought a new journal today, from nice Mr Clark on the high street. He had a new colour in, frosted pink, and he showed me the little clasp at the front and the flowers on some of the pages. Perfect for a pretty young woman like you, he said with a wink. He meant well, I'm sure, but I didn't want that one. Instead, I got the darkest grey, black almost, because I know full well that it isn't going to be a frosted pink kind of year. I chose the slightly thicker paper too, even though it was more expensive, because I have a feeling I'm going to need thicker paper this year. Thick, thirsty paper to soak up all the thoughts and the tears and all the awful things that are happening at my house.

I looked at the date and let out a long, slow breath, feeling my shoulders drop away from my ears and my throat open up. Here she was, in 1958, that young girl from Harriet's story, sad and shaken up already, and even in these first few lines I could feel her story taking shape, could see the downfall coming and my heart went out to her.

I knew people were waiting for me downstairs, but I couldn't resist leafing through the pages slowly, reading my young mother's story. Elizabeth arriving at Hartland, cautious and sad, then the glorious day on the water, Constance dying and John waiting for her at the bus stop. Snippets jumped out at me – my mother hiding in the rose garden because people would insist on keeping her company, and riding in the open-topped car with her new scarf and having her first glass of champagne, and I was both smiling and crying, because here, finally, like an unexpected gift, were memories for us to hold on to, collected and strung along the decades like shiny pearls. I dabbed at my eyes, but they were dry, and I felt my heart lift until I thought it would burst.

Oblivious to the minutes ticking by, I picked up the next book, flicked through the pages.

Dulwich, 8 April 1969
Perfect day in the Park. J a bit fractious. Another tooth coming?

Dulwich, 12 April 1969
Chickenpox! Might have known.

Dulwich, 14 April 1969
Forgot how tedious children's illnesses are, especially in such a small place. G and I have both had it, thank god.

London, 28 May 1969
Looked at the house on Rose Hill Road again, even more beautiful than I'd remembered. Graham loved it. Now that we have Aunt Lavinia's money, we might scrape it together. Although I'd much rather have Aunt Lavinia than a house. I miss her so much.

London, 3 September 1972
It would have been Mummy's birthday today, and I took the children to St Paul's to hear the choir singing. Didn't go up in the gallery, despite A begging to. She'll have to go on a school trip or

something because in all my life I won't ever go near those windows and all those memories. The service was wonderful, though, and even Venetia was quiet the whole hour long! 'Abide with me' was beautiful as ever, so comforting. She would have loved it.

St Paul's. Another tiny piece of the puzzle slotted into place. I picked up the next diary and the one after, not really reading now because I wanted to save them to savour later, but nonetheless mesmerised by the small details of family life. Each book contained several years and the later entries were never very long, sentence fragments in small writing, tiny capsules of days and weeks, some of them so brief that they were clearly only meant to jog a memory. Back and forth across time, the entries zigzagged. Jas being born. Mum graduating. Dad promoted. People I'd known for years flitted through the pages, like characters in a book, and I was on almost every page. I found the entries for my first day of school, first time riding a bicycle, birthdays, Christmases. 1975. 1980. 1985. 1990. 1995. A new dean. Jas's wife pregnant. Back operation.

And then, without warning, George Holloway's funeral. I stopped skimming the entries, brought the book closer to my eyes.

London, 20 April 1996
Father has passed away. Got a call from the lawyer. Funeral next week.

Then, later:

Went to Father's funeral today, sat at the very back. I told Graham and he came with me, dear man. There weren't many people there. Saw old Mr Throgmorton (still alive!). Wants to talk about Father's estate.

A week later:

Had to go in to see Mr Throgmorton today for Father's will. He couldn't understand that I'm not interested in the remains, bodily or otherwise, that I don't want to go back to Bough Road. But he insisted, although he's really rather kind.

A few days later:

Throg on the phone again about the house. Finally to go over there. Some situation with his 'assets'. Throg a pain.

London, 10 May 1996
Went to the house on Bough Road. All very orderly of course, the way Father kept it, so not too big a hassle. Unbelievably, when I went into my room I found that no one had discovered any of my hiding places in the years I've been gone. All those little things I hid, photos and letters, even an old library book I never returned, it was all still there. And when I went into Mum's room, I saw that he'd kept all of her things, too, hadn't even got rid of her clothes in the cupboards or her books on the shelves or any of her knick-knacks on the dressing table. It made me cry for the first time in a long while, because it was so sad to see them. How can it still be so sad, after all these years, to see her bed, her chair by the window looking out into the garden?

It's like time stood still in that house, like Father never even went back into my room or into hers after we were gone and instead preserved her death in here, as if she'd only passed the year before . . . before it all went wrong.

I took some things back with me. Not much, a few photos and books belonging to Mum, letters I wrote to her, the old glass vials of perfume from her dresser, a small painting of her as a young woman. I lifted up the old radio because I thought it would be lovely to have it in our kitchen at home, but it had got stuck to the top of the dresser and the wooden shell came apart at the edges, so I left it. And I took the book of Christina Rossetti's poems, which was still sitting exactly where I had left it, the rose still inside, and which, after all these years, still brings tears to my eyes. Maybe if I'd been able to mourn her properly, with love and support and a real family around me, and without the horror that followed a year later, I'd feel more at peace with the fact that she's gone. But I still don't, I still miss her, sometimes unbearably so, and maybe I always will.

Her writing blurred in front of my eyes but I read on, skipping everything that didn't have to do with the Limpsfield house.

London, 10 September 1996
Throg looking for more paperwork, so I had to go back through Father's ledgers, much as I didn't want to. Found the doctor's report of the stillbirth. Father had just filed it away, like any other paperwork, and it brought it all back to me, all my hatred and rage against him, which was so futile in the end. How I wish I knew where she was buried. And another very strange thing: he'd taken out a lot of money, right before 14 February. £300 pounds. That'd be almost six and a half thousand pounds today. What on earth did he need that much money for? I also found something else that seemed strange: some notes from Harriet back in 1960. Why would Harriet write to me, after all that I'd done to her?

London, 30 November 1996
Turned house over to Throg, he'll sell it off.

London, 12 January 1997
I can't work it out, but there's something bothering me about the notes, and the money. He was always so obsessively mean. I wish I hadn't disposed of the Bough Road house so quickly now. Did a bit of research and neither the women's home nor the hospital would have cost a fraction of that amount. The hospital should have not cost anything at all, really, because of the NHS. Maybe he had to pay for the little room off the side. But never that much. Where did the money go to? Could it possibly be that there was something else there – that he did something terrible and had to pay for it? But the paperwork for her death was there in his files, I saw it. Surely he wouldn't have said that she was dead when she

wasn't? Even he wouldn't have done that, even he wouldn't have been so cruel. I simply cannot believe it.

London, 14 January 1997
I've been trying to look up Harriet, but I have no idea where she is. All Saints & Sisters of Hope are gone. I've almost convinced myself now that Father did something terrible. Perhaps she is still alive? Haven't slept in days. Graham keeps asking whether I'm sick. I don't really want to tell him, not after all these years, because I don't want to re-open all those old painful wounds.

London, 15 March 1997
Graham up at F's. Decided to try and find Dr Miller and some of the nurses.

London, 30 September 1997
I'm going to hire a detective. I've thought about it for a while but I won't bother Graham with it. There's more than enough money in Father's account, I can just pay the detective quietly out of that. I hardly dare believe it myself, and if it is nothing, then I couldn't bear having to share the disappointment with him, not when we agreed so long ago not to ever dwell on the past. And Addie. I couldn't tell her without being certain, without a shadow of a doubt, that her sister is still alive. If she's not, then no one need ever know. If she is, then I'll sit down with Addie and explain it to her from beginning to end, all at once. It's a story that needs to be told properly and if her sister is still alive, then Addie deserves to know. But if it is nothing, then I will leave it at that. At nothing. Because not everyone needs to be burdened with Hope . . .

London, 2 November 1997
I found someone, a James Merck, who seems a bit pedantic but at least he's a perfectionist. And supposedly very good at finding missing people. I still hardly dare hope that that's what this is turning out to be.

Quickly, I flicked through the rest of the book. At first, James Merck was mentioned almost daily and she continued to seem in turns excited, nervous and anxious, then, about twelve months before she died, their interchange started tapering off a little.

London, 28 May 1998
Dead ends all around, it's beyond frustrating and I'm so glad I insisted on keeping it away from Graham, because maybe then I can just quietly try to go back to the way things were before.

Then, later:

London, 15 November 1998
The lovely nurse who helped me simply cannot be found. And she was so young, how can she possibly disappear? If only I could remember more of those days at the hospital, more names, but it's all such a blur. Why can adopted children, with all these new laws, now look for their birth parents but not the other way around? Seems unfair to me, as if mothers didn't want to see their children. But maybe not all do. I do, though, I do! And I can't seem to be able to.

The following year:

London, 30 January 1999
February is coming round once again and I'm bracing myself for its dark nights and all the unwelcome memories. This is my least favourite time of the year, and February is the hardest month, always has been. Merck and I have agreed that he will continue looking but I've asked him not to get in touch again until he finds something real, because waiting and living through each returned letter and each dead end has been too painful for me. I don't hold out much hope, though, because somehow I know, in my heart of hearts, that she really is dead.

I started turning the pages again, quickly at first, then more slowly, not only because I'd already heard and seen so much in the last hour but also because I knew that just further on, the diary would come to a stop and the blank pages would start.

But then, as I turned one of the last few pages, my heart didn't squeeze quite as painfully as I'd expected, because there was something else. Tucked right between the last two diary entries, it was an A4 sheet of paper folded small to fit in here the day before she died. My fingers trembled as I pulled it out, scanned down the page to the name at the very bottom.

Sarah Mason.

Arbroath, 1 May 1999

Dear Mrs Harington,

I am sorry it's taken me so very long to write, but your letter came in quite a roundabout way and only recently found me in Arbroath, which is where I now live. I left nursing quite some time ago (I wasn't ever really cut out for it, to be honest) but I am very glad you got in touch.

That week you asked about at All Saints Hospital I was about to finish up my rotation on the maternity ward and you were one of the last of the girls from the home that came through while I was there. They always treated them so badly, the girls that came to us from the women's home. I think it was the ward sister, she was such a dragon, always on top of you and breathing down your neck, and Matron wasn't much better. Nursing can be wonderful, I'm sure, but you've got to be made of strong stuff, as a nurse in training.

I remember February 14 1960 quite clearly, because while I'd seen a lot of midwife-assisted births, you were only my third Caesarean, and it still seemed so wonderful to me, that a human was cut open and a baby emerged, or, in your case, two babies. The little ones were passed back to me to clean and wrap and it was a lovely sight, these two little bundles lying in their cots. Every birth was a miracle to me, but two babies sharing was double the miracle. The doctor took a long time sewing you back up but when I wanted to take the babies into the nursery, they told me to tell your father about the birth and then get on with my work on the ward. Your father was waiting for news of you. He seemed very nervous about the whole thing and taken aback when I told him about the twin babies. Sometimes even the fiercest fathers came around when they saw their grandbabies, but not this one, he wanted to speak to the doctor as soon as he was finished. He didn't even ask to see the babies, didn't want anything at all to do with them.

Later, Sister told me very curtly that one of the babies was now in the nursery, but that the second hadn't survived and to go clean the sluice before my shift ended. It happened sometimes, that a baby didn't make it and it was disposed of quickly without much fuss over the mum, and so I didn't question it at first, only that they both had seemed fine, crying and looking, well, fine. But then I was very young and inexperienced and afraid of the older nurses, and no one, not even those very same older nurses I was afraid of, ever dared to stand up to the obstetricians. We just all kept our heads down and got on with whatever we were told to do.

It wasn't for another day or so that it began to dawn on me that something odd had happened with your babies and it was when another woman, someone I'd wheeled out a few hours before you to recover from a stillbirth, suddenly had a real, live baby brought out to her. And I'm sorry to say, and more ashamed than I can ever express, that I didn't do anything about it. I knew already, you see, what was going to happen to your babies back at the home, and it seemed to me at the time that the inevitable had simply happened sooner than it would have anyway. Only very few of the mums kept their babies and took them back to their families. Most of them went back to the home to wait for baby's new families there. Some infants were adopted right then and there at the hospital, but they weren't really meant to be, because the mothers were supposed to have several weeks to think about their decision. The adoption process was nowhere near as strictly controlled as it is today.

Your letter made me think it over again, though, and looking back, I'm not sure that there even was an adoption in this case, private or otherwise. I think Dr Miller simply swapped your daughter with the little stillborn girl born earlier in the night. It's the only thing that makes sense. The other mum, her name escapes me, was so distraught and so very unhappy because she'd lost her baby that same night. She'd have done anything to get a child, I'm sure, and I wouldn't blame her. Your father must have been anxious to solve the situation as quickly and quietly as he could. And doctors back then sometimes did things they weren't supposed to, especially on the private wing. Abortions for example, to add to their salary. I saw Dr Miller doing it once, where the mother wanted it and she paid for it. It was illegal at the time, and it was never spoken of after. It's not hard to imagine that he saw a similar opportunity here, struck a deal with your father in exchange for a special 'fee', and quite a big one from the sounds of your letter.

The swap could have easily been done because us nurses never ever questioned what a doctor did back then, particularly if it concerned a single mum. There was no reason to, those mums were going to give up their babies anyway, and then going back to their normal lives. And even if someone had wanted to speak up that night, there weren't too many people around who'd have been able to put together all the pieces.

I'm not quite sure why they didn't call it a private adoption and be done with it, why they added the pain of telling you the baby had died. But they probably feared that you'd make trouble and unrest, especially if you knew that the other baby was just at the other end of the ward, being held by another woman.

Afterwards, the doctor must have been glad he'd done it that way, secretly, under the table, rather than signing off on a private adoption, because the police came looking for you when you didn't turn up at the women's home. He'd surely have got in trouble about the private adoption and this way, there were still two birth certificates and a stillbirth certificate, only the names had changed. But the police didn't know that last bit, especially as the other woman had already left. She didn't stay her allotted ten days and I helped her get ready with the baby, who was the sweetest little thing. Maybe it'll be a comfort to you that the woman seemed overjoyed with it and very gentle, the new dad too, who was a shy, very quiet man. I knew that she'd be a good mum for it and I gave her the bundle you wanted buried with the baby. I thought you might have liked for it to accompany her to her new life.

Sadly, no one would have given you a thought in all this, because unmarried pregnant girls didn't have a say at all. On the contrary, they were seen to be a burden on the hospital and the state and to be deserving of everything they got, which, some said, might make sure they'd behave better next time. The things I've heard on that score would fill a whole other letter, and this one has turned out to be such a long one already. It's been a relief to get it off my chest, although I hope I haven't made it more difficult for you, telling you what I knew? Perhaps it would be better to talk about it in person. I've been trying very hard to remember the name of the other lady but for the life of me I cannot think of it, after forty years. I am so very sorry. You could try and find the names of women who gave birth at the hospital during that month in the birth register and I could try to see if any rings a bell? I really would very much like to help you. And if you'd like to come and see me up in beautiful Scotland, then I would be very happy to have tea with you.

All the very best,

Sarah Harding, formerly Mason

Chapter Thirty-Eight

My fingers shaking slightly, I folded up the letter and was about to slot it back into the diary when I saw the very last entry, written a week before my mother had died. I blinked away those stupid tears that just kept on coming, and read on.

London, 8 May 1999
I'm still reeling from Sarah Mason's letter. I've been thinking about it these last few days, about what happened, what I knew and didn't know and never saw. I'm still not sure why the doctor did what he did, and why my father asked him to do what he did. I can only think that he was nervous about Harriet having been there, that he was looking for a quick way out, and, seeing the chance, he gave her away. He certainly didn't expect his wayward daughter to run off.

I try to remind myself that she went to a good family, that she has probably had a good life, and amidst everything else that at least makes me so happy and very glad. I'm going to tell Graham, soon. Finally, I have something to tell him, something good and real, and it'll be such a relief to talk about it. I know he won't be disappointed that, after all these years, I'm still thinking of her, still want to talk about her. It doesn't take anything away from what we, he and I, have together after all. I'm thinking about my baby, not her father.

Reading Sarah Mason's letter brings it all back to me, that terrible time in the hospital, my father and John and Harriet, my escape from the home. After these last decades with Graham, my time with John has faded almost completely from my memory. There was never anything solid about it, nothing real, nothing compared to being married for forty years to a lovely, wonderful, kind man. If I'd known back then how different a relationship could be, how different to the one my parents had, different to Hartland, I might have acted differently myself, might have seen it for what it was right away. A silly fling that never stood a chance but had such devastating consequences.

I'm going to wait until after the anniversary party tonight. Tonight is for celebrating us, our many years of a wonderful marriage, and not about what happened just before them. Graham's had to put up with such a lot from me over the years, the poor, kind man, and he does deserve to know now, as much as Addie does, but not until our celebration is over.

I'm not sure whether her sister will even want to see me or her, if indeed we'll ever find her, but finally Merck has something to go on and he's off to look through registers and records, to try get in touch with the women who were on the ward. I told him only to come back to me when he has a proper, solid name and someone willing to speak, because I don't think I could take much more in the way of disappointment. And as soon as I know who she is, where she is, I will sit down with Addie and tell her the entire story. I can't even imagine what it would be like, a meeting between them. My solid, cautious daughter and her mystery twin. I'm hugging that thought to myself and keep on hoping for it to happen soon. Hope, that faithful fickle friend of mine, has returned to be, as ever, by my side.

I closed the diary and set it on top of the other ones. So my mother had finally found out. She'd found out the truth, she'd have finally been able to shed her guilt, to let go of the past. George Holloway had paid the doctor the princely sum of £300 for his cooperation, his silence and fake paperwork for a baby's death. He had wanted to give away the second baby as well, but my mother had disappeared with me before he could do it. She'd gone on to live her difficult, burdened life and, considering the circumstances, she'd done it well. She was a survivor, my mum, and I was proud of her, proud of her pushing up her chin and squaring her shoulders.

I should have been angry or sad and I would be down the line, I knew that, but more than that I was filled with a deep sense of relief, because not only would my mother finally have been able to lay the ghost of the dead baby to rest, but she'd known, even if only for a week, that her other baby was alive, that she'd gone to a loving family and was most likely thriving and happy, maybe even close by. She'd known that if both had been willing we'd have met in due course. And we had.

There were a lot of questions still but enough answers for the moment. I scooped up the stack of diaries and tucked them under my arm. I had to find my phone and call Phoebe. I tiptoed down the stairs, very much hoping not to run into Venetia until I'd been able to hide the diaries, because, selfish though it was, I wasn't quite ready to share them yet. My bag was right where I'd left it under the hallway table. The books safely stowed away, I found my phone.

'Phoebe?' I said when she picked up after the fourth ring. 'Are you back home?'

'I'm at my mum's. We're sitting in the garden, hang on, let me go inside.' There was a small scrabbling noise. 'Yes, Mum, I'll be right back. No, it's fine, honestly. Just a second.' More scrabbling, then she came back on the line.

'Listen,' I said quickly. 'I found something.'

She listened in silence, then finally exhaled shakily. 'That sounds amazing . . . I wish . . .' There were tears in her voice. 'I wish I was there right now.'

'I do too. But your mum,' I said, 'is she, I mean – is she all right? Are *you* all right?'

'We've been talking for ages and she told me a few more things about that night. She said the doctor told her just to register me under her own name, that that's how it was done. So when the registrar came by, she just gave him her name and my dad's and mine and that was the end of that. It was never registered anywhere as an adoption. They really did just swap one dead baby for a live one. That's why I'm not in the register.'

She paused and I could hear her struggling for breath.

'The doctor told her to go early, not to stay the ten days, that she didn't need to hang around. He must have been a bit nervous, having both of them on the ward. And she was worried too, so she just left with me, never looked back until that second letter from Merck. She said she just couldn't lie a second time. That she was going to see Elizabeth Holloway before Elizabeth found me herself.'

She sighed. 'I guess it was too late anyway, it was after the accident, so I'm just going to put it out of my mind.'

'She loved you,' I said quickly. 'She did. Just like my dad loved my mum when he made her focus on the future by shutting away her past. It doesn't change who they are, you know, they're still who they always were. The person who really suffered was Mum. She was never quite right again, all her life.'

'Yes,' Phoebe said. 'And at least she knew that I was alive and taken to a loving home. What do you think, could I come and stay with you for a bit, maybe tomorrow, after I leave here?'

'I would love that,' I said, my eyes filling, yet again, with tears.

When I hung up, I stood at the hallway table for a second, thinking of Phoebe. I imagined her slipping her phone into her well-organised bag and walking back into her mother's garden, and tomorrow leaving to take the train to London. Suddenly, I wanted nothing more than for her to be here. I missed her. But the rest of my family was waiting downstairs and at some point I should probably join the party that I had organised. I didn't seem to have a very good track record for family gatherings.

I was just putting away my phone, when the door coming up from the kitchen opened and Andrew appeared.

'Hey.' He smiled when he saw me. 'Everyone's getting plastered downstairs. No one's missing you at all. Everything all right? I came to find you.'

He was carrying a plate heaped with Mrs Baxter's coconut cream cake and two glasses. A small bottle of champagne was tucked underneath his arm. He juggled everything gracefully for a second before managing to kick the door shut with his foot.

'How come you always know when to bring me food?' I said, taking the plate out of his hands and setting it on to the hallway table.

'I like feeding you,' he said simply. 'Somebody has to.'

He pushed his hair back from his face, his eyes crinkling at the edges the way they always did when he was pleased with himself, and when he smiled down into my face, a bubble of happiness floated up from the pit of my stomach and burst with a delicious pop.

'Is Venetia foaming at the mouth that I'm not down there?' I said to cover my confusion.

Andrew was still grinning to himself. 'Everyone's drunk, except for your father, of course, and Venetia's so busy eating cake she's forgotten all about you.'

Doubtful.

'And that apple cake you made is heaven, Ads.'

'Is that why you're being so nice?' I said, regarding him warily. 'Are you trying to get me to rethink Le Grand Bleu?'

'God no.' He waved dismissively, deftly opening the champagne and pouring some into the glasses. 'In fact, I'm very glad we've put it behind us.'

'Is that so?' I eyed him suspiciously.

'Yes, glad,' he said firmly and handed me a glass. 'Drink.'

He raised his glass and I toasted him back, still watching him over the rim of my own glass as the champagne pearled down my throat, wonderfully sharp and cool. I drank it all down, greedy for the coolness against the roof of my mouth. Almost instantly, the buzz hit my foodless veins and I swayed. Andrew put out an arm to steady me and I realised that we were standing very close and that the hall was very quiet in the late afternoon sun.

'So, er, you're glad?' I said, more to break the gathering silence than anything else. I didn't dare move back and confined myself to looking down at his faded jeans instead.

'Yes,' he said and I watched his knees bend as he sagged to look straight into my face. 'I am. And you should be too. After all, two chefs shouldn't be in a relationship.'

'So you said,' I mumbled, 'and what—'

But I'm not entirely sure what I wanted to say because suddenly, in a very strange and completely unpredictable turn of events, Andrew's face was so close to mine that I could see his blue eyes and all the fine lines around them, and then he kissed me, very hard and very long, and I closed my eyes, only just managing to think that I had never,

ever been kissed like that in my life, before falling and falling, and when I finally resurfaced I'd forgotten what I wanted to say altogether.

'But a café owner and a chef, I think, would be fine.' He smiled.

'I . . . yes,' I said, breathing hard and leaning into his arms because I wasn't entirely sure whether I'd be able to stand.

'Want to go down and find the others?' He cocked his head towards the kitchen door. 'No? Are you sure?'

He smiled and pulled me closer, kissed me again, and I held on tightly, feeling the soft, faded cotton of his shirt and smelling his clean-laundry smell, wanting to free fall like that forever until I wrenched open my eyes in a panic, because I didn't want to miss anything either, and found that he was looking straight into them, his own eyes so blue, so warm, so happy that, absurdly, I wanted to cry. Finally, reluctantly, he pulled away. Not letting go of my hand, he set the glasses down on to the table and bent to pick up my bag.

'Come on, then,' he said, pulling me towards the door. 'Let's go quickly before anyone notices. And let's take some cake for the road.'

Epilogue

'It's got to be here *some*where! I think we turn left here . . .'

'Oh, yes, look, there's the little road Harriet mentioned.'

I sat forward in my seat and pointed across the road, where a sign was just visible through a break in the hedgerows, and Phoebe screeched into a hair-raising turn, then bumped along the narrow track that would take us down to Hartland.

This is how I imagined my mother to have come down here in her father's Morris Minor all those years ago. But instead of a young girl looking out of the window feeling empty and sad, it was the two of us now, driving through the sunny English countryside with the top down, music on the car stereo and an enormous picnic basket sitting in the back. Phoebe, who'd picked me up a couple of hours earlier in her little Boxster, looked sleek and tanned and completely at ease behind the wheel, her test-tube baby bump wedged against the steering wheel.

Wearing big sunglasses and my mother's prettiest scarf to hold back my hair, I was buckled into the passenger seat, handing out a steady string of chewy caramels and prawn cocktail crisps, which, despite my best efforts, was Phoebe's pregnancy diet. Andrew had taken one look at the two-seater, the family pack of crisps and Phoebe giving him an excited thumbs-up from behind the wheel and had swiftly declined the offer of a lift, taking his own car and my father instead, with strict instructions for Phoebe to please not kill me along the way. She did drive fast, my twin sister, much the same way I liked to think of her behind the steering wheel of a Boeing 747.

We'd made good time, but Harriet was already waiting at the big ornate gate at the end of the lane. She waved and came around to open Phoebe's car door and helped her up while I got out more slowly, my eyes on the gate and what was beyond. Harriet started unlocking the padlock on the big rusty chain and Phoebe came up to me and slipped her arm through mine, and we just stood there together, taking in the house and the gardens where everything had begun.

There was a riot of greens and browns and everything in between as far as you could see, trees and bushes growing madly, wild grasses and creepers surging over the remnants of sheds and outbuildings on the side, flowers and blooming shrubs and bushes and wild rhododendron spilling around trees and clinging to crevices in crumbling walls. And amidst the gardens, which were hardly gardens any more but an exuberant, joyful wilderness, sat the house, exactly the way my mother had described it in her diary: two small wings tucked behind the main building, the sweeping pebbled drive up to where the front door had been. But the honey-coloured stone and white-washed window frames, the slate-coloured roofs with doves tapping across as my mother woke up in the morning to write in her diary, all that was no more. Hartland was a shell now, crumbling and falling apart, the windows empty gashes. What remained of the stone walls was blackened and grey and the entire left wing, where the fire had started, had almost completely disintegrated. Here, too, the gardens had taken over, had advanced on the house, cautiously at first I'm sure, then more daring until climbers and creepers had started to spread unchecked in every direction. Seeds, blown into crumbling walls by the sea breeze, had taken a hold and what looked like a kestrel had built a nest on the highest wall that still remained on the right. It should have been a devastating sight and maybe to Harriet, who had come up next to us and was resting her hand on Phoebe's shoulder, it was. But there was something so alive about the ruins at the same time, so green and lush as the remains of the house lurked amidst and half beneath the wild gardens surrounding it, that you couldn't help but smile at the sheer abundance, which was, in some strange way, a faint echo of the exuberance we'd found on the pages of my mother's diary from the summer of 1958.

There was the crunch of tyres behind us and a moment later, Andrew and my father joined us by the gates.

'So this is it?' Andrew said, after a moment of awed silence. 'Wow, look, Graham, that entire side has collapsed.'

'That must have been one enormous fire,' my dad said. 'And all of this still belongs to you, er, Mrs Sinclair?'

He offered her an arm and, with a quick, surprised smile, she accepted.

'Oh, do call me Harriet, please. After all we're almost related, aren't we? You know, it was an electrical fault, very small, really, but only Abel lived here at the time and he was too late in stopping the fire in the end. We weren't even here, we were in America. Came back for Abel's funeral. I haven't been here in years,' we heard her say as the two of them slowly made their way down the drive towards what was left of the house. 'I'm keeping it for Carrie, but she's thinking about moving back to America herself, so who knows . . .' Their voices grew fainter as they followed a grassy path to the right. My dad had his head inclined towards Harriet and was listening and smiling, and I was very glad that he'd wanted to come along.

'Could you grab the picnic, Andrew?' Phoebe said over her shoulder. 'I can carry the blankets, but the basket's a bit heavy.'

Andrew waved her off gallantly. 'Of course. You two go ahead. I'll take it all through there on the right where, I think, the garden was.'

He gave me a quick smile and a wink before he turned to go back to the car, watched with almost maternal pride by Phoebe, who, predictably, had taken to Andrew like a magpie to silver.

'Oh, he's just so lovely, you lucky, lucky thing,' she said longingly, giving her bump a quick absent-minded pat as we started slowly walking down the driveway. Despite her best efforts, her soulmate had turned out to be elusive and after a series of highly unproductive dates – showcasing once more the complete and utter absence of any good men on this earth, she said – she'd found a sperm donor and had eventually rolled up on my doorstep with a bottle of non-alcoholic champagne and a red and blue T-shirt that said *Super Aunt* on the front. In true Phoebe-fashion, she'd orchestrated the whole thing beautifully, scoured library and shops for every single pregnancy book available, negotiated a complicated maternity package with her company and had already turned a room in her house into a nursery, which was now eagerly awaiting the arrival of little Charlotte.

'Yes, he is,' I said happily, falling in step next to her. 'And I might as well tell you that we decided to move in together. Last night.'

'Whoohoo,' Phoebe said. 'You're finally giving up control over your mouldy dishcloth dough thingies. I've been telling you and telling you, you have to hold on to that man.'

'She is,' Andrew's voice sounded right next to us, 'and she's agreed to keep our kitchen clear of mouldy dough now that she's got the café.'

He gave me a swift, one-armed hug as he passed us with the picnic basket and a bundle of blankets, then veered off to the right, cutting a track straight through the jungle of grass and ferns to where Harriet and my father were milling about, inspecting the ruined walls from a careful distance.

'Down that way,' I suggested and pointed in the opposite direction. Without talking, we circled the house in a wide arc around the left side, taking in the empty spaces of windows and doors, the blackened and burned insides of rooms. Where the wing had come away, it had opened the side of the main building, exposing the rooms there like a ravaged, burned-up version of a giant doll's house. On the ground floors, whatever could have been salvaged or pilfered had been taken, but the above floors had clearly been unsafe for anybody to enter and from a distance, you could see the charred remains of furniture, half-burned oil paintings, a torn curtain, hanging off-kilter on a rail.

'Look, I think that must have been the library,' Phoebe whispered, pointing towards a big, open room with a steel framework for a small glass cupola. The glass had long gone and the floor-to-ceiling shelves were badly damaged and half-burned, rows of book skeletons that had melted together into random wedges of charred leather covers, the remnants of which had rotted away in the last few decades.

I thought of my mother sneaking into what must have been a beautiful, airy room, to debate between Ivy Compton-Burnett and Lady Dorothy Mills, and Phoebe must have felt the same because she sped up towards the terrace, which we could just see ahead. You could still make out the flagstones and parts of the low wall around it, but the grouting had weathered away and the balustrade had crumbled and fallen apart in many places, giving way to creeping ivy and grasses sprouting up everywhere.

'We shouldn't go up there,' I said doubtfully. 'I'm sure it's not safe.'

'Just up those steps,' she pointed. 'I think it's okay.'

I helped her up the uneven boulders, which had worn away in places and wobbled dangerously, and we stood for a moment at the very top, looking down into what remained of the Hartland gardens.

'Oh,' I breathed. 'It's still so . . . so very lovely.'

The croquet lawns were overgrown, the orchards a tangle of gnarly trees and shrubs, but the graceful downward sweep of the grassy terraces was still the same. The sky was an impossible blue, the sun was warm on our backs and a small lake twinkled at the bottom. Phoebe pressed my arm and she nodded towards the right-hand side of the lawn where Harriet and my father were spreading out several blankets beneath the shade of an old plane tree. My father was wrestling with a stubborn fold-up chair he'd brought along for Phoebe and Harriet touched his elbow, pointed in our direction, gave a wave. Andrew was unpacking the picnic, then he looked up too and waved. They'd found a spot on the edge of what had been—

'The rose garden,' I said in wonder. There, too, nature had reclaimed man-made order in cheerful chaos, but from where we stood up high you could still see the outline of hedges and flowerbeds, espaliered trees against walls. And everywhere, there were roses, flowering and climbing up trellises, a profusion of red and pink and white blooms.

Phoebe put her arm around me and I rested my head against her cheek, and we stood and looked at the rose garden that had made our mother's life, for just a few short weeks, so very happy.

Author's Note

Sandwiched between the war on the one side and the rebellious sixties on the other, the 1950s were a funny decade. Many remember it as a cosy and innocent era, where children played on the street until their mums called them in for tea, where the bobby walked the beat and the nurse cycled by with her bag perched on the handlebars and you could hitchhike to the Isle of Wight without a second thought. After the deprivations of war and the austerity of the post-war years, people had money to spend and a brightly lit, colourful world to explore, a world full of new music and mod cons, of new cars and television.

In many regards, those years *were* safe and exciting and innocent, but they had a darker side too. Lace-curtain respectability and pre-war propriety relegated women, who'd gained a foothold in the male-dominated society during the war, who'd worked and played and propped up their country, back to home, hearth and family, subjecting them to the hypocrisy and double standards of a Victorian morality that tolerated little errant behaviour.

Sexual education was practically non-existent and premarital sex was demonised or ignored – until it resulted in an illegitimate pregnancy. Then, punishment came down hard on the head of the unfortunate expectant single mother, disproportionately severe given how inadequately girls and young women were prepared for the real world. 'Falling for a baby' without a husband, and this included rape and sexual abuse within a family, even sometimes an early baby with a fiancé and a marriage date already set, was seen exclusively as the woman's fault. It was a sin, a sign of depravity and moral weakness – after all, not too long before this, single mothers could still be sent to mental institutions or the workhouse.

Some families might choose to discreetly absorb the new arrival into their clan, raising a baby as a much younger 'sister' or a distant 'cousin,' but for many women, the only option was to have the baby in secrecy at one of the many mother and baby homes around the country, give it up for adoption and return to society for another – a last – shot at 'normal' life. No matter how they found themselves in their situation, no woman came back from this experience unscathed, all suffered to varying degrees from the treatment received at the women's home, the judgement of their own families, the grief and trauma of pre-natal, birthing and post-natal experiences under the supervision of deeply disapproving nurses and doctors and, finally, the heartbreaking ordeal of having to hand their baby over to strangers. At the end of it all, they would go back out into the world, carrying the memory of their lost babies with them, often in silence, for the rest of their lives.

Mother and baby homes dedicated to this process continued to exist until demand for them finally lessened at the end of the 1960s, showing a shift in moral values that would begin to ease the stigma of the single mother, although stories of mistreatment and judgement do exist until well into the eighties.

With the Children Act 1975, adopted persons in England and Wales were able for the first time to view their birth and adoption records, subject to counselling, but it wasn't until the Adoption and Children Act 2002 that mothers were able to try and trace the babies they left behind. In many cases, the connection between those mothers and their children was forever lost, especially as private or third-party adoptions were not always properly legalised until the early 1980s when new adoption laws tightened the process considerably – small consolation to children and mothers searching for each other in the disjointed paper jungle of private adoptions.

Of the many books I've read on the subject of women in the 1950s, illegitimacy and adoption, several were very helpful for anyone wishing to know more about what is now generally accepted to be a difficult and painful aspect of that decade. Jane Robinson's *In the Family Way* and Sue Elliott's *Love Child*, Sheila Toffield's *The Unmarried Mother*, Helen Edwards & Jenny Lee Smith's *My Secret Sister*, Angela Davis's *Modern Motherhood* and Arthur Marwick's *British Society Since 1945*, Paul Feeney's *A 1950s Childhood* and Mary Hazard's *Sixty Years a Nurse* are but a few that help paint an historical picture of what might have been Elizabeth Holloway's upbringing and the problems she faced. Some fictional licence had to be taken. All characters are entirely fictitious. The Charitable Sisters of Hope and All Saints Hospital, although modelled on a variety of real-life institutions, are purely a product of my imagination, and while most of the geography has been duly respected, Porthallow, Tideford Cross, Brimley and Hartland do not exist.

I've always been fascinated by family history and the way it personalises the 21st century as told through our history books. Viewing family secrets and difficult choices against the complex tapestry of an everyday life so very different to ours gives us a new perspective on these secrets and choices. And yet, in an odd way, they remain timeless as well, moral dilemmas of the kind that most of us will relate to in one way or another during the course of our lives.

There are many personal stories out there, both in print and on the countless reunion websites, dealing with the often painful journeys of mothers and children in search of each other, decades of secrets, uncertainty and yearning, followed by the often difficult task of getting to know each other – or indeed choosing to not go down that road at all.

In *My Mother's Shadow*, Elizabeth, Addie and Phoebe's fictional lives were forever changed by what happened that night in 1960. What they experienced and what they learn is as different as the real-life stories, which are by turns harrowing and uplifting, but the three women show, in their limited fictional universe, just how far-reaching, how intricate and devastating the legacy of these forced separations of mother and child really were.

Acknowledgements

If it takes a village to raise a child, then it takes at least that many people to get a book out into the world and I'm endlessly grateful for all the amazing encouragement along the way.

I'd like to especially thank my editor, Marion Donaldson, for always being just a phone call away, for her many words of wisdom – and for making my dream come true. The brilliant team at Headline for welcoming me to the Headline family. My marvellous agent, Caroline Hardman, for all her support.

A huge thank you to Jenny, who helped the story survive, and to Frances for not letting me give up. To Maresa for her creative inspiration, and Rebecca and Hannah for lovely lunches and many kind words.

My most heartfelt thanks, as ever, goes to my family. To my parents for believing in me from the very beginning and being my most loyal and wonderful early readers. My in-law family for all their good cheer from the other side of the world. My two amazing boys, who introduced me long before this book had even taken shape as 'my mum, the author' and who generally make me endlessly proud. And lastly, my husband Paul, without whom nothing would ever be possible. To him especially, I dedicate this book with all my love.

A Q&A with Nikola Scott

What first inspired you to write this novel? And did the focus of the story change as you were writing it?

I usually carry bits of ideas around with me for ages before they take shape, so it's not always easy to pinpoint the very first inspiration of a novel, but the first seed of Addie's story stemmed from a conversation with a friend a few years ago. She'd recently learned of an older sister she hadn't known existed, a woman who was now eager to become part of my friend's life. It kept coming back to me, the thought of this person who has no immediately clear place in your life and yet seems to have the strongest claim on it that there could possibly be. I was wondering how I would feel in that strange no man's land between family and strangers. Would I be thrilled and excited? Would I be indifferent? Jealous? Eventually, the story changed and became a novel about mothers as much as sisters, but this little initial kernel still remains – and I'm still not quite sure how I'd feel if it happened to me . . .

You explore both the joys and difficulties of mother-daughter relationships in the book through the different characters and their experiences. Did you draw on your own experiences of family to help portray these relationships?

Mothers are often romanticised in literature, sanctified or demonised, when real life is rarely that simple. I've had several strong female figures in my life but, rather than actually basing any one character on them, it was more the complexity of those relationships that found its way into the portrayal of the mothers in the book; how these relationships changed and developed over the years, what they taught me to do or do differently, the fallibility of motherhood versus its unchanging core values. I wanted them to be humans rather than figures. If you take Elizabeth, for example, she'll inspire an array of emotions ranging from respect, empathy and admiration, all the way to dislike and impatience. Similarly, we might feel deeply for Madeleine Roberts because of her history, while perhaps not particularly liking her as a character.

There is a whole other aspect behind the mothers in the book, however, and that is the difficult and sad journey of unmarried mothers in the 1950s and 60s. Liz's experience is an amalgamation of the many heart-wrenching stories in history books, novels and online forums about what unmarried mothers went through during a time when extramarital pregnancy – and that included sexual abuse, rape and even a pregnancy by a fiancé – was condemned by church and society. Unmarried mums had to cope with the notion of their motherhood as a 'sin', which could only be washed off if the product of that pregnancy was made to disappear. Unfair stigma and prejudice would close all doors, jobs and housing to them, reiterating over and over again that they were unfit to become mothers and didn't deserve to keep their children, until they believed it themselves.

Forced adoption in its many shades and gradations had a devastating effect on most women. Many continued to love their baby even if it was forever lost to them and many suffered their entire lives from that one moment when the mother-child bond was severed. Reading their stories, I was deeply moved by the power of that bond and that, too, has inspired the mothers in my book.

In your Author's Note you discuss some of the books that you used for historical research for the novel. Did you draw on any real-life stories to help form Addie, Phoebe and Elizabeth's narrative?

There are no real-life models behind Addie, Phoebe, Liz and Madeleine Roberts; they're purely a product of my imagination. Still, a lot of their individual and shared experiences surface as common threads in my historical research. Phoebe's drive to look for her mother is that of many adopted children looking for what they feel might be a missing piece of their identity. Liz's difficulties in relating to Addie mirror some of the struggles that young women forced to give babies for adoption might have faced in subsequent relationships. And Madeleine's dreadful experience with her miscarriages was a small but nonetheless heart-wrenching aspect of motherhood in those days.

Addie and Phoebe look to the past to find answers about their family and how their lives began. Why do you think family history is important to our identity?

I've always been fascinated by family history, partially by the stories themselves and partially because I think they give our lives an extra dimension that helps us understand who we are. Whether we want to or not, we all are a product of our family, our parents, our mothers. Their own experiences directly impact what they think is important to teach *us* and will thus surface in our lives in different ways. I think that understanding those experiences better helps you understand yourself and that is, in essence, Addie's story. Discovering what fed into the psychological and emotional make-up of her mother finally makes her understand what drove the relationship between the two of them. It enables her to make her peace with it and, most importantly, grow and develop in the course of the story.

In the novel you write about the material items that connect characters to those they have lost, such as the Hermès handbag that Addie finds in her mother's study. Are you sentimental about objects and their past?

Yes, much to my husband's despair! I have a cupboard full of little mementos which I'm sure other people won't think remotely spectacular – an old nut grinder, an ancient driver's license, my grandmother's first camera, a chipped sherry glass – but which all come with a story or a memory that makes them special to me. The shiniest, glitziest piece of jewellery isn't nearly as exciting to me as the simple gold chain with the funny tassels that my grandmother bought with her first ever proper salary. She started her own photography business in her twenties, which was incredibly tough in a time when women were not meant to be career women. I just love the image of her walking into the grand entrance hall of the opera, perhaps a little shy and definitely very young amidst all the grand society ladies, but more excited and proud in her new tasselled necklace than any of them could ever have been in their expensive finery.

Hartland is such a vivid and enchanting setting. Is the house a creation of your imagination or is it based on any real locations?

When my husband and I first moved to London we fell in love with the English countryside. We took out a National Trust membership and we've been on every country walk and to every manor house and garden within a fifty-mile radius of London, and many beyond. Hartland was partially inspired by a particularly lovely place called Polesden Lacey, a very leafy, green country house in the North Downs, Surrey.

Are you working on any more novels at the moment?

I'm currently working on another book that brings together a historical plot and a contemporary story. In the late 1930s, a group of friends come together for a last glorious country house weekend at Summerhill, a beautiful, remote estate on the Cornish coast. Summerhill belongs to the young Hamilton sisters, Madeleine and Georgiana, and promises safety and shelter against the looming threat of war. Before the weekend is over, however, tragedy has struck and none of their lives will ever be the same. Seventy years later, in 2009, Chloe – a struggling, young photographer living in London – crosses paths with old Madeleine Hamilton, now a famous children's book artist. An unlikely friendship develops as they uncover an intricate web of love and loyalty, secrets and lies.